He stared into the fire, trying not to count his losses.

A man could, for a little while, forget all the lessons he had learned and think about a lady with cinnamon hair and mossy green eyes and an oddly gentle way of talking. He could, if he wanted to, feel sorry for himself. But he didn't want to. Instead he wanted to dream of silken thighs and soft sighs and the welcome to be found only in this woman's warm body.

He could indulge himself shamelessly in fantasy, and, for a brief while, he did, seeing himself and seeing her in the sinuously twining flames of the fire. His body grew heavy with hunger, while his imaginings filled hollow places in his soul.

For now, for just a few minutes, he refused to remember that Janet Tate was the daughter of a Judas.

RACHEL LEE

A CONARD COUNTY Reckoning

Silhouette Books

Published by Silhouette Books
America's Publisher of Contemporary Romance

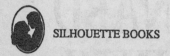 SILHOUETTE BOOKS

ISBN 0-373-48317-1

A CONARD COUNTY RECKONING

Copyright © 1996 by Susan Civil

This edition published by arrangement with Harlequin Books S.A.

Printed in U.S.A.

To Anna Skinner, friend and teacher,
for words of wisdom and a hefty dose of confidence.

And

Leslie Wainger, friend and editor,
for a lot of help and so many good laughs.

Prologue

Something was wrong.

Marge Tate stopped dead just as she entered the kitchen. Reaching back, she caught the screen door before it could slam shut, then listened intently, not moving a muscle.

Something was wrong.

In all the years she had lived in this house, in all the years that she had come home alone, she had never felt this way before.

Something was very wrong.

The feeling was inescapable, but she couldn't find any cause for it. Standing very still, with the sounds of the quiet spring day coming through the open door behind her, she strained every sense, trying to determine what it was that made her so uneasy. There were no unusual sounds from within the house, nothing she could identify as the source of her discomfort.

Her husband, Nate, had always told her that if she ever thought someone was in the house she should leave immediately and call him from somewhere else. Part of her wanted to do that right now, but another part of her couldn't forget that she would feel like an absolute fool if Nate showed up with a couple of his deputies, only to find no one and nothing.

If someone was in here, she would hear them, wouldn't she?

No.

The answer was stark, a quiet word of warning in her own mind. She took a quick step backward, then caught herself. This was utterly ridiculous! This was Conard County, Wyoming, for heaven's sake, not New York or Los Angeles. Out here most people didn't even bother to lock their doors when they went out. Yes, they had crime, but violent crimes were rare....

Squaring her shoulders, she stepped into her kitchen and let the door close quietly behind her. Without finding at least something to support her sense that something was wrong, she would feel like a fool for calling Nate and starting a ruckus. On the other hand, if she *did* find anything threatening, or if she heard something, she would hightail it out of here faster than a jackrabbit scenting a hound.

The next part was going to be harder, though. Next she had to walk through the rest of the house and prove to herself that there were no bogeymen in the closets.

The feeling wouldn't leave her. As she walked through the house, her footsteps silenced by the deep plush carpeting she and Nate had installed last year, she wondered why her sense of invasion didn't diminish as she found each and every room empty.

She reached the master bedroom, the last room in her search. Quickly, before she stepped over the threshold, she scanned the entire room. No one.

But when she entered, the smell of perfume greeted her. Her favorite, spicy scent, one she reserved for special occasions, wafted faintly on the air.

Her scalp prickled, and she had to battle down the urge to flee. She hadn't used that perfume in a couple of weeks. There was no reason why it should be fresh on the air now, stronger than the scent of the lemon oil she had rubbed into the dresser only this morning.

Someone had been in here.

The closet door stood open, but she had left it that way in her hurry to get to her appointment this morning. From where she stood, she could see that no one was in there. The bathroom, too, was open, and by turning her head she could see that it was also empty.

No one was here.

Had she somehow knocked the perfume bottle while cleaning earlier? Had Nate perhaps stopped in for a few minutes to get something he'd forgotten?

Yes, she thought, relief washing through her. That was all it was. Nate had come home for some reason and had knocked the bottle over. If she hadn't tightened the cap properly...

Yes, that was it. Relieved, she turned to go back to the kitchen. That was when she saw that the silver-framed wedding photo of her and Nate was sitting on the bedside table.

Her heart climbed into her throat. For nearly thirty years she had kept that photo on her dressing table. Never had she placed it anywhere else.

Nate could have moved it when he came home, she argued with herself. He could have picked it up to look at it and absently placed it on the night table.

He could have.

But she didn't believe it.

Someone had been in here.

Chapter 1

The back of Janet Tate's neck prickled, and she whirled around, certain she was being watched. No one. Just the scattered shacks of the abandoned mining town and the dark depths of the forest that rose all around. She shivered a little as the cold breath of the spring breeze snaked under the collar of her jacket.

No one.

"Silly," she muttered to herself, turning back to her camera and tripod. The late afternoon light slanted across the ghost town, only minutes from disappearing as the sun sank behind the peak of Thunder Mountain. The shadows were long, heightening the contrast and making the buildings stand out in brilliant relief. Behind the tumbledown shack she wanted to photograph, the green pines rose mysteriously, the shadows beneath them already impenetrable. Before much longer everything would become twilight flat.

The baby within her womb stirred gently, distracting her briefly with the merest flicker of sensation, little more than the feeling of a champagne bubble deep inside her. She closed her eyes for a moment, smiling, then bent to the eyepiece of her camera.

She'd been photographing this mining town for more than a decade, ever since she'd received her first 35mm camera for Christmas. The passion for photography had never left her, and this town had become one of her favorite studies. She had photographed it in all seasons, in all kinds of light, and in the process had caught the inexorable deterioration of the abandoned buildings and the inevitable encroachment of the surrounding forest.

She snapped the shutter, catching the scene in the instant before the sun yielded to the press of time and twilight slipped over the land.

Ice trickled down her spine again. She told herself it was just the chilly breeze that was blowing off the snowfields higher up the mountain. There was no one else here. There was never anyone else here.

Still, it would be a great place for a drifter to hide out. The shadows were deepening as the sun sank lower behind the mountain, and she became acutely aware of the loneliness of this place. The wind whispering in the trees and the soft gurgle of the creek were the only sounds. With the absence of the sun, the air was growing cold. Time to pack up.

She put her camera away in its bag and collapsed the tripod. One of these days—soon—she would have to come up here and take some shots at night during the full moon. Just thinking of the way this place would look in the silvery moonlight caused her to shiver and glance around again. If there were ghosts here, she thought crazily, they were active right now.

Swiftly she tucked her camera equipment in the back of her Explorer and shivered again as the cold wind found its way into her jacket. She was running, she thought. Running the way a child ran from formless fears. Running from the bogeyman in the closet.

There was no reason at all to think anyone was really watching her. The prickling of her scalp was nothing but some new trick of her seven-months-along pregnancy. In all the years she had been coming here, she had only once encountered another soul.

But the black holes of the windows and doors in the tumbledown shacks stared hollowly back at her. If someone wanted to hide here, there were plenty of places to do so. But why would anyone want to? The reasons a person could have for wanting to hide all the way out here...well, none of the ones that occurred to her were reassuring.

So just leave, she told herself. Just get out of here and worry later about whether her flight was foolish.

But she had never been the kind of person who ran from the dragon under the bed or the bear in the closet. Her dad had always taught her that the only way to conquer a fear was to face it. Feeling ashamed of her own cowardice, she decided to walk around the ghost town one last time before leaving. The twilight lingered a long time in the mountains, and she had more than enough light left.

The back of her neck continued to prickle as she walked among the ruins, but she forced herself to ignore it. There was nothing here but memories of the time a century ago when a few hundred people had mined the area, looking for the mother lode that didn't exist. Except for a few birds, nothing moved. Except for the memories, nothing stirred.

She never came here without thinking of all the broken dreams. So many broken dreams. Like her own.

The girl child within her moved, stretching, reassuring Janet with this display of vitality. The baby was a new dream, placed there by a man who had dashed all her old ones. Sometimes it wasn't easy, but she'd promised herself that she wasn't going to be bitter about it. No point in that. Dreams were meant to be lost and replaced. So few of them ever came true.

A derrick rose above an old mine shaft, weathered gray, but still strong. The pulley wheels had rusted dark red, and the rope had long since rotted away. Someone had once worked hard to build that mine, had sweated and bled and hoped and prayed. Now it stood abandoned and forgotten.

Despite herself, she felt the sting of tears behind her eyes. Self-pity. Disgusting. She blinked hard, drew a deep breath and marched on, determined to vanquish the demons.

That was when she saw the man. He stood near the edge of the forest, not far from a caved-in shaft over which a wooden derrick tilted crazily. Phantomlike, he appeared to be a dark shadow—just a black silhouette against the forest depths. Arms akimbo, feet splayed, he looked powerful and subtly threatening.

Janet took an instinctive step backward, her hand flying with maternal protectiveness to her swollen womb. Why hadn't she left as soon as she began to feel that someone was watching? Why had she been so determined to be brave? She took another quick step backward and stumbled, nearly falling.

He didn't move a muscle. "I'm not going to hurt you," he said. His voice was dark and deep, quiet, faintly impatient. Except for that impatience, she would have wondered if it was part of the forest.

Her mind scrambled rapidly around, calculating the distance to her car, calculating her various options for escape. They were slender. "Who—who are you?"

He still didn't move. "I'm just camping out here. I didn't mean to startle you."

"You've been watching me!" Her words were accusatory, and she almost flinched at the way they sounded in the serene quiet of the mountainside.

"If I'd been watching you, lady, you never would have seen me." Now he *did* sound impatient. "I can't be the only fool on this mountain besides you."

If he hadn't been watching her, then who had? The question flashed across her mind, leaving her even more shaken. She had to get out of here. Now. Backing up another step, she asked, "Are you a friend of Billy Joe Yuma's?" If he was one of the vets who lived in these mountains, then he was probably acquainted with her sister Wendy's husband. That was a connection that might protect her.

"No." The answer was one syllable, flatly spoken. It did absolutely nothing to reassure her.

She backed up again, wishing she had the courage to turn her back on him and head for her car. Somehow she couldn't quite believe it was safe for anyone to turn their back on this mysterious man. "Have you been camping here long?"

"No."

He still hadn't moved, and it began to dawn on her that if he meant her any harm, he surely would have sprung by now. "You're . . . not from around here, are you?"

"What is this? Twenty questions?"

In her experience, most campers tended to be friendly and communicative. This man didn't fit any of the norms she was accustomed to. He was intimidating somehow, but offered her no overt threat. He was camping, but she had seen no signs of a campsite, and he displayed none of the ordinary friendliness of people who escaped to the woods for their vacations. In fact, he had a hard city edge to him.

She took one more backward step. "Well, I come up here a lot to take photographs. I'll probably see you around." Turning swiftly, not waiting for his reply, she headed for her car, walking as fast as she could without running.

In the dimness, however, she failed to see a sharp dip in the ground until her ankle rolled over and sent her sprawling. She caught herself with her hands and cried out as she felt gravel cut into her palms. She took the entire force of the fall on hands and knees to protect her womb. To protect her baby.

The next thing she knew, the strange man was squatting beside her, not touching her in any way. "Are you okay?" he demanded roughly. He sounded irritated, as if he would rather not have bothered.

"I'm fine. I'm fine. . . ." She rolled over, staring up at the darkening sky, waiting for the pain in her hands, wrists and knees to subside. Waiting to see if anything else started to hurt—if there were any stirrings of trouble in her womb.

It had been a while since she had fallen so hard, and she suddenly found herself remembering all the skinned knees of her childhood. She wondered if you could skin your knees through jeans and decided probably not.

Pointless mental wanderings. Reasonably certain that she had done no serious damage, she sat up.

"Here." Strong hands grasped her under the elbows and lifted her to her feet in a breathless rush. Lifted her almost as fast as she had fallen. This man had frightening strength.

"Thank you," she managed to say. "Thank you."

He let go of her abruptly and stepped away. "You shouldn't come to out-of-the-way places like this all alone. Now get out of here."

In an instant, like the striking of a match, her temper flared. "Who the hell do you think you are? This is public land, mister, and I'll come here whenever I want."

For the first time she looked directly into his face. In the fading twilight he was a study in shadows, his eyes little more than dark hollows in a sharply etched landscape. He was tall, imposing—and deadly looking.

"More guts than brains," he said shortly, and turned to stalk away.

Janet stared after him, wanting to argue with that insult but having too much intelligence to pick a fight with a total stranger. Contrary to his opinion, she *did* have more brains than guts. Besides, for all that he was grumpy, he had come to her aid. She wouldn't forget that. Sighing, sure now that her knees and hands weren't seriously injured, relieved to feel no troubling pains, she turned again for her car. It was well past time to go home.

Thunder rolled down the slopes of the mountain into the deserted mining camp. The last of the fading twilight was swallowed by the heavy storm clouds that always seemed to swirl around the peak. Tonight they swept down to the lower altitudes.

Beneath his feet, Abel Pierce felt the rumble of the thunder like the heartbeat of the mountain. The power of nature surrounded him with its ferocity, whipping the trees with the lash of the wind and piercing the night with spears of lightning.

He had nearly forgotten, during his long years on city streets, the absolute strength of nature unchained. He had forgotten the brooding atmosphere of a forest, the sense that here another law prevailed.

Inside one of the tumbledown shacks, he sat on an upturned log with his down jacket wrapped tightly around him and watched the fury of the storm through the uncovered windows and the cracks between the boards. It was cold and getting colder, the way spring could be in the mountains, but he had long since taught himself indifference to the elements.

Except that tonight, for some reason, he didn't want to be indifferent to the storm, or the cold, or his own discomfort. Most of his life, he had been denying his body's most basic instincts, instincts for warmth when it was cold, food when it was hungry, rest when it was tired. He had even learned to deny the basic needs of the human psyche for safety and companionship.

He existed behind a wall, focused on the task at hand, letting nothing get between him and his mission. But it was not really living; it was living death.

Tonight he wanted to be alive. Tonight he wanted to feel the cold and yearn for fire. Ache with hunger and savor food. Breathe the damp, pine-scented air with an awareness of the forest—and without an awareness of fear.

He wanted to build a fire, wash his face in hot water and then cook a meal. But caution stayed him. Even though it was unlikely the light or smoke of a fire would travel far on a night like this, he still chose to wait until a later hour, when it was even less likely that anyone would be out and about.

For now he sat in the cold, shivered a little and allowed himself to be human.

That woman who had been poking around the camp today might be a problem, he thought. He tilted his head, listening to the forlorn wail of the wind as it slipped through the treetops, and tried not to think of her as anything except a problem. If she came up here often, he would have to find another camp. He didn't want his solitude to be invaded all the time.

But she probably wouldn't come again soon, not now that she knew he was here. She'd been a bit of a spitfire, facing him down with more spirit than smarts, but he figured that was more an attack of adrenaline than a natural mode of conduct for her. Of course, he could be wrong. It sure as hell wouldn't be the first time he'd misjudged a woman.

She was kind of pretty, though, with cinnamon hair and bright green eyes that were almost the shade of tree moss. Delicate. She had such delicacy of facial structure, and her hands had been tiny, looking hardly strong enough to hold the camera she had been using. But there was steel there, a backbone that would stand up.

Why was he even thinking of her? She was a complete stranger, one he would probably never set eyes on again. She belonged to a world that he had never been allowed to enter, as if he lacked the necessary passport.

Not that he wanted to belong. He was satisfied with the way he lived his life, and with his purposes and goals. But the night was chilly and empty, filled with the wildness of the storm and nothing else, and his mind seemed to want to think of softer things. Gentler things. Warmer things.

Like a woman with cinnamon hair and green eyes and a touch of temper. An image warm enough to make him forget that he wanted a fire.

Janet almost didn't go home. The problem was, there really wasn't any other place to go. She pulled up at last on the street in front of her parents' house and looked at the lighted windows. It was true, she thought sadly; you couldn't go home again.

But there was no point in delaying the inevitable. Swallowing her somber thoughts, she retrieved her camera case from the back of the car and walked reluctantly to the front door. A welcome was waiting for her in there. Mom would be in the midst of cooking dinner, but would immediately insist Janet put her feet up and drink something warm. Dad was home, his official Blazer parked in the driveway behind Mom's red Fiero, and he would be watching the TV news with one eye and chatting with the younger girls about their days. Predictable as the rising of the sun.

Her throat tightened a little. She no longer belonged here. That was the saddest result of the changes in her life; events had distanced her so that she now felt like a guest in the only home she had ever known.

Slipping through the front door, she hoped to be able to dart through the foyer to the back of the house and her bedroom without being spied, but Marge Tate was just coming through the kitchen door into the dining room and saw her.

"Janet! I was beginning to get worried."

"Sorry. I was up at the old mining camp taking pictures, and I lost track of time." Hiding, Mom, she added silently. I was hiding. It was quiet there, and peaceful.

"Go get comfortable and I'll make you something warm to drink. You shouldn't wear yourself out like this."

Caring and love shone from her mother's beautiful face, and Janet felt like the worst sort of ingrate for wanting to escape it. "I think I'll just lie down for a few minutes, if that's okay." She would have preferred to help with dinner, but so far she hadn't been allowed to. She hadn't been allowed to do much of anything, actually. It made her feel even more like a guest here.

She fled to the bedroom she had once shared with her older sister, Wendy, and stretched out on the twin bed that had been hers all her life. It wasn't the same. Nothing was the same. Maybe she should have stayed in Boulder with her friends. Instead she had fled the place that had brought her so much pain and come running home like a child seeking comfort and reassurance.

There was plenty of both here, but they were turning out not to be what she needed at all. She needed to find her own place, for one thing. A place where she could deal with the lessons of the past year inside the solitude of her own mind. A place where she wouldn't be constantly interrupted by caring family members who didn't want her to feel lonely or ignored.

A familiar knock at the door told her that she wasn't going to be left alone right now, either. "Come on in, Dad."

Sheriff Nathan Tate walked into his daughter's room. He was a tall man, still powerful as he approached fifty. All her life he had symbolized safety to her, and all of a sudden she wanted to just hurl herself into his arms and sob her heart out the same way she had when she had been small. To feel safe in a great big bear hug, sure that her father would protect her from every evil.

Another illusion chipped away by the reality of adulthood. There was no absolute safety, and a pair of arms could hurt as much as they could protect.

Nate must have seen the anguish on his daughter's face, because he perched on the edge of the bed, took her by the shoulders and drew her onto his chest, just as he had all during the years of her childhood. "I wish I could fix it, honey. Honest to God, I wish I could."

"I know, Daddy. I know." Tears ran down her cheeks, salty and hot. Then the sobs started coming, soft hiccups of sound.

"All I can promise is that the hurt will heal. Time fixes damn near everything, Jannie. You know that."

"Yeah, but it takes so long!" The words were half laugh, half sob. "Sometimes I want to kill him for what he did to me. You know that? Sometimes I'd find it easy to kill him."

"I'm not surprised." He stroked her hair gently and rocked her slowly back and forth, the way he had been doing for his daughters all their lives. "I imagine your mother felt like that about me a few times after she discovered she was pregnant with Seth."

Janet tipped her face up so she could see him. "What exactly is the story with Seth?"

Nate turned his face away, and it was apparent to her that it still troubled him to discuss it. He and Marge had given their daughters only a sketchy outline of what had happened. "We've told you, Jannie. I got your mom pregnant right before I shipped out for Nam. She heard that I'd been killed in action, so she gave Seth up for adoption. Back then, an unmarried woman couldn't keep her baby. It just wasn't done."

"But didn't she get letters from you? Weren't you writing to her?"

He hesitated visibly. "Yeah," he said finally. "I was writing to her, but she wasn't getting the letters. We didn't want to speak ill of the dead but...frankly, honey, your grandfather Whelan was destroying my letters to her and throwing hers away without mailing them, so I didn't know she was pregnant, and she didn't know I was alive."

"How awful!"

He patted her shoulder. "It was a long time ago, and we've got Seth now, so..." He shrugged. "One way or another, things work out. Just keep telling yourself that."

Janet straightened, drawing back from his hug. She looked down at her twined fingers. "You must both be...embarrassed that I've come home this way. Disappointed." Some things about small towns hadn't changed. An unwed mother...

"Your mother and I aren't disappointed in you, Jannie. And we're certainly not embarrassed. We're just concerned that you not have to go through this alone. Now wash your face and come to dinner before your mom gets mad because it's all getting cold."

And that, thought Janet, was why she was being suffocated in concern. Her father and her mother were absolutely determined that she would have everything Marge had lacked during her pregnancy with Seth. It was suddenly all so clear to her. Why couldn't her own course of action be just as clear?

* * *

The entire family had gathered for dinner that evening, even Wendy, who was married and had a home of her own across town.

Sheriff Nathan Tate had long jokingly complained that with six daughters he was outnumbered in his own home. But he didn't look beleaguered at all as he presided over the table and caught up with all the news from his "girls." Carol and Mary were home from college and bubbling over with news to share. Patty and Krissie, the youngest, were hanging on every word.

"Have some more milk, Janet," Marge Tate said, passing the pitcher. "You need the calcium."

"Mom, I get plenty of calcium in my prenatal vitamins." The impatience she was never far from feeling seeped into her voice.

Marge looked rueful. "I'm sorry. I'm nagging you to death."

Guilt pricked Janet, making her squirm inwardly. Why did her parents have to keep on being so nice? She didn't deserve all this niceness. At least if they got mad at her, she would have an excuse to be snappy and grumpy. "I'm sorry, Mom. Just tired, I guess."

Marge's eyes were warm and understanding. She gave her second-oldest daughter a smile and turned her attention back to the conversation among the other girls.

It was just as it had always been, Janet thought, looking around the table. Her dad and mom presiding over six giggling, laughing, sometimes bickering daughters. Except that it didn't feel the same anymore. She sat there and watched the familiar scene as if it were on videotape, somehow removed from it. Distanced.

She didn't belong anymore.

Even as she had the thought, even as the nostalgic sorrow began to bloom in her, she realized she was indulging in self-pity. It was ridiculous to sit here feeling sorry for herself because she was growing up, ridiculous to feel lonely when she was surrounded by a loving family, and downright ungrateful of her to feel annoyed by all the caring and concern being showered on her. She was acting like a spoiled child.

Her mother's voice yanked her out of her morose thoughts.

"You know, the strangest thing happened today," Marge said. "It's enough to make me wonder if I have Alzheimer's."

"Oh, come on, Mom," Mary said. "Anybody who can remember all the birthdays in this family couldn't possibly be getting senile."

Patty giggled.

"I'm serious," Marge said. "It was unnerving."

The humorous mood fled. She had everyone's attention now, including her husband's. Realizing it, she glanced around the table and gave a self-deprecating laugh.

"It's probably nothing. Really. It's just that...well, you know that wedding photo I keep on my dressing table? I found it on the nightstand when I came home this afternoon. Did one of you girls move it?"

In the Tate household it was understood that the master bedroom was absolutely off-limits except when an invitation was issued. Countless times over the years one of the girls had snuggled into bed with Marge and Nate to be comforted after a nightmare, or through a cold or stomach upset, but under no circumstances did they trespass. The question indicated just how disturbed Marge was feeling.

Six heads immediately shook in denial, and Nate frowned. "I know I didn't move it," he said. "Was anything missing?"

"Nothing as far as I could see. It's just...well, I guess I could have moved it while I was thinking of something else. Frankly, I don't know which idea disturbs me more—that I might have done it without realizing it, or that someone else was in the bedroom while I was out today."

"But if nothing was missing..." Nate said, trailing off, reluctant to argue that his wife was just forgetful.

"I know." She gave another quiet laugh and shrugged. "I must have done it. I just wish I could *remember* doing it."

Wendy looked almost as disturbed as Marge did, Janet noticed, and wondered why. Wendy spoke. "You've had a lot on your mind lately, Mom, what with Seth coming home for a visit, and Carol, Mary and Janet being home...."

And with Janet being pregnant... The words were left unspoken, but Janet heard them hanging in the air anyway. The baby in her womb was at once a promise and a betrayal. Instinctively she crossed her arms protectively over her swollen belly.

"Of course," Marge said, laughing more genuinely this time. "I've been feeling a lot like a chicken without a head lately. I probably just got distracted by the phone or something and set it down without thinking."

She was still nervous about it, though, Janet realized, watching her mother return her attention to her meal. Still unconvinced that this was a harmless, meaningless event. Why?

Her baby stirred gently and kicked. The most thrilling feeling she had ever known. She looked down, forgetting everyone else at the table, and smiled inwardly. Quit with the self-pity, she told herself. *This* is what really matters.

The man stood in the shadows beneath a cottonwood. The curtains at the windows of the Tate house hadn't been drawn against the night, and light spilled across the lawn, not quite reaching him. He could see the family within, gathered around the dining table, smiling and laughing.

Happy.

From a distance, he watched, sharing those precious moments caught in the amber lamplight.

It should have been him.

Chapter 2

Morning dawned chilly and dry, the sun peeking beneath a band of pink-and-purple clouds to cast a soft glow across the mining camp.

Abel Pierce hunkered down beside the campfire he was coaxing to life, trying to think about the hot coffee he would soon be drinking, about the bacon he was going to fry, and how everything always tasted so damn much better in the fresh morning air.

Trying to think about anything except his reasons for being here.

Birdsong frolicked on the breeze, joining the rustle of the pines and the rush of running water. He looked up from the fire and let his senses drink in the sights and sounds and sensations of a clear Rocky Mountain morning. Thousands of feet above him, the peak of Thunder Mountain brooded beneath its ever present mantle of clouds, but here, on the low slopes, the morning was crystalline in its clarity.

Pine trees seemed to stand out with unusual sharpness in air so clear that not even dancing dust motes caught and splintered the dawn light. The shadows beneath the trees remained dark and thick, but the sky overhead was lightening from indigo to azure.

It was unlike him to avoid the hard edges of reality, but this morning it would have been obscene to do anything else. Disturbing the atmosphere with mundane concerns would have been nearly sacrilegious.

Not that his concerns were mundane, he thought almost wryly. Oh no. He'd never learned to live a mundane existence.

Wood smoke wafted up from his small fire, stinging his nose and eyes, filling him with a nostalgic tug of memory. The fire was a gift from the forest, a gift of dry, dead wood to be used with care to bring warmth and life. In all things there was a balance.

How had he forgotten that?

Impatient with the direction of his thoughts, Abel pushed the question aside. Forget it. Forget it all. For now, just exist and take the bounty that nature offered.

In the back of his mind, dark things lurked, held at bay by force of will. He had constructed a prison around parts of himself, walling them off rather than allowing them to torment him. Some folks would probably tell him to stop burying all that stuff, that it would be better to deal with it than to lock it away. In fact, he expected that someday it was all going to force its way out, like a backed-up sewer, seeping through all the cracks and crevices he hadn't been quite able to seal. Someday he would probably drown in the sludge of his own past.

But not now. For now it was going to stay buried deep in the darkest dungeons of his mind. Later. He would deal with it later—if he had to. Funny thing was, some things could be put off until you didn't have to deal with them anymore. Watching a bullet explode a person's head taught you things like that. It taught you to play hide-and-seek with memory. It taught you that tomorrow was an illusion, a will-o'-the-wisp that only fools chased.

But all this philosophy on an empty stomach was going to give him a headache. Smiling sourly at himself, he set the cast-iron fry pan on the fire and laid a half-dozen strips of bacon in it. The water in the nearby stream ran down from the snow-fields high above and was cold enough to make refrigeration a simple matter. He didn't even need to get ice for his cooler; he simply used a mesh bag to keep meat and milk in the icy water.

A flash of movement at the corner of his eye caught his attention, and he turned his head swiftly. A doe. She stood frozen at the tree line, her nostrils quivering as she picked up the unfamiliar scents of the bacon and the man. Poised for instant flight, she stood statuelike for several seconds, then darted back into the shadows, gone in the blink of an eye.

It was as if something were settling in him, as if something that had long been twisted out of shape by necessity were slowly returning to its natural configuration. As if something that had been crabbed and knotted inside him were stretching and relaxing.

Maybe he was just losing his edge. It seemed kind of quick to be doing that, but it was possible. Up here, on the lonely side of this mountain, he felt as if he could safely breathe without looking over his shoulder every minute. Maybe it was safe enough here to do that, but relaxing could be a dangerous indulgence. What if he couldn't get the edge back when he needed it?

But all of that seemed so far away now. What seemed infinitely closer and infinitely more important were the words of his childhood *sensei*. "The rocks, the trees, the water that runs down the hillside, and even you, child, are one. Open your mind and heart and feel it."

When he had been small, those words had made infinite sense to him as he had run virtually free up and down the hills of Okinawa. Then the world had been his to enjoy in all its beauteous aspects, and it had not seemed at all strange that he and it were one. That unity had been lost, though, lost in the harsh realities of adulthood and under the pavement of city streets. He had forgotten, until this very moment, that he could open himself up and relax into the harmony of nature.

But he couldn't afford to lose his edge. Nor was he, he assured himself; he was simply responding to the peace being exuded by the forest just as he responded to the threat when he was on a darkened city street. No one knew that he was here, and that meant he didn't have to live in expectation of attack. He could afford to let the peace overtake him. Briefly.

It was hard to let go, hard to relax the wary alertness that had kept him alive for so long, almost impossible, given the risk that there might indeed be something out there that wanted to harm him. Still, he forced himself to do it. It was a good meditative experience, and it had been too long since he had meditated. Too long since he had honed any skills other than those he needed for survival.

Too long, it sometimes seemed, since he had lived as anything but a hunted animal.

Closing his eyes, he breathed deeply of the pine scent of the forest, of the tangy wood smoke of his fire, of the savory frying bacon. Good smells. Reminders that there was good in life, too. How could he have forgotten that?

Without warning, released by a moment of relaxation, anger rushed up from the depths of his soul, filling him, driving him to his feet. Blindly he kicked at a rock and sent it flying. When it struck a nearby shack, it sounded like a gunshot.

The sharp sound brought him instantly back to his senses. Okay, so he'd had a couple of bad breaks. No need to act like it was the end of the world. He'd known the risks when he'd taken the job, but he'd taken it anyway.

But that uprush of violent anger had been a warning. He looked down at the dusty toe of his hiking boot, the one with which he had just kicked the rock, and acknowledged that buried feelings didn't have to stay buried. They could rise from their graves and pounce when they were least expected. Better not to relax, then.

Returning to the log he was using for a stool, he sat and flipped the bacon strips with a fork, enjoying the sting of spraying grease on the back of his hand. Pain, even minor pain, served as a focal point, clearing away the useless anger. Reminding him that he was real.

Hanging around up here was giving him too much time to think, too much time to brood. It was time to put his plan into action and get on with it. Time to take care of old business and clean up loose ends.

Everything else could wait.

* * *

The nicest thing about returning to Conard County, as far as Janet was concerned, was being reunited with her lifelong best friend, Darlene Llewellyn. The two of them, seeking adventure, had gone to college together after their graduation from high school, but Darlene hadn't quite made it through freshman year. Her mother had died, and Darlene had come home to help raise her two younger brothers.

The boys were in high school now, the eldest just a year away from graduating. They both held jobs at their father's veterinary hospital, so Darlene had the days to herself.

"So let's blow this joint," Darlene said mischievously, snatching up her purse and a light jacket. "I don't care what we do, just as long as it's someplace else."

"The only thing I've even thought about doing today is starting the hunt for a place of my own."

"Oh, goody! I'd enjoy that. Hunting for a place for you, I mean, although to tell you the truth, I'd be delighted to have a place of my own, too. It's high time!"

It was on the tip of Janet's tongue to suggest they move in together, but she stopped herself. The simple truth was, she had never had a bedroom all to herself. When she had left home to go to college, she'd had to have a roommate. Soon she would have a baby to share her life. In the little time left to her before she gave birth, she wanted to know what it was like to live all by herself. To answer to no one. To use all the hot water when she took a shower without worrying that she was depriving someone else.

She had circled possible rentals in yesterday's newspaper, and they headed out to the first of them, Janet driving.

"The boys don't really need anyone at home anymore," Darlene told her. "I think this fall, after they go back to school, I'll move out."

"Just into an apartment around here, you mean? Or are you going back to school?"

"I haven't decided." Darlene glanced out the window, tossing her long chestnut hair over her shoulder. "It's kind of scary, Jan. Five years ago I was ready and fearless. Now I'm scared to death."

"But why?"

Darlene shrugged, as if she couldn't explain it. Then, suddenly, words burst out of her. "Take a bit of advice from me, Jan. Don't stay home and play mother. It's terrible what it does to you. My brain feels like it's rusted, for one thing. I'm not sure I could go back to school now. For another, I don't have a shred of confidence left in myself. It struck me the other day that I don't feel attractive anymore. I don't feel interesting anymore. I can't imagine why anyone would want to spend two minutes with me, let alone be actually interested in me."

"Darlene, that's not true! You're the same person you always were."

"Except that I haven't been out on a date in five years. Except that I haven't done anything interesting in five years. Talk about dull . . ." She shook her head. "It may be silly, but it's how I feel. So I get scared at the thought of trying to go it alone, of trying to pick up where I left off when Mom died."

Janet wheeled them into the parking lot of an apartment complex, stopping right in front of the office. "I guess I can understand that." And she could, sort of. Look what Scott had done to her own self-confidence. "Maybe you shouldn't try to pick up where you left off."

"What do you mean?"

"Well . . . maybe you should start out slowly. Get yourself a part-time job but keep living with your family for a while. You know, get your feet wet a little at a time."

Darlene smiled wryly. "That's probably about the max I'll be able to manage anyway." Suddenly she realized where they were. "Oh, you don't want to even look at these places!"

"Why not?" This complex had been built while Janet was in college, and she figured the apartments were still in pretty good condition.

"I have some friends who live here. The walls are paper-thin. If you want to listen to other people snore, and want them bellyaching all the time about your baby . . ."

Janet turned on the ignition. "I think I'll pass."

"Wise choice. There's an apartment building over on Fuller that's nicer. It costs a little more, though."

"Actually, I'd rather live in a little house outside of town than in an apartment complex."

"Then why are you even looking at apartments?"

"Because they're available?"

Darlene laughed. "Gads, Jan, it's not as if you don't have a place to sleep! What's the rush?"

Janet laughed, too. "I was just trying to be methodical and practical. You know—look at all the possibilities, compare them, then make a reasoned decision."

"But you don't *have* to rent something you don't like, do you?"

"Well, no..."

"So quit being practical. I'm the practical one, you're the impulsive one, remember?"

"I remember." She felt a bubble of sheer happiness rising from somewhere deep inside her. "I've missed you, Dar."

"I've missed you, too, Jan. Now let's quit being maudlin and find someplace you'd *like* to live."

The last place she had scheduled to look at that day was a log cabin on the edge of the Bar C Ranch, at the foot of Thunder Mountain. They were met there by Jeff Cumberland, the county's wealthiest rancher, owner of the Bar C.

He was leaning against a hunter green late-model pickup, waiting for them when they jolted down the narrow track. Pushing close to forty, he was a handsome man with dark hair and friendly eyes, and had the lean, weathered look that proclaimed his occupation. He smiled from beneath the brim of a black cowboy hat when he saw Janet.

Jeff was a good friend of her father's and had been part of Janet's life for years. It was suddenly difficult to get out of her Explorer. She didn't know whether her dad had told Jeff she was pregnant, and she didn't know how he would react to the news. He'd always been like a beloved uncle to her, and she was so afraid he would be disappointed in her.

But if he was, he didn't show it. As she eased out of the car, his quick gaze took in her pregnant state, then returned to her face, warmth undimmed. When he opened his arms wide, she didn't hesitate to accept the big bear hug he offered her. He wasn't going to judge her, she realized. A tight little knot of fear deep inside her relaxed.

"You two planning to rent this place together?" Jeff wanted to know. He gave Darlene a big hug, too.

Darlene shook her head. "Just Janet. I'm not quite ready to move out on my own yet."

Jeff paused, key in hand, as he turned toward the cabin. "Janet, this is a long way out of town. I don't know that I'm too keen on having you out here by yourself."

"I'll be just fine." It was ridiculous, she thought, the way people wanted to smother her. "In the first place, I'm perfectly healthy. In the second place, I'll have a telephone, so if I need anything I can get it. In the third place, when my due date approaches, I'll move back in with my folks."

He searched her face a moment, then nodded. "I guess. You can always call up to the ranch, too. I can have someone here in five minutes. Well, maybe ten."

Apparently discarding his concerns, he led the way to the front door. "This place was built by the first Cumberland to settle here. The family's been using it off and on ever since, and renting it out from time to time. I just had it cleaned up and refurbished since the last tenant, so I think you'll find it's in pretty good shape."

A hollow boom of thunder rolled down the mountain from the clouds that swirled around the peak. Thunder Mountain seemed to make its own weather; everywhere else the sky was still blue. The shadow the mountain cast, however, was steadily creeping toward the cabin's front door as the sun sank lower in the western sky.

"It's beautiful here, Jeff," Janet said as they walked up a narrow gravel path to a low covered porch. The cabin was made of rough-hewn logs, but the window frames, looking relatively recent, were made of finished wood that was painted hunter green, and the plank floor of the porch was also freshly painted the same green. Someone had troubled to plant petunias and pansies along the walk, and the yard was a carpet of wildflowers.

Behind the cabin, the ground sloped gently down to a mountain-fed stream that was sheltered by cottonwoods. It would be a beautiful place to spend the summer.

"I lived here for a while myself," Jeff said as he unlocked the door. "It's wonderful in the summer. I don't know about the winter, though, not if you're going to be here by yourself with a baby, Janet. Getting in and out could get to be tough."

"I'm young, I'm healthy, and I can handle a snowblower. I'll manage, Jeff."

He must have heard an edge in her voice, because he flashed a grin. "Is everybody treating you as if you're fragile?"

"As if I'm an invalid and suddenly have the IQ of a gnat!"

The instant she crossed the threshold, she knew this was where she wanted to live. The cabin wasn't very large, just two bedrooms and a spacious living and kitchen area, but it was just right for her and her baby. The furnishings were old, but not decrepit. They simply looked well-used and comfortable. Bright yellow curtains were hung at the windows, and brown braided rugs had been tossed here and there on the plank floor. The kitchen appliances weren't brand-new, but they were of recent vintage and in good condition.

"I just put in new countertops," Jeff remarked.

"I thought they looked new." Not a cut or a scratch to mar the pristine surfaces. She would have to get a cutting board. She ran her hand over a counter, feeling possessive already.

"You know how to use a woodstove, don't you?" Jeff continued, indicating the black stove that stood in one corner of the living room. Janet nodded. "There's propane heat, of course, and this old cabin is about as weathertight as they come, but it'd be cheaper to heat it with a stove—unless you don't want to. Might be a problem with a baby. Hadn't thought about that."

"Not immediately. Later I could put a safety fence around it." It would be a problem with a small child learning to walk. Would she even be here that long? Probably not. Her plans right now were to go back to grad school after Christmas.

"I've put a couple of cords of wood out back to season, so you can have a fire if you want. Propane tank is full. Do you know how to read the gauge?"

He knew, she thought. Jeff knew she was going to rent the place.

He took her outside, showed her the shed and the propane tank, warning her to call for a fuel delivery before the gauge got too low, because it could take the company as long as a week to get out there.

A couple of minutes later she was handing him a check and he was handing her the key.

"Oh, sigh," Darlene said as they stood in front of the cabin watching Jeff drive away. "I wish he was ten years younger, or I was ten years older."

"He is kind of a hunk," Janet admitted, "but he's also a man. That's the last thing I want in my life right now."

Darlene turned to her. "Scott was a creep, but he's hardly representative."

"Well, there was the creep before Scott, too," Janet reminded her.

"Bud wasn't a creep. He just—"

"Just cheated on me is all!" Realizing that her voice was rising, Janet forced herself to speak more quietly. "Men are cheats. Liars."

"Not all men."

Janet was in a mood to argue about that, except that she found herself thinking of her father. "Okay, there are a few exceptions. My dad. Your dad. I refuse to go any further than that."

Darlene giggled. "Well, it's a start. Then there are my two brothers. Your sister Wendy's husband. Jeff Cumberland . . ." She turned her head and looked down the dusty, rutted driveway. Jeff's truck was no longer visible. "I wonder why he never married."

"Every single woman in Conard County, with the exception of *moi*, would like to know the answer to that. This is ridiculous, Dar. I've got to find you a boyfriend. It's obvious your development has been arrested."

Darlene looked at her. "Arrested? How?"

"You still haven't learned that men are liars and cheats."

She really meant that, too. Sort of. Or at least she was trying to believe it. The real question, of course, was who was truly to blame for what had happened. The piranha for being a piranha? Or herself for not recognizing a piranha before she got bitten?

Except that the piranha had been masquerading as a goldfish. Scott had come to her as a friend after Bud had left her. He had held her, soothed her, inserted himself into her life in a way that filled a lot of empty cracks, and helped her get over her initial pain. How was she supposed to have guessed that that was merely his method of seduction?

But apparently it was, to judge by the tales she had heard since he had walked out on her over her pregnancy. It was amazing how people would rush to tell you everything they had known when it was too late to do you any good. Of course, there was always the question of whether she would have even listened to them while Scott was being so sweet to her.

Basically, she felt she ought to hate men, but despite the way she talked about them, she didn't. What she really felt was hurt deep inside in some very tender place. What she really felt was a lot less trust for the world at large.

What she really felt was that there was something wrong with her. Otherwise he would have stayed.

Well, she didn't want to think about that now. It wouldn't do a damn bit of good if she started brooding.

Instead, spying her dad's familiar silhouette in the window of Maude's Diner as she drove by after dropping Darlene off, she decided to stop. A piece of pie would taste wonderful right now, and it would give her a chance to tell her dad she was renting Jeff Cumberland's cabin.

She had forgotten about her pregnancy, though, and remembered it only when Maude gave her belly a pointed, disapproving stare. At once she felt as if her stomach were painted in neon green.

"Hi, Maude," she managed to say, hoping her voice didn't sound as stifled as it felt.

Maude nodded in return but didn't say hello. Not that that meant anything; Maude had never been one for wasting her breath on greetings and small talk. "You want something?"

Only years of familiarity kept Janet from interpreting that the wrong way. For all its belligerence, it was Maude's usual request for an order.

"Blueberry pie, please? With a scoop of vanilla ice cream."

Maude nodded. "Your dad's over there."

"Thanks, I saw him." As she walked across to the table by the window where her father sat, talking with someone she couldn't see, Janet was sure every eye in the place was following her. The hard part about being the sheriff's daughter in a place this size was that just about everybody knew who you were. And knew you weren't married, because if you had been, they would all have heard about it. She felt like Hester Prynne.

But her father's smile reassured her as he stood up to greet her. The man with him stood, too, and turned, and she recognized the stranger from the mining camp.

An electric shock ran through her as their eyes connected. It was utterly silly, but it was as if they shared an illicit secret. She wanted to look away, but instead she felt as if she were falling into his gaze, into eyes as dark and deep as a midnight pool. She shivered and dragged herself back from the precipice, afraid of what might lurk in those dark depths.

"We met briefly yesterday, Sheriff," she heard him say. "I came across Ms. Tate in the old mining town where I'm camping out. We didn't introduce ourselves, though." He gave Janet a smile that wasn't quite a smile, a curvature of his lips that was more wary than pleasant. "I'm Abel Pierce," he said to her.

He moved a little too close when he shook her hand, betraying that he was a city dweller, accustomed to a smaller personal space. Despite recognizing it for what it was, it still made her nervous, and she was relieved when her dad held out a chair for her on the far side of the table from Abel Pierce.

"Pierce is working on a book," Nate told his daughter.

The other man nodded. "My idea is to tell a history of the Vietnam conflict from the perspective of a single unit."

"That's . . . interesting." Vietnam. So long ago, yet forever rearing its ugly head. She thought of her brother-in-law, Billy Joe Yuma, of his veteran friends on the mountain. Of her father and his friends, Micah Parish and Ransom Laird, three men whose friendships had been welded in the Nam. "Is it about Dad's unit?"

Pierce nodded. "I have all the official history, but I need the personal recollections to make it memorable."

Janet looked at her father. In all the years of her life, he had been largely silent on the subject of the war. She had gotten the distinct impression that it wasn't something he cared to dredge up. "I thought you didn't like to talk about it?"

"I don't, as a rule. Most of the memories aren't what I'd call pleasant. On the other hand, pleasant or not, it was important to everyone who was involved, and I think that deserves to be recognized."

"There are survivors and heirs with a great interest in what happened," Abel observed. "They want to know more than they can learn from official reports."

"Oh, I can see the point of it," Janet said. "I'd want to read it myself. It's just that Dad doesn't usually want to talk about it."

Maude interrupted them with Janet's pie and ice cream, which she slapped down on the table, and a demand to know if anybody else wanted anything.

"That pie looks good, Maude," Nate said. "I think I'll have a piece, too."

"Make that two," Abel said.

"Her curiosity must be just about killing her," Janet remarked when Maude had retreated to the kitchen. "She knows everything that goes on in this county, and now there's a stranger eating pie with the sheriff." She fought back an irrepressible giggle of good humor. "Put her out of her misery, Dad."

"She knows how to eavesdrop. Besides, anything she doesn't manage to find out by listening in, she'll get from Velma." Velma Jansen was the dispatcher in the sheriff's office, and she and Maude were as thick as thieves.

Abel Pierce had a good poker face, but Janet could still tell he was a little surprised by the sheriff's easy acceptance of eavesdropping and gossip. He didn't say anything, though. If she hadn't been looking directly at him, she would have missed his reaction.

"So what brings you in here?" Nate asked his daughter. "Maude's pie?"

"Partly. And partly to tell you I've rented a place of my own."

The look that crossed his face was one of sheer exasperation. "Janet, I've told you—"

"I know you have. And I've told you that I need to be on my own." She didn't want to discuss the issue in front of a stranger and tried to answer her father pleasantly enough that he would drop the matter, at least until later. Apparently she succeeded, because he just nodded and asked where she would be living.

"Jeff Cumberland's cabin." As she'd expected, his face darkened.

"That's a long way out from town."

"Jeff's only a few minutes away, and said he could get someone out to me if I needed anything. Dad, I'll be okay. I'm a big girl now, and I've been on my own for a long time."

"There's a difference between being on your own and being on your own pregnant," her father growled, but with that he let go of the issue for the moment.

Maude slapped two more pieces of pie on the table and refilled their coffee cups.

"Is she always this grumpy?" Abel asked quietly.

"Grumpy?" Janet couldn't prevent a laugh. "Actually, Mr. Pierce, she's in a good mood today."

"That's a fact," Nate agreed. "When Maude's in a bad mood, they know it at the far end of the county."

"I heard that, Nathan Tate," Maude snapped as she came out of the kitchen. "You watch that tongue of yours or you'll need to be watching your food here from now on."

"You threatening to poison me, Maude? Me, an officer of the law?"

"I said no such thing, and you know it. You might just find salt instead of sugar in your pie, is all."

Nate grinned. "You'd never do that. You take too damn much pride in your cooking."

Maude sniffed and disappeared back into the kitchen. Abel chuckled. "I get the picture. Reminds me of my uncle."

He seemed so different today, Janet thought, watching him converse with her father. He seemed so open and friendly, unlike yesterday, when all he had appeared to want was to be left completely alone in his hermitage. The contrast made her uneasy, as if there were something dishonest about him.

But that was ridiculous, she decided. He was probably still a man who very much wanted to be left utterly alone, but today his job required him to be pleasant in order to get what he needed. Simple manipulation.

It didn't raise her estimation of him all that much, but it at least put him in the realm of the normal.

She watched his hands as he talked to her father about the Special Forces unit Nate had been in. Abel was trying to ascertain which people Nate had known personally, and Nate was occasionally hesitating over a name, trying to place the person.

Abel was holding a pencil, slashing a check mark next to names on a roster, scribbling the occasional note on a yellow legal pad. He didn't look like a writer. Which was a stupid thing to think and made her wonder just what kind of stereotypes she was harboring. But somehow, in her mind, she couldn't connect writing with danger, and this man looked dangerous. Not threatening. Just dangerous.

Those dark eyes of his were entirely too alert—and entirely too distant, as if he had removed himself far beyond the reach of humankind. When those eyes flicked her way, she felt their touch like a zap of electricity.

"My mother was Japanese," she heard him say to Nate. "Well, according to her she was." A very faint smile lifted the corners of his mouth. "More accurately, she was Okinawan. I lived the first six years of my life on the island."

"Then you're familiar with the base."

"As of thirty years ago."

"Well, that's when I was there, son."

Son. Her dad was calling him son, which meant Nate Tate liked Abel Pierce. The word seemed to strike Abel, too, because his pencil paused noticeably as he wrote something down.

He glanced at her again, and she felt the same electric jolt. Suddenly she had to get out of there. Pushing her pie plate aside, she mumbled an excuse, dropped a couple of bucks on the table and rose.

"My treat on the pie," Nate said, stuffing the bills back into her pocket. "Honey, is something wrong?"

"Just tired, Dad. Really, I'm fine. I just need to get started on my packing."

Actually, she was losing her mind. Outside, she climbed into her car. An instant later, she changed her mind, climbing out again to cross the street and enter Good Shepherd Church. There she slid into a pew and tried to deal with the fact that she had somehow managed to mess up her entire life.

A year ago she would have wanted to get the attention of a man like Abel Pierce. From the instant she set eyes on him, she would have enjoyed the sparkle of sexual attraction and would have wanted him to notice her.

Now she looked at him and felt those things, but instead of intriguing her, they frightened her. She felt as if she had slammed up against a big concrete wall.

Which was just as well. From here on out, she had to be a responsible adult. She was going to be a mother, after all. The time for childhood was past.

And that hurt like hell.

Chapter 3

"I wish you wouldn't do this," Marge said to Janet. "If you need a doctor in a hurry—"

"Wendy and Yuma will get in their helicopter and come flying to my rescue." Her sister and brother-in-law headed up Conard County's emergency response team. She would get the best service possible. "Mom, women have been pregnant for thousands of years without hospitals nearby. My doctor says I'm perfectly healthy. Will you relax?"

"But you're going to be all alone!"

"No more than a phone call away from help." Janet paused suddenly and looked at her mother. "What's wrong, Mom? You're not usually this nervous about things."

Marge hesitated, her green eyes dark with some hidden feeling. "It's just...oh, I don't know, Janet. I've been uneasy ever since I found that picture moved. It's too ridiculous to even think about, though. I mean, it's not as if somebody was in here. If they had been, they'd have stolen something—and heaven knows, your father and I have managed to accumulate a few things worth stealing over the years!"

Janet almost smiled, except that concern for her mother stopped her. "And?"

Marge blinked, hesitating. "And what?"

Janet dropped the blouse she'd been folding into the box and perched on the edge of her bed. "You're convinced no one could have been in the house, right?"

"Isn't that what I just said?"

"Then the only possibility is that you or Dad moved that photo when your mind was focused on something else. There's no reason to worry about it, Mom. Like Dad said, with all that's been going on, it's hardly to be wondered at if you forget doing some little thing like that."

"I know that! And I'd like to just dismiss it, but I can't. It's making me edgy about everything, including having any of you girls out of my sight." Marge turned away from her, looking out the window at the backyard, where the swing set still resided, painted and repainted over the years, and the weathered redwood picnic table stood beneath a cottonwood. "Alzheimer's can start at my age, I've heard."

"Mom—"

"No, Janet, let me finish. It can start at my age. Little things that won't really be noticeable for years, probably. But, Janet, if I can forget moving a photograph out of the place where I've kept it for nearly thirty years, then I could forget anything. Like my kids or. . ." She trailed off.

Janet stood up and moved to stand right behind her, taking her gently by the shoulders. "Mom?"

"Hmm?"

"Your family all lived to be really old, didn't they? All of them?"

"Except for Great-Uncle Liam. A cow kicked him in the head, and he died three days later."

"Of all the relatives you have who lived to a ripe old age, did any of them get senile?"

"Not that I know of."

"Well, they say Alzheimer's is inherited, so I seriously doubt you could have it. Besides, to get this upset over one little incident—"

Marge turned and looked straight at her. "It's not just one little incident, Janet. If it were, I'd laugh it off."

"You mean you've forgotten other things?"

"I guess. I've been keeping this house a certain way for all these years, and there's no reason on earth why I'd suddenly up and start putting things out of place—certainly not without realizing I was doing it. It just doesn't make sense! But nobody in this family would play that kind of trick on me, and nobody else has been in here to do it."

The hairs on Janet's arms prickled as if a cold wind had just blown over them. "Have you told Dad?"

"Why would I? It's just too ridiculous to be believed, and there's no point getting him all upset until I figure out what's going on."

"What could possibly be going on? A thief would steal something, wouldn't he?"

Marge smiled sadly. "That leaves *me,* doesn't it?"

"No, it means something else is going on." Janet's back was beginning to ache from being slightly bent over while she packed, so she sat on the edge of the bed again. "I'll stay here, then, Mom. You need somebody with you."

Marge looked suddenly appalled. "Oh, Janet, no, I didn't mean . . . Oh, heavens, this all started because I was worried about you, and now you feel you have to be my keeper. No, I won't hear of it. If you feel comfortable with moving out to Jeff's cabin, then go. I'll be perfectly all right. How could I not be? Any time I holler for help, the entire sheriff's department shows up!"

Janet smiled at her mother's attempt at humor, even though it was true. And not only would the sheriff's department show up if Marge Tate needed help, probably three-quarters of the county would, as well.

But that wasn't the point. "Mom, if it isn't you moving the stuff, and it isn't a thief, then someone is trying to make you think you're going crazy. If someone wants to upset you that badly—"

"Oh, that's ridiculous," Marge said vehemently. "Utterly ridiculous. I'd commit myself if I started to get that paranoid. No, it's me. I'm just getting forgetful or distracted or something. I'll make an effort to pay better attention, and it'll probably all stop."

"But if someone . . ." Janet trailed off as Marge shook her head.

"No," her mother said. "There's no one who would want to do such a devious thing. What I need to do is get myself to a doctor and have him check me out. It's probably something very simple—like too much going on at once. I'm trying not to make too big a thing out of it, Janet. It's just that it leaves me feeling uneasy, like I can't quite trust myself, and the uneasiness got transferred to your moving out. You go ahead. The other girls will look after me if I need it. You just be sure to come stay with us when your time gets closer. I don't want you going into labor out there by yourself."

Janet smiled. "I hear a woman has plenty of time with her first baby."

"There's an exception to every rule, Janet. On the off chance you might be one, I want you near the hospital."

"Yes, ma'am."

Marge's face softened, easing the worry lines. "Honey, your dad and I worry about you. No matter how old you get, you'll always be our baby. We understand that you need a place of your own, that you feel like a child again living with us, but we're going to worry anyway."

Janet averted her face, feeling perilously close to tears. "I'd like to be a kid again. That sounds really good right now."

"I can imagine." Marge sighed and sat down on the bed across from her.

"I messed up, Mom. I messed up really bad."

Marge was silent for a moment. "I don't think so," she said finally. "The only mistake you made was one of trust, and I don't believe that's a mistake you should ever apologize for."

"But I had to drop out of school. My baby doesn't have a father. I'm not married."

"Have you been reading Victorian romances again? Listen to me, Janet. What you are doing is living. I don't care what anybody else says, life isn't measured in goals reached. Life is measured in living. In experience. In learning from experience. You haven't dropped out of school. You've postponed your degree so you can deal with matters that are more pressing right now. Your baby has a father who turned out to be a poor excuse for a human being. That child will be better off without him. As for marriage... Well, you know, it's nice if everything works out according to a neat little plan, with all the loose ends tidied up, but I've seldom seen it work that way. As the man said, 'Life is what happens when you're making other plans.'"

Janet looked at her mother. "You're not ashamed of me?"

"Why should I be? You gave yourself to a man you loved. At the time you trusted him and believed him worthy. It's not *your* fault that he wasn't. He's the only one with anything to apologize for. Now if I could just get my hands around his throat..."

Janet nearly laughed at the thought of her diminutive mother trying to strangle the huge, football-playing Scott. And the desire to laugh made her feel ever so much better. "Thanks, Mom."

Her sisters all helped her move, as did Wendy's husband, Billy Joe Yuma. Nothing was particularly heavy except boxes of books, but no one would allow Janet to lift a thing. The cabin lacked bookshelves, but Billy Joe said he would slap a couple of bookcases together for her and have them out there in a day or so.

"See?" Darlene whispered to her. "Not all men are creeps."

"I already knew Billy Joe was an exception. We agreed to exceptions, didn't we?"

Jeff Cumberland, or possibly her father, must have pulled some strings at the phone company, because the phone was operational the minute she plugged it into the wall jack, even though she had been told it might be several days.

Her sisters insisted on making up the bed for her. Her boxes of books were stacked neatly against the wall, and the only reason her kitchen utensils and dishes weren't unpacked was that she insisted she wanted to do it herself.

Her R. C. Gorman and Amado Peña prints decorated the walls, along with a Mexican serape that hung colorfully behind the couch. Eclectic but warm. She liked it.

Exhausted, she flopped into the rocking chair and looked around with great satisfaction. Darlene left early, because she had to go home and cook dinner for her father and brothers. Wendy and Yuma left because they were scheduled to be on call after 6:00 p.m. Her other sisters stayed just long enough to make sure a casserole was cooking in the oven, and then they, too, left.

The doors and windows were wide open, letting in the last of the late afternoon. The sun had disappeared behind the mountain peaks around three o'clock, leaving her cabin in shadow, but the sky was still bright, and the air, though rapidly cooling, was dry and fresh. She could smell the pines, smell the grass and wildflowers, hear the soft gurgling of the stream out back.

It was heaven. Simply, perfectly heaven. Everything she loved about Wyoming was epitomized in her new home and its surroundings. No matter how far she might travel, she would always come back just so she could feel day give way to cool evening, just so she could smell the freshest air on earth and hear nothing at all beyond the sounds of nature.

Her baby kicked. Resting her hand on her stomach, she smiled as she felt a tiny foot poke her palm. A little girl, the doctor had said. Emily Jane. At least so far. Little Emily's name had already changed twice and might change yet again— although she doubted it. In finding the name Emily Jane, she'd had the feeling she had found the name that had been meant for her daughter.

"Hi."

She nearly jumped out of her skin, gasping and turning her head quickly to the open door. Abel Pierce stood there, hands on his hips, pelvis canted to one side, a dark figure against the shadows and the brilliance of the sky.

"Sorry. Didn't mean to startle you. I was driving by on my way back up the mountain and just figured I'd stop in and see if you needed anything."

She couldn't speak, couldn't think of a thing to say. Her heart was still hammering wildly, and conflicting feelings left her unable to respond. On the one hand, he was just being neighborly, exactly what she would expect from a resident of Conard County. But he wasn't a resident. And she had learned lately not to trust.

"Nice place," he said, remaining where he was. "Look, I'm sorry I disturbed you. I realize you don't know me. It's just that . . . well, you're pregnant and I . . ." He shook his head, trailing off.

Another couple of heartbeats passed while Janet tried desperately to think of how she wanted to deal with this. The last time she had felt this addled was when she had first discovered that Scott had another girlfriend and that he wanted her to have an abortion. Which was ridiculous, some other portion of her mind pointed out. All *this* man had done was make a neighborly offer.

"I . . . oh, hell." He paused, shifted his weight to his other foot. "I just thought maybe you'd be tired after moving. My girlfriend was pregnant, and I kind of got used to considering those things. Sorry if I intruded."

He started to turn away, but Janet's voice stopped him. "What happened to your girlfriend?"

He didn't turn to look at her but tilted his head back as if he were contemplating the heavens. "She ran off with my . . . best friend."

Her voice grew soft. "And the baby?"

His hand lifted abruptly, a gesture of denial. "It wasn't mine."

Then he was gone.

The first time Seth Hardin had pulled up in front of the Tate house on an August day several years ago, he had come unknown and unwelcomed. When he returned this time, the entire family was there to welcome him home. Crepe paper streamers had been hung in the living room and dining room, bunches of balloons hung in the corners near the ceiling, and the dining table groaned beneath a holiday feast.

Seth, standing tall and proud in the uniform of a chief petty officer, his SEAL trident glimmering on his breast, took in the festive sight and grinned. "Gee, I feel like the prodigal returning home. Did you kill the fatted calf, too?"

"No, we saved him," Nate said, draping his arm around his son's shoulders. "Krissie got too attached to him."

Krissie, now nearly fifteen, still giggled as if she were twelve. "Oh, Daddy . . ."

They looked so much alike, Janet thought, watching her father and her newfound brother standing together. Seth was twenty years younger than Nate, but apart from the age difference, they were as alike as peas in a pod.

Marge was swallowed up in a bear hug by Seth and squeaked, "When you only come home once a year, it seems like time to celebrate."

But there was more to it than that, Janet thought. There was the fact that Seth had been lost to them for all those years after Marge had given him up for adoption when he was born. This festivity was an attempt to make up for that in some small way. The girls could have resented it, but none of them did. They'd had their parents all their lives. Seth had had parents, too, but now they were dead, and special things needed to be done to make him feel a part of the birth family he had only recently discovered.

When Seth turned to Janet to hug her, he paused a moment to eyeball her pregnant stomach. "I get to be an uncle soon, huh? That's really great. So why didn't anybody bother to mention it to me?" He hugged her more gently, as if worried about hurting her.

"Well, I kind of kept it a secret until a couple of weeks ago," Janet admitted to him.

Seth's expression grew wry. "That's a long time to keep something of this magnitude secret."

Janet glanced down at herself, feeling her spirits rise at Seth's easy acceptance. "It *is* kind of magnitudinous, isn't it?"

"And getting more so daily, I expect."

"Magnitudinous isn't a word, is it?" Krissie asked.

"I don't think so," Carol answered. "But maybe it ought to be."

"Well, come on everybody," Marge said, her eyes bright with unshed tears of happiness. "I'd planned an hour or so to gab and relax before dinner, but—"

"But I'm late," Seth interrupted. "Sorry about that. There was a rock slide on the highway, and we got held up for over an hour while they cleaned it up."

"That's not a problem," Marge said. "As long as we eat now before the turkey gets cold!"

It was springtime, but it felt like Thanksgiving as they gathered around the big table. The afternoon breeze blew through open windows and stirred the sheer curtains, setting the meal apart from traditional holiday feasts, making it uniquely memorable. Seth was home.

Evening arrived while they were still at the table. The dishes were cleared away, candles were lit, and dessert was served with plenty of coffee.

"I need to be on my way," Janet said, pushing her chair back from the table and rising. There was a half-hour drive home facing her, and at this stage of her pregnancy she got fatigued easily.

Seth was instantly on his feet. "I'll follow you in my car."

Apparently, Janet thought as she tried to ease a kink in her back, he was going to smother her, too. "You know, I've been going home by myself every night for the better part of the last six years."

"But you weren't going home to an empty house," Marge said. "Thank you, Seth."

He flashed a grin. "No problem."

Janet threw up her hands. "What does the rest of the world do without all of you? How do billions of women go home every night without Seth to protect them?"

Laughter rolled around the table, but it was Nate who had the final word. "Billions of women don't have a choice. Thanks, Seth."

Outside, the stars were lighting up the heavens. Candles in God's windows, someone had once told her. Their glow was pale, pristine, overwhelmed by the light shining from the houses around. At her cabin, nothing else competed with the light from the stars. The Milky Way was so brilliant and thick, it looked like a gauze drape across the sky. Out there, she began to realize just how many stars there were . . . and just how insignificant she was.

"Am I annoying you?" Seth asked as he helped her into her car.

"Not really. It's just that lately I've been feeling hovered over all the time. I've been on my own for a while, and I'm not used to it anymore. I'm used to being able to decide my own comings and goings and not having to account for every little thing."

Seth squatted beside the car and helped her with the seat belt. "Well, I'm a little concerned about you being out there all by yourself, too, but probably not as concerned as the rest of the family. I've only known you as an independent adult.''

''Which I am.''

''Of course.'' He smiled at her. ''But the real reason I'm tagging along is I needed to get out of there myself. I'm not used to so much family in such big doses. Besides, I want to hear what the hell is going on with you, and I could tell I wasn't going to hear a word of it there.''

He was throwing a sop to her pride, Janet thought as she waited for him to get into his own car. The thought, however, was a fond one, and it brought a smile to her lips. Seth Hardin was definitely a Tate. It had to be something in the genes that caused the mother-hen streak. It certainly couldn't be an accident that he had the trait as strongly as any of them.

Darkness crept across the world, giving him the protection he needed. He stood beneath the cottonwood in the shadows near the picnic table, watching the family within as they laughed and talked around the big table. Occasionally the breeze would whip one of the sheer curtains across the windows and he would see them through a veil, as if they belonged to another world.

He saw the young man and the pregnant woman rise, saw them a few minutes later as they crossed the lawn toward the street. He watched the man squat beside the woman and talk to her as she sat in the car, but the breeze snatched their words away. Then they drove away together in separate cars, and he wondered why. The family within continued to talk and laugh.

They lived in a safe, special little world of their own, he thought as he watched the curtains blow in the breeze and listened to the easy sound of their laughter. They didn't know what it was like to be on the outside, to be cold and alone. They didn't know what it was like to lose everything.

Old anguish filled him in an agonizing rush, causing his eyes to prickle with the tears he had never shed. Everything had been stolen from him. Everything. His past was blighted, and his future stared at him with the hollow, empty eyes of a death's-head.

Those people inside the warm circle of light didn't know what it was like. It wasn't fair that they didn't know. It wasn't just. But that would change.

Because he had come here to find justice.

Janet had left lights on in the cabin, and they welcomed her and Seth as they drove up the rutted driveway. The first thing she did when they stepped inside was to reach for the phone and call her folks to tell them she had arrived safely. After she hung up, she turned to look at her brother. "I didn't have to do that every night when I was living in Boulder."

He laughed, then looked around. "This place is neat."

"I think so." Billy Joe had brought the promised bookcases just that morning, and she had made a small stab at unpacking her books.

"Do you have any method for this?" Seth asked, indicating the books with a tilt of his head.

"Just alphabetical order within subjects."

Without further ado, he started transferring books from boxes to shelves. "Stop me if I do it wrong. You just relax. You look pooped."

She was. Her back ached, her feet felt as if they had swollen to the size of blimps, and her eyelids felt too heavy to stay up. Emily kicked vigorously, a series of sharp raps across the front of her womb, as if the baby were turning over. Or jogging around the inside of her balloonlike home. Janet nearly laughed at the image that filled her mind, and she was suddenly conscious of an incredible sense of well-being. Nothing, she realized suddenly, mattered as much as the little girl growing inside her.

"Can I get you something?" she asked him. "Coffee, tea, milk, juice?"

"You can sit down in that chair right there with your feet on the ottoman and supervise me. Mom just filled me to the gills with food and drink. If I tried to swim now, I'd sink like a lead balloon."

For once Janet wasn't inclined to argue with someone who wanted to look after her. With a contented sigh she collapsed as directed and watched while he dealt steadily with her library.

"So what's the story?" he asked finally. "Last I heard you were happily involved with some guy and wildly in love."

"I thought I was. I guess I wasn't."

He shot her a wry look. "That speaks volumes. Sort of."

Janet shrugged. "What I mean is, it suddenly struck me that his betrayal didn't hurt as much as it should have. I think I was infatuated."

"How did he betray you?"

"You mean the other women, or the fact that he dumped me because I refused to have an abortion?"

"Ouch." He shoved a couple of volumes on a shelf. "Either one is enough."

"Well, I got both. I refrained from killing him, finished up the school year and then came home to lick my wounds."

"I like that."

"Like what?"

"The way you said that, that you refrained from killing him."

Janet laughed quietly. "Believe me, Seth, it was a struggle for a few days there. I think I was more furious than hurt."

He smiled over his shoulder at her. "It wouldn't surprise me. I've felt that way a number of times."

"How come you never married?"

"Wouldn't be fair. I'm not home as often as a woman has a right to expect, and my job is dangerous."

"Some women can handle that."

"And some can't. There's no way to be sure which is which, so I'll just wait until I retire."

Janet propped her chin on her hand, finding the steady rhythm of his movements as he shelved the books almost hypnotic. "I don't think you've ever really been in love, Seth."

"No, I haven't. Which is why my life is so neat and orderly and moving according to plan."

She glanced sharply at him, then saw the teasing twinkle in his dark eyes. A whoop of laughter escaped her. "That's the truth!"

Right then she determined to introduce Seth to Darlene while he was home on leave. The two of them could have some fun together, and Darlene could rediscover her dating skills with someone who was safe. And while she was at it, she needed to convince Darlene to start building a life of her own. Admittedly, it wasn't always so wonderful, but Darlene had always had a thirst for adventure that would never be satisfied by staying at home to take care of her father and brothers.

And then there was Abel Pierce. Remembering how the man had stood in her doorway just a couple of days ago, she felt a tugging sensation in her chest. Something about him...

When she woke, she was alone. A fire burned in the stove, and the books had all been put neatly away. A note at her elbow said only, "Sleep well, Sis."

She got up just long enough to go to the bathroom, undress and tumble into her bed. Oh, she was tired, a good kind of tired that made the bed seem so soft and welcoming. Thunder rolled down from the mountain with a low rumble that sounded like a feline purr. Emily stirred sleepily, a soft little ripple of movement that let Janet know her baby was okay.

Another roll of thunder, quieter this time, but it drew her thoughts up the mountain to where Abel Pierce was sleeping tonight. Something about him...something drew her at an almost subliminal level so that she was aware of it only in moments like these, when it drifted gently across the quiet sea of her mind.

A connection. She felt some kind of connection to the man. Which was ridiculous, since she hardly knew him. But it pulled at her anyway, as if he were a forgotten friend whose memory she couldn't quite bring to full awareness. As if they had met and parted in another lifetime.

She drifted off to sleep again, but this time Abel came with her, a dark presence she couldn't quite identify. Like her destiny.

Or her doom.

Abel Pierce threw some more wood on the small fire he had built on the nearly destroyed hearth of the shack he was calling home. The night had begun to grow wild, alive with the moan of the wind and the creaking of the trees that bent before its force. Thunder rumbled again and again, quieter than on previous nights, but far more frequent. Forks of lightning danced among the clouds overhead. When it flashed, the shack filled with blinding white light.

The wildness of the night called to his soul. It reached out to him in invitation, like a lover who felt his yearning.

Where had he lost the child who had heard voices in the thunder and seen visions in the lightning? Where had he lost himself in the long years of a journey to find justice? When had principles become more important than anything else?

The night offered no answers. Sitting alone before his fire, listening to the wildness without, he wondered why it felt as if his very foundations were teetering. It wasn't as if he believed life should be fair. No such thing was inherent in the human condition.

No, whatever fairness there was, it was wrested from the chaos of an uncaring universe. Whatever justice could be found was created by men with a determination not to be ruled by the vileness within them. By men, like himself, who sensed the gleaming purity of true justice and struggled to meet its standard. Sometimes they failed—he certainly had, and endured nightmares of blood on oily gray pavement as a result—but the struggle must never be abandoned.

His rewards in this struggle were few and far between, but he didn't think about that. Just as he didn't think about the fact that he was a hunted man. Just as he refused to consider the price he had paid. His ideals were all he had, given to him by his father, long dead. By the uncle who had been his first *sensei.*

"You know, son, a man ain't nothing without principles. If he don't know right from wrong, then he's nothing but vermin, and he don't deserve to live."

"The difference between a man and a beast, nephew, is a man's ability to judge his own behavior."

Abel closed his eyes, hearing the teachings with which he had been raised. He hadn't failed them. He had served justice all his days, and when others failed to distinguish right from wrong, he made sure they paid.

The long road of principle, far from being straight and narrow, however, was beginning to appear crooked and winding. It had, of all things, brought him to this remote mountain. It had, in one way or another, stripped him of nearly everything. All in the service of justice.

But the cost of compromising one's principles was even higher.

He stared into the fire, trying not to count his losses, and let the night call to him with its untrammeled wildness.

Men might be set apart by their ability to judge themselves, but a man could still long to be as free as the trees in the forest, as wild as the spring storm building overhead.

A man could, for a little while, forget all the lessons he had learned and think about a lady with cinnamon hair and mossy green eyes and an oddly gentle way of talking. He could think about a woman's belly full of baby and wonder why he'd been denied even that.

He could, if he wanted to, feel sorry for himself. But he didn't want to. Instead he wanted to dream of silken thighs and soft sighs and the welcome to be found only in a woman's warm body.

He could indulge himself shamelessly in fantasy, and for a brief while he did, seeing himself and seeing her in the sinuously twining flames of his fire. His body grew heavy with hunger, while his imaginings filled hollow places in his soul.

For now, for just a few minutes, he refused to remember that she was the daughter of a Judas.

Chapter 4

Morning sun drenched the courthouse square and fell warmly across Abel Pierce's shoulders as he sat on a wooden bench and watched the comings and goings. His legs were stretched out before him, and one arm lay along the bench back. He looked for all the world like a man with nothing to do.

People nodded to him as they walked by, many called out an easy "howdy," or "nice day," to which he responded in kind. Friendly folks, friendly even though he looked utterly out of place and even though he was a stranger. It was odd to be sitting here without the skin-crawling uneasiness he would have felt in L.A. Without feeling it was necessary to glance around every time he heard footsteps approach.

He had an appointment with Nate Tate in an hour, but for now he was content to sit here on a park bench and watch the doings of the local people. The sheriff's office, on a corner across from the square, was continually busy. Deputies came and went frequently, but so did many other people. He wondered what those people would think if they knew the truth about their sheriff.

But he was boring himself. He would do what he had come here to do, but that didn't mean he had to think about it every second of every day.

Turning his attention in another direction, he watched two old men play dominoes on a folding table they'd set up in front of the benches. A sudden, piercing envy struck him. Those two old men made life look so simple.

When he lifted his eyes from them to a point beyond, he saw a man leaning against a lamppost. And suddenly he was hyperalert, every sense and every thought focused on the man who lounged against the pole.

Why? He depended on his senses, on the intuition that had never yet failed him, but he could see nothing about the other man that justified his reaction. The guy was probably just waiting for a friend to turn up or his ride to arrive. Nothing overtly suggested a threat, and the fact that he was dressed a little differently from the local folks didn't mean diddly.

Nonetheless, Abel's antennae were quivering, and he never ignored his intuition. Eventually, though, the man turned, strode briskly down the street to a battered old pickup and drove off.

Probably an assignation gone awry. Regardless, the explanation was the only one he was ever going to get, unless he chased after the guy and asked him what he'd been doing. And if he was stupid enough to do that, he would probably get exactly what he deserved—a pop in the nose.

Letting go of his tension, Abel relaxed and allowed his mind to wander over what he had seen in an attempt to figure out what had alerted him. It couldn't just have been that the guy was dressed in camouflage. Hell, you saw plenty of people dressed that way on the streets of L.A. And it wasn't as if everybody on the street here were sporting a cowboy hat and boots. Like him, a lot of folks were wearing work boots and baseball caps.

Something about the casual yet not casual enough way the guy had been leaning against the lamppost? Naw. He would have stood exactly the same way himself if he'd been waiting for a girlfriend and getting angrier by the minute.

A cackle of laughter drew his attention back to the two guys playing dominoes. One of them was grinning victoriously.

This place, Abel found himself thinking, was so positively bucolic it could drive a man to drink. Probably the last exciting event around here had been Christmas.

Life in Conard County remained calm until it was time for him to cross the street and meet with Nathan Tate. Now that man was an enigma, he thought as he stepped into the sheriff's office. He appeared to be as open and aboveboard as it was possible for a man to be. Judging by the comments of people to whom Abel had mentioned the sheriff, he was loved, honored and respected among the residents of Conard County.

But that was now. What about *then?* What about more than a quarter century ago, before people here knew much about him? What about events that had happened so far away that news of them had never trickled home to this backwater community? What kind of man had he been then, when he had done awful things?

One thing for sure, Abel promised himself; he was going to find out.

The sheriff's office smelled like coffee and cigarettes. A thin, wizened crone sat at the dispatcher's desk, puffing on a cigarette and talking through her headset.

"I know, Beau," she was saying, "but Greta Hawley says she saw two of them foolin' around behind her shed, and now there's a mess of torn-up toilet paper blowing every which way. Don't ask me what you're supposed to do about it. Put the fear of God into 'em, I reckon. If you can figure out who they are."

"Something we can do for you, mister?"

Abel was astonished that he could have overlooked the deputy who was standing behind one of the desks and looking expectantly at him. No one could have missed this guy in any crowd. He had to be five or six inches over six feet, with black hair that reached to his shoulders and a face that could only have belonged to an Indian.

"The name's Pierce," Abel told him. "I have an appointment with Sheriff Tate."

"He should be back in a few minutes," the deputy told him. "He radioed a while ago that he was on his way. Grab some coffee and pull up a chair."

"Thanks." He filled a disposable cup and took a chair that gave him a view of both the deputy and the dispatcher. The woman was still talking away, but now clucking like a mother hen over something someone else had told her.

The deputy seemed oblivious of his surroundings as he worked on reports. As big as he was, he looked capable of dealing with just about anything.

Abel's gaze settled on the other man's name tag, and it was as if a fist drove into his gut. *Parish*. This was another one of the men he had come here looking for. He spoke.

"Are you Micah Parish?"

The big deputy raised his head and regarded him steadily from eyes as dark as his hair. "Yes."

Abel mustered a smile. "Great. You're the next person I wanted to talk to after the sheriff."

Micah leaned back in his chair, pen still in hand, and waited expectantly. Abel felt a glimmer of admiration. Not many people had mastered the art of silence.

"I'm writing a book about the Special Forces in Vietnam," Abel told him. "It's going to focus specifically on a couple of teams, one of them yours."

Not a muscle in Micah's face flickered. "I know. Why?"

"Because it'll make for a different type of book than has been written before. Instead of concentrating on the strategy, or the high points of large units or entire years, it'll concentrate on what it was like to be there day in and day out."

Micah made an impatient gesture. "I understand why the book would be different. The question is, why my team? Why not some other one?"

"Because your team saw some of the heaviest action in that time frame."

Micah nodded noncommittally.

"So, can we get together in the next few days and talk about your experiences?"

"I don't talk about them."

"I realize they must be uncomfortable for you—"

"Look," Micah interrupted him quietly, "whatever they are for me, they're past, and I like to leave the past in the past. Besides, I have no desire to spew my guts for the entertainment of a pack of voyeurs."

Abel was startled. He'd expected a lot of different objections, but he hadn't expected this one. He wasn't quite sure how to deal with it. An instant later, he decided to go on the attack. "What about the incident at the falls in Area 71? You guys didn't go back after your buddies."

Micah waved an impatient hand. "You expect me to defend my actions in your book? At this late date? Forget it. I have nothing to explain." He dismissed Abel by simply leaning forward and returning to his work.

Abel was on a rush, the same as when he was about to break a case and was putting everything on the line to do it. The lack of resolution to his conversation with Micah did nothing to satisfy the adrenaline in his system, and he was left feeling edgy and angry. There had to be some way to break through this man's reserve and find out what had really happened.

Before he could decide how to pursue the issue, the door opened and Sheriff Nathan Tate walked into the room. Behind him came a tall young man who was his spitting image.

It was the difference between night and day as Micah Parish rose to greet the young man. His face broke into a smile as he said, "Good to see you again, Seth." Hearty handshakes were exchanged. "Are you following your dad's footsteps and joining the department?"

"Not yet, but I'm sure giving it some thought. I don't know, though. I doubt you guys can give me as much excitement as the SEALs."

A SEAL. Tate's son, a SEAL? It wouldn't be surprising.

"Oh, no?" Nate asked. "This county is going to hell in a handbasket, son. Where else can you deal with toxic waste dumping, devil worshipers and foreign agents, all without leaving home?"

Nate turned to Abel and made swift introductions. "My son, Seth Hardin. Seth, this is the writer I told you about, Abel Pierce."

Abel shook his hand firmly. "I guess I need to suck up to you."

"Why?"

"Because you have a pretty sister."

Seth began to grin. "Which one? I've got *six* pretty sisters."

The sheriff led the way down the hall. Abel wasn't exactly pleased to find that Seth was joining them, but there was no way he could protest. He was, after all, supposed to be collecting information for a book, not for a classified document.

Hardly had they settled into seats around Nate's desk, however, when the scrawny dispatcher buzzed Nate on the intercom. "Ransom's here," she said.

"I asked him to come along," Nate told Abel. "He was there, too, and I figured you'd want to interview him."

"Thanks. I asked Parish if he'd talk to me, too, but he wasn't inclined."

"Ransom may not be, either. None of us like to talk much about those days."

Ransom Laird was leaner than either Tate or Parish, with golden hair and a golden beard, but his blue eyes had the same steady look as the other two. He shook Abel's hand and nodded in response to Nate's explanation of what Abel was looking for, but he had something else on his mind.

"Before we get into that stuff, I was wondering, Nate. Do you guys have any recent reports of drifters?"

Nate shook his head. "I haven't heard any. Why? Did something happen?"

"Yesterday, when I was away, Mandy saw some guy standing out along the driveway. She wouldn't have thought much about it except he stayed there for a long time. Finally she got nervous enough to lock the doors."

"Did he do anything?"

"Not that I can determine. Just stood there and stared at the house, like he was waiting for something to happen. You know, Mandy's pretty steady, but now she doesn't even want to let Justin out to play."

"You didn't leave her home today, did you?"

Ransom shook his head. "No way. She's taking Justin and Amy shopping while I take care of business. But, Nate, you know damn well I can't always be with her. Somebody has to go out and look after the sheep."

"What about those shepherds you hired?"

Ransom smiled. "Come on, Nate, you know any man who leaves his business entirely to someone else to manage winds up without any business to manage. The guys I hired are good, but it's knowing I'll know if they aren't that keeps them in line." He sat on the one remaining chair and crossed his legs. "I figure he was probably just some drifter looking for a handout or a meal who couldn't get up the nerve to come to the door. Maybe. But I honestly don't like the way Mandy said he was staring at the house. As if he was fixated or something.''

Nor did Abel. His antennae were vibrating madly again.

"Well," said Nate, "I don't see why a drifter would have trekked up that endless driveway of yours and then not asked for the food or the money or the work. It doesn't add up. I'll see about getting the patrols to swing by your house more frequently...say every couple of hours.''

"Thanks." Ransom nodded. "I don't see what else anyone can do. I'd dismiss it entirely except that . . . hell, I've probably still got a lot of old enemies."

"Old enemies?" Abel asked. "From what?"

"My days with Central Intelligence. I'd be surprised if any of 'em were still looking for me, but anything's within the realm of possibility."

Central Intelligence. Abel suddenly had an unsettling feeling in his gut that the man he was talking to was not the man he had come here to find. But then, Nathan Tate wasn't at all what he had expected, either.

"It happened once before," Nate said. "I certainly wouldn't sneer at the possibility."

"I'm also not going to live as if I'm under siege, not without a little more to go on." He turned to Abel. "You're the guy writing the book about our unit?"

Abel nodded. "I was hoping you'd talk to me a bit about your recollections."

"Micah's refused," Nate told Ransom.

"He's never been one to talk about things," Ransom said. "That's his right."

"What about you?" Abel asked him.

"I'll need to think about it. I'm not sure I see anything to be gained by raking it all up."

Nate picked up a pencil and began to rap it idly on his desk. "On the other hand, it'd be a chance to tell it the way it really was. I get a little chapped at times with the way things got distorted. I sure as hell object to the general perception that we were all doing drugs and killing babies. That's what my kids hear, and that's what yours are going to hear, too."

"On the other hand, I don't feel any particular need to defend myself. We did what we had to do, Nate. We did it the best we could, and then, if we were lucky, we came home. It's in the past, and the past can't be changed."

"But it could be presented in a different light," Abel argued. "The past isn't as immutable as we tend to think. It's made up of people's recollections—which are never precise—and of whatever facts and memories others choose to share with us. It's a fluid thing, Mr. Laird, and one man's perception of it may be very different from another's."

"Which means?"

"You can shape the past by sharing your recollection of it."

There was a silence in the room as the three other men pondered what he'd said. Presently, Ransom looked at Nate. "You going to talk to him?"

"I think so."

"Well, I'll think about it. I don't feel I can do this without discussing it with my wife. If you publish this stuff, it'll put her in the spotlight, too."

"Well, there is one incident I'd especially like your input on," Abel told him. "Because it could wind up making you all look bad if someone doesn't deny it. One man's denial would help, but having someone to back him up would be real useful."

Both Nate and Ransom stiffened a little. "What are you saying?" Nate asked.

"That there's been an allegation that you left your comrades behind to be taken prisoner."

"Well, I'll be double damned!" Nate erupted from his chair and stalked to the window. His anger was evident in the way his jaw worked. Finally he was able to swing around and glare at Abel. "One time. One damn time, and it happened because we were misinformed!"

"Tell me what happened."

"No."

"Why not?"

"Because someone else is involved, and I'll be damned if I'm going to smear his name for a stupid thing he did when he was nineteen years old and terrified out of his mind! You say the past is fluid? Well, it isn't. Not at all. There's no way on God's earth I can change what happened that day, and heaven knows I've wished I could more times than I can count.''

''But—''

''No, you listen to me, son. Telling what happened that day means naming names, and I'm not going to do it. If I'd known Doyle and Bryant were alive, nothing on earth could have kept me from going back for them, and the same goes for Ransom and Micah. Two good men paid, but at this late date I'll be damned to hell if I'm going to ruin another life over something that can't be changed!''

He didn't know where he was going. Or maybe he did. When he found himself driving along the edge of the Cumberland ranch in the general direction of Thunder Mountain, he thought he was going back to his campsite. The truck seemed to have a mind of its own, however, and tugged him down the driveway to Janet Tate's new home.

She wasn't there. He debated whether to leave or to wait for her to return. He didn't even know why he wanted to see her. When he considered what he thought of her father, it made even less sense. She would hate him when she knew. And she *would* know. Somehow she would find out, whether it was from her father or from him—because he would feel obligated to tell her what he thought of Nathan Tate, and why, if he were to start getting close to her. It was the only honest thing to do.

So if he had half a brain, he would get back in the truck right now and leave. Instead, he sat down on the porch, in a rough-hewn rocker, and waited for her to come home.

She was a beautiful woman, he thought, and made more beautiful by her pregnancy. He knew from experience that women felt ugly and fat and awkward during pregnancy, but as far as he'd ever been able to see, they simply grew more beautiful. Janet Tate had become breathtaking.

He half closed his eyes and watched the breeze ripple through the tops of the trees. The spot was both lovely and isolated, an idyllic setting. Why the hell didn't he give up city life and find himself someplace like this? The desire tugged at him, reminding him that life *could* be simple, and that not every day had to be lived on a knife edge.

He was also unsure how to deal with what Nate Tate had told him. He'd expected some kind of denial, and he supposed that was what he'd gotten, but the form of it spoke of a sense of honor every bit as developed as his own. Which didn't mean anything at all, he supposed. He'd known honorable people who'd failed to live up to their own code. Honorable people who'd done very dishonorable things.

Nate Tate could well be one of them.

Part of the problem, he acknowledged, was that he didn't know what he was hoping to find here. He had no idea what he thought would be accomplished by tracking down the men who had been responsible for what happened to his father. It wasn't as if he expected some magic answer, because he didn't. He didn't believe in magic answers.

But he did believe in right and wrong, and what had happened to his father had been wrong. It need never have happened. He held Nate Tate, Micah Parish and Ransom Laird responsible for that. They had violated their code as Green Berets. They had not returned for their fallen comrades.

What he hadn't expected to discover was that at least two of them had not forgotten the event, either. And that Nate Tate, at least, not only had not forgotten it, but had apparently agonized over it.

Shades of gray. He hated shades of gray. Did a crime become less heinous because the perpetrator felt remorse? No. Never. The man who wept because in a fit of fury he'd hit his wife and killed her could not be forgiven. What he had done was wrong. The parent who shook a baby and killed it could not be forgiven because it was an accident.

He didn't forgive *himself*, after all, for such things. Like the cop who had taken a bullet two years ago when she had stumbled into the middle of a drug deal he was working undercover on. He hadn't pulled the trigger, but he had failed to anticipate a possibility. Yes, it had been a remote possibility and probably wouldn't have occurred to anyone else, either, but she had taken a bullet in the chest, and he had seen her fall and die, and he knew it was his fault. He would never forgive himself for that. Nor would he probably ever stop having flashbacks of blood on pavement.

Nor should he. What good was a principle if you could manufacture exceptions to it? Might as well not have any at all.

The soft sigh of the breeze through the trees and the gentle rushing gurgle of the stream out back were as soothing as a lullaby. He might have dozed, he didn't know, but the next thing he was aware of was the sound of a car engine. Opening his eyes wider, he watched Janet's Explorer pull up next to his truck.

She hesitated a moment before getting out, and he couldn't say he blamed her. This was the second time he'd shown up here unannounced, and they didn't exactly know each other well. At what point did his behavior become obnoxious? Or even frightening to her?

Disturbed, he stood up and spread his hands in a gesture of apology. "Sorry," he said. "I was driving by and just got an urge to check in on you and say hi. If I'm scaring you, just tell me to vamoose and I'll stay away from now on."

She stood by her vehicle, hand on the door, as if pondering. "Are you stalking me?"

Damn it, didn't she have brass... whatevers? Admiration brought a smile to his lips. "That's certainly not my intention, but it struck me just now that it could look that way."

"Why *did* you come?"

He figured the only way to handle this now was to be perfectly blunt. "Because you're an attractive woman. Because I'd like to get to know you better."

"What if I don't feel the same way?"

"Then I'll leave and won't trouble you again."

She smiled then, and relaxed. "Could you help me carry in my groceries?"

Everything was packed in plastic bags with handles, so she could have managed it all herself, but it was nice to have the help. Nice to have someone help her unpack the bags and help put things away. Abel Pierce didn't look as if he were domesticated, but apparently someone had managed it in the past.

She supposed, if she really thought about it, she ought to be a little nervous about having a near stranger show up at her place like this. Thing was, he'd shown up once before and left when he realized he was intruding. And he knew her father. Maybe it was dumb, but that always made her feel safer.

When the groceries were put away, they went to sit on the porch. Because there was only the one rocking chair, he settled on the steps with his elbows resting on his splayed knees.

He still looked dangerous, Janet thought, but not threatening. He had never threatened her. She was dying to know more about what had happened with his girlfriend and the baby, but she didn't dare ask about it, so she resorted to more casual questions. "Where are you from exactly?"

"Los Angeles."

"I've always wanted to visit California, but I'm not sure I'd want to live there. I worry about things like earthquakes."

One corner of his mouth lifted into a wry smile. "It's a fact, you can't live there if you're going to worry about quakes all the time. You'd be a basket case."

"Doesn't it worry you at all?"

He shrugged a shoulder. "I wouldn't build a house on a hillside, and I'd avoid having natural gas lines nearby, but . . . disasters happen everywhere, Janet. Even here."

"Not often."

"Maybe not on the scale of an earthquake, but you have serious blizzards that kill people, and sudden drops of temperature that can do the same. And when it comes to death, does it matter whether it happens in a large-scale disaster or a small one? I doubt it. It still comes down to a very personal thing, namely dying."

"I hadn't thought of it that way. But living in a serious earthquake zone raises the probabilities, doesn't it?"

"Life is full of risks. We each find some of them more tolerable than others. You minimize your exposure as much as possible and then get on with it."

"I suppose you're right. I keep getting behind the wheel of my car, after all."

He laughed. "Yep."

She liked the way he laughed, the way it relaxed him and softened the hard angles of his features. She never would have guessed his mother was Japanese, so little of it showed in his face . . . until he laughed. Then she could see the hint of his ancestry and found it attractive. And when he glanced at her, just for a second or two, he didn't look haunted. It was then, in seeing the startling change in him while he smiled, that she recognized how closed in and haunted he ordinarily looked, as if he had ghosts that pursued him mercilessly. If only she felt free to question him.

"Your dad mentioned you were going for your master's degree," he remarked.

"Yes, in special education."

"You have the patience of Job?"

It was her turn to laugh. "No, I just like kids. They're so unspoiled and eager and full of life. I figure if I hang around with them enough, some of their magic might rub off on me."

Again he smiled, but so faintly she almost didn't see it. "Yeah, they're magic, all right. If you catch 'em before life does."

She paused for a minute, trying to interpret that. "I guess you see kids on the streets who've been knocked around pretty badly."

"I've seen plenty of kids who look at you with the eyes of old men who've lived too long and seen too much. I don't know what the answer is, though. We keep trying to get rid of the poverty and the abusive parents and the drugs and all the other things that make kids grow up too quickly, but nothing seems to work."

Emily stirred, kicking her mother sharply a couple of times, and then punching her solidly. Janet gave a soft laugh and placed a hand on her belly.

"It's moving?"

She looked up and found Abel staring at her stomach. "*She's* moving, yes. Kicking and punching, from the feel of it. Emily, meet Mr. Pierce."

"You know it's a girl?"

"Well, I'm not a hundred percent sure. The ultrasound isn't always that accurate. But boy, is she going to be surprised if her name changes to Tom."

"She'll probably be scarred for life. If it turns out she's not a girl, maybe you'd better call her Emmitt. You can always claim Emily was a slip of the tongue, and then the shock to her won't be so great."

Janet felt a bubble of laughter rise from the pit of her stomach. She liked the way he fell in with her absurdity. She also liked the way he was willing to allow the conversation to lag. There was no pressure to fill the silences.

"How long do you think you'll be here?" she asked him. "Will it take long to do your research?"

"I'll be here a few weeks, at least. If I could swing it, I'd like to spend the summer."

"It's a wonderful place to spend the summer." She hoped she didn't sound too eager. Heck, she didn't want to *be* eager to have him stay. Wasn't her life messed up enough?

He turned to look at her, but this was no casual glance. This time his eyes bored into hers, as if seeking something deeper. Then his gaze traveled lazily over her, licking at her rounded contours like black fire. Everywhere his eyes settled on her, she felt their heat.

No, she thought. This man could not possibly find her sexually attractive. Not in her present state. She must be imagining the heat in those dark eyes.

"You're one hell of a fine-looking woman," he said abruptly. His voice had softened slightly, had grown just a little bit husky in an unmistakable way.

The rippling edges of panic began to fill her stomach. She didn't know him. She was all alone out here with him. And she certainly wasn't ready for anything like . . . this.

"Have—have you written any other books?" she managed to ask, trying to divert the conversation from dangerous channels.

"No." With that one uncompromising syllable, he rose to his feet. "Why?"

"I, uh, just wondered. I mean, if you'd written something else, I'd like to read it."

He seemed to let go of some kind of inner tension, but he didn't resume his seat. "I've got to be going. Is there anything you need me to do before I go? Bring in some wood?"

"No, nothing. Really. But thanks so much for helping with the groceries."

"Anytime." He gave her an unsmiling nod. Moments later, he and his truck were heading down the driveway, leaving Janet all alone in her sunlit spot in the woods.

* * *

The dappled light beneath the trees made a perfect camouflage. He was close enough to see Janet Tate clearly, yet, unless he moved suddenly, she would never see him. Now that he knew where she lived, he could deal with her at his leisure.

The only stumbling block was her pregnancy. Of all the unexpected possibilities he had considered and tried to correct for, this one had escaped him. And now he was discovering it to be a major sticking point.

He didn't want to harm a pregnant woman. What a stupid thing to get hung up on, given all the other things he was planning to do.

But stuck he was and, as he watched her nap in her rocking chair on the porch, he realized he was going to have to find a way to get over his reluctance.

Some way. He would find one.

He always had before.

Chapter 5

"Do you remember my friend Darlene?" Janet asked.

Seth was using a scythe to cut the thick grass and undergrowth out behind the cabin. The afternoon was warm, almost sultry, and he'd shed his shirt, baring his gleaming back to the sun.

"When did I meet her?" He never paused in the steady, swinging movements of his arms.

"Christmas the year we all learned about you. She came over for a couple of hours on Christmas Day. Dark hair and blue eyes?"

"Maybe. Maybe I remember her. That was a pretty confusing time, upsetting. My recollection isn't the best."

"Well, she's coming over this afternoon to visit. I'd like you to stay and meet her. In fact, I'd like you to do me a favor."

The scythe never paused. "What kind of favor?"

"She's been out of circulation for five years now, ever since her mother died. All she's done is play housekeeper for her dad and mother to her younger brothers. She feels as if she has nothing interesting to talk about, and she's forgotten that she's attractive. I was wondering if you could . . . well . . ." Now that she was saying it, she couldn't find a way that didn't sound like an awfully big imposition.

The scythe stopped, and Seth turned to look directly at her. "You want me to date her?"

"Well...maybe help her get her confidence back." It was an *awful* lot to ask, now that she thought about it. Would she never stop being impulsive?

"Yeah, I'll do it," Seth said, absolutely flooring her. "As long as you tell her that's exactly what I'm doing."

"That'll ruin the entire thing!"

"It'll protect her from the possibility of hurt. You can't expect me to string her along into thinking I'm seriously interested."

"You could be!"

"No, I couldn't be. I'm not going to allow myself to get interested until I retire."

Not going to allow himself? Janet stared at Seth's back as he bent again to the scything. If it wasn't just like a man to think he could control such things. The last thing she'd wanted to do after her breakup with Bud was fall in love again, yet she'd promptly fallen for Scott. She was doing slightly better this time; it had been six months since she had discovered she was pregnant and that Scott was cheating, and she had managed to remain unattached. It was to her pregnancy, however, that she credited that fortunate state of affairs. It was her guess that men were avoiding her as much as she was avoiding them.

Not that she was an easy mark. It was just that she knew from her experience with Scott that love wasn't something you chose to do at a convenient time. You didn't put it in your appointment book and then, when the big day arrived, tumble head over heels with someone. Nope. Love kind of came at you sideways and didn't even bother to blow the horn in warning before it knocked you thirty feet into the air.

"Okay," she said to Seth. "Forget I asked."

"You got it."

He'd insisted on clearing the backyard from the cabin to the stream because of snakes. Janet felt guilty, watching him work so hard while she lounged around with her feet propped up on an overturned bucket, but there was no way she could swing that scythe in her current state, and the yard was far past a lawn mower. "You know," she told him now, "you're supposed to be on vacation."

"I am. A vacation by definition is any period of time during which you don't go to your job."

She laughed. "You're easy to please. When I think of vacations, I think of sun-drenched beaches. Or long auto trips."

"Well, I all but live on the beach in Virginia, so coming to the mountains sounds good. And I took a long auto trip."

"From the airport."

"Long enough."

Just then Darlene came around the corner of the house. Dressed for an afternoon of helping Janet plant flowers, she wore a sleeveless blue blouse and jeans. Her hair was caught back in a headband, and she carried soiled gardening gloves. "Hey!" she greeted Janet breezily, then stopped dead as she saw Seth.

"That's my brother, Seth," Janet said. "You met him at Christmas a couple years ago."

"Oh . . . that's right. I remember. Vaguely."

Janet had a sneaking suspicion that Darlene's recollection of *this* meeting was never going to be vague. If there was one thing you could say about a navy SEAL, he was in good condition. Excellent condition. The kind of condition that looked pretty good stripped to the waist. Darlene wasn't immune.

Seth turned as he heard their voices and smiled. "Darlene? Nice to see you again." Then, that easily, he turned back to his task.

Darlene leaned down and whispered to Janet, "Why, didn't I remember what a hunk he is?"

"I don't know. Maybe we were all too busy thinking about other stuff . . . like the fact that Seth even existed." She pushed herself out of her chair. "Seth?" she called. "I'm going to fix some cold drinks. You want anything?"

"Ice water. A bucketful, please."

"You got it."

In the kitchen, she poured fruit juice for her and Darlene, and a huge mug of ice water for Seth.

"He's gorgeous," Darlene said almost wistfully. "If he's half as nice as he looks . . ."

"Oh, he's every bit as nice and more. A lot like my dad, actually. Except... Listen, Dar. In the first place, he's absolutely determined not to get involved until he's ready to retire in eight years. He doesn't think his life-style is fair to a woman."

"It probably isn't." Darlene shook her head. "Will you relax? I'm not trying to put a ring on his finger. I'm just drooling. Seeing as how I'm still single, I'm allowed to drool, right?"

Janet laughed. "I guess. I've been doing a little drooling myself lately."

Darlene's eyes widened. "Over who? Janet, are you keeping secrets?" She took a playful swipe at her friend's forearm. "We've always shared everything! Who is it? Is he drooling back?"

"You wouldn't know him. He's just here to do some research on his book and take a vacation."

"A writer? Is he a writer?"

"Apparently."

"Would I know his name?"

"He hasn't published anything yet."

Darlene leaned back against the counter. "So he's a hunk?"

"Sort of." Janet closed her eyes for a moment and thought back to the afternoon Abel had sat on her porch. "Not hunky like Seth, just... Oh, I don't know how to explain it. I think he's attractive. Not that it matters."

"Why not?"

"Darlene, get real! I'm seven months pregnant, getting darn close to eight, as big as a barn, and I have all the grace of a beached whale!"

"Actually, I was thinking how much better you move than when you see an actress on TV who's pretending to be pregnant. You get up out of a chair the way you always have, without all that awkward back-bending stuff they do."

"Probably because I've grown into this gradually and had time to adjust," Janet said a little dryly. "The fact remains, I ain't no sex object."

"You'd be surprised. Some men think pregnant women are very sexy."

Inevitably Janet found herself remembering how Abel had looked at her the other day, as if he were hungry. As if he wanted to devour her. A pleasurable little thrill trickled through her and settled right at her center. Being pregnant hadn't killed her sex drive. Not at all.

But who needed the complication? she asked herself. She had enough going on without getting involved, and she didn't believe in casual relationships.

She managed to suppress a sigh before it escaped her and picked up Seth's mug. "Let's get this out to my brother before he thinks we've forgotten him."

The afternoon turned into a kind of mini party as the three of them laughed and joked their way through planting marigolds, daisies and gladioli along the front of the cabin. It was the first place Janet had lived on her own that she had been able to indulge her passion for gardening, and the satisfaction was immense.

During the late afternoon, they all collapsed on the porch, dirty, exhausted and happy.

"I vote we clean up and catch some fast food for dinner," Seth suggested.

"Oh, I can't," Darlene said regretfully. "I've got to get home and put dinner on the table for Dad and the boys."

Seth looked at her. "Why don't you put pizza on the table for them?"

"I suppose I could, but I already thawed chops. You and Janet go ahead. It was great to see you again, Seth."

After she drove away, Seth looked at Janet. "Somebody needs to take care of her."

Janet nodded.

"What's wrong with her father?"

"Nothing. He's a great guy. I just don't think he's really thought about what's happening, is all. When she first dropped out of college to take care of her brothers, he was too wrecked over his wife's death to really think about it. It was only supposed to be temporary, after all. I don't think anyone expected it to go on this long, except Darlene. She didn't want a stranger raising her brothers."

"But what about *her* life?"

"I get the feeling she's giving some thought to that right now. That's why I wanted you to date her. She's feeling unattractive and dull."

"Well, she's not. But I'm not going to date her anyway." He looked at her and smiled faintly. "It wouldn't be fair to her, Janet. She doesn't have any defenses."

"You're out of her league, huh?"

That made him scowl. "I didn't say that. Don't be a pain. Now go clean up so I can feed you!"

There were people watching him. Abel felt it at the base of his skull, a prickling awareness that wouldn't quit. Earlier he had thought he'd caught sight of movement among the dappled shadows beneath the pines, and now he was sure he had. He kept walking, eyes forward, as if he didn't know he was being stalked, making his way steadily back toward the mining town and his vehicle.

No one could have traced him to this place. No one. He'd been smart enough to use cash every step of the way from L.A. He hadn't told a soul he was coming here, or even called anyone back home. Unless, by some strange circumstance, someone he had run into here knew someone back there who was trying to track him down....

No way. That was so farfetched even a paranoid would know better than to believe it. Unless they had somehow managed to tail him every step of the way, no one could have found him.

So who was watching him? Who was stalking him along these isolated mountain trails where he was hiking in the hope of finding some kind of peace with himself?

He hadn't gone back into Conard City to talk to Nate Tate or his buddies again, but he needed to. Needed to hammer away at the problem until he got some kind of answer.

But what if there was no answer? That, he realized, was the concern that kept him from forcing the issue with those men. He needed answers. He'd always needed black-and-white, solid answers he could rely on. What if the events that had eventually cost his father his life had no answers at all?

Micah Parish, he had learned, had made a career of the Special Forces and then had retired to Conard County to become a well-respected cop. Ransom Laird had evidently spent his days in Foreign Intelligence and was now ranching. Nathan Tate had come home from Vietnam to become his county's sheriff, living in the public eye. Could these men be the cowardly monsters his father had always painted them as?

He doubted it.

The prickling at the base of his skull intensified. Every instinct he had learned in the Special Forces and developed on the streets of L.A. came to the fore now, making his senses preternaturally alert. His eyes were out of focus, looking at nothing in particular, ready to detect the slightest motion from any direction. His footsteps had grown as light as a dancer's as he silenced his own movements so his ears could pick out alien sounds better. His hand, appearing to rest relaxed on the hilt of the hunting knife strapped to his belt, was not relaxed at all.

The woods were alive with sound. Wind rustled in the tops of the pines, sounding like rushing water. The life force of the forest was as perceptible to him as the pounding of the blood in his own veins. Over there, a fallen log supported a cluster of mushrooms. Wildflowers, so small they almost looked miniaturized, sprang up on fragile stems in the unlikeliest places. A squirrel froze on a tree trunk, tail twitching nervously. A chipmunk peered at him over the edge of a rock. Life abounded, and he could feel its vitality in his very bones. The forest was a magical place.

Thunder Mountain shrugged lazily, sending a quiet roll of thunder down its slopes. The clouds that normally hung around the peak had been absent for days. Now they gathered again, promising rain.

Movement. He whipped his head around and looked. He wasn't sure, but he thought he saw something melt away into the shadows. A deer?

He figured he could handle just about anything short of armed attack from a group, which was unlikely to happen anyway. There might be some lunatic running around these hills who liked to stalk and kill, but he figured that if anyone really wanted to kill him, they could have put a bullet in him an hour ago and saved themselves all this trouble.

That didn't mean he was going to relax his guard. It *did* mean that he'd feel a whole lot better if he could get to his car so he'd have a way out of here if things got nasty for some reason.

What he wanted to know, though, was who was stalking him—and why? Just who was up here in these mountains?

He kept walking, a brisk pace that would make it difficult for his followers to keep silent and out of sight. If he could get them to expose themselves . . .

But he reached the mining camp without incident. The growing storm made the tops of the trees toss like the masts of ships on a restless sea, and clouds began to swallow the sun. If the stalkers were still there, they remained invisible.

All of a sudden he heard a sound from one of the tumble-down shacks. He froze, hand tightening around the hilt of his knife. Probably just some tourist poking around. Probably. But just in case . . .

He headed in the general direction of the sound, trying to keep out of the line of sight from the shack windows, trying not to let whoever was within realize that he had heard them.

Another sound, this one of something being scraped against wood. Whoever was there wasn't trying to be quiet, and that relaxed him a little—but not much. It could be a trick. A trap. After having been followed for the last hour, he realized his paranoia level was a little on the high side. Anything, after all, was possible.

Whoever was there apparently didn't see him coming. Damn, he thought as he rounded the corner of another building and came as close as he could get without crossing open ground. Damn, he was going to feel like a fool if it was a raccoon or a lost beaver.

Moving swiftly, he closed the last distance and burst into the cabin.

Janet Tate gaped at him in utter shock. She stood, one hand on her camera tripod, the other on her swollen belly, and looked as if she couldn't believe her eyes.

Which maybe she couldn't, he admitted uncomfortably. He was standing crouched in the doorway, knife in hand, ready for an attack. To her, his defensive posture probably appeared to be a terrifying threat.

"Sorry," he said, lowering the knife and straightening.

"You—" The word was a short, breathless gasp. "You—you frightened me!" She swayed a little, her eyes going even wider, and he instinctively reached out to steady her.

"Don't you touch me! Don't you dare touch me!" Anger rescued her, raising her blood pressure to normal again. The urge to faint passed.

"Damn it, Janet, you ought to know by now that I'm not going to hurt you!"

"No? Then why creep around like someone who has something to hide? Why sneak up on me like a thief?" But she was angry, not afraid, and the questions were merely a means of throwing her anger in his face.

"I didn't know who was in here! And someone's been following me through the forest for the last hour!"

"Why would anyone do that?"

"How the hell should I know? All I know is someone's been following me. How was I to know there wasn't some kind of trap waiting for me?"

"Are you always this paranoid, Pierce?"

"Yes, damn it! I have to be!"

Stunned, she took a moment to gather her wits. "Why?"

"Never mind." Scowling, he turned and stalked out of the shack, leaving her frustrated and angry and with nothing to vent her feelings on. Wishing she could shake him, she stood there until she realized her teeth were clenched so tightly that her jaw was beginning to ache.

She was losing the light. The nagging thought tugged at her, trying to pull her back to her reason for coming here. Arguing sensibly against the urge to race after him and demand an explanation.

Did she really want to know why he felt he had to be paranoid?

Reluctantly, she turned back to her camera. She'd come here to take a picture through the window of one of the cabins, to frame the fantastic late-day shapes of the decaying mining town in the dark shadows that were a part of it. Short of major catastrophe, she was going to do precisely that.

Why should he be so paranoid? She could understand him being nervous about being followed, but she was amazed that he would think anyone would set a trap for him. That went far beyond the usual expectation of trouble. A person could think he was being followed by someone who wanted to mug him, but there had to be a reason to think someone would lay a trap for you.

Unless you were mentally ill, of course.

But she didn't think he was. Something in the depths of his gaze was haunted, but he appeared entirely too rational to have a disordered mind.

So why would he think someone would lay a trap for him? Probably because there was someone in his life who could and would. Someone who wanted to get him.

So maybe he was up here not to write a book, as he claimed, but to hide? And maybe she ought to be smart and get out of here right now.

She turned to her camera, deciding to take a couple of quick photos, then leave, abandoning the rest of her planned shoot. In fact, she didn't think she was going to come up here again until he left for good.

On the one hand, she didn't think he wanted to hurt her. On the other... well, if he was irrational, then all bets were off. There was no accurate way to predict what he might do. This business about being followed... No, he didn't sound completely rational.

Why did her hormones always get stirred up by the wrong men? She swore at herself under her breath and snapped the photo she had come up here to take.

"They're still out there."

This time she was marginally less startled when Abel spoke from behind her. She closed her eyes for a moment, then asked, "Do you think you could knock, or make some noise when you walk, so you don't scare me half to death when you come up behind me?"

He ignored her. "Whoever followed me is still out there. I want you to get your stuff together now and get the hell out of here before something happens."

Unease tingled along her nerve endings, making the warm afternoon feel chilly all of a sudden. "Why do I get the feeling this is a new and creative way of getting me out of here?"

"It's not."

Suddenly he was there beside her, taking her shoulders, turning her around to face him so that his black eyes could bore into hers, riveting her with their intensity. "Someone followed me through the woods for an hour this afternoon. They're still out there, watching. It might be innocent, but it might not be, and if it's not, I want you out of here. I don't want anything to happen to you, and I don't want to have to worry about you if there's a fight.''

She believed him. Whether the threat was real or not, he was genuinely concerned, and he wanted her safely out of the way. "Okay." What else could she say?

It didn't take all that long to put her camera in its case and fold the tripod. Abel picked up the case and the tripod as if it were his duty—or his right—and walked her briskly to her car. His eyes never rested on any one thing for long, and the slightest sound caused him to tilt his head attentively. This was no mere attempt to get rid of her, as she had suspected. He really did believe someone was watching, and that they posed a threat.

He put her into the driver's seat of her Explorer before he walked around to the back to put her equipment away. Then he came back to stand beside her rolled-down window.

"You'd better not come back up here alone," he said. "Not until I figure out what's going on."

"But why would anyone want to hurt you?" As soon as she asked the question, she knew he wasn't going to answer. He didn't trust her that far. "Look, I'll call my dad and ask him to send someone up here."

"Don't bother. They won't find anything. Whoever's been following me will be long gone by the time anyone can get up here."

"Then get out of here. You can stay in town."

He shook his head. On the off chance that someone did manage to trace him to Conard County, he would be too easy to find in a motel. Nor did he want Janet to know any more about who he was. It wasn't so much that he thought she would deliberately do something to get him into a mess, but each person who knew who he was and what he was doing here created another possibility for a slip that *might* get him into trouble.

She looked at him for a few moments longer, then turned the key in the ignition and drove away.

He stood in the cloud of dust she left behind, a man trapped between worlds.

* * *

"Dad, what do you know about Abel Pierce?"

Janet tried to be casual about it, but something in the way her father's eyes narrowed at the question told her that she hadn't succeeded. At his invitation they had met for a late breakfast at Maude's on Saturday morning. Janet watched with near envy as he put away biscuits and gravy, eggs and bacon. She settled for an English muffin.

"At the moment, not a whole lot. Why?"

"I'm just a little curious." When he looked at her, she gave a small shrug. "He just . . . arouses my curiosity, that's all."

"Well, he arouses mine, too." Nate smiled as Maude appeared with a carafe full of fresh coffee. "You make the best coffee, Maude."

The woman sniffed. "Quit lying, or I'll tell Marge." She ignored his chuckle, filled his cup and stomped away to the next table.

"It takes all kinds to make a world go round," Nate remarked.

"Why does he make *you* curious?" Janet asked, ignoring the interruption.

"Hmm? Oh, Pierce. Well, his questions seem just a tad too focused for my taste. Like he's mining for a particular piece of information to confirm what he already knows or believes. That kind of thinking always makes me a bit nervous."

"I guess I can see that. What is he after?"

"Beats me. I just don't like the feeling, is all."

Janet spread some blackberry jam on her muffin, taking more than usual care. She had to stay away from Abel. That was all there was to it. If her dad had doubts about him, she would be wise to listen.

"It's not that I think he's a bad guy or anything," Nate continued. "It's just that I don't see any reason for him not to say what he's after, unless I'm not going to like it."

"I can see that. Do you think he could hurt you?"

"With stuff published in a book? Naw. Not as long as it's true and complete. Now, if he wants to twist things around . . ." Nate shrugged. "Nothing I can do about it. I'll just have to let my deeds speak for me."

"What could he hope to gain? It's not as if you're some nationally recognized figure who everyone would want to hear a scandal about."

Nate grinned. "Actually, you could get real poor writing a book about me, since it wouldn't interest anyone outside Conard County."

Janet felt herself smiling in response. "Yeah, you'd sell maybe two thousand copies, and then only if the sex scenes were good."

Nate tried to look scandalized that his daughter had mentioned such a thing to him, but he failed. "Well, I'm not really worrying about it. I *am* doing a background check on him, though. There's something going on here that I don't know about, and I don't like that."

He was on his third cup of coffee by the time they finished their breakfast. "How do you like living out there all alone?" he asked her.

"All alone? When? Darlene has practically moved in with me, and Seth is there more often than not. I'll let you know what it's like to be alone when I finally discover it. How's Mom, by the way? Is she home this morning?"

"Off to Cheyenne with the church youth group. She'll be back sometime tomorrow." He looked past Janet, staring into space. "You know, she's edgy again. The last time she got this jumpy, I found out about Seth. Now I'm wondering what in the hell could be going on."

It was on the tip of Janet's tongue to tell him about the things Marge felt were out of place, but she caught herself. If Marge wanted her husband to know, she would tell him, and telling Nate that his wife was worrying about such things would only get him worried while she was out of town overnight and he couldn't do a damn thing about it. Best to keep her silence on the subject.

Best, too, not to ask any more about Abel. Maybe best just to completely forget about him. He acted as if he had reason to be afraid, and something about the questions he was asking had her dad concerned. And Sheriff Tate wasn't a man to get concerned about trifles.

"Now we have a prowler out at the Laird place," Nate said.

"A prowler? All the way out there?" Complaints about prowlers usually came from in town, and usually turned out to be kids, although there had been a few Peeping Toms.

"All the way out there. Mandy's the one who saw him, so I beefed up the patrols out that way. She's seen him twice since, and we don't have a clue what he's about."

"What did he look like?"

"He wasn't close enough for her to get a really good look. Ransom's debating whether to move her and the kids into town for the time being."

"That sounds like a good idea to me."

"Me too. Which leaves you."

Janet sighed. She had known this was coming. "I'll keep my doors and windows locked, and if I see anyone, I'll call you immediately."

He gave her a fatherly scowl. "You do that. I have an uneasy feeling about this."

"I'm clear at the other end of the county, Dad. I'll be fine. There's no reason to think that any prowler out at the Laird property would come clear across the county to prowl at my place."

"The problem with being as young as you are," Nate said severely, "is that you think you're indestructible. If I had any inkling that prowler might come out your way, I'd hog-tie you to your bed at home."

Janet and Darlene had decided to spend the day making sourdough bread together. Janet loved fresh bread, but it was too much trouble to make just for one. She'd been easy to entice into the task by the promise of a fresh loaf just for her.

Darlene was accustomed to baking bread once a week, so her request for Janet's assistance was really a request for company. Her brothers had gone with the youth group for the weekend, and her father was out making the rounds of ranches that had called for him, so she had been facing a long day of solitude.

The sourdough was already working by the time Janet arrived after her breakfast with her father. She helped Darlene scoop some of the fresh mixture back into the crock, where it would be kept until the next time it was needed. Darlene's sourdough starter had come down to her directly from her grandmother, and she took good care of it.

"Now sit," Darlene said, and pointed Janet firmly into a kitchen chair. "I'm boiling over with curiosity, and all I want from you today is the gossip."

"Hey, you're the one who lives in town. What makes you think I'm up on any gossip?"

"Because your dad is in the middle of this. Who's the stranger he was talking to at Maude's and then at his office last week? Why was the guy asking around about him?"

"He was?" Janet felt a queasy sensation in the pit of her stomach. Maybe her father was right to question Abel's motives.

Darlene, standing with her hands in a huge mound of bread dough, darted a concerned glance her way. "Oh, don't worry about it, Jan! Most of the people in this county think your dad walks on water. That guy'd have a hard time trying to find someone who'd say anything negative about Nathan Tate."

"Yeah, he'd have to look as far as Jed Barlowe."

"Jed? The town drunk? Oh, for heaven's sake, Jan! Who'd believe him? Not even a stranger! The man is never sober long enough to tell a coherent story, anyway. Now tell me, who is he?"

"He's a writer doing a book about Vietnam. He says he came to gather some recollections."

Darlene nodded, her face growing pinker by the minute as she kneaded dough. "That would explain why he was asking about Ransom Laird and Micah Parish, too."

"He was? Well, it fits, I guess." It fit with him doing research for a book. Maybe there wasn't anything suspicious about Abel Pierce after all.

She was surprised to realize just how important that was to her. She should have been indifferent, but somehow she wasn't. She wanted Abel to have no dastardly secrets, to be just an ordinary man doing ordinary things. Not someone she needed to be afraid of.

Just the other day he had taken her by her shoulders to warn her of danger, and now she found herself all too able to remember the warmth of his firm grip on her. Well, having the hots for him certainly couldn't get her into trouble right now. Not with Emily making her the size of a walrus, and about as graceful.

"What's his name?" Darlene asked. "Where's he from?"

"Abel Pierce. Los Angeles, I guess."

"Ooh, the big city. Do you suppose I'll ever get there?"

"Why shouldn't you? You can leave anytime you want now, Dar. You know that."

"I don't want to talk about me. I want to talk about exotic strangers from exotic places. I want to talk about why your voice changed when you said his name. Janet, do you know him?"

Janet hesitated, then wondered why. She vaguely remembered discussing Abel with Darlene once before. "I've run into him a couple of times. I wouldn't say I know him."

"What's your impression?"

"He's . . ." She hesitated again. "I don't know, exactly. Basically, I think he's as protective as my father."

"Of you?" Darlene turned around, forgetting all the flour and dough that clung to her hands. "And just how did you manage to discover that he's protective? What have you been doing? Tripping in front of oncoming locomotives?"

"No, nothing like that. He's camping out at the old mining town on the side of Thunder Mountain."

"You go up there all the time to take pictures!"

"That's how I ran into him. He was concerned about me being up there alone."

"So am I, now that I think about it." She turned back to her kneading. "You take me along next time."

"Dar, you can't spend the rest of your life baby-sitting people."

"Why not? There are an awful lot of people who seem to need it. Chalk it up to my curiosity about exotic strangers. Come on, Jan, share the excitement. I'm apt to spend the rest of my life in this kitchen and working at the library. Miss Emma's offered me a job."

"That's great!"

"Yeah. Except that I'll probably never get out of this town."

Not too many years ago they had been young girls dreaming of escape from their boring, humdrum lives. Now Darlene still yearned for escape, but Janet would have been happy to settle down to an existence as simple and happy as her mother's.

"You should go back to college, Dar."

"Maybe. I guess I'm a contradiction. I want an exciting life, but I want to be a traditional wife."

"And I want a quiet life, but I don't want to be a traditional wife. I'd go out of my mind doing what you do, Dar. I'll always need a job. A career."

"Well, I'd like to find a husband with an exciting job," Dar said wryly. "Maybe an astronaut will come through town."

"Or a foreign correspondent."

"Now that would be really neat! Someone assigned to the Paris bureau. Or Tel Aviv."

"That's definitely too exciting for my taste. I don't like bullets."

Darlene giggled. "You're right. Okay, the Paris bureau. Or what about a diplomat assigned to Russia?"

"That could certainly be exciting. The thing that concerns me, though, is that I don't think you'd like the excitement quite as much if you had kids."

"It would depend on whether the kids were at risk, I guess." Darlene now had a smooth mass of dough that sprang back like rubber every time she punched her hands into it. She lifted it into a huge stainless steel bowl and covered it with a clean, damp towel. Janet started helping her clean up the flour that had scattered everywhere.

"What didn't you tell me, Jan?" Darlene asked after a minute or so. "What aren't you telling me about Abel Pierce?"

What wasn't she saying about Abel? How about that, much as she'd been trying to ignore it, he was the most attractive man she'd ever met? She couldn't even isolate why she felt that way, but feelings were never easy to explain. How about that she kept feeling that something was eating him alive and she wanted to do something about it?

"I don't know, Dar. What haven't I said?"

"That was *my* question. I get the distinct feeling that this guy is more than someone you just ran into a couple of times."

"No, he's too much of a mystery. I've learned my lesson. The next guy I get involved with will come with a detailed five-hundred-page biography and a pedigree attached."

Chapter 6

Marge Tate often took a short nap in the afternoon. It was a habit she'd developed when the children were small, taking advantage of their nap time or school hours to refresh herself for the rest of the day.

Usually she woke up feeling chipper and ready to go, but this particular afternoon she wished she'd never lain down at all. She had a dull pounding headache, the kind she only got when she was sick, and she felt as wrung out as an old dishrag. Sitting up on the edge of the bed proved difficult, making her feel as if she had a heavy, sharp-edged brick in her skull. She had to hold still for a couple of minutes before the throbbing in her head settled down enough to make standing a possibility.

Her neck hardly felt strong enough to hold her head as she rose and began to make her way toward the kitchen. A cup of herbal tea might help. And maybe a couple of aspirin.

She was halfway down the hall when she smelled gas. The pilot light on the stove must have gone out, she thought. It happened once in a while, and the stove was too old to have an automatic shutoff. She and Nate frequently talked about getting a newer model, but with the girls going through college, they tended to avoid any extra expenses.

She passed the door to the basement and rounded a corner into the den. There was no odor of gas here. She paused, finding that odd, since the den opened directly into the kitchen.

The hairs on the back of her neck began to prickle. It wasn't the pilot light on the stove. Quickly, ignoring her headache, she turned and headed back up the hall to the basement door.

As soon as she opened the door she was hit in the face by the unmistakable odor. The basement was full of fumes.

Swiftly she closed the door, aware that at any moment the water heater in the basement might turn on. She was standing right above a huge bomb.

Emergency vehicles filled the street in front of the Tate home. Nearby houses were evacuated. The propane feeder line was shut off at the tank. The basement windows were broken to let the fumes escape. When the fire chief judged it safe enough, two of his men went into the house, opened the rest of the windows, then headed down into the basement to find the leak.

Janet, who had been coming to visit her mother, stood down the street behind the cordons with the rest of her family, waiting. She, too, thought of the water heater in the basement. If that had switched on while her mother was sleeping . . .

She shuddered and felt Emily kick softly. Nearby, her father and Micah Parish were talking, heads together and voices low. She eased closer to them and eavesdropped unabashedly.

"I'm getting a bad feeling about this, Micah," her father said. "There was the prowler at Ransom's place, and Marge feeling like somebody had been in the house—hell, I should have paid more attention when she said that. She just told me she's had the feeling a couple more times."

Micah nodded. "I didn't listen, either."

"You mean Faith thought someone was in your house?"

"She's been complaining we have a ghost, that things are out of place too often. I've been brushing it off because of Sally...that little girl gets into just about everything. But maybe it isn't Sally."

"I don't like the way the trouble seems to be circling around the three of us," Nate said.

"Like that stranger who's asking questions about our unit in the Nam."

Janet caught her breath sharply. What were they suspecting Abel of?

Nate sighed exasperatedly. "I don't like it when my scalp prickles. I hate this damn niggling feeling at the base of my skull. Something's going on."

"Did you find out anything about this Pierce character?"

"He doesn't have a criminal record, he was in the army for six years—special Ops, as a matter of fact—and he has a California driver's license. I'm waiting on additional information."

"Then maybe he's legit."

"I'm not ready to trust that right now. I'm going to keep digging."

They moved on to other subjects, and Janet turned back to her mother and sisters. "You told Dad about things being out of place?"

Marge nodded. "I guess I was silly not to tell him sooner."

"You think the gas leak has something to do with that?"

"Maybe. I don't know." Marge shook her head. "I don't know what to think any longer. But how could a gas line just break? If someone had been doing renovations at something, that would be different, but this…" Again she shook her head.

Bad things sometimes happened to people. Janet hadn't been the daughter of a sheriff her entire life without learning that. But those bad things didn't happen to the people she loved. They didn't happen to her mother.

Feeling sick to her stomach and suddenly very, very cold, she wished she could ignore the ugly possibilities that had been raised. But she couldn't. There was no way back from knowledge.

Long, uneasy minutes kept ticking by as they waited for the fire department to make a determination of safety. Another half hour passed before one of the firemen came up to Nate.

"The gas line to your dryer had gotten disconnected," he told Nate.

"How could that happen?"

The man shrugged. "Must have worked loose over time, and somebody bumped the dryer, I guess. We checked all the other fittings, and they're fine. You can go back in now."

But for several moments no one moved. Then Marge said, her voice sounding strained and distant, "No one's been in the basement since Sunday."

The cabin looked different when Janet came home that evening. Twilight lingered, and the brilliant blossoms of wildflowers stood out against the darker ground as if lit from within. Nothing had changed, but it somehow looked less welcoming.

Because of what had happened to her mother.

Her dad was convinced the threat was directed at him, and it was the only thing that made sense. Why would anyone in the world want to stalk Marge Tate, who had never harmed a soul? No one could possibly want to hurt her, so that left her husband as the intended target.

But the gas leak could have killed Marge. Marge, who had never hurt anyone.

If that could happen to Marge Tate, then no one was safe. Including her. And her child.

The cabin had a lonely look to it as she parked in front of it. Even the light that she had left on in the living room didn't quite dispel the sense of isolation she now had. Nothing had changed, and yet everything had changed.

A paradox. Life was full of them, she thought as she sat in her car and stared at her home. Another paradox was the fact that she had so desperately wanted to be on her own to lick her wounds and sort out her life, and now she was wishing she didn't have to come home alone. That she didn't have to come home to an empty house.

And the worst paradox of all: she never wanted to let another man into her life to make a mess of her feelings and betray her trust—yet she desperately wanted a man to come home to, one who would greet her with warm smiles and a hug. One who would stick through thick and thin and bring laughter with him.

So it made no sense that she was drawn to Abel Pierce, she thought in disgust. The man looked as if he couldn't laugh if his life depended on it. Yep, she sure had her head together.

Giving herself a mental shake, she climbed out of the Explorer, grabbed the sack of groceries from the back and let herself into the cabin. It was home and was going to be home for months to come. She just needed a little time yet for it to *feel* like home.

At some point she began to grow uneasy. The shadows cast by the lights she turned on seemed somehow full of threat. They became harder and harder to ignore. As she stood at the sink preparing a salad, she kept wanting to turn around to see who was behind her.

But no one was there, she told herself, and refused to look. The doors and windows were locked, and she was all alone. Through the window over the sink she saw that the darkness had nearly swallowed the forest outside. Unnerved, she couldn't stop herself from drawing the café curtains closed to seal out the night.

Briefly, she felt better and was even able to convince herself it was just nerves over what had happened with the gas. But as she sat at her dinette eating, the darkness seemed to grow in the corners, to be reaching out toward her.

That was when she noticed that the thumbtacks holding one of her Peña prints had been moved. Each one had been offset by an inch. She would have thought she was crazy except that the original holes were there to confirm it.

Slowly she put her fork down. After a moment she rose and went over to the print to stare at the thumbtacks. Seth had helped her move in and hang these prints. He could have put the tacks there. Except that he'd been so careful to put them through the holes that were already there with all the other prints.

She turned around, her skin crawling with unpleasant awareness, and looked for something to confirm what she suspected. No, everything seemed to be just fine. So the tacks must have been an accident. Maybe Seth had been hurrying and hadn't noticed.

She was, she told herself firmly, just edgy because of what had happened with the gas line at her folks' house.

But she sat up well into the night anyway, wondering.

Abel Pierce thought of himself as a lone wolf, but sitting on the windy side of a mountain in a ghost town was a little more alone than he wanted to be, at least for any appreciable length of time. It gave him too much time to think about things he would rather not be thinking about. It gave him time to get in touch with parts of himself he'd buried or forgotten a long time ago. It was like opening the rusty-hinged doors on an ancient crypt and discovering only death within. If he had any treasures buried in his psyche, he sure couldn't find them.

For the last couple of days he'd occupied himself by stalking his stalker. What he'd found was that there were a number of men keeping an eye on him, and that when he got too close they melted back into the mountains. He had to conclude that they didn't mean him any harm but were worried about his intentions. For now he decided just to keep an eye on them.

But that left time heavy on his hands again. Finally he decided to head into town and have a couple of beers at Mahoney's. Maybe he could have some casual conversation with another human being, even get up a game of darts.

The drive into Conard City gave him more time to think, though, and he found himself thinking about Janet Tate. About her fresh, pretty face, fiery hair and ripening body. He wanted her. His loins tightened every time he thought of her, filling him with a yearning he would never be able to satisfy. Even her pregnancy didn't dampen his hunger. He merely thought her womanly, fulfilling a purpose more important than any he had ever served.

His ex-girlfriend's pregnancy had fascinated him, and he had eagerly tracked every change and shared every new development. Some long-dormant part of him had come to life at the prospect of a child, and now he felt much like any parent who had lost a baby. The part of him that had burst to life had been left unfulfilled.

He tried to tell himself that was why Janet appealed to him. That he was merely drawn to the possibility of completing an interrupted process, the hope of finding a fulfillment that had been stolen from him.

But he didn't believe it. He wanted Janet Tate—pregnant or unpregnant. Had she been as slender as a willow wand, he still would have wanted the feel of her curves beneath his hand and the taste of her flesh in his mouth.

He wanted *her*.

And it was pointless. He wouldn't be here long. He would be leaving just as soon as the trial started in L.A. All he wanted to do here was find out the truth about events back in Vietnam, events that had cost his father his life—events that Nate Tate refused to discuss.

What he wanted was to confirm the iniquity of Tate, Laird and Parish, the three men who could have saved his father. What he *didn't* want to do was discover that they were good, honest, honorable men. And that was exactly what he seemed to be finding out.

But good and honorable men didn't do the kind of thing his father had accused these men of. Did they?

He had for some time been aware of a rigidity in his moral character, a tendency to paint things all in black and white. Until now he had never been willing to consider that gray might be an acceptable coloration. The only way, he firmly believed, that it was possible to maintain a high standard was to be strict about it. Once you allowed shades of gray, you could slide all the way into iniquity and still justify yourself.

Was that what these men had done? These otherwise good and honorable men?

Damn, he wished he could get one of them to discuss events with him. If anything, it seemed more important now than it had when he arrived.

He hit Mahoney's just before five, before the evening crowd started to congregate. Only two other people were there, sitting together in a booth. Sad country music played quietly as Abel took a stool at the bar and ordered a sandwich with his beer.

He was halfway through his sandwich before he realized the bartender was watching him as if he were a deadly snake.

"Something wrong, friend?" he asked the man finally.

"Could be," was the unrevealing answer.

Abel put his sandwich down. "Did I do something?"

"You been asking around about the sheriff."

"Yeah. So? I'm writing a book."

"You wouldn't know anything about the gas leak at his place, would you?"

Abel absorbed the implicit meaning of that question, and only years of practice kept him from showing his reaction. "I guess I need to straighten a few things out," he said presently. Putting down his sandwich, he left his beer untouched and walked out of the bar.

His next stop was the sheriff's office. It was close enough that he decided to leave his truck parked where it was and walk. He would undoubtedly miss Tate, who must be on his way home right now, but at least he could take the first step in dealing with this misapprehension.

But Nate hadn't left the office yet. He was standing by the front desk, talking with one of his deputies, his car keys in hand and hat on his head, obviously delayed on his way out.

When he saw Abel, his eyes narrowed. "I want a word with you."

"That's what I'm here for." Abel nodded to the deputy and strolled over to the window, waiting for Nate to finish his business.

The guy in camouflage was back on the street corner, waiting for something or other. As Abel watched, however, he turned and walked away in the direction of Maude's Diner and Good Shepherd Church. The old men playing dominoes had long since folded up their game and abandoned the courthouse square. At the stores facing the square, shopkeepers were closing up, chatting with one another when they met on the way to their cars.

Life looked so damned uncomplicated from here, Abel thought. He wished his own could have been half as peaceful as what he saw through this window. *Blood on oily gray pavement.* The vision that haunted him intruded even now.

"Come on back to my office, Pierce."

Abel turned and followed Nate down the hallway. He took the chair the sheriff indicated, sitting with his legs casually crossed and his fingers loosely laced across his belly.

"I think it's time we got down to brass tacks here," Nate said. "Who are you, and what exactly do you want?"

"I'm a cop, and I'm here because there are some people who would like to see me dead before their case comes to trial. I'll be here until I'm needed to testify."

"I can verify this?"

"You can verify that there's a detective by my name who is on indefinite leave just by calling the department. If you want anything more specific it'll have to wait a few more weeks, because any serious inquiries by you would give away my whereabouts."

"Convenient," Nate said doubtfully.

"Actually, it's damned inconvenient."

"Who's after you?"

"Cops. I'm with Internal Affairs."

Nate sat back, absently tapping the eraser of a pencil on his desk. "So I'm supposed to believe you needed to hide out and just decided to come to Conard County to do it. And while you were here, you had a brainstorm about pretending to write a book about my Special Forces unit."

"I didn't say that, Sheriff."

"Then maybe you'd better start speaking for yourself."

"My dad was a Green Beret, and so was I. I went to a reunion of his old unit a couple of years ago in San Diego and heard stories about you from a number of people. When I needed an out-of-the-way place to go to ground, this seemed to be as far as I could get from anywhere, and once I got here, I thought it might be a good time to start researching my book. I *do* intend to write a book."

Nate tapped the pencil again, staring steadily at Abel, pondering. "What brought you over here this evening?"

"I was at Mahoney's having a sandwich and a beer when I heard about the gas leak at your house. From the way the bartender was looking at me, I figured I was probably the likeliest suspect in the county."

"You are." Nate tossed down the pencil and leaned forward. "You got anybody who can vouch for you personally?"

"Right now, Sheriff, there isn't a soul in the world I trust enough to vouch for me. That's why I'm hiding out. I couldn't even trust my own bodyguard."

Nate knew what few people outside law enforcement did: cops in Internal Affairs were sometimes assigned bodyguards. Abel's knowledge of that cleared some of the frown from his brow... but only some.

"I don't like this, Pierce. I don't like it one bit. Something in my county stinks, and the stink started the same time you showed up. I'm going to check you out as far as I can without alerting anyone to your whereabouts... and you'd better by God keep your damn nose clean while I do."

Abel nodded. "What's been going on that has you concerned?"

"It doesn't concern you... unless you're involved."

"It concerns me, Tate. I just got looked at as if I were responsible for a crime. Why are people getting suspicious, and why are they getting suspicious of *me?* Was there something strange about the gas leak?"

"Gossip spreads too damn fast in this county." Nate hesitated, then finally said, "A prowler's been seen around our house. This afternoon a gas line was jarred loose from the back of the dryer in my basement... but nobody had been down there in three days."

Abel nodded slowly. "That's serious."

"You're damn straight. So keep your hands where I can see them, Pierce, because right now you're high on my list."

He never finished his dinner. Nor did he feel like going back to the bar for those beers and the game of darts. Instead he picked up some provisions and began to drive back to the ghost town. If he thought about it, he might conclude that he was one of the most unpopular people on the planet right about now. Wanted dead or alive by criminal types in L.A., and suspected of attempted arson by the Conard County sheriff.

He couldn't help it; he had to laugh. Years of pretending to be a sleazeball must have finally transformed him enough that even strangers thought he was one. He'd better just hide out on the mountainside and keep his head low. Every time he poked it up, somebody used him for target practice.

Aw, whine, whine, whine. The simple truth was that a man made his own choices and then paid for them. He'd chosen to take on Internal Affairs. He'd chosen to breach the "Blue Wall" of silence his comrades honored and go after dirty cops. He'd compromised his loyalty to his fellow officers in favor of a greater loyalty: his oath to serve and protect. Now there probably wasn't a cop in the world who would step out of his way to aid Abel Pierce if he were bleeding to death on a rain-soaked city street.

Abel was as alone as a man could be, but he didn't blame anyone other than himself for that.

He was driving past the expanse of the Bar C Ranch when he thought again of Janet Tate. Night had fallen on the world, and the stars were coldly bright. Up on the side of that mountain he would be alone with only the chilly companionship of the moaning wind and the small warmth of a wood fire. He, who had always believed himself to be solitary, was discovering that he wasn't solitary at all.

On an impulse rooted deeper than thought, he turned into Janet's driveway. She was probably going to become convinced, if she wasn't already, that he was some kind of weirdo who just wouldn't leave her alone.

He was prepared to risk that. She was light and warmth and vitality, and he needed to bask in her glow, if only for a few short minutes. He needed, just briefly, to touch upon all the good things in life, the things he devoted himself to protecting. The things that were denied to him because of the life he had chosen.

The lights were on at her cabin, an inviting golden glow that seeped through drawn curtains. It seemed to cast an aura around the building and to hold at bay the encroaching shadows of the forest. Magical. Something deep inside him stirred.

He knocked on the door, trying not to sound threatening. She must have heard the approach of his vehicle, he thought, and he was surprised she hadn't looked out already.

There was no answer, so he knocked again, this time louder. A short while later a curtain twitched, and he assumed she was looking out. Finally the door opened a crack.

One sleepy eye peered out at him. "Yes?" She sounded groggy, unsure.

"Sorry," he said. "I was driving by and thought I'd drop in. I didn't mean to wake you."

"I shouldn't have been asleep." Her smile was apologetic as she opened the door a little wider. Her caution remained, though, and she didn't invite him in.

"I wanted to tell you that the men who were following me on the mountain apparently live there."

"Oh." She blinked, then nodded, pushing her hair back from her face. "I know who you're talking about. There are some Vietnam veterans who live up there. They're okay."

"Do you know them?"

"Not exactly. I've met a couple of them. My brother-in-law used to live up there with them."

He hesitated, feeling like an intruder, yet reluctant to leave. "Can you sit out here for a little while? That is, unless you think I'm to blame for the gas leak at your parents' house today."

She drew a sharp breath, her eyes widening. "Are you?"

He was a man who didn't feel he should have to defend himself, yet already today he had defended himself against the suppositions of a sheriff he suspected of being responsible, however indirectly, for his father's death. Now he was going to defend himself to a woman he scarcely knew. "No," he told her flatly. "Absolutely not."

It took a few seconds, but at last she nodded. "Thank you," she said.

He let the subject die right there. "It's a beautiful night, just a little chilly. Come out?"

She hesitated, then smiled, an expression that lit her entire face with warmth. This woman took his breath away.

"Sure," she said. "Just give me a minute."

She didn't invite him in, he noticed, but that was okay. She was willing to come out here and sit with him. Suddenly the night didn't seem chilly at all.

Abel sat on the step again, while she curled up in the rocker with a blanket around her legs. It *was* a beautiful night, cool enough to be invigorating but not uncomfortable. The breeze gently whispered through the tops of the pines, and an owl hooted in the distance.

"How's Emily?" he asked.

Janet was touched. She battled the softening in her heart, because she didn't want to ever again allow a man to touch her emotions, but she softened anyway. If he had just asked about "the baby" it wouldn't have been anything special. His acknowledgement of Emily as a person said something about him that reached her deeply. "She's fine. Strong and healthy and very active."

"That's good."

Oh, Janet, she warned herself, don't let him get to you this way. This was the man who had let his pregnant girlfriend go because the baby wasn't his. He couldn't really be interested in someone else's child.

"A lot of people—" He broke off, cleared his throat and spoke again. His voice was gritty and a little thick. "I guess a lot of people wouldn't understand that...well, it's hard to explain."

Again that tug beneath her breastbone, a touching in places where she didn't want to be touched. Janet wanted to reach out to Abel Pierce and hold his head to her breast and tell him it would all be all right. The impulse terrified her.

"I feel...I feel like I lost my child."

Janet felt as if the night were holding its breath, waiting for the sudden tension inside her to settle. She couldn't imagine why he was confiding this obviously painful feeling to her. "I'm sorry," she finally said.

"So am I."

The owl hooted again, a sad, eerie sound in the night forest.

"Are you sure the child isn't yours?" Janet dared to ask.

His voice remained rusty. "I thought about...forcing the issue. Demanding genetic testing. Insisting on my rights."

She waited awhile, then prompted him, "But?"

"But I got to thinking about the kid," he said flatly. "I got to thinking about how Louise and my friend were getting married, about how Barry believed the kid was really his. About how Barry would make a better dad than I ever could. I mean...what did I have to offer? I'd have to stay away for weeks at a time . . . anyway, I figured I wouldn't even make a good uncle to the kid. So I let it be."

Janet's heart squeezed. "That was very generous of you."

"Was it?" He gave something like a snort of laughter. "I don't know about that. Maybe it was purely selfish. Sometimes I think I have a martyr complex."

"Why's that?"

He turned and looked at her, astonishing her with a smile. "Because I do everything the hard way."

She couldn't help it; she laughed. There was something so incredibly engaging about the way he'd said that, something that invited her to share in his humor about himself. "I think I do everything the hard way, too."

"Have you ever thought about why that is?" He shook his head, as if he didn't like the direction of his thoughts. "I've had a lot of time to think, sitting up on that damn mountain. Maybe too much. It's a strange kind of place up there. When I was just a kid, living in Okinawa, I spent a lot of time with my uncle. He was my first *sensei,* or teacher. He taught me martial arts sprinkled with a liberal dose of his world view. He was a . . . mystical man, I guess is a good description. He would have loved sitting up there in that ghost town and listening to the voice of the wind."

"What about you? Do you love it?"

He shot her another wry look. "Me? I'm not sure. You don't have to be there very long before you start thinking the wind is talking to you and that the trees are listening. When I was a kid I believed that kind of thing wholeheartedly. Now . . . well, maybe I've spent too much time on city streets and gotten too cynical."

"Maybe I have, too." Janet smoothed her hand over the blanket, over her rounded tummy, and smiled as Emily stirred. "When I was a young girl, I used to think the wind spoke to me. If I sat still long enough, and was quiet enough, I could hear things. When I got older, I decided that I was really just listening to myself."

"That's about how I figured it, too. And it's been too damn long since I really listened."

Janet looked down at her hands, folded now across her stomach as if she were hugging her baby. "I guess I haven't been listening too well, either. You get so busy living that sometimes you forget to take time out to just think about what you're doing and where you're going." She raised her eyes and looked at Abel. The light from the windows illuminated his back, but his face was turned toward the night and hidden in deep shadows.

"I don't know where I'm going." He spoke slowly, quietly, as if he'd forgotten she was there. "I always figured I had a duty to make things right, but somehow, no matter how many things I make right, there's always another one that's wrong."

"I think that's a condition of the human race."

"Maybe. Maybe it's too much to expect people to always do the right thing. To be honorable and honest."

"It may not be too much to expect, but expecting it is bound to lead to disappointment."

"So it seems. But it's not just that. I mean . . . if you do everything right, if you hold to your ideals and do your damnedest to live up to them, you shouldn't discover you've made a big mistake, should you?"

Janet hesitated. "Do you mean that holding to your ideals was a mistake?"

"It may have been."

His bleak tone shivered through her like a cold wind. "What happened, Abel?"

The owl hooted again, sounding so lonely in the dark, chilly night.

"Never mind," he said presently. "I've got to work this one out for myself."

"Nothing's ever as black or white as it seems."

"Maybe that's my problem. Maybe I see things as being too black and white." He shrugged and glanced at her. "Enough of me. What happened to Emily's father?"

The change of subject threw her off-balance, and the bluntness of his question wasn't something she had expected. So far everyone, with the exception of Darlene and her family, had scrupulously avoided asking why she had come home alone and pregnant.

"You don't have to answer," he said. "It's really none of my business, and I won't be offended if you tell me so. I just can't imagine that any man in his right mind would want to leave you."

Again she felt that warm tug inside. Another breach in her recently constructed defenses. But what he said was just flattery, she told herself. She shouldn't take it seriously. "He didn't want to get tied down in a mountain of bills and diapers." She didn't mention Scott's infidelities. That was one humiliation she didn't have to share.

"He sounds like an ass to me—a juvenile ass," Abel said. "A kid who isn't ready to grow up."

"That's one description." She laughed a little harshly. "Jerk is another."

"Are you down on men now?"

"Are you down on women now?" she countered.

He shrugged. "I'm in a bind on that one. My best friend and my girlfriend were fooling around behind my back. Am I supposed to get down on both men and women? Or just on friends?"

Little by little she was coming to realize that this man was mature, not only in his years but in his thinking. He was quite a change from most of the people she'd gone to school with. She wondered if he found her utterly juvenile.

And she wondered why she should even care.

"Were you going to marry her?" she asked him.

"Of course." Bending, he scooped a rock from the ground and tossed it into the shadows. "From the instant I learned she was pregnant. I still don't understand why the two of them took so long about telling me that they were going to get married and that the baby wasn't mine. Maybe they were just chicken."

"I can kind of understand that."

He laughed. "So can I. However it was, yeah, I'd have married her."

"But if she hadn't been pregnant?"

It was a long time before he answered. "Probably not. Things were never quite . . . right. She kept wanting to change me."

"That never works."

"No. It's one thing if I want to change myself. It's another if someone demands I meet their expectations. That gets a little hairy after a while, to feel you're always falling short."

"It would sure be nice," Janet said, "to be loved just the way you are. Bad and good together. Not to have to feel that if you get up on the wrong side of the bed and bark a little, your lover is going to walk out."

"Sounds like you've had the same problem."

"Who hasn't? I suspect it's part of the reason for the high divorce rate in the first year of marriage. The hormones calm down a little and people discover that they've married a human being, and that the human being isn't going to become perfect just to suit them."

"Or that he's not going to change his work habits."

"Ah!" Janet laughed. "I hear the bone of contention. Are you a workaholic?"

"Sometimes. I know it's not easy to live with, but that's the way I am." Slowly he pushed himself to his feet and came to stand in front of her. "It's getting cold, and it's getting late, and you really need to get inside. Thanks for keeping me company."

"Thanks for stopping in."

He tossed the blanket over his shoulder and reached out with both hands to help her up from the rocking chair. The contact of skin on skin when she slipped her hands within his was electric. His flesh was warm, dry, firm. And his strength was evident in the easy way he tugged her to her feet.

They were close, so very close, and it somehow seemed utterly natural when he turned her a little to the side so that her stomach wasn't between them. She caught her breath when his arm slipped around her shoulders and drew her against him. Instinctively she tipped her head back and looked up at him.

His eyes were dark hollows, his face an angular mask of shadow and light. She could feel his heat, though, could feel his desire. She should have been frightened. Some little corner of her mind tried futilely to remind her that she was all alone with a near stranger in the middle of nowhere, that she was completely at his mercy.

Instead, all she could feel was the absolute wonder of being wanted. The dizzying, heady feeling of being desired. His heat was a promise, not a threat. It felt so *good* to be wanted, and it had been so long since she had been.

His other hand came up to slip along her cheek and into her hair. "You're beautiful," he said simply. "Beautiful."

She wanted him to kiss her. Every fiber in her being yearned for the touch of his mouth on hers, yearned to feel his strength wrapped around her as he held her close in a moment of intimacy. Every other consideration was lost in the hunger that sharpened her senses. He smelled so good, like wood smoke and man. He felt so good, hard and warm. He held her with such gentle strength. . . .

Just a kiss. One kiss.

But his hand slipped from her cheek to her stomach, to rest there gently. "Good night, Emily," he said quietly. "Good night, Janet."

The kiss came then, just a light brush of warm lips over the cool skin of her forehead. It wasn't nearly enough, but he stepped back and dropped his arms.

He waited until she was safely locked inside. Only then did she hear him drive away, leaving the night empty.

Chapter 7

"It could just have been an accident," Marge Tate told Janet. They had gotten together to spend a couple of hours browsing at Freitag's Mercantile more than a week after the gas incident. Janet's time was drawing near, and she still needed to get a crib. "Your dad's really concerned, and I know he's linking it up with things that Faith Parish and Mandy Laird have noticed, but... Well, I just don't see why anyone would want to do such a thing. I could understand it when he was suspicious of Abel Pierce—after all, the man was asking questions about Ransom and Micah, too, and it would all have fit together reasonably well, but now..." She shook her head. "It just doesn't make any sense, especially now that he seems to think that Pierce is okay."

"He does? When did that happen?"

"Apparently he came by after the gas leak and talked to your dad. Nate seems satisfied, at least for the moment."

Janet heard that with a surprising amount of relief. Ever since Abel Pierce had kissed her, she hadn't been able to think about much else. The warm pressure of his mouth on her forehead seemed to have been engraved on her soul, and every darn time she closed her eyes, she felt it again. Where before she had felt emotionally drawn to him somehow, now she also felt physically drawn. She wanted another of his kisses with an intensity that made her ache, wanted to feel his mouth not just on her forehead but on her lips. Yearning to be that close to him again haunted her. Suppressing a sigh, she forced her thoughts back to the conversation with her mother. "Then what does he think is going on?"

"I don't know. I don't think he does, either." Marge shook her head and looked at her daughter with worried eyes. "I'm concerned about him, Jan. He's not sleeping well, and I know it's because of what happened with the gas, and the business with Faith Parish and Mandy Laird. He's convinced there's a stalking going on."

"I know." She hadn't forgotten the conversation she had overheard between her father and Micah Parish. "But there would have to be a reason for it, Mom! I mean... it's not a random kind of stalking, like when a guy gets a fixation on some woman. This is directed at three families in a way that seems to indicate a logical link."

"I know. Your dad's thinking about sending us all to my cousin Lou in Colorado, except that the younger girls would have to quit their jobs, and Wendy wouldn't go, of course, because she's not going to give up her job heading the emergency response team for any reason. Besides, you couldn't persuade her to leave Billy Joe behind. She just wouldn't do it. Of course, your dad's afraid that if this loony is trying to get to Micah, Ransom and him through their families, it wouldn't be safe to leave anyone behind, Billy Joe included."

"But—" Janet's mind was beginning to rebel against the whole notion. "But how can anyone be sure something really *is* going on? The gas leak is weird, I grant you, but it *might* have been an accident. If the hose had come loose enough, eventually anything at all might make it slide the rest of the way off. Just the rumble from a passing truck on the highway."

"We've discussed that possibility."

"And the prowler that Mandy Laird saw a couple of times could just be a drifter. Lord knows, enough of them pass through here hoping for work or a handout. What she's seen might have no relation whatever to what happened to you!"

"I know. But what about Faith Parish feeling like things have been moved around her house? Just the way I felt?"

"Faith Parish has a three-year-old daughter, Mom. She doesn't need a ghost or a prowler to move things."

Marge faced her daughter squarely. "A mother knows these things. You'll see. There isn't a doubt in my mind that Faith would know it if Sally were moving things around. Anyway, Faith's been blaming it on a ghost."

"Seriously?"

"What else is she going to blame it on? I think she's kind of joking, actually. Anyway, enough of that. Why don't you get that natural oak crib?" She pointed to a crib off to the left. "With that finish, it'll be perfect for both boys and girls."

"It's too expensive. Besides, Emily's going to be my last one for a long time."

Marge's green eyes, so like her daughter's, were suddenly twinkling. "That's what *you* think. Well, your dad and I have already decided we want to help you with baby furniture, so don't worry about whether that one costs more. The question is whether you like it."

Janet loved it, and before long it was being loaded into the back of her car.

"I'll ask Seth to drive out and help you with it," Marge said. "If I can pry him away from Darlene for a little while."

"Darlene? I thought Seth didn't want to get involved."

Marge shrugged. "I don't know anything about that. I just know he took Darlene to the movies two nights ago, and last night they went out to dinner, and today they drove over to the national park to go hiking. I'm surprised she didn't tell you every little detail. The two of you used to share everything."

"Times change. People change." But she felt hurt anyway. Left out. Kind of silly, she supposed, when she hadn't shared all the gory details of her own messy relationship with Dar. Long periods of separation had broken that bond of intimacy and placed a distance between them. Not a huge distance, but a small one that allowed for privacy.

Of course, she reminded herself as she drove back home, she hadn't told Dar everything about Abel, either. In fact, she'd been quite careful *not* to tell her everything. It wasn't so much that she thought Dar would give her a hard time about it as it was an almost superstitious feeling that she would jinx herself if she admitted her feelings out loud.

What were her feelings, anyway? A desire to be held, a need to be loved, a yearning to feel emotionally safe with someone. Those feelings had nothing to do with Abel Pierce specifically. How could they? She hardly knew the man. No, what she was doing was directing a very general set of needs and wants in his direction. He was just a target of opportunity.

She couldn't help it; a giggle tumbled past her lips at the notion of Abel Pierce being a target of opportunity. She had an absolutely ridiculous mental picture of him wearing a huge archery target on his back and trying to dodge her attentions. Nope. That wasn't him. Or her.

She was still giggling to herself when she pulled into her driveway and stopped in front of the cabin. Home sweet home. Flowers bobbed gaily all around the house—the pansies planted by Jeff along the walk, and the glads, marigolds and daisies she, Darlene and Seth had placed all around the foundation. And scattered all over her yard were Indian paintbrushes, a gift of nature.

It was a beautiful day, warm enough to dangle her toes in the frigid stream out back. The rocks at streamside were slippery and unstable, though, so she thought better of the idea. When Seth came over to help with the crib, maybe . . .

When she stepped through the cabin door, every hair on the back of her neck suddenly stood up. *Somebody had been in here.*

If things had been tossed around, if something had been vandalized, the feeling would have been just as shocking but far less creepy. Instead she stood there and looked frantically around, wondering what was wrong.

A part of her mind argued that she was feeling this way only because of the things that had happened to her mother, Faith Parish and Mandy Laird. She was uneasy because of her discussion with Mom this morning. That was all.

Another part of her mind wasn't buying it. Never in her life had she been suggestible enough to feel what she was feeling simply because of a conversation. Something was very, very wrong.

Dad had always said to clear out. Just get out, call him, wait for help. Under no circumstances should she venture farther into the house, in case an intruder might still be there.

Might be hiding behind the bedroom door, which was only partially open. Might be hiding in the bathroom down the hallway, or behind the kitchen counter...

Stepping to one side, she reached behind her for the door latch, lifted it and backed out of the house, afraid to turn her back for even an instant.

Her keys were still in her hand, clutched tightly. Turning now because she had to, she hurried down the steps toward her car. Never had she felt as ungainly as she did right then, torn between the need to be careful so she didn't fall and injure her child and the need to get the hell out of there.

Just as she was rounding the front of her car to the driver's side, the sound of an approaching engine reached her. Someone was coming up the driveway!

For an instant her relief was so great that her knees almost gave way. Then she realized she didn't know who was approaching. It couldn't be her brother—he was still hiking in the national forest—or her father, who was working....

Galvanized by renewed fright, she climbed rapidly into the front seat of her Explorer, just as the vehicle rounded the last bend in the driveway and came into sight.

It was Abel Pierce. He pulled up nearby, climbed out of his truck smiling that incredible smile and walked toward her. As he approached, his expression gave way to concern.

She ought to just drive out of here now, Janet thought. Just leave him standing in her dust as she headed for town and help. But she didn't. She couldn't, not when he was looking at her with such patent concern, a frown furrowing his brow. "Janet? What's wrong?"

After a perceptible moment of hesitation, during which her mind and emotions warred wildly, she lowered the window just a crack. If he tried anything, she would drive away and never look back. "I have the feeling somebody was in my house."

His head swung sharply around as he looked toward the cabin. "When? You mean just now? I'll check it out."

The change that came over him was amazing. He crouched slightly and moved toward the cabin with all the sinuous grace of a stalking cat. He moved like a man who knew exactly what he was doing, and that disturbed her even more. How was it he knew such things?

When he reached the door, he pressed himself against the wall and peered cautiously around the corner. Moments later he disappeared within.

All of a sudden the clearing seemed isolated. Desolate. The ceaseless breeze tossed the tops of the trees, but nothing else moved. Shadows were gone, the sun hidden behind Thunder Mountain. The brilliant blue of the late afternoon sky seemed to have nothing to do with the deepening twilight in this clearing. Even the flowers, which had looked so cheerful only a short while ago, now looked bizarrely out of place. Something evil had passed this way.

She shivered.

"Janet?" Abel appeared in the doorway of her cabin. He came toward her at an easy lope, jumping the stairs to the ground as if they were no more than a curb. He was long, lean, elegant in his movements, she thought. In his element.

"Janet, whoever was there is gone. It's safe to come inside. You can tell me if anything's been disturbed."

Something inside her abruptly unlocked. Anger, buried so deep she hadn't been aware of it, came seething upward from the dark places of her soul, born of betrayal and unleashed by fear. "Why should I trust you? Who the hell are you? How do I know you weren't the person who was in there? How do I know you're not trying to kill my family? How do I know—"

She broke off abruptly as he thrust something angrily at her, pressing it with an audible slap against the still partially rolled-up window.

"I'm a cop," he said flatly. "LAPD. I don't hurt people. I *help* them!"

Maybe it took forever. Maybe it only took a few seconds, but his words finally penetrated. She stared at the badge before her face. "A cop?"

"A cop. Just like your dad. Believe me, it's safe for you to come inside and tell me if anything is messed up."

Her knees still felt like soft noodles. Emily kicked mightily, as if angry over the fright her mother had experienced. The lower part of Janet's back ached dully from all the time she had spent on her feet that day, and her feet, in full agreement with her back, had become so swollen that her shoes were too tight.

And quite suddenly, all Janet wanted to do was put her head down and bawl her eyes out. She fought the need, closing her eyes tightly, but tears seeped out anyway.

"Aw, hell . . ." Abel muttered the words and pulled open the door of her car. Idiot that she was, she hadn't even locked it. Moments later, much to her astonishment, she was being lifted gently from the driver's seat. "Shh," he said quietly, carrying her toward the cabin. "Shh . . . It's okay. Hey, *I'm* here. What could possibly be wrong?"

The outrageousness of his question startled a teary laugh from her, but the strength of his arms elicited a whole lot more. She felt safe, wonderfully safe, as he carried her up the steps and into the living room. It had been so long since she had felt so safe. . . .

Huge tears forced their way past her eyelids and rolled hotly down her cheeks. The dike had been breached, and it seemed nothing was going to stop the flood.

Instead of just putting her down, he settled on the couch with her in his lap. All of a sudden she felt small, precious and protected, and not at all ungainly. Somehow he was big enough and powerful enough to accommodate both her and Emily on his lap and still be able to tuck her face into the curve between his neck and shoulder.

"Hey," he said softly. "Hey, hey. It's okay. Really. I'm here, and I'll be damned if you have to face this whatever-it-is alone. Anybody who wants to get to you is going to have to get through me first."

Another wave of hot tears poured down her cheeks as she fought for control. She ached inside, deep inside, in the very center of her soul. Ached for dreams lost, ached for promises betrayed, ached for the end of childhood and the beginning of adulthood in a frightening world. Everything she had ever wanted had turned to ashes in her hands, leaving her alone and scared to face the biggest responsibility in life.

She could hardly concentrate on the soothing promises Abel made. Nor did she believe them. Never again was she going to believe the easy promises made by a man. But he shouldn't be promising such things, anyway. He hardly knew her. . . .

A sob escaped her, a gulping sound, and Emily kicked sharply at her side, pinching Janet between a tiny foot and Abel's hard-as-granite belly.

"Feisty little kid, isn't she?" he murmured. A moment later his hand settled warmly on Janet's tummy, spread flat, as if he were holding Emily, too. And somehow the intimacy didn't seem out of place. "It's all right," he said quietly. "It's okay. Nobody's gonna hurt either one of you...."

Vain promises. Empty promises. But she didn't want to argue with him. Nor did it really matter. All that mattered now was her need to cry, her need to be held as if she mattered.

Abel held her close, one arm wrapped snugly around her shoulders. The other hand he lifted from her belly so he could rub her arm soothingly as she sobbed against him.

"Talk to me," he murmured eventually. "Tell me what hurts so much. Maybe I can't fix it, but I can sure listen."

But so many painful things inside her were warring for expression, and they'd been held inside for so long, that it was as if there weren't words in the language to begin telling anyone how wounded she felt.

And, as usual, her pride reared its head, telling her to quit wallowing in self-pity. She didn't have it that bad. Not bad at all. She had a loving family and friends, and all of them were concerned about her and eager to help her. The world was full of people who didn't have nearly as much as she did. Young women who were utterly alone, penniless . . .

But betrayal and loss don't listen well to reason. She gasped, drawing deep breaths of air to calm herself, and little by little her eyes began to dry. Finally, her head stuffy and eyes sore, she lay weakly against Abel.

"So tell me," he said.

"It's nothing, really. Nothing. Old story."

He lifted his hand and gently stroked her hair. "I guess you must feel betrayed twice over. I mean, not only did he ditch you, which is bad enough, but he ditched the baby, as well. A classic double whammy."

Janet drew a shuddery breath and blinked away the last of her tears, drying her cheeks with her sleeve. "You had a double whammy, too."

"My girlfriend and my best friend? Yeah, I guess. Life dishes those up from time to time."

Suddenly self-conscious about sitting on his lap, she wiggled, trying to slide back onto the couch. At once he slipped an arm under her legs and moved her over so that she sat beside him. Some corner of her mind was disappointed that he'd been so quick to set her aside. Silly, she told herself. Don't be silly.

Her eyes felt swollen, her head throbbed, and her nose was as stuffy as if she had a bad cold. In all, she felt miserable and stupid, stupid for giving way to tears over things that couldn't be changed.

"Are you all right now?" he asked.

She nodded, sniffled and managed an embarrassed smile. "Sorry."

"For what? Reaching the end of your rope? Everybody gets there sooner or later. Mind if I get a glass of water?"

She watched him cross the plank floor and braided rugs into the kitchen area. He found the glasses in the cupboard to one side of the sink as if he'd lived there all his life. But of course that was the logical place for them to be—all six of them. She wasn't exactly swimming in an embarrassment of possessions.

"Would you like some?" He held a glass out to her.

"No thanks."

He drained a couple of glasses himself, remarking how good the water here tasted.

"There's a well," she told him. "No chlorine. Just pure, untreated Mother Nature."

"Cold, too." He flashed one of those incredible smiles that made her insides quiver pleasurably. Emily must have felt it, too, because she kicked several times in rapid succession. "Okay," Abel said. "Let's check the place out, together. Take your time, and see if you can figure out what gave you the feeling that someone had been in here."

She didn't want to do this. A cowardly urge to just dismiss the whole thing made her resistant to the notion of hunting for the cause of her feeling. If she actually found something to justify her fear, then it would become concrete, inescapable. In its present state, her fear could be brushed aside as imaginary, as the result of her conversation with her mother earlier. But if she discovered something . . .

Somehow she couldn't be cowardly with Abel standing there, patiently waiting for her cooperation. Somehow she couldn't ignore the very real possibility that someone had been in her little home since she'd left this morning, and it might well be dangerous to dismiss that.

Pushing herself up from the couch, she looked at Abel, trying not to appear as plaintive and reluctant as she felt. "Okay."

"Stand where you were when you first had the feeling someone was in here," he suggested. "It's probably something you saw."

Calm now, less concerned that someone might actually be *in* the house, she noticed the cause of her fright almost immediately.

"My books," she said, turning to look at Abel. "Someone put them out of order. Why would anybody want to do that?"

He walked to the shelves and scanned them. "Which ones?"

She pointed out three volumes, each moved slightly out of the alphabetical order in which she had placed them.

"You're sure?" he asked. "You're positive you couldn't have made the mistake yourself?"

She looked at the shelves with a sense of growing uncertainty. It was possible, she supposed, that they had been out of order all along and she had only just now noticed it. "It's possible," she said reluctantly, her voice heavy. "It's possible...." She trailed off, suddenly swamped in a nightmarish feeling of not being able to trust her own perceptions.

"But you don't believe it." Abel astonished her by nodding. "Okay. Someone was in here. Do you see anything else?"

She turned slowly, surveying the room with a growing sense of horror as it began to dawn on her what it might mean that someone had come into her house only to shift things around. To leave signs of his invasion like silent threats.

"I thought—I thought once before that someone had been in here," she said, her mouth suddenly so dry that it was difficult to speak. "The thumbtacks on that print weren't in the right place." She pointed to the Peña print. "It may just be that Seth didn't put the tacks through the holes that were already there, but he was so careful to do it on all the other prints...."

Abel crossed to the print and peered at it intently. "This was no accident," he said finally. "All four of those tacks are offset by exactly the same amount from the holes. No way did that just happen. Somebody had to do it deliberately.''

A chill trickled down Janet's spine, and she instinctively pressed her hands protectively to her womb.

Abel faced her. ''Maybe you ought to go stay with your folks.''

''What good will that do?'' The words burst out of her. ''This same thing has been happening to my mom for weeks, and then the gas leak . . . What good would it do?''

''Someone moved things around at your parents' house, too?''

Janet nodded, biting her lower lip to keep back the tears that were threatening again. ''Just like this. Little things. Mom thought she was getting Alzheimer's!''

''Is there any place else you could go?''

''What, and bring this threat with me?''

''I guess not,'' he agreed after a moment. He turned around slowly, not really seeing the room, thinking about the situation. ''Given what happened with the gas, I don't think we can safely dismiss this as some kind of prank.''

''No. Oh, no,'' she said tautly. ''This is vicious. This is designed to make me feel unsafe in my own home. That's no little prank, Abel!''

He hesitated, a struggle visible on his face. A second later he strode across the room to her and took her into his arms. Holding her carefully yet securely, he astonished her by dropping a kiss on her forehead.

''It's all right,'' he said huskily. ''I'll stay here. I'll camp on your couch or on your front porch, but I'm not going to leave you here alone.''

It was insane to trust the man this way. Janet rode alongside Abel in his truck up the side of Thunder Mountain to retrieve his gear, and bit her lip until it was sore as she argued with herself over her inclination to trust him. What did she have to go on, after all, except instinct and an LAPD detective's shield? Good grief, police the world over were corrupt. A shield was no guarantee that a man was law-abiding and honorable.

But she couldn't forget the way he had laid his hand on her belly. That gesture had been so protective, so caring. It was impossible to rustle up any real fear about Abel when she remembered how he had touched her.

Evening was falling. Even in the shadow of the mountain it was possible to tell that day would soon be over. The blue of the sky was darkening, the light dimming steadily. The forest depths to either side of the road had become impenetrable, mysterious.

Abel drove slowly up the last several miles of rutted road, taking care not to jolt Janet unnecessarily. When they rounded a bend and saw the mining town in the clearing ahead of them, Janet suddenly couldn't repress a shiver.

"It looks spooky," she said. "It always does at this time of day, but..."

He braked at the lip of a gentle hill, which gave them a slightly elevated view of the ghost town. It sat in a hollow carved by ancient glaciers in the side of Thunder Mountain. Whatever might once have grown there was gone, and little would grow there for centuries to come. All the tailings that stood in stark mounds near the mine shafts were poisoned with metals and minerals brought up from deep within the earth. Even grass couldn't grow there.

It looked like a lunar landscape that was punctuated with tumbledown buildings. Stark. Empty. Haunted.

"It's fantastic in this light," Abel remarked. "I wish you had your camera."

"Me too. I've never been up here this late. My next project was photographing this place by moonlight, but this is...eerie."

He released the brake and drove down the gentle slope into town. Janet had, in the past, driven past the buildings and wondered about the faces that had looked out those windows so long ago. Now she looked at those windows and wondered who was peering out right now.

Abel braked in front of the shack where he had made his camp. "You just wait here," he told Janet. "It won't take but a minute to get what I need."

"Don't leave anything you don't want stolen. Someone might think it's abandoned and just take it."

"I didn't bring much to begin with."

Inside the shack he reached for the duffel that held his clothes and froze. Someone had been going through his things. It was subtle, but he knew he'd closed the zipper all the way that morning. His index finger remembered the way the tab had pressed against it when the slide would go no farther.

Immediately he scanned the rest of the room, taking in the aluminum pot that held his cup, plate and other utensils. It had been tipped over.

It took him only a few minutes to discover that nothing at all had been taken. Not that he had left anything here anyone would want. Disturbed, he picked up his duffel, his sleeping bag and the pot and carried them out to his truck.

He wasn't sure whether to suspect that the same person who had gone through Janet's place had gone through his things. On the face of it, it seemed ridiculous...until he considered the proximity of the two events and the fact that he and Janet were acquainted. Had the vendetta against her family somehow been extended to him?

One thing he *did* know for certain: he wasn't going to tell Janet about this. She had quite enough on her plate right now. Besides, it was probably totally unrelated to what had happened at her place. The *modus* wasn't the same, for one thing. No, someone had just been curious, probably one of those guys who had followed him the other day. He couldn't blame those vets. Given their state of mind, they were bound to be paranoid and want to know everything possible about the stranger on their mountain.

He gathered up the rest of his stuff and shoved it into the back of the truck. It was a meager pile of possessions, and the sight of it as he dumped the last items onto the truck bed gave him pause. It wasn't the knowledge that it was everything he owned in the world, but the realization that there wasn't a whole hell of a lot more at home waiting for him. Except for the time he'd spent with Louise, he'd never tried to make a home for himself. And all he had left from that venture was a stereo that took up most of the room in the efficiency apartment he currently kept. So what was there? A few dishes, a few suits he seldom wore, more street clothes that weren't appropriate anywhere outside L.A., a couple of uniforms... Zip. Zilch. *Nada*. What a hell of a lot to show for thirty-six years on this planet.

He swore under his breath and stomped around to the driver's side of the truck. Who needed this? Why now? Stuff like this had never troubled him before, and now it could damn well wait until after the trial. Once he'd taken care of that business...well, he would be damned if he was going to go back into covert operations for Internal Affairs. Let somebody else do it.

Of course, he'd screwed himself royally by going to work for IAD. It might well be that he could never again do anything else. At least, not in L.A.

"Something wrong?" Janet asked as they drove down the mountain.

"Nope. Just thinking about the mess I left back home."

"I wanted to ask you..." She hesitated, aware that it was really none of her business.

"Go on, spit it out. I don't bite except on Saturdays, and last I checked, it's Tuesday."

Impossibly, she felt herself smiling. "I just wondered what you're doing camping out on Thunder Mountain." And why he had been so paranoid about being watched the other day, but she didn't dare ask that outright. That was simply *too* rude.

"Well . . . it's kind of a long story. I've been a cop ever since I got out of the army."

"Like my dad."

He glanced at her and nodded. Ahead of them the road was a tunnel carved out of the night by the beams of their headlights. "Like that. Anyway, at some point or other I made the mistake of getting fed up with all the corruption in the department. It happens everywhere, you know? Big town, small town, whatever. Some cops shouldn't be cops. They were always criminals at heart, and they take advantage of their position. Sometimes it's just protection money. Sometimes it's drugs or women, or fencing stolen goods. Usually it's just one guy or two. Sometimes it's worse."

"I've heard about it."

"Everybody has. Wherever people are involved, you're going to have corruption. But...I got fed up with it. Fed up enough to go to work for the Internal Affairs Division."

"Ooh."

"Exactly. *Ooh.* It was bad enough when I was picking up guys in singles, but then I stumbled on a really big operation.

Thirty, maybe forty or more, cops were involved in an organized criminal network. Drugs, prostitution, bootlegging—hell, there wasn't a whole lot they didn't have their dirty little hands in, and they had some big-time organized crime connections.'' He shrugged a shoulder. ''Anyway, my life isn't worth a plugged nickel until after I testify. IAD tucked me away in a safe house, but there was a hit on it just twenty-four hours after they stashed me. They figured they couldn't protect me, and I agreed. So here I am.''

Janet was silent for a few minutes, absorbing what he'd told her. ''I've heard that it can get dangerous, working for Internal Affairs.''

''A lot of people have a lot to lose.''

''Because of the code of silence, I mean.''

''The Blue Wall? Yeah. Even the straight cops won't forgive you for crossing that line.''

''So I've heard. Do you really think you'll be safe after you testify?''

''Sure. Everything I have to say will be out in the open and on record. There won't be any reason to put me away then. It won't do any good.''

''Unless they want revenge.''

He shook his head, tossing her a smile. ''Nope. Revenge doesn't pay. The harm to them will already have been done, and they'll only get themselves in more hot water by wiping me out. It's not as if each one of them wouldn't be on the primary suspect list if I met an untimely demise.''

A small laugh escaped her at his phrasing. ''I'm sorry. I'm not laughing at your situation but at the way you said it.''

''I was hoping you'd at least smile.'' He sent her another glance. ''It'll settle down, but I'm thinking about getting out of Internal Affairs. Trouble is, I don't know if I'll ever be able to work as a cop again.''

''The resentment, you mean?''

''That's about it. They're not going to forget I was a rat.''

It sounded like an untenable position to her. ''What will you do if you can't be a cop?''

''Hell, I don't know. Work in corporate security or something.'' He shook his head. ''These are the things we never think about when we make a decision in a moment of honest, passionate conviction. Putting on a white hat sounds real good until the bill for it arrives."

"Sort of a 'good guys finish last' philosophy?"

"No way. I never finish last."

There was no moon. The stars seemed cold and distant above the black tops of the pines as they jolted down her rutted driveway.

"You need to get this damn thing graded," Abel remarked.

"Jeff says he's going to do it one of these days soon."

"Jeff?"

"Jeff Cumberland. He owns the Bar C ranch. He said this place was where his ancestors homesteaded when they first came to Wyoming."

"He's kept it up pretty good." He braked in front of the cabin, then turned off the engine and lights. The night was suddenly silent and dark. "You wait here while I check the place out."

She nodded mutely and handed him her key. It didn't escape her that he locked his truck when he climbed out. His caution comforted her somehow, letting her know that he wasn't dismissing her feeling that someone had been in her cabin.

He returned a few minutes later. "All clear." He did not follow her into the cabin.

It was only later, as she stood in her kitchen with her growling stomach, that it occurred to her that they hadn't sorted out anything about the terms of this arrangement. Did he expect her to feed him and cook for him? She didn't like that idea at all. In the first place, she couldn't afford to feed another mouth, and this guy was no ninety-pound weakling. He probably had an appetite to match his size.

And then there was the question of where he would sleep. On the sofa bed? Other than the floor, she had no other place to put him, and she didn't feel entirely easy with that. After all, she hardly knew him, and she wouldn't feel comfortable stumbling to the bathroom at 3:00 a.m. in her nightie.

Which was silly, she assured herself. Given that she liked flannel nightgowns that reached her ankles, she would hardly be immodest.

But what could she feed him tonight? She hadn't planned on making anything but a single chop, a small salad and a glass of milk. She wasn't prepared to offer sustenance to half an invading army!

But as she stood there worrying the question to death, Abel poked his head in the front door.

"I'll be out here if you need anything," he told her. "Good night."

The door closed with quiet finality, leaving her absurdly disappointed that he was making this too easy.

Chapter 8

Janet couldn't leave him out there. It got cold at night at this elevation. And what about food? Did he have anything he could eat for dinner? How would he cook it? Good grief, her front porch wasn't some kind of campground where he could build a fire to cook on. Or to keep himself warm with.

Disturbed, she put her chop back in the fridge and went to the front door. Leaning out, she found him spreading out his sleeping bag.

"What are you going to eat?" she asked.

"I have some jerky and some canned beans. I'll be fine."

"That's ridiculous! Jerky and canned beans! A cold meal on a chilly night."

He looked at her, a smile creasing the corners of his eyes. "I'll be fine. It won't be the first time."

She chewed her lower lip for a moment. "At least let me heat up your beans."

"Janet, I'll be okay. Really. Just forget I'm out here and look after yourself. This is no different from camping out up in the ghost town."

"But up there you could have a fire!"

He shrugged. "Sometimes. It's not that cold out here, and I've been through worse."

"When? On the streets of L.A.?"

A snort of laughter escaped him. "Depends on what you mean by worse. In terms of camping . . . I was in the Army Special Forces."

"Oh." Feeling a little silly, she went back into the house. Special Forces, like her dad. She knew how Nathan Tate felt about being mollycoddled. For some reason those guys didn't seem to be able to appreciate a woman's natural concern about such things.

Well, there was no point arguing further. He wouldn't yield, and he would only get irritated if she kept bothering him. She ate her chop and salad, drank a full glass of milk, and washed the dishes. Standing at the sink with her hands in warm, soapy water, she stared at her reflection in the window glass, beyond which there was nothing but the chilly darkness of night.

This is ridiculous! she thought. She shook the excess water and soap bubbles off her hands and dried them quickly. A moment later she was leaning out the door again.

Abel was sitting in the rocking chair, the empty bean can and fork on the floor beside him. He was rocking slowly and steadily, his right ankle resting on his left knee.

"Beautiful night," he commented. "I thought I heard a wolf."

"We have a pack up on Thunder Mountain. They usually stay up really high, though."

"Maybe the wind's carrying the sound down the slope."

A familiar rumble of thunder reached them, sounding distant.

"This place is weird," Abel said after a moment. "The way there nearly always seems to be a storm around the peak of this mountain."

"It's a sacred mountain. I guess it can have any kind of weather it wants."

In the dark, she saw the gleam of his teeth as he smiled. "Is it? I like that."

"Some Indians think so. Gray Cloud could tell you more about it than I can. He's a medicine man who lived on the mountain."

"Maybe I'll look him up one of these days. I think my uncle would think this place is sacred, too. Maybe I'll bring him here sometime."

"Where does he live?"

"In Okinawa. He taught me never to forget that all living things are my brothers. It's funny, but I'm just beginning to realize how much I've missed having bare ground beneath my feet instead of pavement."

Janet nodded and tentatively offered something she'd never said out loud before. "Sometimes I think—well, I have a hyperactive imagination, so this is silly, I know—but sometimes I think that we need to walk on the bare ground, to have our feet touch the soil with nothing in between. As if we're flowers that can move around but sometimes just need to get our refreshment from the earth."

He nodded slowly. "That describes it perfectly, this feeling I've been having lately. Getting in touch with the earth. Getting in tune. Well, if you're being silly, then so am I."

She liked him then. All along she'd found him appealing and attractive as a man, but right then she really *liked* him. "You come in and sleep on the couch," she told him. "It's going to be cold out here, and it's utterly ridiculous for you to sleep in a sleeping bag when I have a sofa bed inside."

He shook his head. "It's not ridiculous."

"Whyever not?"

Even in the near darkness she could feel the sudden heat of his gaze. He looked her over from head to foot as if he had all the time in the world. As if she were standing there naked and slim, rather than in maternity clothes and a ragged sweater. Instinctively she pressed her hand to her stomach, touching the fullness that housed Emily.

He couldn't possibly be looking at her that way, not when she was so pregnant. He couldn't possibly find her sexually attractive.

But the woman in her responded to his look anyway, and warm feelings spiraled to her center, causing a deep, delicious throb, a feeling she hadn't allowed herself in many months. He wanted her, and she desperately wanted him. She needed warm, loving hands to stroke her all over. Wanted a hot, hungry mouth on her full, aching breasts. Longed to be filled by a man's hard strength. Yearned to be loved.

Emily kicked sharply, bringing her back to her senses. She didn't know this man at all. Certainly not enough to give herself to him. Turning quickly, she went back into the house without another word.

He was right; he was better off outside.

The morning dawned cool and misty. Wispy fingers of fog stretched downward, appearing to graze the treetops. The wind had stilled, leaving the world silent. To Janet it felt as if her little clearing were isolated from the rest of the world, cast adrift on the sea of clouds.

She hadn't lit a fire last night, and the damp this morning made the chill seem bone-deep. Wearing a blue sweater and fleecy pants, she threw some sausage patties in her electric frying pan and whipped up some pancake batter. After the briefest hesitation, she went out to the front porch.

Abel was sitting in the rocking chair, wearing a denim jacket and jeans. He looked as if the morning suited him just fine.

"Good morning," he said when he saw her. "Beautiful day, isn't it?"

"That's a matter of opinion. Listen, I'm throwing some pancakes together for breakfast. If you'd like to join me, I'll make coffee."

He smiled, a warm, easy expression. "My willpower's at an all-time low right now. That invitation is too good to pass up."

He filled the kitchen. No matter where she stood or in what direction she looked, she was acutely aware of him sitting at the wooden table with his legs stretched out and crossed at the ankle. He looked dark and dangerous, and when he unbuttoned his jacket she expected to see a black shirt. Instead he wore a gray sweatshirt that looked as if it had seen a few better days. It was somehow disarming. She decided they'd better discuss something neutral.

"How exactly do you work undercover?" she asked him. "Are you on the beat with the cops you suspect?"

"Actually, they don't know I'm a cop at all. They think I'm a punk. A street wart."

A laugh escaped her at the term. "I've never heard that one before."

"I think I invented it. No, I just pretend to be a sleazeball for hire and make myself real available where it counts."

She placed a plate of sausages and pancakes in front of him and poured him a cup of coffee. "How did that affect you?"

"Me? What do you mean?"

"Well, it can't have been easy living that way, pretending to be something you aren't. Did you ever start to believe your own acting?"

"You mean, did I ever start to feel like a genuine street wart?" Syrup dripped from the piece of pancake on the end of his fork. He stared at it, trying not to remember blood as it ran from Delia's crumpled body.... "Yeah, I got to believing my own press. That's the danger of working undercover like that. You can't quit long enough to remember who you really are. Some vice cops get it really bad."

"What about you?" She slid into the seat facing him and poured a small amount of syrup on her pancake. "Did you get it really bad?"

"No. There was always something to wake me up...." Like watching Delia stumble into the middle of the deal, like watching her shock as she recognized her fellow cops, knowing that her fate was sealed in an instant, being unable to do anything at all because it all happened so fast.... But he would have done something if he could have. He would have blown the whole damn investigation, would have blown his cover, would have stood between her and that damn bullet.

He would have. But there wasn't time.

He was a failure. A major failure. Everything he'd been trying to accomplish had become as important as sawdust in those split seconds that had taken Delia Burke's life. If he couldn't protect one innocent person, what did it matter how many crooks he put away?

But that was why they were so damn eager to wipe him out. He could identify the gunman who'd killed Delia. Who'd killed a fellow cop. They would all go down on that one, all of them, as principal accessories to murder. Every last one of those bastards was going to get it for Delia. He was going to make sure of that.

"Abel? Are you all right?"

With a start he came back to himself and found that he was still staring at the same piece of dripping pancake on the end of his fork.

"Abel?"

He lifted his eyes to Janet's concerned green ones. "I'm fine. Just thinking." Without further explanation he began to eat.

Two cups of coffee and a half-dozen large flapjacks later, he was feeling like a new man. All the stiffness left in his joints by the cold, damp night had vanished, and a sense of well-being filled him. Damn, he couldn't remember the last time he'd felt this good or this relaxed. Just went to prove he wasn't living right.

"This was fabulous," he said. "It was the best meal I've had in a while."

She smiled. "You're easy to please."

"And you need to learn to accept a compliment." He smiled to take the sting out of his words. "You make a great pancake. Not everyone can. You're also very pretty and sexy as hell. Now, don't argue with me, because it could get embarrassing. When exactly are you going to get around to telling me what happened to the bozo who happens to be Emily's father?"

That caused the smile to drain from her face. She looked away, as if she couldn't bear to have him see into her eyes. Into her heart. It shamed her to admit she hadn't been woman enough for Scott, but she needed to admit it—so Abel wouldn't be misled about her. "I was apparently only one of a number of girls he was having an eternal love affair with. Three or four, I guess. We were each under the illusion that we were the 'one and only.'"

"Kind of hard to be the 'only' when there are so many others."

"Exactly." She dared to look at him and found only sympathy on his face. "I think he wanted me to find out about the others. It happened shortly after I told him about the baby, and he started backing out, telling me he wasn't ready for fatherhood. I thought he'd change his mind if I was just patient enough...." She shook her head. "What an idiot."

"He was, certainly. Not you, though. You're not an idiot. So he couldn't quite convince you the baby was a serious problem vis-à-vis his perspective on your relationship, so he very conveniently let you know that he'd been merrily cheating on you with several other women."

"That's about the size of it."

"Son of a bitch deserves to have his *cojones*... Never mind. He's going to pay child support, of course."

"No, actually, he isn't. He's denying paternity, and I'm damned if I want him to have anything at all to do with Emily anymore. He's disgusting. Loathsome. A lowlife. The only question in this is how my judgment could have been so far off the mark."

He reached across the table and pressed a gentle fingertip to one of her clenched hands. The touch was warm, electric. She caught her breath helplessly as that simple contact set off a firestorm of yearning. He didn't seem to even notice.

"Your judgment wasn't off," he said. "From the sound of it, this guy is pretty smooth. Why should you feel bad that you couldn't see through him? I'm sure he's had plenty of experience at manipulating people, but how much experience have you had at seeing through a con? Don't beat yourself up over it, Janet. You're not to blame for anything."

"It'll be a long time before I trust my judgment about anyone again."

He withdrew his hand suddenly, remembering that she had no cause to trust him. "I can understand that."

Janet had no idea that he thought she might be speaking about him. All she knew was that she missed that small contact. It was amazing how much such a simple thing could mean. "He wanted me to have an abortion."

"Probably wanted to make sure you couldn't sue him for paternity." The disgust he felt was in danger of showing on his face, so he took a moment to get it under control. "You *are* better off without him."

"I think so." But none of that, of course, addressed the wounds she had suffered and how much they still hurt. On the other hand, she was getting tired of wallowing in her own misery. "The worst part of this is that I feel so angry so much of the time now. I'd like to just put it behind me."

"You will." He tried to look reassuring but felt like a complete sham. How long now had he been nursing his own grudge about Louise and the baby that wasn't his? Too long. He was hardly one to tell anybody else that they would get over betrayal. In fact, it was beginning to seem to him that betrayal was the hardest thing in the world to get over.

They were also avoiding some pretty important issues, he thought as he helped clear the table before insisting on washing the dishes himself. They weren't discussing the fact that she was afraid someone had broken into her home twice. They weren't discussing how this might be linked to what had happened with the gas leak at her parents' home. Nor were they discussing whether he would spend another night playing watchdog.

She was afraid to bring those things up, he realized. She was afraid that he was going to say he had to go back up on the mountain, as if there were something inherently better about sleeping on the cold side of a mountain versus sleeping in the cold on her porch. He smiled inwardly and scoured a plate.

He didn't have anything better to do with his time right now than watch over her, but as soon as he needed to go back for the trial, she was going to be all alone with her fears. With the intruder. With whatever was threatening her, threatening her parents. At this point he was ready to believe they were the same thing. After all, how much was likely to happen in a backwater like Conard County?

"We need to get to the bottom of this," he said over his shoulder.

"The bottom of what?"

"Who's been in here. Who might be stalking your parents."

"You think they're related." It wasn't a question but the voicing of a thought that she hadn't really wanted to face.

"If this were L.A. you might persuade me these things were simply coincidence. Out here? Not in a million years. At this point I'd say it's pretty certain that someone has a grudge against the Tate family, wouldn't you?"

"And not just us!"

He turned from the sink, ignoring the soapy water that dripped from his hands. "What do you mean?"

"Micah Parish and Ransom Laird. Some funny things have been going on with them, too. Dad and they think that it has something to do with something that happened in Vietnam. There's no other link."

He stared at her for a long, hard moment, then remembered his hands. Quickly he dried them and wiped the floor with a paper towel. "Tell me. What's been happening with Parish and Laird?"

"Not much, really, but it's made them suspicious. Ransom's wife has seen some kind of prowler several times. Micah's wife has begun to think they have a ghost, because things keep getting moved around. That's the same thing that happened to Mom before the gas leak."

"The same thing that's happening to you." Troubled, he frowned. "And your dad thinks it has something to do with Vietnam?"

"That's what I heard him say. They thought it might be you, because of the questions you were asking."

"I can see why. What about you? Do you still believe that?"

Janet shook her head. "No, I can't. I just can't."

"It's possible, though, you know. It's entirely possible I could have a grudge to settle. Just because I don't seem like a killer..."

She stared at him with widening eyes, her heart suddenly hammering. What was he telling her? That she was all wrong about him? That he really was the stalker?

He shook his head. "I told your dad who I am. I told you. You can verify it, if you want. I realize that my being a police detective really isn't any kind of guarantee that I don't have a personal agenda here, but maybe you can believe that if I were that kind of person, I wouldn't be in Internal Affairs."

And that, she realized, was the most persuasive thing he could have said. No, she really didn't think that any man who could value ethics highly enough to make an outcast of himself could be the kind of man who would stalk three entire families this way.

She kept a roll of paper and a pencil on the counter beside the refrigerator for making shopping lists. He yanked a strip of it loose and scribbled on it. "Here," he said, handing it to her. "This is the phone number of my boss. He'll acknowledge that I work there and tell you that I'm presently on indefinite leave.

He won't be able to tell you anything else, though. Nobody knows where I am right now."

She accepted the scrap of paper and tucked it into her pocket, but she made no move to go to the telephone. The simple truth was, she believed what he was telling her. Later she would probably doubt him again, and that would be soon enough to call. Right now she would feel like a fool doing it.

Abel pulled out a chair and straddled it, folding his arms across the back. "Tell me about Parish and Laird. I know they were with your dad in Vietnam. I learned that much in my research. But what brought them here to live? What are they like now?"

"They're . . . almost legendary around here." She shrugged deprecatingly, always reluctant to say anything that sounded like bragging. And talking about her dad, Ransom or Micah somehow always sounded like bragging. "Especially Micah. He's half-Cherokee, you know, and when he first arrived here a lot of folks were suspicious of him. Bigotry exists everywhere."

"I've noticed."

"But he joined the department, and little by little people really came to respect him. He's very honest, honorable, decent. . . ." She shook her head. "There isn't enough good stuff to say about him. I know I'd trust him with my life. So would my dad."

"And Laird?"

"He was in Intelligence for a long time. He came here to recuperate after being a prisoner in some awful place for years. He wound up marrying locally and staying. I've heard that Micah wouldn't be alive now except for Ransom."

"Why not?"

"Because Micah was wounded and captured in Vietnam during a heavy firefight. Ransom went back to get his body, thinking he was dead, and instead found him being held prisoner and tortured. He got Micah out of there and carried him for miles through enemy territory."

Abel was staring at her as if transfixed. "He did that?"

Janet nodded. "They all did things like that. They don't like to talk about it, but other people do sooner or later. I heard about Ransom and Micah from my dad. I've also heard some pretty neat stuff about my dad from the two of them."

It seemed to her that something she had said had seriously disturbed him, but she couldn't imagine what. He fell silent for a while, scowling almost fiercely at the table. Finally he appeared to shrug internally. "There's no other way that the three of them could be linked except for Vietnam?"

"I don't know." Janet cocked her head, thinking. "I can see why the assumption would be that it has something to do with Vietnam. It's the only time the three of them have acted together in ways that might give anyone cause to hold a grudge. I'm sure plenty of people could hold grudges against my dad and Micah for things they've done in law enforcement, but Ransom was never with the sheriff's department. He's been raising sheep since he came here."

"That doesn't seem like the kind of occupation that would raise this kind of vendetta."

Janet couldn't repress a giggle. "Actually, it might. Talk to a cattleman."

A smile flickered over his dark face. "Point taken. The bottom line is, their current activities in this county can't really explain why all three of them would be targeted."

"Not in any way that comes to mind."

"And now, judging by what's happened to you, it appears their families are targets. Not just their wives, but their children...unless it's their wives who are the targets to begin with. Do all three of the women have any activities in common?"

Janet hadn't even thought of that, but after a minute she was able to shake her head. "Mom is real active in community affairs, but neither Faith nor Mandy is heavily involved. They're too busy with small children, for one thing, and Mandy's a novelist, besides. Faith does some work with the battered women's shelter, but neither Mandy nor Mom is involved in that."

"Well, if you can think of something that links them other than that their husbands go way back together, let me know. It could be significant."

It suddenly struck her that he was investigating. She had heard her father speak just this way to victims as he tried to ascertain what had happened.

It also struck her, even harder, that she'd been playing a potentially deadly game of ostrich herself, hiding from the reality of her situation. Whoever had caused the gas leak at her parents' house had intended fatal harm. Because of that, there was a deputy assigned to watch the Tate house twenty-four hours a day.

And whoever had tried to hurt her mother was now turning to her as a target. A shiver of apprehension passed through her, and she rose from the table, needing to move. It was a blind, pointless attempt to escape, but it carried her out onto the porch, where she stood in the chill, damp air as anxiety clawed at her.

Someone had tried to kill her mother. Apparently that same someone had now targeted her. The denial that had insulated her since yesterday afternoon blew away in the hurricane of awareness that ripped through her. She had been targeted, possibly for death.

God, how self-indulgent she had been these past months, licking her wounds and expecting the world to give her sympathy and the space to heal. How juvenile she had been in her narrow focus on her own petty problems. She had a life growing in her that needed protection! How could she have become so...so...self-centered?

It was as if, at the moment that Scott had told her to get lost, she had retreated into some kind of la-la land. It was a wonder her friends and family had even been able to stand her these past five months. She was ashamed to realize just how self-absorbed she had been.

Now this.

In facing the ugly possibility that someone wanted to kill her, she came face-to-face with what really mattered. Yes, Scott had hurt her, and hurt his child, but what mattered was the child. The baby within her deserved a chance to be born, to live, to grow and someday have children of her own. And Janet was the only person who could give her that.

She closed her eyes, shivering again as the day's chill seeped through her sweater. The memory of the way she had drifted through the past months was not something she could be proud of. Like a rudderless boat, she'd drifted on the current of the moment. Awful as it was to admit it, she'd been feeling as if the universe owed her something in exchange for Scott's betrayal.

But the universe didn't owe anybody anything. The only debt that was owed was hers to her child, and other than minding her nutrition and taking her vitamins, she hadn't been doing a hell of a good job at that. Somewhere or other she had heard that pregnant women become bovine, but this was ridiculous!

Abel was suddenly beside her, just as she heard the engine of an approaching vehicle.

"Get inside," he said.

Yesterday she probably would have argued. Today she simply hurried indoors. Abel followed her and took up his post beside the front window, peering out to see who was approaching. Janet peered around him.

"That's Darlene!" The instant she saw her friend's dark blue car, Janet felt a letting go of tension. Her best friend was exactly the person she needed to be with right now, and it would be a great distraction to ask her all about her day with Seth yesterday. Wouldn't it be great if Darlene became her sister-in-law?

"Isn't it an icky day?" Darlene asked when she walked up to the porch from her car. Then she froze as she saw Abel Pierce standing in the doorway behind Janet.

Only then did Janet even consider that Abel's presence might be difficult to explain. Not embarrassing—she had nothing to be embarrassed about—but definitely awkward.

"Let me guess," Darlene said. "This must be the mountain man."

Abel stepped out so that he stood beside Janet. "In some quarters I'm known as Abel Pierce."

"Like I thought. The mountain man. Everybody in the county must be talking about you, and I get to meet you. Neat." She turned her attention to Janet. "You okay? You don't look so good."

"I'm fine. Really. Come on in. I've got some fresh coffee."

They gathered in the living room with steaming mugs of coffee for Darlene and Abel and a cup of herbal tea for Janet. Abel squatted before the woodstove and began to build a fire to take the chill off. He was very handy, Janet thought. You would never guess he was a city dweller.

"So what's the story?" Darlene demanded. "Are you guys living together?"

Before Janet could do more than open her mouth, Abel responded. "No," he said. Just the one uncompromising syllable.

Great, thought Janet. That really clears things up. "It's just that..." Just that what? she wondered. She didn't want to explain to Darlene that she feared for her life. But why not? Why should she feel as if that were some kind of dirty secret that she needed to hide from her dearest friend?

"Someone broke into Janet's cabin yesterday," Abel said into a silence that had grown too long. "I'm just here to keep an eye on things until we're sure it won't happen again."

Darlene made a distressed sound and turned at once to Janet. "For heaven's sake! Why don't you just come stay with me? Or go home to your parents? Janet ... this is silly! There's absolutely no reason to stay out here by yourself!"

"I'm not by myself," Janet reminded her. "Abel is looking after me."

"But who is Abel?" The words apparently slipped out before Darlene was aware that she was going to say them. The look of horror that passed over her face might have been comical under other circumstances.

Maintaining his squatting posture, Abel pulled a slim leather wallet out of his hip pocket and tossed it to Darlene. It fell into her lap. He turned back to the fire he was meticulously building.

Darlene flipped the wallet open and stared at the shield. "LAPD? What are you doing all the way out here?"

"Taking a vacation," he replied easily enough. "At least, I was until yesterday."

Darlene tossed his wallet back to him, then turned to Janet. "You've told your father about this break-in, haven't you?"

"Not yet."

"For heaven's sake, why not?" Darlene leapt up from her chair and began to pace rapidly, gesticulating with her hands. "As soon as he hears about this, he's going to insist you come home, and I'd feel a whole lot better about that than having you out here by yourself depending on a total stranger if something happens. No offense to you, Mr. Pierce," she added as an afterthought.

"None taken," he allowed. He struck one of the fireplace matches that were stored in a canister beside the stove and lit the kindling he'd laid so carefully.

"Well, I wouldn't be safer at home," Janet said. "Have you forgotten about the gas leak?"

"I heard about that, but it was just an accident, wasn't it?" She paused midstride and looked at Janet. "Wasn't it?" she repeated.

"My dad doesn't think so."

Darlene sat down abruptly. Her voice was hushed when she spoke. "Somebody actually tried to hurt your mom?"

"So it appears."

"And you think this same person may be after you?"

"It's a possibility. The point is, I won't be any safer at home."

Darlene shook her head as if she couldn't believe what she was hearing. "My God, this is horrible! Just come stay with me, Jan. Please!"

"And put you at risk?"

Darlene leaned back in her chair and covered her mouth with her hand, as if to silence all the protest inside her. The fire began to crackle as the kindling burned hotly, igniting the logs above it.

"What you're saying," Darlene said, "is that someone is stalking you and your family."

"So it appears."

"So tell me, Jan, just how is it you know that this stalker isn't the very man who is here with you now."

Chapter 9

The only sound in the cabin was the pop and crackle of the fire. Outside it began to rain, and the drum of raindrops on the roof, at first a gentle patter, gradually became a steady pounding.

Janet was the first to speak. "You know, Dar, that's a really dumb question to ask in these circumstances. I thought *I* was supposed to be the impulsive one."

Darlene blushed brightly. "It is dumb, isn't it?"

"It's okay," said Abel. "It's not Saturday."

Darlene looked at Janet. "What's that mean?"

"He only bites on Saturday."

Darlene giggled, at first hesitantly and then more comfortably. Just that easily, the balloon of tension burst. "I'm sorry. It's just that I don't know you, Mr. Pierce, and there's been all kinds of talk and speculation about you everywhere, because you're camping out in the old mining town and because you've been seen talking to the sheriff. Some people are pretty convinced you're up to no good."

"So I heard when I went to the bar the other night. You're not the first person to hold me responsible for the gas leak." He looked at Darlene over his shoulder. "I didn't take offense.

Don't worry. You'd have to be terminally stupid not to wonder about me. I gave both Janet and her father a place to call to check out my story."

Darlene looked at Janet. "Have you called?"

"Not yet."

Abel looked at her. "There's no reason on earth why you should trust me, Janet. I used my shield to get your immediate cooperation, but maybe you ought to make sure the shield is real."

"Call," Darlene urged her. "Right now."

Janet felt awkward about it, especially since Abel genuinely seemed to have her best interests at heart. It wasn't easy to question someone's honesty right in front of him. On the other hand, she *would* be terminally stupid if she didn't check it out.

The only phone was on the wall in the kitchen. When she went to use it, both of them followed her, which only made her feel more awkward. Nevertheless, she picked up the receiver and dialed.

"Internal Affairs Division," said a pleasant woman's voice.

"May I speak with Detective Angelo Rossellini, please?"

"Detective Rossellini is away from his desk right now. Would you like to leave a message?"

"Well, perhaps you can help me," Janet said, making up her mind in an instant. Why go directly to the man Abel suggested? If he worked for Internal Affairs, someone else would know that, as well. "I'm trying to find out if you have a Detective Abel Pierce working for your division."

There was a pause. "One moment, please. I'm transferring you."

Janet looked at Abel. "She's transferring me."

"That's why I sent you to Rossellini. Just anyone shouldn't be able to find out about me."

Suddenly understanding why, Janet was about to hang up when a male voice came on the line. "This is Detective Juan Emory. I understand you're inquiring about Detective Pierce?"

"I just want to know if he's really a detective."

"Yes, he is. Can you tell me where you're calling from? We really need to locate him."

The instinct to respond opened her mouth, but in a flash she recalled why Abel was hiding, and from what. Without saying another word, she hung up.

"What happened?" Abel asked immediately.

She looked at him, feeling a new kind of uneasiness. "Did I make a mistake?"

"Why?"

"I spoke to some guy named Emory. Juan Emory."

"I know him. I thought he was pretty straight. What did he say?"

"That you're a detective. Then he wanted to know where I was calling from. He said they really needed to locate you. I shouldn't have talked to him, should I?"

Abel ran his fingers through his hair.

"Abel?"

"It would have been best," he said carefully, "if you had only talked to Rossellini. It's my fault. I should have made that clear."

"You were trying to when I started talking to this other guy. They can't find you, can they?"

"I'm afraid so. All they need to do is trace the call. It's relatively easy when it's long distance."

Janet felt her stomach sink. "How long will that take?"

He shrugged. "Who's your long-distance company?"

"It's a local company, not one of those big national ones."

"Then it'll take a while. Probably until the trial."

"Is there some way you can find out?"

"Yeah. I'll talk to Angelo tonight."

Janet bit her lip. "Maybe there's a good reason for them to want to find you. Maybe something's happened."

"That could be," he agreed, and gave her what was probably supposed to be a reassuring smile. "If so, Angelo will know. I talk to him regularly."

"Will someone please tell me what I'm missing here?" Darlene asked. "Why are you worried about anybody tracking you down?"

While Abel explained, Janet listened with only half an ear. It was too much, she thought. Just too much. Someone stalking her and her family, and probably the Parish and Laird families, as well. Someone wanting to kill Abel . . . It was an incredible set of circumstances. An incredible confluence of events. How had the world suddenly become so unsafe?

Emily stirred, giving her a few soft pokes. For so long Janet had been sure she would eventually hold her baby in her arms. Now that was in doubt. Everything was in doubt. Icy fingers of panic kept clawing at her, but she didn't dare give in to them. There had to be *something* she could do about this.

"There's got to be something that can be done, at least about some of this," Darlene said when Abel finished explaining. "I can't believe Janet just has to sit here like a stationary target and wait for something to happen. Or that her family has to."

"I'm not going to," Janet said flatly. "There is no way I am simply going to wait for something awful to happen."

"But what can *you* do?" Darlene asked worriedly. "You're pregnant."

"Pregnant doesn't equate with paralyzed and helpless!"

"But you have to take care of the baby."

"I know that!" She could have growled in her frustration, but she kept a tight rein on herself. "But I *can* tell my dad what's happened so he'll know Mom isn't the only target in the family. Something about this might be an important clue. And then I can talk to Mandy Laird and Faith Parish and see what else I can learn about what's going on. I can use my brain and try to get to the bottom of this somehow!"

Abel spoke. "There's no point in you sticking your neck out, Janet. Your dad is looking into this, and you can be sure I will, too. Just leave it to us."

"Stick my neck out?" She threw up her hands. "Damn it, Abel, I don't have to stick my neck out. It's apparently already stretched over the chopping block!"

Rain continued to fall throughout the day. Darlene departed shortly after lunch, and Janet fell asleep in the rocker in the living room, soothed by the fire Abel kept brightly burning in the glass-fronted woodstove. Abel wandered off somewhere, but she really didn't have the energy to quiz him about it. Besides, he didn't go too far. Periodically, as she dozed, she was aware that he looked in on her.

His concern made her feel safe, safe enough to let go of the tension that had been keeping her on edge since she'd found signs of intrusion the day before. Her dreams were soft dreams, dreams of her baby and some shadowy figure who shared the joy with her. She even had one dream where Emily was a little girl in a lavender dress. In her dreams nothing was missing. Everything was there, including the things that Scott had so ruthlessly stripped from her.

When she awoke, the first sight she saw was Abel sitting in the armchair on the other side of the woodstove, reading one of her books. He looked up instantly, as if he had heard her eyes open. "How're you feeling?"

"Pretty good, actually." And she was. Her dreams had filled her with a wonderful sense of well-being . . . until she remembered what was really going on.

She looked away from Abel, closing her eyes against the sudden rush of memory. Someone wanted to kill her entire family. Someone wanted to kill *her*. And someone else was trying to find Abel to kill him. Alice couldn't have felt any more shocked when she fell down the rabbit hole.

"I need to call my dad," she said.

"It would be a good idea."

"He's probably going to give me hell for waiting so long."

"I wouldn't blame him."

She scowled at him. "Why don't *you* call him?"

"Because he'll take it a whole lot better coming from you. At least he can be certain you're okay, instead of getting the news secondhand."

She sighed, giving up the argument. "He's going to chew my ear. How can I explain why I didn't call him right away? I can't even explain it to myself."

"How about you simply couldn't believe it? I think you were in a state of shock, Jan."

"Maybe." Her dad was also going to have a fit about Abel Pierce playing bodyguard for her. How was she going to deal with that? He would probably want her to come home—although precisely how that was supposed to help matters, she couldn't imagine. What a situation!

"Someone's coming." Abel was out of his chair like a shot and moved swiftly to the window. "You expecting anyone?"

"No." She strained but couldn't hear anything except the drip of rain and the crackle of the fire. Seconds ticked tautly by. Finally she, too, could hear the engine over the rain.

"It's a man in a blue Cherokee," Abel said. "I can't quite make him out. Maybe a couple years younger than me, brown hair, square jaw..."

"That's my brother, Seth. Mom said she was going to send him out to help put up the baby's crib."

Abel turned to look at her, his eyes suddenly piercingly intent. "You could have asked me."

One part of her registered that he had no right to say such a thing, or to feel that way, but another part leapt with an excitement that terrified her. She didn't want to become involved with this man. No way. In a few days or weeks he would be heading back to Los Angeles and leaving her here nursing a new set of wounds. Despite that, part of her kind of enjoyed his interest and enjoyed indulging in vague fantasies about passionate lovemaking or quiet, comfortable evenings by the fire. The danger was that those were generalized fantasies she could have about anyone. They didn't mean she wanted Abel Pierce. But if she let the fantasies guide her, as they had before, she was going to pay for her folly.

Did she never learn?

"What the hell is going on?" Seth demanded when she opened the door.

Janet instinctively stepped back. Never before had she seen her brother angry, and he was an intimidating sight.

Abruptly, Abel moved between them. "You shouldn't shout at her."

"What the hell are you doing here?"

Seth was angry, but he was in control of himself. Abel, however, wasn't angry at all. His posture was relaxed, his expression pleasant, yet he looked as immovable as Thunder Mountain. He didn't answer Seth directly. "Shouting is a form of intimidation and classifies as an act of violence."

The two men measured each other with long looks, and then Abel stepped to one side, no longer interposing himself between Janet and Seth. It wasn't a surrender but an acknowledgment that Seth was through shouting.

"I didn't mean to shout at you," Seth told Janet. "I've been worried sick about you since Darlene told me what was coming down. Damn it, Jannie, you should have come straight to town and told your dad about this. What are you thinking of, staying out here by yourself?"

"I'm not exactly by myself."

"A total stranger doesn't count."

"Abel's a police detective. That's about the best protection anyone can have."

She returned to her chair and sat, wondering if she looked as mulish as she was suddenly feeling. She absolutely *hated* to have anyone order her around or try to tell her what to do. It was an attitude she was always trying to temper, and Seth *did* have her best interests at heart, but she didn't like being treated as if she were a child.

Seth closed the door, shutting out the gray, rainy day. "Have you told Nate about this yet?"

"No."

"Why the hell not?"

"I don't know how to."

Seth stared at her as if he were seeing some strange life form for the first time. "What's to know? Just tell him."

"It's not that easy! For heaven's sake, Seth, I'll be dropping a bomb in his lap, and there isn't a damn thing he can do about it! Would I be any safer at home, given what nearly happened to Mom? If I move in with someone else, will I just make a target of them?"

Abel was standing in the far corner, hands on his hips, just watching. Janet wondered what he was thinking.

"This is important," Seth said. "Your dad needs to know, whether he can do anything about it or not. At the very least he could give you police protection."

"She *has* protection," Abel said. "She's not stirring one foot in any direction without me."

Seth turned on him. "What gives *you* the right? How do any of us really know you're what you say you are?"

"Seth," Janet interrupted, "I hardly think Abel is paying a bunch of people to say they're the Internal Affairs Division of the LAPD. I talked to them on the phone this morning."

"But does that mean that *this* man is Abel Pierce?"

Abel cocked his head. "Good question."

"Hell, you look more like a street thug!"

"That's generally how I make my living. Look, Seth, sooner or later you have to take somebody at their word. My word on this is that if anyone wants to get to Janet, they're going to have to get through me first."

"Why?" Seth jabbed his index finger at Abel. "That's easy enough to say, but doing it is a different matter. Tell me, Pierce, just why you should want to do any such thing. Tell me why I should trust you to do it."

Abel looked at Janet and felt his heart turn over. Why would he put himself on the line to protect her? His reasons couldn't be measured in words. The need to protect her was an imperative that guided him now, perhaps born of his desire for her. Perhaps born of her spunkiness. Born, maybe, of just the sight of her with her tousled red hair and moss green eyes as she watched the two men argue about what was best for her.

It was foolish. Maybe it was insane. But for whatever reason, he would lay down his life to protect this woman and her child. Yeah, he was crazy. And her brother would never believe it.

But maybe Seth saw something in Abel's hardened face, because he dropped the question. Instead he turned to Janet. "Maybe it wouldn't be any safer for you to come home. What we really need to do is solve this damn mess!"

"Exactly what I was thinking," Abel said. "There's got to be some way to figure out who's behind this. Or maybe to get this guy to tip his hand."

Seth again turned to Abel. "You got any ideas?"

"Not yet. I need to know more about how he works and what he's after. What I'd like to do, though, is get an introduction to those veterans up in the hills."

"Why?"

Abel glanced at Janet, hesitated, then said, "Well, somebody went through my things yesterday while I was in town. At the time I tried to dismiss it, figuring they were just curious about me. Now I'm not so sure."

"Why not?"

"What if somebody checked me out because they've seen me visiting Janet?"

Janet felt every hair on the back of her neck stand up. "Are you saying that someone is watching me?" The idea that someone had broken in a couple of times to frighten her was bad enough. The idea that someone might be out there watching her was even more unsettling.

"At least some of the time. He'd have to be. This stalking is being deliberately drawn out so that everyone knows what's happening. Why else would the guy get into your cabin and move things just enough to let you know that he'd been here? He wants to terrify you. He wants you to know you're helpless."

"He wants Nate to know," Seth said. "I get the feeling he wants to terrorize the women so that the men can feel helpless and trapped."

Abel nodded. "I'll buy that. And he's doing a damn good job so far. I understand your dad has a full-time watch on his house now."

"And now you're watching Janet full-time. Which means he's probably going to have to do something to someone else."

Janet sat up straight. "No! You mean he's going to go after the Lairds or the Parishes?"

"That would be my guess. Why try to slip past the watchdogs when you've got plenty of other targets?"

"But they have small children! We should warn them, tell them to be extra careful!"

"It's already been done, Jannie," Seth said. "Dad thought of that, too."

"So now the game gets more difficult," Abel remarked. "The stakes are rising, for him and for us." He went to stand at the window, staring out at the rain-drenched world. Night was beginning to fall, and his reflection in the window glass was as clear as the view from the other side of the pane.

"What does that mean?" Janet asked.

"I don't think we're going to see any more fooling around with moved objects and mysterious prowlers. With his victims alerted to his intentions, everything he intends to do has become markedly more difficult. And each time he does something he runs an increased risk of being caught. No, there's going to be no more playing poltergeist."

Janet's stomach growled, reminding her that it was dinner-time. The sound was noisy and caused both Seth and Abel to look at her. She blushed, and they both laughed.

"Come on," Abel said, "let's go into the kitchen. You tell me what you want me to do, and I'll cook your dinner."

She didn't want to eat. She felt nervous and unsettled, and scared...none of which were conducive to appetite. But she had more than herself to consider, so she shoved herself up from her chair, wincing as her back protested briefly, and shook her head. "I'll cook. Just don't you two discuss anything when I'm not around to hear it."

She made a relatively easy meal of bacon sandwiches, mentally kissing her food budget goodbye. She hadn't exactly shopped with the appetites of two large, active men in mind.

It was soon apparent that the men had reached a kind of truce. Janet wondered whether to fume silently or loudly over the way they were excluding her from their decisions. She listened with interest when Abel talked about his background in the Special Forces, but became distinctly restless when they started divvying up the task of watching over her.

Finally an objection burst from her.. "Maybe I don't want to be watched twenty-four hours a day!"

"You don't really have any choice," Seth said.

She glared at him, aware that she was being stupidly stubborn about this, but unable to stop herself. She was sick of other people ordering her life. "Maybe I can take care of myself!"

Abel suddenly leaned over, covering her hand with his. The touch made something deep inside her go all soft, and her inclination to be difficult began to evaporate. "I'd worry, Janet. I'd worry myself sick about you. So would Seth."

Her defiance wilted. She wasn't stupid, just irritated. Nor did she really want to have to deal with this threat alone. "Sorry. I don't mean to be perverse. It's just that you two are sitting here making all these decisions, and no one's even asking what I think about them."

Abel squeezed her hand. "What *do* you think about them?"

"That I'd like to be involved. There are things I can do, even though I'm pregnant. Like go visit Mandy Laird and Faith Parish and get the details of exactly what's been happening to them. Maybe if we knew more than just that weird things are happening we'd figure out something useful."

"Dad already went out there and questioned them," Seth said. "Nothing's shed any great light on matters."

"I still want to talk to them."

"It wouldn't hurt," Abel said. "A different person learns different things. Could you do it on the phone, though? I'm not sure I want you going out there. It would just put two targets in the same place."

"But we'd know if we were being followed," Janet argued. "There aren't that many cars on these roads."

"But what if the stalker is already at one of these places watching, and he sees you come up? I don't like it, Jan. Let me think about it some."

She was content with that. At least he wasn't dismissing her, the way Seth was wont to. Seth, in fact, had too much of the commander about him, probably from being a chief petty officer in the SEALs. The two men, she found herself thinking, were as different as night and day. Seth was open, uncomplicated, a take-charge type who was used to giving orders. Abel, on the other hand, was closed, very much keeping his own counsel. He took charge when he felt he had to, but the rest of the time he was willing to listen to arguments and adjust his position if he decided it was wise. Seth was more physical, Abel more cerebral. Interesting.

After dinner Abel excused himself to take a walk around the property, giving Janet and Seth time for some private conversation.

"What exactly did Darlene tell you that sent you hotfooting it out here?" Janet asked.

"I was coming out here anyway, to help you put that crib up...which we still haven't done, by the way."

"That isn't what I asked."

Seth flashed a grin. "Well, Dar told me that you had some strange man who claimed to be a cop staying with you, and that someone had been in your house moving things, just the way it happened to Mom. My alarm bells all went off at once."

"You and Dar are hitting it off, huh?"

His smile faded. "I told you, I don't have time for that stuff right now. After I retire, maybe. We're just hanging out together for the hell of it. She knows I'm married to the navy."

"With her brain, maybe."

"Hey, wasn't this your great idea? To give her some dating experience so she'd build some confidence?"

"Now it's *my* fault? You said you wouldn't. It was a dumb idea, anyway."

"Well, it was. But we have an understanding. She knows I have to head back in a few weeks. We're just having some fun."

"And now everything I tell her gets passed on to you?" The thought was more than a little irritating.

"I doubt it. Aw, come off it, Jannie! This was different. She came out here today and found out all this stuff, and she was worried!"

"Not too worried to leave me here alone with Abel! And what about you? You seem to think he's okay, too."

"Well, I kind of do. Dad checked him out and seems to think he's straight. But even with that, there are still some question marks. The way I figure it, now that he knows that two other people are aware he's staying here, he wouldn't dare harm a hair on your head. It has the added advantage of letting you keep an eye on him. As far as helping him get to the bottom of this problem . . . well, that'll give *me* an opportunity to keep an eye on him."

"I don't think I like this at all."

Seth shrugged. "Too bad. It works. If Abel Pierce is the threat, I've just made you about as safe as a baby in its cradle. Or damn near, anyway. If anything happens to you while he's staying here, he's going to be the primary suspect, and he knows it." He smiled suddenly. "Damn, I'm brilliant!"

She reached for the dish towel that hung nearby and threw it at him. "Do they hand out oversize egos as part of a SEAL's standard equipment?"

"Yup." He looked smug. "Great stuff, huh?"

"I refuse to join your list of adoring admirers. I'm your sister, remember? My job is to remind you that you have feet of clay."

He glanced at his polished hiking boots. "Nah. More like webbed feet. Quack, quack."

They were both laughing when Abel came into the kitchen. Their laughter died as they saw his expression.

"Someone's been out there," he said. He tossed some muddy, soggy cigarette butts on the table. "This afternoon somebody stood out there in the woods long enough to smoke three cigarettes."

Seth looked at them, his brow furrowing. "Why would he leave evidence? Why not fieldstrip them?"

"Maybe it never occurred to him," Janet said.

"Or maybe," Abel said heavily, "he wanted us to find them. He couldn't get in here to leave another calling card, so he left one out there."

"Which means he knew you would check things out," Seth remarked.

Abel nodded.

"How would he know that?" Janet asked. "How would he know that Abel walks around out there every few hours. I just realized it myself." She clapped a hand to her mouth as she understood.

"My God," she whispered, "how long was he out there watching us?"

Night settled in, gusty and rainy. Thunder rumbled down the mountain, but it was a quiet, unthreatening growl, almost a purring.

Janet and Abel sat before the fire, reading. From time to time Abel would go outside for a while, then return with his olive drab rain poncho dripping. His restlessness disturbed her, and finally she gave up all attempts to read. She tossed her book irritably aside, and it landed with a thud on the table at her elbow.

"I'm sorry," Abel said. "I'm disturbing you."

She looked at him. He was disturbing her all right, but not in the way he meant. Besides, he wasn't at the root of her dissatisfaction. "It's not you," she said. "It's me. I feel like I'm on a runaway train. Nothing in my life is in my control anymore. Nothing has been since Scott and I split. Maybe since before that! I don't know. I just know that I feel as if life is pushing me this way and that, and I can't even push back!"

His nod was encouraging, his expression understanding. Janet rose and went to stare into the flames of the fire, unconsciously resting a protective arm over her womb.

"It sounds stupid, I know," she continued. "I've always believed that we have control. Whether we want to admit it or not, we make the decisions that direct our lives. And it's true. I decided to go with Scott. I made the decisions that led to Emily's conception and my coming back here. If I hadn't made those decisions, I wouldn't be where I am right now. I know that. But I still feel like I'm on a runaway train, and I don't like it!"

Her voice had risen with her frustration, and she had begun to gesture with her hands, but all of a sudden strong arms closed around her from behind, wrapping around her belly just beneath her breasts.

"It's okay," Abel said, his deep voice gentle. "It's scary. And there's only one thing you can do when you're riding a runaway train."

She shivered deliciously as his warm breath tickled her ear, felt reality slipping away within the strength of his arms. How she wanted to be held! "What's that?" she asked, her voice little more than a wisp of sound.

"Enjoy the ride."

Was that a kiss? she wondered almost dreamily as she felt something warm on her earlobe. It had been so long.... Instinct and need caused her to lean back against him, and his shifting stance made her feel welcome.

"I've found," he continued quietly, "that it's tension that makes life exciting. Good tension, bad tension."

She drew a shivery breath as one of his hands began to gently stroke her stomach in slow, hypnotic circles. Did he have any idea what he was doing to her? Every cell in her body was beginning to melt, and everything in her was narrowing its awareness to his touch and his voice.

"We'd all die of boredom if nothing ever went wrong," he murmured. "We'd never value life if we couldn't lose it. If you let it, this experience will awaken all your senses. It can be as exhilarating as it is terrifying."

His touch on her tummy was both exhilarating and terrifying, she thought hazily. He was making her want things she knew better than to want. Making her yearn to just melt into him. Tempting her to beg him to do as he would with her.

Ah, that thought speared her with desire. To beg him to have his way with her.... Fantasies spiraled upward from the depths of her mind, fed by a desire to have him take her and, by taking her, relieve her of the responsibility of doing anything at all. She wanted to ride the tide of his desire, to be a plaything for his needs and thus be free to simply experience whatever he gave her. Free to just be.

Images floated through her mind—his hands slowly rising from her belly to her breasts, squeezing gently, then playing with her tender nipples through her sweater until they were so hard they ached. Strong, rough, masculine hands lifting her sweater over her head while she stood mutely, captive to his needs . . . and her own. Hands, slightly callused, on bare flesh, causing shivers of desire to race through her. Heat pooling at her center the way she had always dreamed it could.

"Somehow we'll get to the bottom of all this," he murmured reassuringly. "Somehow we'll find the bastard and put him out of action. It'll be okay, Jannie. Then you can get on with your life."

His hands continued to soothe her. Their movements were utterly asexual, meant only to relax her, but the tension they were creating in her had become the paramount thing in her universe. She wanted those hands lower. She wanted them higher. She needed to feel them on her breasts and between her thighs. Oh, nature had a cruel sense of humor to allow sexual feelings to run so high when a woman was at her least attractive.

Another warm brush on her earlobe. A kiss? Oh, please, another one. Warmer yet, and on her neck, please? The wishes grew in her, threatening to take voice at any moment, and only fear kept her silent. Fear that he didn't want her after all. Fear that she would look like a fool if she let him know how he affected her.

Hadn't Scott already made a fool of her? Hadn't he taken advantage of her weaknesses and used her brutally? Hadn't she vowed she would never be so frail again?

All those thoughts raced through her head but failed to diminish her growing arousal as his soothing hands kept stoking the fire with touches that might well have been innocent.

She sighed. As if he heard it, he bowed his head and pressed a kiss on the curve between her shoulder and her neck. The spot was exquisitely sensitive, and the kiss sent out ribbons of delight that curled her toes and made her very nerves strain toward him for more.

Talk about a runaway train! She was headed for perdition and couldn't get there fast enough. The realization, poking its head through the fog of her desire, brought a gurgle of laughter to her lips.

"That's better," Abel said gently. "Laugh, Jan. Laugh in the face of the threat. We'll get you through this. You'll see."

She was never sure whether they were as far apart in their moods as it seemed, because just then the phone rang. She wanted to ignore it, but knowing it was bound to be family, who would go into a tailspin if she didn't answer, she drew reluctantly away from Abel.

Her dad's voice nearly barked at her. "Janet, I want you to get into your car right now and come to my office. Something's happened."

"What? Dad, what happened? Is it Mom?"

"Good Lord, no. But someone laid a booby trap at Ransom's place. It's a miracle he and Mandy aren't dead right now."

Chapter 10

The ride into town through the dark, rainy night seemed to take forever. Abel insisted on driving, and Janet was grateful. A booby trap! Only now, when the threat and intent were unmistakable, did she realize how reluctant she had been to believe that the gas leak at her parents' house had been deliberate.

Talk about denial!

Her teeth were chattering, even though the night wasn't that chilly, and her hands were knotted together so tightly that her fingers ached. Emily stirred, a soft reminder of sanity amid a world gone mad.

"I didn't believe it," she said aloud.

"Didn't believe what?" Abel asked.

"That the gas leak was deliberate. I had myself nearly convinced that it was some kind of accident. God, what a fool!"

"You're not foolish," he told her. "Your reaction is perfectly normal. Some things just aren't easy to believe." *Blood. Everywhere. Running from the throat, head and chest of a woman who was still too young to be a cop. Too young to be dead.* "It's a kind of protective mechanism," he continued. "An overload reaction."

"Well, it's just plain foolish not to believe the truth when it's right in front of you."

"But what *is* the truth? There was a gas leak. It *could* have been accidental. And if you want my opinion, Jan, I think your father's been having just as much difficulty believing it." He would believe it now, though, Abel knew. He wondered what kind of reception the sheriff was going to give him after all this. Probably not a very warm one.

"This is...this is scary," she admitted, shivering again. "Terrifying. Booby traps! What kind of booby trap? How do you guard against things like that?"

"You hang out with someone like me, who knows all about making booby traps, so we know what to look out for. Why do you think one of the Lairds *isn't* dead? Because Ransom—that is his name, isn't it?—knows all about booby traps from his Special Forces days. Something tipped him off. Now we'll all be on the lookout for more of the same."

Janet tightened her arms across her womb, suddenly wondering if she was going to live long enough to actually hold Emily. "Booby traps catch even experienced people."

He didn't soften his answer. "That's a risk."

The stark reality of the situation was almost too much to contemplate. Her insides were twisting into knots, and the urge to flee was overwhelming. Right now, if she'd had the option this very minute, she would have leapt on a plane for the other side of the globe. Anywhere away from all this.

But as soon as she had the thought, she felt horribly guilty. How could she even contemplate leaving her family to face this alone? Flight might be a natural reaction, but so was fight, and it was time to fight. They had to get this SOB before he really hurt someone.

"It'll be interesting," Abel said, "to see what kind of booby trap it was."

"Why?"

"Because that'll tell us a lot about the man who laid it. What did he use? Where could he have gotten his materials from? What was his method, and where was he likely to have learned it? All very useful information for tracking a perp."

"I'm having just a tiny bit of difficulty seeing this development as something for which I should be grateful."

He chuckled and reached over to pat her thigh briefly. The touch warmed her, easing some of the chill of fear. "You'll see. The guy has to leave *some* evidence. Eventually it'll be enough for us to nab him."

"I hope it's soon." She turned her head and looked out at the dark, wet countryside. There wasn't a whole lot to see out there, although once in a while she caught a glimmer of light that must have come from a ranch house. "Dad thinks it's somebody from when he was in Vietnam. But why would anybody turn up after all these years to do something awful like this? It's hard to imagine anyone bearing a grudge for so long."

Abel felt a twinge of guilt; after all, he had come here seeking answers to things that had happened when he was just a child. Things that had involved her father and his friends. He didn't find it at all surprising that someone else had come here in search of a different kind of answer. Admittedly, it was hard to conceive of the kind of hatred and anger that their stalker must have been nursing all these years. In his own case, time had made the questions calm, and his desire for the answers was merely a normal need for closure. Never would he have dreamed of actually harming someone over what had happened to his father.

Abel seriously doubted that whatever had happened to this guy in Vietnam could have been nearly as bad as what he had inflicted upon himself through all these years of nursing his hatred. God, how he must have suffered!

Janet spoke. "What you said earlier, about enjoying the ride?"

"Hmm?"

"Are you addicted to danger?" His answer seemed incredibly important, though she wasn't sure why.

"What do you mean by 'addicted'? That I need it to feel good? No. Actually, I'd prefer to have a lot less of it. But in my job, that isn't exactly possible, so I make the best of it. What else can anyone do?"

Indeed. Janet found herself wondering about his life in Los Angeles, whether he had friends, or if he was the solitary creature he seemed to be. Of course, there had been Louise, the baby and his best friend. Maybe he hadn't always been as isolated as he seemed now.

Every so often something sad would flicker in the depths of his dark-as-night eyes, something that hinted at regrets and losses . . . and sometimes hungers. He seemed cool, contained, thoughtful and melancholy. Why, then, did she feel that intense emotions filled him, that his controlled exterior was nothing but a facade?

A soft sigh escaped her, and she let go of the questions. Anything she decided about Abel Pierce would be pure speculation and more likely to misguide her than help her. She'd faced that once before, imagining she knew a person, only to discover that everything she had assumed had been dead wrong.

Emily stirred, and Janet pressed her hand to her womb. Not much longer and she could hold her baby the way she so desperately wanted to. Maybe she ought to forgive Scott. After all, he had given her Emily.

The sheriff's offices were ablaze with light and full of movement. Whatever was going on in his county, Nate Tate was bringing everything he had to bear on it.

Gage Dalton, the department's chief investigator, was just inside the front door, listening to something one of the deputies had to say. He looked less dark and melancholy now than he had before he married Miss Emma, the librarian, but his face was still scarred, and the unceasing pain he suffered had etched it deeply.

He had a smile for Janet, however, and a measuring look for Abel. "I don't believe I know you," he said to Abel.

"Abel Pierce, detective, LAPD. I'm here on a sort of vacation and seem to be getting dragged into this mess one way or another. I've even been accused of being the perp, so I guess I'd better help get to the bottom of things."

The truth was, he would have wanted to get to the bottom of things even if he weren't an obvious suspect. He would do whatever was necessary to make Janet safe.

Gage nodded, plainly reserving judgment. His stormy eyes returned to Janet. "Your dad'll be back in a minute. He told me to sit on you and make sure you stayed put."

"What exactly happened, Gage?"

"Somebody pulled the pin on a fragmentation grenade, put it in a tin can with the spoon compressed so it wouldn't detonate, and hooked it to a tripwire. The idea was that somebody would walk through the wire, yank the grenade out of the can, and boom! The only thing that saved Ransom was feeling that wire just as soon as it brushed the front of his shin. If his stride had been a little bit different, he wouldn't be talking about it now. He would have felt it too late."

"My God." Janet barely breathed the words as she closed her eyes. The same person who had done that had probably been standing outside her cabin today, smoking cigarettes and watching her.

"It had to have been laid sometime today," Gage continued. "The really chilling thing is that it was right across the path Mandy always takes out to the chicken coop, and she walks that way twice a day. She'd have been the one walking out there tonight except that Justin and Amy have come down with some kind of flu, so Ransom was filling in for her. *She* wouldn't have noticed the tripwire."

It wasn't at all what Janet had imagined. She had envisioned something a little more benign, such as Ransom recognizing the trap because he noticed something out of place. She had never dreamed that only chance had saved him.

"There you are, young lady."

Her father's stern voice left her with no illusions about what he had heard and what he thought of it. She turned to face him, trying to remember that she'd had good reasons for every decision she'd made.

"What's this I hear about you finding your cabin has been broken into and then depending on a total stranger to look after you? Why the hell didn't you call me? And why the hell do you trust this guy? What do you know about him! Damn it, Janet, he could be the stalker!"

"He isn't! You cleared him yourself! You said he doesn't have a criminal record." As soon as she made the protest, she realized that, as always with her father, she had reverted to being a child. Would she ever outgrow this? "Look, Dad, I called Los Angeles. He's a cop."

"And just what the hell does that prove? Not having a criminal record doesn't mean a person is incapable of committing a crime. And it wouldn't be the first time a cop went outside the law to get what he wanted. It wouldn't be the first time a cop turned out to be rotten to the core. Hell's bells, didn't you even listen to the story he's telling? That he's being hunted by *cops?* Doesn't that tell you something?''

"That some cops are bad? Sure. We all know that. So are some next-door neighbors! But, Dad, I believe him. Besides, someone was watching the cabin today and left cigarette butts behind. Didn't Seth tell you?''

"He told me. Why don't you consider who found them?''

She hadn't thought of that. She honestly hadn't thought of that. Slowly, she turned and looked at Abel, feeling her heart squeeze painfully. Had she been mistaken again? Only as she wondered did she realize how deeply it mattered. How much of herself she had already given this man she hardly knew. Charging ahead impulsively as usual, she might well have messed up again.

Nate turned to Abel. "I want your fingerprints.''

"Fair enough.''

"And then I want you to tell me exactly what you're trying to find out about the three of us in Vietnam, and why you're asking. I want straight answers, Pierce, or I'm going to hold you for questioning.''

Abel hooked his thumbs in the belt loops of his jeans and canted his hips to one side. "What do you want to know?''

"Why were you so determined to find out what happened at the falls?''

Abel knew he could continue to insist that it was simply a tale he had heard at a Special Forces reunion. Or he could tell the truth. Somehow he didn't think Tate was going to buy the re-union story, anyway. Besides, Janet was standing right there, and he didn't want to lie to her. Ever. He'd had enough lies in his undercover work. Enough half-truths and evasions to last a lifetime. Once, just once, he wanted to tell it like it really was and let the damn chips fall where they would.

"My father was Miles Bryant.''

Nate went rigid; his color darkened. "Come into my of-fice—*now!*''

Abel and Janet both followed. Janet suspected she wasn't included in her father's command, but she would be damned if she was going to be kept out of this conversation.

Nate closed the door of his office and turned to face Abel. They were squaring off, neither choosing to sit. Janet, her back aching as it usually did if she stood for any length of time, settled on one of the tattered brown chairs.

"Talk," Nate commanded.

"What's there to say? My dad was Miles Bryant. He never forgave you or the others for leaving him at the falls to be taken prisoner. He was sickly by the time he got out of the POW camp, and he died a few years later as a result of complications from his wounds. If he'd been rescued and gotten decent medical treatment, he might not have died. At least, that's the way he told it."

"How do *you* tell it?"

"I told it pretty much the same way, until recently."

"And what did you come here hoping to do?"

"Put the questions to rest. That's *all*, Sheriff. I wanted reasons for what had happened, whether it was that you and the others were brass-plated bastards, or that you were just young and scared. I needed an *excuse*. I was hoping to find out that you were all evil incarnate."

"Why?"

Abel shook his head. "It would have been easier to swallow. Oh, not because of what happened to my father. I just prefer to have my bad guys bad and my good guys good."

"It doesn't always work that way."

"No, I guess not."

Some kind of tension let go of Nate, because he relaxed a little and rounded his desk to take a seat. After a moment Abel followed suit. Janet bit her lip, holding back a million questions, refusing to consider whether Abel had just been ruthlessly using her as a way to get to her father, leaving everything in abeyance until later, when she could think things through, when she could question Abel. It wasn't easy to do, and she felt as if she could have exploded.

Nate spoke. "I'm supposed to believe you just want answers." It wasn't a question.

The other man nodded.

"It's a little thin, Pierce. Why is your name Pierce, anyway?"

"My mom remarried after my father died. It was important to her, so I let her husband adopt me."

Let her husband adopt me. The words were stark and plucked at Janet's heart. He hadn't felt loved by his new father. Or had resented him too much to permit it.

"Honestly, Sheriff, I already told you the truth. When I had to go to ground someplace where nobody could find me for a few weeks, this seemed like the ideal place." He spread his hand. "You have to understand that for years I heard from my father about the three of you, about how you'd failed in your duty. He painted you all about as black as you could be painted. Which was fine. Black and white is an easy way to paint a world."

"It sure is," Nate muttered.

"But lately...well, lately I've been running into a lot of gray. It's as if...oh, hell, I really can't explain it. I just needed to see the three of you and judge for myself what kind of men you are. You're all doing a lousy job of fitting into the all-black category, I can tell you."

"Gray will do just fine," the older man said dryly. "None of us really belongs in any other category."

"So it's beginning to appear. Anyway, everything I learned about you creates a completely different view than the one I got from my father. So now I'm wondering how it is that you didn't come back for my dad and Larry Doyle. Why *did* you abandon them?"

Nate passed his hand over his face in a way that told Janet he was disturbed. His eyes had a distant look in them, as if he'd gone far back in memory. As he probably had. "I'll tell you this because Miles was your father and for no other reason. Don't you ever print names."

"You got it."

"Six of us were sent out on a two-pronged mission. My group was to kidnap a highly placed ARVN officer. Your dad's group was to blow up a bridge. Somebody on the team must have let word slip somewhere, because the ARVN was waiting for us. We managed to snatch our target and get away, but your dad's group wasn't so lucky. Only one of them returned, and he said Bryant and Doyle had been blown to smithereens so small he couldn't even find their dog tags."

"And you believed him?"

"Unfortunately. We had no reason not to. He'd never lied before that any of us knew."

"This is the scared nineteen-year-old you were talking about before?"

"The same."

"Dad mentioned him a couple of times but didn't seem to feel as much anger toward him. Warren Roth."

"That's him. Roth was brand-spanking-new. None of us expected a whole lot of him until he got seasoned a bit. But none of us thought he'd get scared enough to lie, either. Anyway, we didn't have a whole lot of time to question him or think about it, because our position was under attack. We had to get the hell out of there."

Nate shook his head, staring off into space. "I found out about Doyle and Bryant a long time later. Nearly a year, a year and a half. Some intelligence came in on the POW camp, and I was . . . pretty shook to see their names turn up. I was Stateside at the time, and I tried to mount a rescue operation, but command wouldn't hear of it." He turned burning eyes on Abel. "I never even left a corpse behind. If I'd thought there were enough pieces of your dad and Doyle to bury, I would've brought 'em out. If I'd had any idea they might be alive . . ."

Abel wanted to believe him, but belief didn't come easy. He'd seen too much betrayal in his own life to accept anything that easily. "Do you know what happened to Roth?"

"Living in Florida, I think. We get a Christmas card from him every year." Nate smiled mirthlessly. "Why? You want to check out my story? He'd have plenty of reason to refuse to talk to you."

"I guess he would. Just wondering."

"But that's neither here nor there," Nate said. "We've got a problem that's a hell of a lot more immediate than what happened nearly thirty years ago."

Janet spoke. "Gage said there was a grenade. Dad, where in the world would someone get a grenade?"

"No place legal." He looked sternly at her. "I'm upset with you, miss. You should have come home immediately and told me what was going on."

"I don't see the point in coming home," she argued stubbornly. "It's hardly any safer."

Nate couldn't very well argue with that, so he scowled even more darkly. "This is a hell of a situation. I don't think I have enough deputies to put guards on everyone who needs one. I'm thinking about shipping everyone out of the county for the duration, but—"

"If you do, he'll just stop and bide his time," Abel interrupted. "You won't be able to catch him if you remove all his targets. All you'll do is postpone the problem."

Nate nodded grimly. "That's about the way I figure it. And I don't want to bunch everyone up together just to make it easier to guard them, because it'd also make it a hell of a lot easier for him to take them all out. Damn, I wish I could get my hands around that bastard's throat."

There was a rap on the door, and Gage poked his head in. "Nate? There's no way to tell where that grenade came from. The perp could have gotten it from almost any arsenal. It's standard U.S. military issue."

"Probably some jerk at some post somewhere is selling matériel for drugs," Nate said disgustedly. "God, I wonder what else this guy has in his tote bag."

"Could be just about anything if he has an in with someone who has access to an arsenal," Gage said. "Listen, I figure the next incident has to hit Parish. It's the only way the stalker can be sure everyone involved is on notice that he wants them. Come daylight, I want to take a team out there and see what we can discover."

Nate nodded. "Do it. That'll probably be Micah's inclination, too, and I'm sure he'll appreciate the help."

"I'll let you know if I come up with anything else useful." With a nod, Gage departed, closing the door behind him.

Nate turned his attention to his daughter, a frown creasing his brow. "Now what the hell am I gonna do about you? As it stands, I'm trying to figure out how to get the younger girls out of this mess. I hardly want to tell you to move back in. You sure as hell wouldn't be any safer."

"Actually, she might be even less so," Abel told him. "You'd be concentrating the targets, like we were saying before."

Nate nodded. "What I'd like to know is who his targets really are. Is it me he wants? Or my wife? Or my kids...? It doesn't add up, Pierce. Not at all."

"That's because we don't know who he is."

"Well, it sure as hell can't be one of my neighbors, unless one of 'em has suddenly blown a gasket. Nope, it doesn't make any sense that it would be someone from around here. The only way the three of us could be linked in some way that would make somebody this angry goes back to Vietnam, and I'd know if any of my neighbors had a grudge against any of us over that.

"That leaves strangers. Where have we got strangers?" He jabbed a finger at Abel. "There's you. There's a couple of truckers who've been hanging around the Lazy Rest Motel a little too long. I'm checking them out. There are a few tourists in the national park campground. And there's the vets in the hills. I wonder if there's anyone new up there."

"Billy Joe would probably know," Janet said.

"I know that!" At once his face softened. "I'm sorry, I shouldn't have snapped. I'm just so damn worried I'm barking at everybody. And I still don't know what the hell I'm going to do with you."

"I'm going to stay right where I am, Dad," Janet said firmly. "It won't get any better if I come home, and there's no place else to go."

"Not since Cousin Lou got sick last week. She needs surgery of some kind." He shook his head. "God, talk about being caught betwixt and between!" Abruptly, he turned again to Abel. "I'm going to have a deputy run by Janet's place every hour or so. If I so much as get wind that one little twig isn't where it ought to be, if you so much as twitch wrong, I'm going to haul you in."

The night was chilly and misty when Abel and Janet stepped out of the sheriff's offices later. It was as if the clouds that had been raining on them all day had now reached down to touch the ground.

"I don't want to go back to the cabin tonight if we can avoid it," Abel said. "Is there someplace we can put up?"

"The motel. But why?"

"Because the place has been unattended for a few hours now. If the perp happened by and left a little surprise package, I'm not sure I could find it in the dark."

Janet shivered. Suddenly the cost of a motel room didn't seem astronomically high. "It's not the Hilton."

"I don't need it to be."

He made Janet wait in the car while he checked them into one room at the Lazy Rest. "Everybody in this damn county probably recognizes you," he explained as he left her there.

No one was out and about, which was hardly surprising, since it was well after twelve on a weeknight. Five minutes later he was ushering her into a room that looked as if it had died during the transition between Western and Southwestern decor.

"You take the bed," Abel said. "I'll take the couch."

The couch barely looked big enough for her, let alone him. "But—"

"Don't argue. Just get some shut-eye. I want us out of here before dawn so that nobody sees you leaving this place with me."

Janet almost laughed. "What the hell difference does it make, Abel?" She patted her tummy. "I'm already a fallen woman, and everyone knows it. What's more, somebody probably wants to kill me. Do you really think I give a damn what people will think if they see me leaving a motel?"

She was getting hysterical. She didn't want to get hysterical. Clamping the lid tightly down on all the feelings she had been holding at bay, on all the questions she hadn't asked or that didn't have answers, she entered the bathroom and closed the door. The lock made a loud *snick* as she turned it.

Alone at last. Alone for the first time in nearly two days, out of the disturbing presence of the man who seemed to be taking over her life in giant leaps. Quietly, safely, peacefully alone.

Oh, God, she had never before realized just how alone it was possible to be.

Janet lay down fully clothed on top of the blankets. It wasn't the most comfortable way to sleep, but she didn't expect to sleep much, anyway. Regardless of being a fallen woman, she didn't feel at all eager to remove any of her clothes around Abel, even if he vowed to look the other way.

Sleeping in someone else's presence was a difficult thing to do, she discovered. She felt exposed and defenseless in a way that not even being fully clothed could defeat.

Despite everything, she eventually dozed off, feeling safe, somehow, because Abel was sitting up in an uncomfortable chair near the door. A twinge of guilt followed her into her dreams because he was losing sleep on her account, but the demands pregnancy made on her body could not be denied.

She awoke during the night to a dim world of flickering green from the neon sign in front of the motel. From the room next door came someone's snore, loud enough to be annoying. When she turned her head a little, even in the dim, uncertain light, she could see Abel's dark shadow in the chair. His eyes glittered faintly, letting her know he was awake.

"Something wrong?" he asked. His voice was a deep, quiet rumble, sounding as if it were part of the night.

"No." And really, there wasn't. She needed to go to the bathroom, but that was normal these days. She *always* needed to go to the bathroom. She pushed herself upright and shoved her hair back from her face. "You can't stay up all night. You need some sleep."

"I'm catnapping. Don't worry about it."

She went to the bathroom, then returned to bed, lying on her side and watching the flickering of the light. Her desire to sleep was gone, even though it was only around three. An edginess filled her, an uneasy sense of impending doom. Something bad was going to happen, and there was no way she could prevent it.

Suddenly she blurted the most pressing of her questions. "Why are you doing this? Why are you protecting me?"

"It's what cops do."

"But this isn't your jurisdiction. No one's paying you to do this. You have every right to keep clear, and no one would blame you."

"I would."

"Why?"

"It wouldn't be the right thing to do."

She didn't know if she liked being "the right thing to do." Kind of a silly attitude, she acknowledged. What had she been hoping? That he had personal reasons for caring what happened to her? How could he? He hardly knew her, after all, and a couple of embraces were meaningless. She, of all people, ought to understand that men separated sex and emotion without any difficulty.

But women didn't, and his touches had been dangerous to her self-imposed isolation and equanimity. They had reached into her heart and made him part of the emotional constellation of her life. Which was not to say that she had foolishly fallen in love, or that she had even become infatuated based on a few touches, but her emotions had become open to him, affected by him, directed toward him.

A fancy way of saying she gave a damn.

Nature, she thought, had played a cruel joke when she made men and women react so differently to physical intimacy. That difference had gotten her into serious trouble not so very long ago, and she would be wise to keep that in mind. Abel Pierce could touch her and hold her and even make love to her without feeling anything at all for her.

Not that he would. Not when she resembled a beached whale. Jeez, Janet, screw your head on straight!

She spoke again. "So you'd do the same for any Tom, Dick or Harry?" Even she could hear the challenge in her words. Half of her wanted him to agree. The other half vainly hoped he would tell her that she was special somehow. Dumb!

With a speed that astonished her, he was suddenly there by the bed, leaning over her, looking down at her, his eyes a dark glitter in the deeper shadows of his face.

"Do you like to play with fire, Jannie?" The words were little more than a harsh whisper, a sound that shivered through her. "Would you like either answer to that question?"

Could you stuff the genie back into the bottle once you'd released it? she wondered wildly.

"It's a matter of honor and duty," he said softly. "I wouldn't stand by and let anyone be victimized the way you are. On the other hand, don't ask a man if he's interested unless you can stand the answer."

In an instant he was behind her on the bed, pressed full-length against her, his mouth near her ear, his arm snug around her middle.

"Am I interested?" he murmured, his breath warm in her ear, sending shivers through her. "Oh, yeah, I'm interested, Jannie. You're the first woman I've wanted in more than a year. But would I take advantage of you?"

She hung breathless, suspended between one moment and the next, waiting for his answer to his own question, wondering if he was about to give her what she both wanted and feared.

"Only if you wanted me to," he said finally. "And even then, I might hesitate, because I don't want to hurt you."

Just that easily, the threat was gone from the moment.

"It's a matter of honor," he said after a moment. "It's always a matter of honor."

Not many people even used the word anymore, Janet thought. Words like *honor* and *duty* seemed to have been relegated to a dusty shelf somewhere, and people got uncomfortable whenever they were mentioned. Except her dad. Her dad used those words all the time, and he had tried to raise his children to believe in them, too.

Abel must have thought she wanted him to take advantage of her, because moments later she felt a warm, moist kiss on her neck just below her ear. She caught her breath with exquisite awareness, poised on the pinnacle of a moment between fear and yearning. She wanted . . . she didn't want . . .

"God," he whispered, "you feel so good to me. So good . . ."

Another kiss found her neck, moister, warmer, firmer. His palm began to move in gentle circles on her tummy. It might have been intended to be soothing, but it wound up being anything but. From that circular caress, waves of desire began to spread through her, warm and compelling, softening muscles to compliance, fogging her mind with a golden haze.

He pressed a little closer, bending his legs at the knee so that it seemed every inch of her back was pressed to him. *More,* pleaded some hungry little part of her. Oh, more . . . please. It had been so long since she had felt truly wanted. . . .

He dropped a string of moist kisses along the side of her neck as his hand grew bolder, sliding upward until it touched the undersides of her aching breasts. She caught her breath and bit her lower lip, afraid even the least little movement on her part might be mistaken as rejection. The rationality of what she was doing no longer mattered. With just a few touches he had carried her to a place where nothing mattered except that these sensations never cease.

"I want to touch you here," he whispered. "I want to fill my hands with your bare flesh and feel your nipples grow hard for me. I want to stroke you until soft little moans come out of your mouth...."

She shivered with pure pleasure and wondered hazily why his hand seemed to be stalled where it was. It was hardly moving, sliding back and forth so that it lightly stroked the undersides of her breasts.

She resented the clothes between them, resented every layer of wool, cotton and tricot that lay between them like a barrier to fulfillment. Her body was beginning to move gently as ancient rhythms pulsed through her, and she could feel his body responding in kind. Somehow that realization gave her the nerve to reach for his hand and move it upward to cover her breast.

She heard the hissing breath he drew, felt the immediate response of his body. Her own leapt, too, and some spring that had been drawn tight suddenly relaxed with exquisite relief as his hand tightened over her flesh, squeezing gently, possessively.

"So sweet," he murmured raggedly. "Damn, you're sweet ... just let me ..."

His hand swept downward, sending a spear of disappointment through her, but almost before she could register it, his hand swept upward again, this time beneath her sweater, across the taut, silky skin of her swollen belly and upward to her breasts.

"Say yes," he whispered roughly. "Let me. Just let me ..."

She was past saying anything at all, but he must have taken her silence for assent. With an easy flip of his wrist he opened the front clasp of her bra, and her breasts spilled free. A moment later his hand brushed over her naked flesh.

She gasped, startled by the extreme sensitivity of her nipples. His lightest touch was almost painful in its intensity. Even so, she didn't want it to stop, dreaded that he might pull away.

"Easy, honey," he whispered. "Easy. It'll get better...."

And it did. Even as he reassured her, desire was taking the edge from his touches and transforming it to something deeper, something at once more satisfying and yet more unsatisfying. More . . . she wanted more. . . .

"Damn, I love how you respond," he muttered raggedly in her ear. "It's like holding fire. . . ."

His words thrilled her as much as his touches, unleashing the part of her that she'd buried after Scott's treachery, making her feel beautiful despite her pregnancy, despite her deep-rooted conviction that there must be something wrong with her or she wouldn't have been treated so badly. She forgot her fears and gave herself up to the building rhythms, ready to follow wherever he led.

His other arm slipped beneath her sweater, and his hand cupped her other breast. She was suddenly ablaze like a torch, filled with exquisite sensations too long denied, filled with a hunger as demanding as any conflagration.

One hand slipped downward, sliding across her tummy with aching familiarity, then slipping lower still. In an instant the universe seemed to freeze, everything halted in its tracks as she hung suspended on the pinnacle of anticipation. She didn't even breathe.

And then, like an answer to all her questions about her own womanhood, his hand slid beneath the waistband of her pants and settled between her legs.

Chapter 11

*W*hat the hell was he doing?

Reason washed through Abel's mind like a fresh wind. He was lying in bed with a woman and doing things he had no right to be doing. Taking advantage of her because she was lonely and human, and because he wanted her. Was he out of his ever-loving mind?

But he felt the tremors of desire passing through her in waves, felt the hunger he had awakened in her body, and even if he went to hell for it, he couldn't leave her like this. Steeling himself against his own desires, he slipped his hand deeper and touched the moist, hot nub of her desire.

God, he hoped she didn't hate him for what he was about to do, but he couldn't leave her this way. He didn't want her to feel rejected, but he didn't want to make her feel humiliated, either. Or wounded. Damn, how had he gotten himself into this position? He'd acted like a damn teenager, letting his loins guide him when he should have been listening to his head. If he'd *thought* first, he wouldn't have brought them to this point.

No matter what he did now, she was going to feel hurt. It was a hell of a place to be, and he had only himself to blame. Hell!

He felt her slip into that place where need controlled her and everything else vanished. He felt her rise higher and higher, and felt culmination snap through her and catapult her over the edge.

It was a moment of infinite beauty for him. Too bad she wasn't going to see it that way.

A sense of horror began to invade Janet's warm cocoon. Moment by moment it grew increasingly apparent that they were through making love. Awful questions began to occur to her. Had she somehow repulsed him? Had she disappointed him? What was wrong with her?

Scott's treatment of her had damaged her self-image as a woman. She had sensed it before in small ways, but not until now, as she lay humiliated in the dark, had she realized just how much she had been wounded. There had been a time when she would have assumed he had other reasons for not continuing. Now she was sure the problem was her.

"I'm sorry," he said huskily into the dark. Gently, taking great care, he removed his hand from within her slacks. His other hand continued to cup her breast, as if to reassure her. "I let this get out of hand. As God is my witness, Janet, I didn't mean to take advantage of you."

That was supposed to make her feel better? That he hadn't meant to do what he had done? There was a logic in there somewhere, she supposed, but it didn't help her. All she wanted to do was crawl into a deep, dark hole, curl up into a tiny ball and never let anyone see her face again.

He had shared such intimacy with her, and now it appeared that he had been standing on the outside looking in while she had . . . she had . . . Oh, she didn't even want to remember the explosions that had rocked her aching, hungry body. Explosions that were meant to be shared, not witnessed. Humiliation scalded her.

"Damn, I'm an ass," he muttered.

No, she thought, she was. She was the ass. How long was it going to take her to learn her lessons about men? How many times would she have to be treated like an object before it penetrated that they saw women only as a means of gratifying themselves, that they just didn't care? Not about her, anyway.

Janet gasped with sudden shock as Abel's strong arms abruptly lifted her and turned her so that she was facing him. Never in a million years would she have believed he could do that, not in her present shape.

Then, as gently as if she might shatter at a touch, he drew her head to his shoulder and curved himself around the fullness of her belly.

"It's okay," he said softly. "It's okay. I know I embarrassed you, but I swear I didn't mean to. I wanted you so much and . . . well, wanting isn't enough, Jannie. You deserve someone who can give you his heart and his life. Someone who'll stick around to take care of you and Emily."

"That's not the most original kiss-off line I've ever heard," she said thickly. Her throat felt as if someone had wrapped a wire around it and was strangling her.

He swore savagely, but his hold on her remained gentle. She ought to get up and move away from him, but she couldn't make herself. For all the pain and hurt he had just inflicted, his embrace still had the power to make her feel safe. Crazy!

"It wasn't a kiss-off," he told her. "I know I can't make you believe that, but it wasn't. Now just go to sleep before I get mad enough to do something we'll both regret."

Like what? she wondered, but had the sense not to ask. She could feel the tension in him, the controlled anger, and much as she would have liked to argue until she had at least worked off her own anger and embarrassment, she didn't know him well enough to take the risk. Scott had hit her once. There was no telling how this man might react if seriously provoked.

As soon as she had the thought, she felt ashamed. So far Abel had been unfailingly gentle and protective of her...except for what had just passed between them. An episode she couldn't even bear to put a name to. Embarrassment flamed in her cheeks once again, but it passed more quickly this time. Maybe he hadn't meant to use her. Maybe he'd been as carried away as she'd been by the magic of his touches. Maybe...

The way he was holding her was kind and caring. She couldn't bring herself to move away, nor did she even want to any longer. Emily kicked gently, as if to say, "Everything's all right, Mom."

It felt that way, too. As the tension seeped away and sleep began to steal up on her, she wondered if, rather than taking something from her, Abel hadn't just given her a selfless gift.

"Let's go."

It wasn't quite dawn, but Abel wanted to get Janet out of the motel before the world stirred and someone saw her leaving. She might think her reputation was ruined because she was pregnant and unwed, but she didn't have a clue. She couldn't even begin to imagine what folks would say if she were seen coming out of a motel with the stranger from Los Angeles. He could imagine all too well.

They were on the road, headed west toward the mountains, when daylight began to creep across the world from behind them. First it was just a pearly glow, hardly bright enough to see by, but gradually it gave way to pastel pink, and then to the blue of morning. Janet kept her face averted, watching the passing countryside as if she had never seen grass and trees and cattle before.

All he could do was ignore it, he decided. He could curse himself for his stupidity during the night, he could explain to her over and over again, but the bottom line was that he couldn't take back what he'd done, and she was just going to have to realize on her own that he wasn't the scuz she believed him to be right now.

Or was he? It would have been fair to say that he was feeling pretty slimy at the moment. He couldn't believe he'd let his needs rule him to the extent that he'd forgotten both his honor and his good sense. Especially his honor.

It seriously troubled him to think that he had failed to live up to his own ethical standards. That was something he couldn't tolerate, and last night he'd done it in spades.

He glanced over at Janet and found himself looking at the back of her head. Maybe she was right to feel this way. Maybe he didn't deserve forgiveness.

A young woman lying in a pool of blood . . . He didn't deserve forgiveness there, either. He should have thrown over the whole operation. Should have found a way to slow time down enough that he could have inserted himself between Delia Burke and the bullets. Should have foreseen, somehow, that she was going to stumble into that hornets' nest. Should have been prepared for something like that to happen. After all, Murphy ruled the world.

When they reached the turnoff to Janet's cabin, he pulled onto the shoulder and braked. He turned in his seat to look at her, and gradually she brought her head around and looked back at him. "When we get to your place, I'm going to leave you in the truck while I check things out, okay?"

She nodded. Her green eyes looked dark this morning. Wounded. God, he hated himself.

"Considering what your friend Ransom found, I'm going to ask you to refrain from dashing around outside and wandering wherever you might feel like it. If you get an urge to spend time in the garden, ask me to check it out first. Got it?"

She nodded again. This time, though, her chin had a mutinous look to it, and he wondered if she was going to be a handful, or if she was going to be sensible about this whole thing. From what he'd seen of her so far, she had a stubborn streak that was apt to get her into trouble from time to time. As a rule, he believed stubbornness to be a good thing, but there were times, like now, when it could be a hell of a handicap.

He left her locked in the truck with the motor running and instructions to take off like a bat out of hell if anything untoward happened.

He checked the perimeter first, moving slowly and cautiously, alert for any indication of a booby trap. He also wanted to make sure that nothing else had been tampered with, such as her propane tank or lines. Or her car.

Something about this guy's M.O. was troubling him, but damned if he could figure out what it was. Maybe it was just the fact that one attempt had been made to appear accidental, while the other had been blatantly deliberate. After all, grenades didn't get tucked into cans and tied to tripwires any other way.

Maybe the first attempt hadn't been meant to succeed? Perhaps it had been intended as an act of sheer terrorism. After all, from what he had heard of the circumstances, the only reason the gas level had gotten so high was because Marge Tate had taken a nap. What if she'd been awake? She would probably have smelled gas long before it reached the explosive levels she had discovered upon awakening.

Maybe.

In most of his police work over the years, he had known his perps, had been able to talk to them face-to-face and figure out what made them tick. He didn't like this business of not knowing who was behind these acts, of having to guess what drove him and how he was thinking. It was like standing in the dark in the middle of an unfamiliar room, inching this way and that for fear you would bump into something and get hurt.

His search was painstaking and turned up nothing. Which didn't mean that nothing was there. Just that things *appeared* to be okay out here.

Inside it was more of the same. As far as he could tell, nothing was out of place. No booby traps had been laid, ready to explode when someone opened a drawer or a door. Maybe the bad guy had gotten enough jollies with his little trap at the Laird place.

He went to the door and signaled Janet to come in. He wanted to help her down from the truck, but thought it highly unlikely that she would tolerate even his innocent touch right now.

She walked past him, headed straight to her bedroom and closed the door. He might have been seriously troubled by that except for one thing—she glanced shyly at him as she passed him.

The sight of Darlene later that morning caused Janet mixed feelings. On the one hand, she was always glad to see her friend. On the other, she was a little irritated that Dar had gone to Seth with her concerns over Abel.

Not that Janet wouldn't have done the same thing in Dar's shoes. But acknowledging that fact didn't help ease her sense of betrayal, as if a confidence had been divulged.

But Darlene hardly even noticed that Janet was glum and distant. She had other concerns on her mind.

"Everybody's talking about what they found out at the Laird place last night. Have you heard?"

Velma, Janet thought. The sheriff's dispatcher must have spilled the beans to someone. "I heard."

"Jan, it's terrifying! Aren't you scared to death? Everybody's saying that someone is after your dad, Mr. Laird and Deputy Parish about something that happened in Vietnam."

Definitely Velma, Jan decided. She wondered if her dad knew that his dispatcher was gossiping again. He'd tried to cure her of it after the toxic waste uproar, when Velma's gossiping had nearly cost Marge Tate her life. Apparently the cure hadn't taken.

"I'm so worried about you," Darlene continued. "You've had the feeling someone has been in here, and there was that gas leak at your folks' house.... Jan, what if the creep is after the families, as well? What if he's after *you?*"

"Abel is keeping an eye on things for me, Dar. Relax, huh?"

"Relax? *Relax?* My best friend may be in mortal danger, and you want me to relax?"

"Well, there's not a whole heck of a lot else that can be done about it." The minute Darlene had arrived, Abel had excused himself to go for a walk. Janet hadn't the least doubt that he was at once giving her privacy and also patrolling the perimeter, looking for signs of danger. He would probably grin if he heard her sounding so calm about all of this. And last night... Wisps of memory flitted around the edge of her mind, as they had all day. The way he'd touched her, with such incredible gentleness ... Impatiently she shoved the memories away and focused her attention on Darlene.

"Let's sit out front," she suggested. The cabin, which normally felt so homey, suddenly felt like a prison. The way things were going, it might well be her coffin. Lord, what a macabre thought.

In sharp contrast to the day before, the weather had turned gorgeous. Not a cloud marred the pristine blue of the sky, and even Thunder Mountain was silent. The air was dry and warm, the sunshine a tingling caress. In only a few more hours the early mountain twilight would fall and it would be too chilly to sit out here without a jacket. That was the only thing Janet didn't like about the location of her cabin—the earliness of evening.

For some reason the thought of the sun disappearing behind Thunder Mountain troubled her today. But then, everything seemed to be troubling her today. It must be a combination of lack of sleep and recent events, she told herself. Anything would appear sinister.

Before she and Darlene had done more than settle into the rocking chairs with glasses of iced tea, Abel emerged from the woods. "Mind if I use your phone?" he asked Janet.

"Help yourself."

When he had vanished inside, Darlene looked at her curiously. "What's wrong? Did I just hear an Arctic freeze in your voice?"

"Nothing's wrong. It's just that after hearing about Ransom last night, I didn't sleep too well." Interesting way of phrasing it. Choose your facts carefully and precisely the wrong conclusion could be drawn. Was that what Abel was doing with the stories of his father? Was he the bad person after all?

As furious as she felt toward him today, still, she couldn't quite manage to believe that.

Fleeting memories of last night tormented her once again. Warm touches and kisses, incredibly soft caresses . . . She felt so damn cheated to have discovered it was a fake. She closed her eyes, fighting off the wave of anger and sorrow, and turned her attention to something else. "So you and Seth are like hand and glove now?"

Darlene blushed brilliantly. That sight was worth a fortune to Jan, who hadn't seen her friend blush like that since she had gotten her first period during gym class.

"I wouldn't say that," Dar answered. "Seth has to go back to Virginia soon."

"So I hear. But you've evidently gotten close enough to him that you went to him after you found out Abel was here."

Dar flushed even redder. "He's your brother, Jan! Who else would I go to when I was worried about you?"

Janet caught herself, realizing she was being a bitch, and for no better reason than that she was upset about other things. Hadn't she admitted to herself that she would probably have done the same thing in Darlene's position? "Sorry," she said.

"I'm in the world's rottenest mood today. So tell me about you and Seth."

"There isn't anything to tell! We just go out together occasionally. Casually. We both know nothing will come of it."

"Sounds good. Why am I having trouble believing it?" This time Janet's voice was gentle. She didn't know who she would kill if either one of them got hurt by this. Herself, probably, since she'd kicked things off by asking Seth to date Darlene.

But these things, which would have seemed of paramount interest to her only a couple of days ago, now couldn't hold her attention. Instead she focused on images of grenades in cans, of warm, knowledgeable hands stroking her flesh, memories of beautiful moments flashing in sharp contrast against moments of sheer terror. Everything was fractured—her life, her mind, her perceptions of the world she had always taken for granted.

A shiver passed through her, a cold wind of foreboding. Only in fairy tales was there a "happily ever after" ending. In life, endings were often tragic.

Emily kicked sharply, as if trying to jolt her mother out of her melancholy mood. Janet's hand flew instinctively to the spot and pressed as if to soothe her child. Emily had become the most important thing in her life. Somehow she had to protect Emily from all of this. She had to stop cowering and start acting.

Except that she couldn't think of a single useful thing to do. Until they knew who this creep was, they were utterly at his mercy, waiting for him to make the next move.

"We could get on a plane and go to Europe," Darlene suggested suddenly. "He wouldn't follow you to Europe."

"He followed me here to the cabin. He followed Dad, Micah and Ransom to Conard County. I don't think it's going to be as easy as that, Dar."

"I guess not." Dar settled her chin in her hand and rocked gently back and forth. "That booby trap could have killed Justin Laird. My God, Jan, the child is barely four. What if he'd run across the yard and tripped that wire? What kind of man would hurt little children?"

Jan didn't even try to answer. Right now she really didn't want to focus on the fact that this stalker apparently had no sticking point. Maybe she was being cowardly not to consider it, but she didn't see how it helped any to brood about whether he would hurt children. The only wise way to look at it was to realize that he would stop at absolutely nothing.

But how did that help in dealing with him? How would that help them to escape him?

"Well," said Dar, "there has to be *something* we can do."

"That's what I've been telling myself. Only I haven't figured out yet what it could possibly be."

Just then she heard the sound of an approaching car. At once she sat up straight and looked at Dar. "Let's get inside. Someone's coming."

Dar didn't argue, but something in her expression told Janet just how much it disturbed her to have to hide from something that should have stirred no fear at all.

Abel was just hanging up the phone when they came inside. "What's wrong?" he asked as soon as he saw Janet.

"Someone's coming up the driveway."

"Get back in the hallway and stay away from the windows."

The women didn't argue; neither of them was a fool.

The engine sound came closer. Abel stood by the living room window and peered cautiously out. Janet didn't believe the stalker would approach openly this way, and she doubted Abel did, either. He just wasn't going to take any chances.

Fool's gold. Why did that pop into her mind all of a sudden? Twined with flashes of imagery from last night. Fear and passion so close together. One feeding the other, perhaps?

Maybe she was attracted to Abel because he was playing the protector, a thoroughly male role? Was she acting like some twit who was drawn to qualities that seemed so awe-inspiring but would be impossible to live with later? Hadn't she yet learned that machismo often made for lousy companionship, that it usually utterly lacked compassion and tenderness?

But Abel didn't lack tenderness. She had discovered that last night....

Oh, God, who was out there?

Her nerves were screaming from the tension, and even her mind's attempts to flee from it by thinking about Abel, about last night, weren't helping. Her nerves were stretched so taut that she felt they might snap at any moment. Please, God, let this all go away. . . .

"Jan? Darlene? It's okay. It's Seth."

Yet another person had arrived at the cabin in the woods. The watcher, careful this time to leave no trace of his presence, slipped back deeper into the shadows. He was surprisingly relieved to discover that she had a man friend living with her. It relieved him of the necessity of acting against her, at least for now. Much as he was determined to complete his mission, much as he meant to show his betrayers just how merciless and implacable he could be—as implacable as their desertion of him had been—he was reluctant to hurt the unborn child.

It was a stupid scruple. He knew it and was fully prepared to trample right over it...but he was relieved that the time had not yet come. His pain had haunted him and goaded him for almost half his life now; he could wait a bit longer to assuage it.

It wasn't that he wanted to hurt these people. He didn't want to hurt anyone at all anymore. He had enough ghosts to haunt him after years as a mercenary. He could lie down at night and close his eyes and see a parade of the faces of his victims.

It was no mystery to him why some cultures believed that when you killed a man you absorbed his life force and power. Everyone he had killed was still with him, part of him. A reminder.

But he hated to kill, and he was going to hate taking these lives. If he could have found some other way to silence his pain, he would gladly have taken it. But there was no other way. For thirty years he had lived with the anguish. These men had cost him his wife, his children, his life. Because of them, he had become a shadow that slipped through dark places and committed dark deeds. The only way he could be free, he had finally realized, was to take revenge. Appease his ghosts.

But he hated to think he was going to take the life of the unborn, as well. He wasn't quite sure why that disturbed him so; after all, part of his plan was to deprive his three betrayers of everyone they loved, and some of those were children.

But this . . . this was different somehow, and it stymied him. As if there were something sacred about a pregnant woman. As if he would be committing sacrilege.

Troubled by the line of his thoughts, he backed away farther. There were other targets. Janet Tate could wait.

The four of them gathered around the kitchen table, Darlene watching Seth as if she couldn't bear to take her eyes from him, Janet doing her level best to avoid looking at Abel. None of them was very relaxed, and currents of tension flowed through the room. Janet rested her hand over Emily and thought of the old Chinese curse, "May you live in interesting times." Right now she would have given her left hand for some good old-fashioned boredom.

At Seth's urging, Abel had just now called his mother and asked some pointed questions about her recollections of what his father had claimed had happened at the falls. When he hung up, he had joined them at the table.

Abel spoke. "My mother can't remember the names of everyone on the mission, and who my dad used to say was at the falls that day. She managed to come up with Nate, Boyle and Warren."

Seth nodded. "Dad's racking his brain to come up with the names of anyone who might bear a grudge like this and still be alive."

"My guess would be that our man is hanging out on the mountain with those veterans. He wouldn't stand out much there."

Seth nodded again. "Dad's doing background checks on all the guys he knows are up there. My brother-in-law, Billy Joe Yuma, is going to check out whether there are any new people in the group."

But Abel's mind had wandered down a different path and come up with a surprising thought. "I think I saw him."

"What?" Seth stiffened. "When? Where?"

"In town. I didn't think much of it at the time, except to notice the guy. He was wearing woodland camouflage and hanging out across from the sheriff's office. I saw him twice, I guess. Maybe three times. No, just twice. Something about him made me notice him." Abel's eyes narrowed in thought. "When you've been a cop long enough, you start to develop a radar for people who want to be inconspicuous. This guy definitely didn't want to be noticed." He looked at Seth. "Do you folks have a police artist around here?"

"There's a woman who does it for us sort of free-lance," Janet said. "There's not enough demand for someone to do it full-time, but Dad can usually rustle up Esther without too much trouble."

"Well then, let's ask him to rustle her up. If we can get a decent drawing of this guy's face, we might find a lot of the answers we need."

Esther Jackson, the artist, lived out near Willis Road on a few acres of land with a barn that she had converted into a studio. She was a young woman with incredibly long auburn hair, hazel eyes and a bad leg on which she wore a heavy brace. It was rumored that her watercolors were displayed in galleries from Los Angeles to Madrid, but if this was so, Esther herself never said so. Janet might never have known she was in the county if her father hadn't mentioned her on several occasions, in relation to some work she had done for him. Several times Nate and Marge Tate had invited her to dinner, but Esther always declined.

"A recluse," Abel said after hearing her story.

"But it's such a shame! She's so young. Just because her leg . . ."

"You don't know it's because of her leg," he reminded her. "She could have a lot of reasons for preferring her own company."

It was true, Janet admitted. Chances were, Esther Jackson had a Scott in her past, too. Or an Abel Pierce. "I'm kind of surprised your mother remembered the veterans' names after all these years."

"I'm not. If I heard Dad's story a million times, she must have heard it ten million."

"That must have been very difficult for her."

"I can't say. She was always a stoic, very Japanese in her concept of marriage. She'd have died before she said a word against my father."

"Is she happy now?"

"Oh, very. My stepfather is very good to her."

"But not to you."

"What do you mean?"

She looked at him. "It just struck me, when you were telling my dad about why your last name was Pierce. The way you spoke of him made me think you're not very fond of him."

"I don't much care one way or the other, to tell you the truth. As long as he's good to my mother, it doesn't matter to me."

"But..." She really ought to drop this, she thought. He clearly didn't want to get into it, and pressing him could be foolish. On the other hand, this man had shredded her soul during the night at the motel. The least he owed her was a glimpse of his. "But why don't you like him?"

He blew an impatient breath. "I never really had an opportunity to like him or dislike him, Jan. He didn't like *me.*"

"But... whyever not?"

"Because I was moody, melancholy, difficult... and because I was living proof that he wasn't the first man in my mother's life, or the only one she had ever loved. He and I both went through that adoption just to please my mother. Neither one of us wanted it. And as soon as I could skedaddle, I skedaddled."

How sad, she thought. How very, very sad. "How old were you?"

"When they married? Fourteen. When I left? Seventeen."

"That's when you joined the army?"

"Right away."

"It was the same for my dad," she told him, not knowing whether he would particularly care. "He and his mother didn't have a very good reputation around this place, and his father left when he was very young. So as soon as he graduated from high school, he enlisted."

"A surprising number of people do that." He looked over at her and smiled faintly. "Your dad sure showed 'em."

Janet felt the first genuine smile in two days stretch her face. "Yeah, he did, didn't he? He's a pretty remarkable guy."

"And what about you? It couldn't have been easy growing up as the sheriff's daughter."

Janet shrugged. "I don't know. There were six of us girls, so I guess we kind of spread it around. I don't think it was that difficult. It wasn't as if Dad was an overprotective nut, so guys weren't afraid to ask us out. Of course, I think we were expected to be more honest than other kids. Not so much by Dad as by the community as a whole. I used to wonder what would happen if I shoplifted something. I kind of figured they must have a special sentence for crooks who were also sheriff's kids."

He laughed at that, a deep sound of humor. "So you played it straight your entire childhood?"

"As far as I can remember. Sometimes I wonder if that wasn't a mistake."

"Why?"

"Because I honestly had no idea just how conniving and underhanded people can be. Because I always assume other people are telling me the truth because that's what I would tell them. I might have been better prepared for reality if I'd cut up a little more myself."

"I don't think anybody is ever really prepared for an emotional knife in the back, Jannie."

"Maybe not." No, she decided, you couldn't be. Because if you were ever really prepared for it, you would never allow yourself to feel enough to make it possible. Was that how it was with Abel?

Her eyes absently wandered over his hands on the steering wheel and in a flash she remembered the intimate way they had touched her at the motel. Color flooded her cheeks, and she looked swiftly away. The worst of it was, she wanted more of those touches. Many more. She had felt the skin on the backs of his hands when she had covered one of them with her own, and it had the most incredible texture, so smooth, like living satin, in sharp contrast to his hardened, callused palms. If the skin on the backs of his hands was that smooth, then she could imagine what it must be like on his back. Her palms itched to touch him.

Wasted yearnings, she told herself. Wasted emotion. He was passing through and didn't give a damn, other than for some nobility of purpose that required him to protect a pregnant woman.

And as for that night...well, she was willing to allow that he hadn't intended for it to happen, that he'd been as caught up in things as she had. Still, he would probably make damn sure it didn't happen again. Which was good, right? She didn't really want to have a brief fling with a man who was going to move on in a few days or weeks, did she?

And what about the rest of this mess? Like a cold slap in the face, she was reminded of the threat they were all facing. She was doing everything short of committing suicide to ignore the situation, but awareness wouldn't relax its grip for long. What did anything else matter in light of the fact that they might all be dead in a few days? She might not live long enough to watch Abel shake the dust of Conard County from his heels.

But instead of thinking about things that really mattered, like survival, she was dithering about whether he had used her that night at the motel or had simply fallen into the same well of passion she had.

Not too swift.

Nate Tate had phoned ahead, asking Esther to see Abel. The woman had agreed readily enough and said any time in the morning would be fine. Abel drove them around in a few circles on back country roads until he was absolutely sure they weren't being followed, then headed for Esther's place.

The woman was waiting for them on her front porch. She sat in a rocker with a blanket over her legs, probably to conceal her brace from inconsiderate stares.

She was a pretty woman, with the clearest hazel eyes Janet had ever seen, clear enough that they appeared luminous. The shape of her face was reminiscent of Botticelli's Venus, though it showed a great deal more character. She welcomed them with a smile, exchanged greetings, then reached for her sketch pad and charcoal.

She didn't want to be sociable, Janet realized. Not even a little bit. This call was an intrusion into her day, and she wanted to keep it as brief as possible.

Abel, being a cop, had observed more of the person he was describing than ordinary, and his description was swift, factual. "Five-ten, weight a hundred and sixty-five, hair and eyes dark. Leathery-looking skin, deep creases around his eyes, and very pronounced vertical creases in each cheek. His nose is a little big for his face and has a bunch of bumps on the bridge. Probably been broken a lot..."

Esther was sketching swiftly, so swiftly that it seemed to Janet like magic. Abel sat hunched over in a chair right beside her, watching each stroke of her charcoal stick, commenting on each line to bring it nearer to his memory of the man he had seen.

Watching Abel, Janet once again felt that achy tug of yearning for things that could never be. She tried to tell herself it was just a generalized feeling of longing for dreams that would never be fulfilled, but a part of her insisted that she was longing for Abel in particular. For the tenderness he had shown her several times. For his surprising gentleness.

And he *was* surprisingly gentle for a man who looked so hard. He had a compassionate heart, a rarity among both men and women it sometimes seemed, and it guided him as much as that notion of honor he talked about...whether he admitted it or not. He gave her the feeling that if she could just curl up within the circle of his arms, he would hold all the bad things of the world at bay.

She stifled a sigh and looked away, telling herself that such thoughts were sheer fantasy. No one could be protected from life to that degree, and she would probably die of boredom if she didn't have any problems to deal with. Life was meant to be thorny, a difficult journey full of experience and learning, but that didn't mean she couldn't yearn for a break from it.

"That's it," Abel said. "You caught him exactly, Esther. My God, do you have talent!"

Esther flushed faintly. "It's fun to do this, actually. Like a brainteaser."

"You're better by far than most police artists I've worked with. If you ever want to change careers, just let me know."

Esther laughed, looking prettily flustered. Janet was surprised, given the woman's reputed success, that she apparently didn't hear such compliments all the time. But perhaps they still came as an utter surprise to her.

Esther was still faintly pink when they said goodbye and drove away.

At the end of Esther's driveway, Micah Parish was waiting for them in his official vehicle. He had stayed out by the road to make sure that no one followed them. Now he climbed out and came over to the driver's side of Abel's vehicle to accept the portrait.

Micah studied it intently while his long black hair tossed in the gentle breeze. "That's gotta be him," he said finally. "Allowing for the years, that's Larry Doyle."

Chapter 12

Once they left Micah, Abel couldn't see the point of taking Janet back home right away. While they were out she could feel some freedom from fear, and she could be distracted from all the dark things that had invaded her life.

But first he wanted to stop by the hangar that housed the Emergency Response Team. It was time to meet Billy Joe Yuma and ask a few questions about the vets in the hills. Besides, though he scarcely acknowledged it, he felt a sincere curiosity about the rest of the Tate family. Maybe it all came back to the unexpectedly honorable man he had once held responsible for his father's death, or maybe it came back to Janet.

He glanced her way and saw that she was no longer attempting to sit as far from him as she could. Maybe she was truly getting past the incident at the motel. He hoped so. He would cut off his own hands before he would hurt her, and he hated to think he had done so for simple lack of self-control.

But damn, she was one sexy woman. It was in the way she moved, the way she smiled, the way she tossed her red head. Pregnant, unpregnant, slim or fat, this woman would be the sexiest he had ever known. She was beginning to haunt his sleeping dreams as well as his waking ones, testing his self-control to its uttermost limits. He just hoped he could get through without succumbing for the short time until he needed to return to L.A.

Billy Joe Yuma—Yuma to everyone except his wife and family—was working on the medevac chopper in the shade of the open hangar. He greeted Janet with a big smile and a warm hug. "Wendy'll be back in a minute. She just ran to Maude's to pick us up some lunch. How're you doing, kid?"

Only from Yuma would Janet take that appellation. He was considerably older than her sister, nearly twenty years, but as a couple, they were perfect. "I'm doing just fine. I think Emily's in a hurry, though. She's getting downright rambunctious."

Yuma laughed and turned to Abel. His greeting to the younger man was cautious and displayed none of the warmth he had showed Janet. "So you're Abel Pierce. I've been hearing a lot about you."

"Mixed reviews, I imagine."

"You could say that. To what do I owe this visit?"

"We think we've pinpointed the source of the recent troubles, and I was wondering if you might have run into him among your friends up in the mountains." Esther had a photocopier and had given Abel several copies of the original charcoal sketch, which was now in the hands of the Conard County Sheriff's Department.

Yuma studied the sketch for only a few moments before nodding. "I saw him up there maybe two weeks ago. Said his name was Larry."

Abel looked at Janet. "Bingo. Now all we have to do is find the son of a bitch."

Wendy contended that she had brought back enough food to feed an army and insisted that Janet and Abel stay for lunch with her and Billy Joe. Wendy was usually so busy with her duties as chief of emergency services that Janet had hardly seen her at all since she had returned to town. It was good just to gab with the sister who had been her closest friend throughout childhood, and a relief that so far Wendy had noticed nothing unusual.

"Maybe this guy hasn't figured out yet that I'm a Tate," Wendy suggested with a shrug.

"I wouldn't count on that for protection," Yuma said. "If any stranger comes within a hundred yards of this place, he's going to have to do some fast talking."

Wendy gave him an indulgent smile. "Cut it out, Billy Joe. You know you'd rather die than hurt a fly."

"If anyone threatened you, I might change my convictions about violence."

The way he said it convinced Janet that he meant business. Wendy was the center of Yuma's universe, and he made no bones about it.

"What I'd like," Abel said to Yuma a while later, as the conversation wandered around recent events, "is for you to take me up there to meet your friends and see if Doyle is still up there."

"And if he is?"

"Then I'll bring him back down with me."

Yuma nodded thoughtfully. "That's a possibility. You're really sure he's behind this? Because frankly, man, if I turn in one of those guys to the law, the rest will never trust me again."

"I'd be awfully surprised if your friends weren't on your side once they hear what this crud has been up to."

"Maybe. Listen, I don't give a damn what anybody thinks if this will make Wendy and her family safe, but I don't want to do this unless you're damn near certain, because there's too much at stake."

"Fair enough. I've got a background check going on this guy right now, and I think Sheriff Tate does, too. If either of us can turn up anything useful in the way of proof, we'll go after him."

Yuma nodded. "I can live with that. It'd be even better if you can figure out a way to get the guy without getting the other vets involved. They have enough reason to be paranoid already."

"How long has he been up there? Do you have any idea? Would they consider him to be one of them in such a short time?"

Yuma shrugged. "There are questions I don't ask because they won't get answers. How long somebody has been there is one of them. As for whether they'd consider him one of them . . . depends on what you mean by that. He'd be one of them by virtue of being a vet. Whether they'd trust him, or consider him worth getting into trouble over . . . I doubt it. On the other hand, he's probably one of them enough that if I were to help turn him in, they'd feel like I'd used privileged information against one of their own.''

''Not so good.''

''No.''

''Well, I'll see what I can do to avoid dragging you into this.''

''You don't need to avoid dragging me into this. Just be damn sure you're hunting the right guy. That's all I ask.''

Before going back to the cabin, they stopped by the sheriff's office to share what little they'd learned. Nate had been looking at the sketch of Doyle and trying to figure out why the hell the man would have borne a grudge for so long.

''I'd like to know why he didn't confront me years ago,'' Nate told Abel. ''All these years, he could have had it out with me at any time. Or he could have gotten over it. We all had stuff like that to get over. Every damn one of us.''

''Some people don't forget so easily.''

Nate nodded, glanced at the sketch again, then looked at his daughter. ''How're you doing, honey? Is everything okay?''

''I'm fine. Just frustrated and angry. I see the doctor again tomorrow, so I'll let you know officially that everything is A-OK then.''

He managed a tired smile. ''Just a few more weeks. Damn, I hope we can get this mess straightened out by then.''

Abel spoke again. ''I've got a friend of mine looking for Warren Roth. I can't think of any reason why he might be involved in this mess, but maybe he knows something about it.''

''We're looking for him, too. He appears to have moved away from Gainesville. But if anything, I'd think Doyle would hate Roth most of all,'' Nate said. ''If Roth had told the truth, we would have gone back for Doyle and Bryant.''

''But does Doyle know that?''

''At this point, I'm not making any bets on what Doyle thinks or thinks he knows.'' Nate shook his head impatiently. ''All I want is to get all three families through this in one piece. I've been thinking about taking a posse up into the mountains to look for him, but that'd be like advertising we were coming. We wouldn't stand an ice cube's chance in hell of finding him up there. I'd ask Micah to track him down, except I don't know anybody better qualified than Micah to protect Micah's family." He gave a snort of angry laughter. "I feel like my hands are tied behind my back. Everybody's on maximum alert. I can't send the families to Timbuktu until this is over, because all we'd do is put the mess on hold. You're right, Pierce. We've got to stick it out."

"How's Mom doing?" Janet asked.

"About as well as you'd expect, given that she and the girls are under armed guard. You probably know by now how that feels."

Janet experienced a fleeting stab of guilt, because she *didn't* feel as if she were under guard. Being watched over by Abel was . . . different. But that was probably because she was so attracted to him. Some puritanical streak in her was embarrassed because she wasn't experiencing at least as much discomfort as her mother.

"We figure," Nate said, "that he's going to hit Micah's place next, or yours. Keep your eyes peeled, and don't go wandering off by yourself, Jannie. If you think you see anyone or anything, or think you're being watched, call me immediately. I've arranged to keep a patrol vehicle within ten minutes of your place at all times, okay?"

Janet nodded, hating the way the prison of fear was closing around her again. Knowing that her brief escape with Yuma and Wendy had been an illusion. If she ever got *her* hands on this Doyle, she would make him sorry—somehow.

During the ride back to the cabin, the cloud of threat seemed to close in around her. She ought to be heading home with anticipation, looking forward to a cozy evening with a good book. Instead, with each passing mile her dread grew.

"He's toying with us!" The words burst from her suddenly, expressing all the anger, fear and frustration that left her feeling so helpless. "Like a cat with a mouse! This is *sick!*"

"It's not exactly sane," he agreed. "What I can't figure is why he's after the wives and children, too. It doesn't make a hell of a lot of sense, in terms of revenge."

"None of this makes any sense! He must be completely bent, not to have been able to make peace with this stuff after all these years. What kind of person sits around nursing a grudge for so long?"

"I've known a few. As a rule, they're not people I care to spend a whole lot of time with."

Emily stirred, giving Janet a feeling not unlike the one that came with a sudden drop. This man, this creep, this vengeful crud, was threatening her child. Damn it, she wished she could get her hands around his throat.

Instead, helpless to do anything but wait, she stared out at the passing countryside and tried to let go of her frustration. The time would come, she promised herself, when she would be able to do something. Anything. Some little thing to assert that she wasn't helpless and that this monster could not control her with his terror tactics.

She waited patiently while Abel once again checked the environs of the house for booby traps and the propane tank for tampering, but then, determined to prove that the stalker couldn't control her completely, she was right behind him when he opened the door of the cabin.

"Wait in the truck," Abel said. "If something happens, I want you to be able to get away."

"No." When it appeared he was going to insist, she set her chin stubbornly. "No. I refuse to let this man dictate my every move from now until whenever we catch him. I refuse to sit idly by while you take risks in my place!"

"Don't be ridiculous."

"This isn't even your problem. You're not the one who's threatened by this jerk, so who's being ridiculous?"

"I'm a cop."

"Not in this jurisdiction."

He stared at her so hard that she was sure he was reading thoughts at the back of her brain...or buried deep in her soul. Finally he turned back toward the door. "Stay right behind me," he ordered. "Don't stray so much as six inches to either side."

What she wanted to do was walk ahead and prove herself uncowed. But that would have been utterly foolish, given that she didn't have the knowledge to recognize a booby trap if it stood up and looked her right in the eye, and she was not a foolish woman. She stayed right behind him as he checked the living room and kitchen. She was still right behind him as they went down the hall.

She was there when they found the teddy bear.

Several weeks before, Janet had bought a soft, plush brown teddy bear for Emily. It was large, and far too furry for an infant. She had bought it fully anticipating that it would be nothing but a cute decoration for the baby's room for some time to come. Until now, it had been standing on a cardboard chest of drawers she was using until she could afford something sturdier.

Now it was hanging above the crib Seth had assembled. Hanging by the neck in a carefully tied noose.

Janet wanted to run. She wanted to take to her heels and run until she was so far away that this bastard would never be able to find her. Would never be able to find Emily. Instead, she backed out of the bedroom and down the hall, until she stood in the center of the living room, shivering helplessly with dread and anger.

Abel followed a few seconds later. "I took care of it," he said. "It's down."

"He's vile," she said, squeezing the words past her clenched teeth. "He is the vilest, lowest, most despicable life-form on this planet. That was a threat to my baby! To my *baby!*"

Abel threw caution to the winds, reaching out to draw her within the protective circle of his arms. She went without resistance, at first remaining stiff in her rage and horror, but gradually relaxing into the warmth of him. Letting herself feel the safety he offered.

He lifted a hand and stroked her red hair gently, wishing there was some way he could take her away from all this. But even if he made her temporarily safe, it would not ease all her terrors for her family, nor would it ease her fear that eventually the stalker would find her again. There was only one solution, but damn if he didn't wish he could find another way, one that would take her completely out of this.

He could hardly hear her when she spoke. "I've been really angry in my life," she murmured against his shoulder. "I've been mad enough to want to smash things. But this is the first time I've wanted to kill somebody. To really kill. I don't like the feeling."

"It's a terrible feeling. And believe me, you don't want to kill. Not really."

"He threatened my baby! Abel, he threatened my *baby*."

She couldn't seem to get past that, as if it were inconceivable that anyone would threaten an unborn child. But Abel had lived in a far darker world, and such things no longer shocked him. They appalled him, but he doubted there was much left in the world that could astonish him.

"Try to think of it a different way," he suggested. "That was intended to terrify *you*. It couldn't hurt your baby in any way."

"At this point, there isn't a whole lot of difference," she argued, but some of the strain had eased in her voice.

"Maybe not, but it wasn't directed at Emily, honey. He just wanted you to feel that it was. It was definitely directed at *you*."

He wanted a better way to reassure her, something more than this measly bone to offer her, but he couldn't think of a damn thing. When he opened his mouth to tell her that he would keep her safe, the words lodged in his throat and died, leaving a bitter taste in their wake. *Blood on stony pavement, red on oily gray.* How the hell could he offer to protect anyone?

She straightened at last, pulling away from him, but he didn't feel rejected. There was a definite sense of determination to her movements, as if she were gathering her resources. If the night at the motel had even entered her head, she didn't let him know.

"I'll start dinner," she said. All the color was gone from her voice.

Abel went around checking locks on windows, drawing curtains against the evening. The guy had broken in somehow but had left no sign of his point of entry. He was good.

When Janet was involved in the kitchen, he took out the teddy bear with the noose around its neck. What she hadn't seen was the note pinned to its back.

In a slashing hand reminiscent of saber strokes was written the chilling threat: *Each day I come nearer.*

The noose itself was made of cheap hemp rope, but was precisely formed, including the thirteen coils that made the noose so much more deadly and inescapable than a slipknot. The deliberation was as chilling as the note.

He tucked the teddy bear, noose and note into his duffel, still exactly as he had found them, taking care not to touch anything that might carry a decent fingerprint. Tomorrow, when he took Janet to her doctor, he would take this to her father. The bear would have to be replaced. He didn't think she would want this one around now. He certainly didn't.

Back in the kitchen, he offered to help Janet with the meal. She was making a stir-fry and readily accepted his offer to chop and slice vegetables.

"Usually I like to do it, but standing for that long gives me such a backache anymore."

"Not much longer," he told her as he picked up the cleaver. "In a few more weeks it'll be your arms that are aching."

She managed a wan smile but said nothing in response. He turned his attention to the job of chopping, but his mind was on the note. On the threat. On the mentality of the person who had hung that bear over the crib.

Apparently hers was, too, because she sat there staring at her hands as if they were the only solid thing in the universe. "I could be dead tomorrow," she said.

"Janet—"

She interrupted him as if she didn't even hear him. "I could be dead tomorrow, and so could Emily. She might never even be born. Does that seem right?"

"No."

"I've been kind of silly, doing so many foolish things, and for months now I've been telling myself that I've learned something, that I won't do this or that ever again. That I'll never give another man a chance to mess me up the way Scott did. That I'll never, ever do those foolish things again." She looked up at him. "Never is an awfully long time, don't you think?"

No glib answer would suffice. He set the cleaver down and faced her.

But she was already racing on. "To never see my daughter grow up. To never again run barefoot through grass and feel the sun on my face. To never again ride a horse through fields of wildflowers. To never take another photo of that old mining town on Thunder Mountain. To never again feel a man's arms around me. Never is a long, long time.''

He had resolved to ignore his own wants and needs, to shelter this woman as he might have sheltered his own sister, but all his resolutions crumbled to dust before the utter anguish of her expression. Crossing the distance between them in a single stride, he reached for her and lifted her into a tight, hungry embrace. The desire for life in the face of death was overwhelming. Consuming. Impossible to deny.

Bending, he slipped an arm behind her knees and lifted her, carrying her down the hallway to her bedroom. He was taking risks, dozens of them, but all of them seemed paltry when the entire future might be as brief as the next few hours.

Janet never uttered even a murmur of protest. She simply pressed her face to the warmth of his neck, and moments later he felt the hot flow of her tears.

The thud of his boots on the plank floor sounded loud in his ears, almost as loud as the thudding of his heart. When he laid her upon her bed, he knew a moment of common sense, an instant of clarity when wisdom chided him for being an ass. But wisdom couldn't overcome the heat he was feeling or even raise a credible argument against instincts as old as humanity. In the face of death, the ultimate expression of life became as imperative as breathing.

He was aware that he might well be betraying her. Later she might despise him—and herself—for the moments to come. She might well feel he had taken advantage of her in a moment of weakness. It was a risk he chose to run, because she needed these moments as much as he did, and because later might never come.

He tugged her boots from her feet before he stretched out beside her. ''I won't hurt you,'' he said huskily, wishing she would open her eyes, needing somehow to reassure her. ''I won't hurt you.''

Slowly her eyes opened, shimmery, wet green pools. ''Yes, you will,'' she whispered.

She wasn't talking about the moments immediately ahead of them. He wished he could tell her that she was wrong, that he would never hurt her, wished he could make the vows she needed, but he knew she would never believe them. This woman had been wounded and no longer believed in happily-ever-afters. But then, neither did he, and that lack of faith kept the promises and vows locked up tight inside him. They had become unspeakable, symbols of dreams betrayed.

Emily kicked, and he felt the magic of her gentle poking against his abdomen. Awed by the miracle of life, he pressed his palm to Janet and waited for Emily to stir again.

There was an important question to ask before he allowed his passion to rule him. A question that was hard to ask but could not be ignored. "Has your doctor restricted you in any way?"

She closed her eyes and shook her head. "No. As long as nothing hurts...."

"I'll be careful, Jan. I swear it." That much he could promise. But what he wanted now was to be done with words and the harsh realities they represented. He drew her close, taking her head upon his shoulder, and stroked her gently along the curve of her fragile back. "Cry if you need to, honey. It's okay. It's all right...."

She did need to. She hated herself for it, hated to be weepy and helpless and all the other things life had made her during the past half year. It was as if the universe had set out to teach her a series of lessons, to shake her from the protected cocoon of her childhood into the harsh reality of adulthood in the most shocking ways imaginable. In such a short space of time she had learned the folly of trusting, the folly of loving, the folly of believing herself to be independent and capable. She could neither rely on anyone else nor get by without them.

Abel held her for a long time, long after her tears had dried and she had relaxed into silence. Somehow the closeness of these moments had cast a spell that he didn't want to disturb. Just then he would have been content to lie there all night and ignore the aching of his loins. If that was what she needed, that was what he would give her.

But gradually, as he held her and stroked her, he felt a change in the tension that filled her. Now he sensed the hush of expectation, the breathless hope of anticipation. She had moved from her sorrow and helplessness into the realm of passion.

"Life is never so sweet," he murmured huskily, "as when we might lose it."

"Is that why you're a cop?"

"Partly..." He allowed his stroking hand to slip from her back to her side. As if to encourage him, she raised her arm and looped it around his neck. "Without valleys," he whispered, "there are no hills. We don't treasure what cannot be lost."

She gasped and arched her head backward as his hand found her swollen breast and cupped it gently. She was his. As simply as that. And they both knew it.

"Have I told you—" He broke off and cleared his throat, trying again. "Have I told you that you've haunted me from the instant I first saw you? Have I told you how beautiful you are? No." He kissed her mouth quickly, silencing her instinctive protest. "Pregnant or not, skinny or fat, you'd be every bit as beautiful to me."

A shiver ran through her, and a soft moan escaped her lips as he kneaded her breast. "I need—you need to know... I'm... not very good... at this...."

"Where'd you get that idea?" His pulse was pounding, his loins so heavy he felt ready to burst, and all he wanted was to feel this woman's flesh against his. How could she be anything but splendid at this?

"I...um..." She blinked, looking confused and embarrassed all at once. "I'm... just not."

"Bull." Even through the layers of her maternity top and bra, he could feel her engorged nipple. Maddeningly, he brushed his thumb across the peak and felt her twist sinuously. "Are you going to take the word of a man who didn't even have the sense to want his own daughter?"

Before she could reply, he had taken her arm from around his neck and pressed her hand to his pelvis. He heard her swiftly drawn breath as she felt how much he wanted her. "All you have to do," he said hoarsely, "is breathe. Just breathe for me..." Deliberately, not caring how coarse he might be, just needing her to come with him to the place she was sending him to, he rubbed her hand along his swollen length, silently cursing the denim that was between them.

It was the most vulgar gesture a man could make, and he knew it, but it served its purpose. Being faced directly with his response to her, discovering the power she held over him, unleashed her from her fears of inadequacy. The pinched look left her face to be replaced with an impish look of delight.

In that instant she became the woman she was capable of being. Freed of fear by the gift of her woman's power, she forgot everything but the man she was with. She blossomed into a flower of passion.

Encouraged, he reached for the buttons of her top, then pulled it over her head. Oh, sweet heaven, she had the creamiest skin and a redhead's adorable smattering of golden freckles. The plain white tricot bra she wore became the sexiest undergarment he had ever seen, because she was wearing it. Impatiently, his hand found the back clasp and released it, freeing her lovely breasts. He tugged the scrap away, wanting nothing between his eyes and her flesh.

Her nipples were engorged, nearly red, as they reached for his touch. Her areolae were small, the color of café au lait. He wondered what color they were when she wasn't pregnant. Pale blue veins etched her fullness, a testimony to the delicacy of her skin.

"Beautiful," he whispered. "You have the most beautiful breasts."

She responded by arching her back in invitation, an invitation he gladly accepted. Pulling back a little, he bowed his head and took her into his mouth.

"Gently," she whispered. "Gently...I'm so tender...."

He loved that tenderness and cherished it with his tongue and lips as the treasure it was. She tasted so sweet, and she was so incredibly responsive, her entire body soon moving in time to his careful sucking.

He, too, was pulsing in time to the movements of his mouth, as if each time he drew on her she filled him with a new wave of heat. He wanted her...he wanted her beyond his ability to explain. His need for her filled him like a blinding white fire, driving everything from his head, lapping at his soul, making him hers for the asking.

His hands roamed over her as he suckled her, his callused hands hot against her cooler skin, leaving a trail of goose bumps behind, causing her to shiver in delight. Higher and higher he carried them both, determined they should arrive together in that place out of time.

Finally he tugged her pants away, then stood by the bed and cast his own aside, letting her see him as he was, fully aroused and hungry. Then, with hands as gentle as he could make them, he turned her on the bed so that her legs hung over the side, one on either side of him.

Bending, he strung kisses over her breasts, then scattered them over her swollen tummy, a rain of warmth and moisture that sent soft shivers pulsing through her.

Lower and lower his mouth moved, and he could feel the growing tension within her. What if she didn't like this? he wondered as his mouth trailed even lower. What if...?

Such questions had no answers unless they were asked, and he asked this one with his lips and tongue as he dropped to his knees and kissed the most sensitive part of her.

"Abel..." His name escaped her on a soft moan as her hands dug into the sheets and her hips lifted toward him.

A gift, he thought hazily. She was giving him the most inestimable gift. Welcoming him to her in the most intimate way. Her response fueled his own, leaving him trembling as he lashed her up the slope of passion with his tongue.

"Please...oh, please..." She was moaning, tossing her head back and forth, clutching at his hair with one hand, pulling, pulling....

Janet wanted him inside her. The realization slammed through him with sharp delight, then clenched his loins in a fierce grip of need. She didn't want to make this journey alone, and, oh, how he wanted to go with her!

And then he slipped into her, into hot, wet depths that cradled him as if they had been meant just for him. Kneeling there between her legs, he moved deeply and slowly in and out, savoring the moment of possessing her, savoring the moment of being possessed by her.

In...out... A hypnotic rhythm gripped them both. She reached for him, and he leaned over her, propped on his hands so he wouldn't harm Emily, dropping kisses on her belly, on her breasts. Her feet lifted from the floor, and her legs twined around his bottom, drawing him even nearer. She moaned his name again, and her nails dug into his upper arms, clutching at him as if he were her lifeline in a universe turned on end.

Higher and higher he rose, wanting it never to end, drawing out these moments as if they were glass to be spun as fine as silk threads. She took him out of himself and gave him back himself all at the same time, making him feel fulfilled as he never had before.

And finally she gave him joyous release.

Chapter 13

They lay side by side beneath the blankets. Night had fully conquered the world beyond the cabin, but inside the bedroom a single oil lamp burned, holding the darkness at bay. Abel held Janet close, as if he wanted to keep her there forever and didn't want so much as a breath of air to come between them.

Nor did she. Janet wondered how she could ever have thought she knew what lovemaking was. Never before had anyone made her feel so cared for as Abel just had. Never had anyone carried her so swiftly to such heights of need and satisfaction. This man was addictive.

"Thank you," he said quietly.

Scott had never thanked her. Scott had always had something critical to say in the name of making her a better lover. Even though she had refused to admit it to herself at the time, she had gotten sick of his postmortems of their lovemaking. Lovemaking? No, it had never been any more than moderately good sex. What she had just shared with Abel had been lovemaking. Each and every step of the way, he had made her feel as if she were more important to him than what he was feeling himself. She wished there was a way to ask him if she had given him the same feeling, because she desperately hoped that she had.

"Hey," he said quietly, catching her beneath the chin with his finger and turning her face up, "don't look like that. Don't let the ghosts into this room. Not now. Not when we've shared something so perfect."

"Was it?" she asked before she could stop the words, hating herself for revealing her insecurity so clearly.

"It was perfect for me," he assured her.

Don't, she told herself. Don't start a postmortem. Remember how much you hated them with Scott. All Scott had wanted was a massive ego stroke. How is Abel to know you aren't hunting for the same thing? Don't ask any more.

"What did he do to you?" Abel asked suddenly.

Startled, she looked wide-eyed at him. "I'm sorry, what?"

"You're a beautiful lover. You ought to know that. What did he do to you that undermined your confidence so severely?"

She felt color stain her cheeks, and in self-defense she closed her eyes. "You mean besides having a bunch of other lovers? Isn't that enough?"

"Maybe. Maybe not. It seems to me that you blame yourself for his infidelity. If you were as confident of yourself as you ought to be, you'd know he was the one who was a failure, not you. There was something wrong with *him,* Janet."

But deep inside she knew there was something wrong with *her.* There had to be. Abel was just being nice to her, but the simple truth was that Scott would not have abandoned both her and their baby if there hadn't been something intrinsically wrong with her. He wouldn't have needed other women if she had been adequate.

Abel spoke, shaking her out of her melancholy reflection. "I don't think I like what you're thinking, to judge by the expressions crossing your face. Come back, Janet. Come back to me and share the evening with *me.*"

"Sorry." She shook her head. "I've become so moody since I got pregnant. My mind wanders off on journeys, and I lose track of everything except what's going on inside me."

"That's pretty normal, I think." He gave her a gentle squeeze. "Why don't you look forward instead of back? Tell me what you're going to do once Emily arrives."

"I'm on sabbatical until January, so I don't really have any plans, except to get to know Emily and be a full-time mom to her for a while."

"Sabbatical from what?"

"I'm a graduate student and teaching assistant."

"What's your area?"

"Special education."

"That's a rough field, Jan. You must have an incredible amount of emotional stamina."

"I don't know, actually. I've never been in full charge of a classroom of my own. Mostly I've been involved in a pilot program with autistic children, experimenting with various means of communication. My exposure has been limited to a few hours a week. It can be wrenching, and I've cried more than once, but it hasn't been overwhelming."

"Do you plan to teach these kids?"

"You mean as a full-time classroom teacher? I might, but I'd really prefer to limit my scope to autism."

"Why?"

"Because . . . I don't know if I can explain it. Those kids are locked up inside themselves, so isolated and alone. They don't respond to ordinary stimuli the way we would. Most of them don't even want to be cuddled. Some respond to even the slightest touch as if it causes severe pain. If I thought they were happy in themselves, I'd leave them there, but, Abel, I can't believe they're happy. Not after spending time with them."

"So you want to help them."

"Stupid, isn't it? But when I can draw one of them out of his or her shell just a tiny bit, when I can bring even the briefest glimmer of awareness to a pair of empty eyes . . . well, I feel great. So I keep on trying."

"I don't think that's stupid at all, Janet. Not at all. You want stupid? Look at what a cop does. It's like trying to hold back a flood with a broom."

"I know the feeling. But somebody's got to do it."

"Exactly. Somebody's got to do it."

Scott had been unalterably convinced that she was wasting her time with autistic children. He was of the opinion that if she wanted to work with "problem" kids, she ought to spend her time with those who had more easily treated conditions. "More bang for the buck," he'd said. But then, Scott had the mind of an actuary and measured everything in terms of cost-benefit ratios—except when it came to his own needs and wants. Then all that mattered was that he get his own way.

What had she ever seen in him?

Abel's hand had begun to move with seeming casualness along her side, from shoulder to knee. Back and forth his hand traveled in a lazy pattern, waking her nerve endings once again to exquisite life. At first she pretended to be unaware, not certain if he meant the touches to arouse her, afraid that if she let him know how she was responding, he would be put off. Men, Scott had taught her, didn't like to feel pressed by a woman's sexual needs. If she let Abel know how he was inflaming her, would he feel she was being demanding?

Not knowing, she tried to remain silent, but her body betrayed her eventually, causing her hips to begin a rhythmic rocking. It was a gentle movement, barely perceptible, but he must have felt it, because suddenly his hand slipped around to cup her soft rump and draw her hard against him. Hard against his arousal.

She gasped softly, delighted by his tumescence pressing hard against her belly. Emboldened, she reached out with her hand and touched him. It was his turn to draw a sharp breath.

Oh, she liked this. She liked this very much! Drawing her fingers along his length, she felt the incredible power of a woman over a man. Felt his need as surely as she felt her own. His response to her zipped through her like lightning, carrying her past all the doubts and fears of the unknown. He wanted her. Again. His wanting made her feel sexier than she had ever felt in her life, and feeling sexy gave her more nerve than she'd ever had before.

She threw back the blanket and filled her eyes with the sight of him, drinking in powerful muscle and sinew. He was a beautiful man, at least to her eyes, and that was all that mattered.

Rising up on one elbow, she ran her hand over him, learning each angle, hollow and plane of his body. Beneath her touch she could feel his muscles twitch and leap in response. His breathing grew more ragged and shallow as she continued to explore him.

"Feels good," he whispered. "Nice touches . . ."

Pointy little nipples reached out to her from small copper areolae. Bending, she dared to take one of them into her mouth and suck gently.

He sucked air between his teeth and arched toward her, his hand rising to clasp her head where it was. "Yes . . ." he hissed between his teeth, leaving her in no doubt that he found this sensation as exquisite as she did.

She sucked and nipped, moving from one nipple to the other until he was writhing on the sheets, as helpless in the face of his hunger as she had been before hers.

And slowly, slowly, she began to trail her mouth downward, over the flat hardness of his belly and down still farther to where there was crisp, curly hair. She nuzzled him there and felt him stiffen. He stopped breathing, as if he were afraid that the merest sound might divert her.

A bubble of sheer delight formed in the pit of her stomach, and she claimed him with her mouth. Giving him all that he had given her. Giving. It had been so long since she had wanted to give.

Sometime later—minutes or seconds, she had no idea which—he lifted her, helping her to straddle him, guiding himself into her, reaching between them to touch her swollen nub with his fingers. She arched almost violently in pleasure as he filled her, as his fingers so exquisitely stroked her.

"Damn, you're gorgeous," he murmured thickly. "So perfect . . . so sweet . . ."

She never heard the rest of what he said. His voice blended with the pounding of the blood in her body and was lost in the raging tide that swept her away. She rose higher and higher and then crested with a long, low moan.

Moments later he followed her over.

No!

Abel couldn't reach her in time. He shouted again and again for her to get back, to leave, to find cover, but no sound escaped his throat. He ran toward her, knowing that he had to get to her before the bullet did, knowing that if he didn't, she would be dead. He ran, straining every muscle in his body, but with each step he took she receded a step. Her badge glinted brightly on her breast, catching the light from above. It made a perfect target.

He ran, but it was as if he were mired in mud, or running at the bottom of a swimming pool. His legs moved so slowly, and no amount of effort could make them go any faster. He shouted again, but no sound came out of his mouth. Instead the words ricocheted around the inside of his head, trapped.

Go back! The bullet was approaching her now, flying through air that was thicker than gelatin, moving slowly, so slowly that he could see its hideous shape and the Teflon jacketing that would pierce her armor. *Stop!*

Nothing stopped. Nothing. The bullet flew toward her. She turned her head slowly, becoming aware of Abel for the first time, looking confused. Because she looked at him, she failed to see the gun pointed at her, failed to see the bullet that was heading straight for her. Failed to see the gun fire again.

The sound filled his head, distorted like everything else. Her eyes widened, looking into his as if she could not believe what was happening, beseeching him for an answer to what she felt in that instant as the bullet pierced her armor and then her chest.

Before she could move, the second bullet found her, burrowing a hole in her forehead, exploding out the back of her head in a geyser of blood, bone and brain matter. The light was gone from her eyes in an instant, and she fell, slowly... slowly... slowly....

Scarlet pools of blood on oily gray pavement. Covered in blood, Janet Tate stared back up at him as the life drained out of her....

He threw back his head and screamed.

Pale dawn light seeped around the edge of the curtain. Janet was sitting up, sheet drawn to her breasts, looking at him with concern. "Abel? Are you all right?"

"A dream," he managed to say in a cracked, parched voice. "Just a bad dream."

Sitting up, he threw the covers back and tried to stand. Nothing wanted to work right, a sure sign he'd awakened too abruptly. It took time for the soul to return to the body, and his was in no hurry this morning. At last he attained his feet.

Janet spoke. "You screamed."

He paused in the doorway, keeping his back to her. "Sorry." Then he headed for the kitchen. He didn't feel like answering any questions. Not now.

Even the simple act of making a pot of coffee seemed to be too much. He spilled grounds and water all over the counter, then cursed quietly as he cleaned them up.

Desperate for distraction, he put in a call to Angelo Rossellini, his boss. Angelo wasn't awake enough yet to want to chat, but he had one piece of important information to deliver—the trial was to begin on Monday. In just a few days, Abel had to head back to L.A.—and leave Janet unprotected. He had known it was coming, but not this soon. God, what was he going to do about Janet?

When he hung up the phone, he found Janet watching him from the hallway. She looked concerned, but not frightened.

"Sorry," he said again. It was all he was up to saying just now, and more attention than he felt he wanted to pay to a damn nightmare.

"Who's Burke?" she asked.

He hadn't allowed that name to cross his lips in over a year. He had buried it as deeply as he could, along with the whole damn memory, suppressing it all except the flashes of bloodstains he couldn't seem to get rid of. *Burke.* Just hearing the name seemed to rip him wide open.

"Abel?"

"A cop," he said hoarsely. "She was just a cop."

"What happened?"

"Drop it, Janet. Just drop it." Drop it, please, don't make me relive it. . . .

She came into the kitchen and poured herself a glass of orange juice from the carton in the refrigerator. The meat that had been intended for last night's stir-fry had been left out overnight, so she threw it into the trash.

"I need to take the garbage to the dump this morning," she remarked.

"I'll take care of it when I drive you to the doctor."

"My appointment's at ten-thirty."

"Okay."

She sat at the table, not looking at him, and drank her juice. It occurred to him suddenly that this was probably not the way she had wanted to wake up this morning. That after the intimacy of the night, his leaping out of bed and refusing to discuss what was wrong could be interpreted in a lot of different ways, none of them very pleasant for her.

God, he hadn't wanted to hurt her! Now here he was reinforcing her belief that there was something wrong with her. It would take so little to reassure her. So little. Why did he feel stuck here on the far side of the room, mired as he'd been mired in that awful dream, unable to do what needed doing?

"Janet..." He trailed off, uncertain how to begin. He didn't want to sound melodramatic, or indulge in a boatload of self-pity, or even give her an opportunity to feel sorry for him. He wanted none of those things; they were utterly useless. All he wanted to do, in as concise a way as possible, was explain to her why he was withdrawn this morning when he should be hugging her close and coaxing laughter out of her.

"Janet, it was just a nightmare. A little over a year ago, I was involved in an undercover operation. During a drug sale, a cop I didn't know walked in and was shot. I couldn't act in time to save her and ... it bothers me a little. Maybe because she was so young and so new on the job." He shrugged a shoulder and pretended to study the pattern of knots in the wood floor.

"Do you ... have dreams about it often?" she asked hesitantly.

"No. This was the first time." And he had a feeling it had more to do with the situation with Janet than it had to do with Officer Burke's death. He was afraid—oh, hell, just be honest about it, Pierce!—he was scared to death that he wouldn't be able to protect Janet adequately. Scared to death that he might see her lying in a pool of blood just that way, looking up at him with eyes that asked why.

Why? The one question for which the universe offered no answers. There was rarely a satisfactory "why" for anything in life.

He sighed and looked at Janet. She was watching him, her face both concerned and uncertain. That uncertainty ripped at him. If, after their night together, she could still be uncertain about how wonderful he thought she was, then he had failed miserably. That was the one thing he had hoped to communicate in the hours past—that she was one of the most wonderful and remarkable women he had ever known.

But he had failed.

The coffeemaker hissed steam and popped a few times as it finished brewing. He opened his mouth to try to tell her all the things for which words were inadequate, to attempt to tell her without making promises he was in no position to keep. God, how could he do that? This was a time when protestations of undying love were due, and he couldn't make them. They wouldn't be true, and she would know it. And even if they were—what good could it possibly do? In a few days or weeks he would return to L.A. She would remain here, and they would never meet again.

The thought caused him a pang, but he ignored it. He cared about her, yes. He cared about Emily, too, come to that. The kid was going to be one feisty little dickens. But he had nothing to offer either Emily or Janet. Certainly nothing that either of them could possibly want.

Janet was no longer looking at him but appeared to be absorbed in contemplation of her glass of orange juice. He knew better. Clear across the room, he could feel the questions buzzing around in her head like angry hornets.

"I'm sorry," he said abruptly, utterly at a loss as to how to deal with this. "I'm sorry. I'm going out to look around."

Janet watched him depart and winced when the door slammed with a crack as loud as a gunshot. What had she done to deserve this? she wondered. Had she demanded anything from him? Had she clung, or started speaking of the future as if it were a given? No! All she had done was ask about his nightmare, and now he was acting as if she had done some unforgivable thing.

Would she ever understand men?

Disgusted, and more than a little hurt, she rinsed out her glass and considered the question of breakfast. She didn't really feel like eating, but she would feel rotten in an hour or so if she skipped the meal. First, though, she was going to shower and dress in something bright and springlike.

Her back twinged, and she reached behind her to rub it absently as she walked down the hall. It was a low, dull ache, probably from her unaccustomed activity last night. Just the memory brought a smile to her lips in spite of Abel's off-center behavior this morning. In fact, remembering made her inclined to forgive him his surliness. He had given her a night of incredible beauty. She could forgive him a few foibles this morning.

Turning into the bedroom, she froze. An instant later a scream ripped out of her throat and she turned to run.

Doyle wanted Janet to leave. Unlike his other intended victims, he wanted no harm to befall this woman. Not while she was pregnant. He could always come for her later, once the child was born, but hurting her in her present state was beyond him. He would never sleep again.

But that meant he had to scare her away, because as long as she was here, he couldn't ignore her without failing to get his message across. If she would just leave the area, he could exempt her. For now.

But his whole purpose was to take from Tate, Laird and Parish the very same things they had taken from him. His wife. His children. They wouldn't fully understand what they had done to him until he had done it to them, and he needed them to understand. For Ida's sake. Ida, who had taken her own life when he was reported dead. Ida, who had never hurt a soul in her life, had paid for these men's dereliction.

He needed to avenge her. She came to him in his dreams and begged him to avenge her death, to avenge the loss of their children to adoption by strangers. To avenge their children, who had lost both mother and father. These men had to pay, and they had to pay in full, because, by God, there was no way he could sleep at night until he did something to ease the pain and anger that had been gnawing at his soul for thirty years.

But to hurt a pregnant woman . . . No. No way. That went further than vengeance demanded.

So he had to scare her away. Unfortunately, the task had become considerably more difficult since the man had turned up. Abel Pierce was the name he had heard in town. No one knew who he was, but Doyle had developed a pretty good opinion of him. He knew what he was doing when it came to protecting the woman.

But he didn't know enough.

When Janet and Pierce were both in the kitchen talking, it was easy to climb in the bedroom window to arrange another little display. He had been sure the teddy bear in a noose would have been enough to scare her into leaving, but the man had handled it somehow so that she hadn't panicked.

He decided to get even more graphic this time. He had a long, ugly hunting knife that he wouldn't mind getting rid of, so he figured he would just drive it into the middle of her mattress. That ought to do it, especially since she would know he had been in the cabin while she was there. If that didn't scare her . . .

But just as he was about to drive the knife into the mattress, he found himself looking into her horrified green eyes, heard her scream and saw her run.

Instinctively he followed, in time to see her tear out the front door toward the woods. In time to see her trip and sprawl facedown on the ground.

In time to see her grab at her belly and cry out . . .

"My baby! Oh, my God, Emily . . ." A long, low groan was torn from her mouth, and she curled up into a fetal position. "My baby . . ."

He hesitated, looking at the phone. He could call for help. . . .

Abel heard Janet scream. The sound turned his blood to ice as he started running for the cabin. Damn it, he hadn't believed anything would happen in the five minutes it took him to check for booby traps or other signs that the stalker had been here. Five lousy minutes!

Blood on oily gray pavement . . .

He'd failed again, this time more critically, because this time he had taken on the responsibility of protecting Janet. This was no unforeseen circumstance; this was something he should have been guarding against every single moment. And he had failed.

God, let her be all right!

The woods were endless. How had he gotten so far from the cabin? Surely he hadn't walked this far in just a couple of minutes? Where had his mind been? Brooding over last night instead of paying attention to the present. Hell, he could have walked into a booby trap without ever seeing it in his present state of mind....

He burst into the clearing at the front of the cabin and saw Janet on the ground, curled up and sobbing his name. The door of the cabin yawned wide. If anyone was in there, he couldn't see him.

He dropped to his knees beside Janet and reached out to touch her shoulder, calling her name as he did so. "Janet? Honey, what's wrong? What happened?"

"My baby... I fell... It hurts! Abel, he was in there!"

"In where? Where does it hurt?" His mind was flying in a dozen different directions as he tried to assess her injuries and her meaning.

"The man! He was in the bedroom with a knife! I saw him...ran... I fell. I hurt. Oh, God, it hurts so bad! Emily..."

In the bedroom with a knife! God. He had to get her into the truck. Then he had to call for emergency help for Janet—except that the guy might still be in the house.

Maybe.

"I'm going to unlock the truck so I can put you inside it, honey. Then I have to call for help. I'll be right back."

Her terrified green eyes looked straight into his a moment before squeezing shut again. Another groan rose from deep within her.

"Do your breathing," he told her. "You took the Lamaze class, didn't you? Do your breathing." If nothing else, it would give her the feeling that she was doing something useful. He unlocked the back of the truck, then returned for her.

Her slacks were soaked with something. Water. Her water had broken. If she wasn't already in labor, she probably would be soon. It was far too early. The baby would need prompt medical attention. He had to make that call, but first he had to make sure Doyle was gone so he wouldn't get stabbed in the back.

As carefully as he could, he placed her in the back of her Explorer, on the flat, carpeted surface, then locked her inside. That would protect her from anything short of a hand grenade.

Then he faced the cabin and wondered what the hell was going on. If Doyle had meant to kill her, why hadn't he? Why hadn't he followed her out of the cabin? Why hadn't he shot at her and Abel? None of this added up!

But maybe Doyle had only wanted to frighten her. In which case he had succeeded and was probably gone now. But that didn't fit, either . . . unless he had wanted Janet to see his face? So that she could describe him to her father? So that her father would know beyond any shadow of a doubt who was after his family?

Yeah, that made a perverted kind of sense, all right.

Or maybe he hadn't intended to be caught doing whatever it was he'd been up to. Maybe Janet had caught him unaware, and he had fled. Maybe he hadn't wanted to do anything but scare her again.

Regardless of Doyle's intent, Abel didn't think he was going to find the man in the house now. Nor did he. Nowhere was there any sign that someone had broken in and driven Janet into terrified flight.

Someday, he promised himself as he reached for the phone, he was going to get his hands around Larry Doyle's neck and wring it.

Abel drove Janet out to the highway and then sat with her, holding her hand and talking with her until the medevac helicopter arrived. She had gone into labor, but the contractions were still five minutes apart. Straining his memory, he recalled the childbirth techniques he had learned in classes with Louise and helped Janet with her breathing.

He sat with her between his legs, resting her back against his chest, and when the contractions came he reached around her to gently rub her taut belly while coaching her on her breathing. And somewhere, deep inside, he gave thanks that he could share these precious moments with her. He only wished they weren't shadowed by the terror that this would harm Emily.

"I'm so scared," she told him between contractions. "I'm so scared that I hurt her when I fell!"

"Shh," he said soothingly. "Hush, sweetheart. You didn't hurt her. She was safe inside a big water balloon."

"But it broke!"

"It also absorbed the impact. It's okay, sweetie. Really." He wished he believed his own words.

"It's too early! She isn't supposed to be born for another four weeks!"

"I know. I know. But it's only a little bit early, honey. Only a little bit. Emily will be fine."

He didn't know it could take so long for a helicopter to arrive. Hell, he probably could have driven her to the hospital faster! But he wouldn't have been able to hold her or help her as he was now. Besides, the helicopter didn't have to make all the bends in the road, and all the stop signs and stoplights....

His mind wandered over all those things like a rat caught in a maze with no way out. He felt so damn *helpless!*

He rubbed Janet's belly when she cried out again, and reminded her of her breathing. "Just think," he told her. "In a little while you'll be able to hold Emily. Will you let me hold her, too?"

She never answered that, but her hand clutched his much tighter, and he took it for an affirmative.

"I'll bet," he continued, "that she's every bit as pretty as you. I just hope she has your red hair and green eyes. Your eyes are so beautiful, Janet. Mossy green. They remind me of cool forest depths, so inviting...."

He talked aimlessly, trying to fill the silence with something besides all the fears that were waiting to pounce. Trying to reassure her.

At long last the helicopter arrived. Abel turned Janet over to her sister's care with a crazy mixture of relief and reluctance. He wanted to share this with Janet, but he also wanted her to have the best care she could.

He drove into town alone, his only companions a teddy bear with a noose around its neck and a vision of bright red blood on oily gray pavement.

* * *

Doyle watched from the shadows in the trees alongside the road. Listening to the woman's cries, listening to her sob out her fears to the man pierced him deeply. He hadn't intended that to happen. He hadn't intended to hurt that unborn baby. When the medevac chopper arrived and landed on the road, it was as much a relief to him as it must have been to her.

When the copter was gone and the man had driven off toward town, he sat on his heels and started to think about just exactly what he was doing and just how far vengeance really needed to go.

The last thing he wanted to do was become worse than the men he was after. The Good Book had been very clear about that: "Eye for eye, tooth for tooth, hand for hand, foot for foot."

He was already a little uneasy at the way he was balancing those scales. After all, his children hadn't died but had simply been taken from him. Still, he couldn't see any other possible way to take these men's children from them now except to kill them. So that was all right.

But the unborn baby? His stomach roiled, and he decided that perhaps he needed to reevaluate his plan. Just a little.

Chapter 14

The corridors of the community hospital were soft blue and beige. The floors gleamed like glass, as did the tile that rose halfway up the walls. Abel could see his reflection in them and wondered when he had become a wild man.

They wouldn't let him see her. He wasn't family, and right now they would only let family into the labor suite with her. Her mom. Her dad. Her sister. It was a family affair and hardly surprising that he was on the outside.

But, hell, hadn't he been on the outside all his life? Well, be fair about it, Pierce. Only since he'd left Okinawa. Before that, hanging around with his uncle and cousins, he'd felt very much at home. But his uncle had died, and he hadn't seen his cousins since his last visit to the island nearly twenty years ago. His only family was his mother, and she mostly belonged to her husband, Bill Pierce.

That hunger for family had probably been the primary cause for his involvement with Louise. Much as it made him a little uncomfortable to admit it, her primary attraction had been permanence—or so he had thought at the time.

Maybe that was all that was going on with Janet Tate. Maybe all his muddled feelings about her and the baby were nothing but a desire for the taste of home she had given him over the past couple of weeks. Maybe he didn't so much want Janet and Emily as he wanted the *idea* of Janet and Emily.

Not that it mattered. No, he would go back to L.A. and his feelings would sort themselves out as he took up his life again. This was all just an aberration born of the strangeness of his circumstances and his recent loss of Louise and her child. He just needed to get back to work.

The soft sound of a door opening alerted him. Nate Tate stepped out of the delivery suite. Just before the door closed, Abel thought he heard Janet moan.

"How is she?" he asked Tate.

"Getting close, I guess. Another hour or so."

"That's quick. I thought this would drag on most of a day."

Nate smiled ruefully, but the expression never quite made it to his eyes. "Janet has never been slow at anything. Come on, let's go hunt up the coffee machine."

Machine coffee, one of the world's great abominations.

"I haven't been asking her too many questions," Nate said as they strolled down the corridor in the general direction of the front lobby. "She's worried about other things right now."

"Has anyone said how Emily's doing?"

"The fetal heartbeat is evidently good, so she'll probably come through this okay, but she'll most likely have to spend some time in an incubator."

"Probably." He had expected that. Like Janet, however, he was concerned that Emily had been injured in her fall.

At the machine, Nate pumped in some quarters and got them each a cup of black brew. It didn't smell as burned as usual, perhaps because it was still relatively early in the morning.

Nate turned to Abel. "She says somebody was in the bedroom."

"That's what she told me. I went out to check the area around the house, and when I'd been out there maybe five minutes, I heard her scream. I found her on the ground out front of the cabin, where she'd fallen, and she said somebody was inside, that she'd seen him in the bedroom."

"You checked it out?"

"Of course. As soon as I moved her into the Explorer, where she'd be safer. She told me she'd seen a man with a knife in the bedroom, but when I checked it out, I found nothing at all. Not that I'm saying there was no one there, because I'm not. Janet didn't imagine what she saw. What upsets me is that he was able to get in the house when we were there. That he was evidently watching closely enough to know which room Janet was in, to know that I had gone out to check around."

"He was going to kill her." Nate's voice was threaded with steel.

"I'm not sure about that."

"Why not? There either was or wasn't a man in her bedroom with a knife! If there was, then what would he be doing there if he didn't mean to kill her?"

"I think he meant to scare her. I'm not even sure he intended to confront her face-to-face. Maybe he was going to leave the knife as another act of terrorism. Which reminds me. I haven't told you about the teddy bear yet."

Nate listened intently, his expression growing darker by the second as Abel described how they had found the teddy bear and the note. "You didn't touch it, did you?" he demanded.

Abel shook his head. "I'm a cop, too, remember? I didn't touch anything that might have retained a fingerprint. I've got it out in the car, by the way. I was planning to bring it to you this morning when Janet came in for her doctor's appointment."

Nate swore savagely. "When I get my hands on that sumbitch…" He broke off. "I've been trying to reach Warren Roth. The last address I had for him is Miami, but it seems he's not there anymore."

"I've been looking for him, too. I've asked a friend of mine who's a private investigator to see if he can locate him."

Nate nodded. "My gut says it's Doyle. If it is, Roth may know something."

"We can hope." Abel tipped his head back, reaching into dim memories from his childhood. "I don't know that my dad held Roth all that responsible for what happened. He seemed to have focused on your team as the culprits."

"Like I said, Roth was just a kid. Nobody expected a whole hell of a lot from him. Maybe your dad never knew that Roth told us he and Doyle were dead, blown to smithereens." Nate shrugged and sipped his coffee. "God, this is awful stuff." He shook his head disgustedly. "I say that every time I drink it. I should know better than to pop quarters into that machine." But he kept right on drinking it anyway.

"I'm pretty sure Dad never heard that Roth had lied. If he had, would he have blamed you so much?"

"I don't know. I don't remember your father or Doyle that well, Pierce. I can remember conversations I had with 'em, I can call their faces to mind...but I never got to know either of them well enough to predict how they'd carry a grudge. I'm not sure I'd feel comfortable doing that even about people I've known for twenty years."

"I don't guess I knew my father all that well, either. I was pretty young, and he was a very bitter man. I don't think he was always that way, so the man you knew was probably pretty different from the one I knew."

Nate nodded, a quick movement of his head. "I'm sorry about that. It's haunted me ever since I learned the truth about what happened. I made the best decision I could at the time. I had to consider the survival of my men versus going back to look for pieces of bodies. So...I'll defend my decision, Pierce. I'll defend my decision to get Roth, Laird and Parish out of there as quickly as I could when we were under heavy attack, and I'll defend it before any tribunal you choose. But I'm not sure I'm ever going to learn to live with the results of that decision."

Abel respected him for that, more than he could say. Life sometimes caused people to make tough decisions without sufficient information. Most people shrugged and moved on even if their decisions led to morally reprehensible outcomes. It was a rare man who could accept his moral responsibility for an unforeseen outcome even when he had made the best choice he could. Abel was a man like that, but he had seldom met another.

Flashes of blood on oily gray pavement... He closed his eyes for a moment, forcing the image into the background. Like Tate, he had things in his past that he was never going to learn to live with, things he felt responsible for even though he couldn't have done a damn thing to prevent them. And now he had a new one: Janet Tate lying curled up and crying on the ground, scared to death that she was losing her baby.

No, he hadn't caused that. It would have taken incredible foresight to know that Doyle would get into the house in those five minutes that he was away. He had been doing the best he could. But if anything happened to Emily, he was never going to forgive himself.

"What's my daughter to you, Pierce?" The question was blunt, as blunt as the man who had asked it. Tate looked him straight in the eye and waited for an answer.

It was like a scene out of an old novel, Abel thought with an errant flicker of amusement. Except that the baby wasn't his, so he shouldn't properly be playing the bounder. Nor did he quite know how to answer. He opened his mouth to say, "Just a woman who needs protection," but the lie wouldn't emerge. That was no longer true, and he damn well knew it.

He stalled, sipping the terrible coffee, trying to explain the unexplainable. Finally he settled for the truth. "I'm not sure."

That seemed to settle Nate's mind in some way, for he nodded. "She's been hurt an awful lot lately."

"I know. Believe me, I don't want to hurt her in any way." But wasn't that what he was doing by making love to her and then . . . panicking? Wasn't that exactly what happened this morning? Panic? Hadn't he felt the strings of attachment wrapping around him? God, the thought of caring for anyone that way made his damn knees knock. People had a way of abandoning him. . . .

It was as if someone had slapped him. The stark understanding of his view of his relationships was shocking to him. Never before had it occurred to him that he carried a concrete expectation of being deserted that caused him to hold back a significant part of himself. He had told himself that he was a little gun-shy because of Louise, but he had never realized until this very instant that he had *always* been gun-shy. Nor had he ever considered that he might have been directly responsible for Louise's departure. That his refusal to open up and completely commit might have left her so emotionally unsatisfied that she had turned to his best friend.

No. He wasn't going to accept that. Maybe he did hold back, but that sure as hell didn't justify what Louise had done to him. And why shouldn't he hold back? Sooner or later, everyone in his life had left him behind . . . even his mother.

Even his mother. God, was this the way his head worked? His mother hadn't left him! She'd remarried, and she had every right to find happiness for herself. She hadn't cut him out…her husband had. Besides, it had been time for him to start growing up and cutting those apron strings anyway. Damn it, he couldn't really be walking around feeling abandoned, like some orphan, could he?

"You okay?" Nate asked him.

Abel suddenly realized he was standing with his head tipped back and his eyes closed, lost in some internal maelstrom of self-discovery. The sheriff was going to wonder if he was completely cracked.

"Just thinking," he said through lips that didn't want to work. "Worrying about Janet…"

Tate nodded, his lips compressing into a thin line. "Don't blame yourself. You were trying to protect her."

How had the sheriff known he'd been doing precisely that? "I did a really great job of it, Sheriff. Really great."

"We do what we can. Nobody can ask more than that. Not even me, and I'm her father."

They started walking slowly back to the delivery suite, cups in hand. Nate paused a few times to poke his head into a room and say hello to someone he knew. Every nurse who passed had a smile for him, and one of the orderlies stopped him to chat for a minute about a church meeting.

This, thought Abel, was the kind of place anybody in his right mind would want to settle down in and live. There might not be a whole lot of excitement, but there were plenty of good people and friendships to be made. In the end, your friends mattered more than whether you could get to a concert on a Friday evening or dine in a five-star restaurant.

"This seems like a special place, this county," he said to Nate.

"It sure is." They stopped outside the door to the delivery suite. Neither of them seemed to want to sit in the waiting room. "Tell me how many places in the world you can go to the supermarket, discover you forgot your checkbook and have the cashier hand you a blank check to use?"

"Not a one."

Nate nodded. "I'm afraid that'll change eventually, but right now folks here know each other pretty well. They know who to trust and who not to. Most of us are pretty trustworthy. Likable, too. And it helps that we've only got one bank."

That drew a laugh from Abel.

"There's one thing I didn't tell you, and I reckon I should," Tate continued. "Last night somebody put a bullet through a window of Micah Parish's house. Nobody was in the room at the time, so it wasn't intended to kill, but . . ." Nate shook his head. "I'm getting damn sick of this cat-and-mouse game!"

"I thought there was protection on his place!"

"There is, but you can't watch every square foot every damn second of the time. The guy used a high-powered rifle, shot from a fair distance away—better than eight hundred yards, we're guessing. Hell, I don't know what more we can do! I want that man's head on a platter before he actually kills someone, but I'm damned if I'm going to use someone as bait in a trap. It's too risky, and for the most part right now, he seems to be after our wives and kids. No way am I going to jeopardize one of them."

Abel nodded agreement. "It's a problem, all right. Are you going to be able to keep a guard on Janet and the baby while they're here?"

"Count on it. The president doesn't have any better protection."

"I have to go back to L.A. on Sunday. I have to testify Monday morning. I don't feel good about leaving Janet behind."

"Nobody cares more about that girl than me," Nate said gruffly. "She's impulsive, always making headlong dashes into trouble and then trying to figure her way out once she's up to her neck. Always grabbing life with both hands . . . until this Scott character. I don't mind telling you, I don't like the way she's been since she came home. She's almost tippy-toeing around life, trying to avoid any more trouble or hurt. Yeah, she moved out on her own, but that wasn't for any reason other than that she wanted to hide."

"It didn't work very well, did it?"

"Hell, no. But it wouldn't have made any difference if she'd stayed home with her mom and me. This problem would have happened anyway. But what bothers me is she used to want to be part of everything. Now she's hiding from her own neighbors, acting like there's something wrong with her."

"Maybe she feels folks around here might disapprove of her being an unwed mother."

"I reckon some of them do. That's still no reason to hide . . . and I can tell you, in the past she wouldn't have."

"Life changes us all, Sheriff."

"Sometimes it's a damn shame. I've never figured out why a woman who keeps her child is somehow more reprehensible than the man who walks away from his responsibility."

"Beats me."

Nate flashed a weary smile. "It's too damn early in the day for cosmic questions. The only question I really want an answer to right now is how I can get my hands around Larry Doyle's neck."

"He won't be easy to track down. We need to draw him into a trap."

"Easier said than done. That man hasn't forgotten his training. If anything, he's gotten better at slipping past security. I was hoping to get him when he made a move against the Parishes. Micah picked that place of his with a military eye. I couldn't have asked for a better place to set up a cordon and catch the guy. Instead . . . Aw, hell, never mind. I'm so frustrated I could spit nails."

Abel leaned back against the wall and crossed his legs at the ankle. "Do you get the feeling he doesn't like to repeat himself? Admittedly, the gas leak thing wouldn't work at Janet's place, because the only gas appliances she has are the stove and the water heater, both in the kitchen, so she'd smell gas almost immediately. Nor would it pay to blow up the propane tank, because the log wall is just too damn thick. The force of the explosion would blow outward, away from the cabin, and the resulting fire would leave plenty of time to escape.

"Now, he could have tried the booby trap again anywhere, but apparently he hasn't. Instead, he shoots a bullet through Parish's window and hangs a teddy bear in Janet's place."

Nate humphed. "It's a good way to keep folks from knowing what to watch out for. That's no guarantee he'll start killing us by different methods. Turning up in Janet's place with a knife doesn't exactly fit with anything, either."

"Maybe he wants to scare everyone into herding together so he can take out the entire group at one time."

Nate froze. A quiet word escaped him, one that could have been an oath or a prayer. "You don't know how many times I've considered bringing everyone together because it would be easier to guard them." Nate swore again.

"Have you learned any more about Doyle's life after he was released from the POW camp?" Abel asked him. "My sources haven't turned up anything yet, but it sure would be nice if we could learn something more about him. It might help us understand what he's after."

"I know what he's after," Nate said flatly. "I got the information just this morning. His wife committed suicide when she heard he was killed in action. There was no other family, so his two kids got put up for adoption. The adoption records were sealed, and as far as I've been able to find out, he was never able to learn what happened to his son and daughter."

"My God." It all suddenly made a hell of a lot of sense to Abel.

"The only question is why it took him all these years to come after us."

"Maybe it took him all these years to become a vengeful man."

Nate nodded slowly. "Could be."

"I've got a friend who's a P.I. Former Treasury agent. I'm going to ask him to track down Doyle's kids. Maybe if we can find them for him, we can talk him out of this lunacy."

Nate snorted. "I doubt it. He seems hell-bent on killing us all."

"I'm not so sure about that."

The sheriff cocked a brow. "Not sure? After that grenade booby trap?"

"If he wanted to kill people, he could do it easily enough. He could have ignited that gas leak at your place. He could have lobbed that grenade into Laird's house. He could have picked off the whole damned Parish family with that high-powered rifle . . . and he could have killed Janet with that knife this morning."

"What are you saying?"

"That he may think he wants revenge, but his heart isn't really in it. It's almost as if he's choosing to do things that will leave the outcome up to fate. As if he wants things to go wrong so that his victims escape."

The older man stared into his cup of coffee, thinking it over. "Could be," he said finally. "Could be, but I can't afford to bet the farm on it. I have to go on the assumption he's playing cat and mouse with us, and that he fully intends to kill each and every one of us."

"I couldn't agree more. It's just that some of the things he's doing could well have proved fatal. The gas leak, the grenade booby trap—each of those goes past taunting to attempted murder, and yet each was designed so that it could fail."

"Maybe his idea of cat and mouse is a little more serious than yours. When a cat plays with a mouse, each bat of its paw is potentially fatal. The game could end at any instant. Maybe that's part of the fun of it for the cat."

The guy's motivation didn't really make any difference at this point. They had to assume that he intended the worst and was fully capable of carrying it out. The fact that Doyle might actually hope to fail in what he was doing made him no less dangerous. Abel filed the notion away, however, as a possible insight that might become useful at some future time.

Seth and Darlene joined them a short time later. Darlene looked seriously worried and gave Nate a big hug. Seth, however, looked furious, and his fury was directed at Abel.

"Where the hell were you?"

"Outside looking for booby traps."

Nate stepped between them. "Take it easy, Seth. It's a mistake any one of us might have made."

"How's Jan?"

"Pretty close to delivering. So far, so good. I expect the baby's going to spend some time in an incubator, though."

"If I get my hands on that son of a bitch..." Seth let the implied threat dangle and paced away up the hall. Darlene stared after him with a kind of hungry yearning that made Abel want to shake Seth to his senses.

He could sympathize with Seth's anger and frustration, though. Seth was a SEAL, a man accustomed to taking action, a man who hated to find his hands tied. Abel was much that way himself, as was Nate Tate. Three men of action, stymied by a lone assailant. Hell, "frustrating" didn't begin to cover it.

The door to the delivery suite opened, and Marge Tate emerged, a pleased smile on her face. "Mother and baby are doing fine. Emily is six pounds, three ounces, and if she's premature, I'll eat my hat."

Abel turned away, astonished to feel his eyes stinging and his throat aching. He didn't want anyone to see how affected he was.

Darlene saw anyway. While the Tate family members hugged in jubilation, she went over to Abel and touched his arm. She didn't say anything, just squeezed gently. It was kind of nice not to be alone.

Several hours passed before Abel was allowed in to see Janet. Family and close friends came first, of course, and no one thought of him as being a close friend. He fell into the category of "acquaintance" in their minds...and even in his own. He didn't feel he had a right to see her, and when Marge Tate suddenly turned to him and suggested he go in, he felt... awkward. As if he had suddenly ceased to be invisible and had taken on a more prominent role than he was comfortable with.

But he wanted to see Janet, wanted to see Emily, to assure himself with his own eyes that they were all right.

Looking tired but happy, Janet was propped up against the pillows. Beside her, Emily lay in a bassinet. The baby was sleeping soundly on her back, her impossibly tiny fist against her mouth. Abel was unexpectedly almost overwhelmed by a desire to pick the child up and cuddle her close to his chest. To try to make her safe.

But he wasn't able to keep anyone safe. Hadn't he proved that today?

"Isn't she beautiful?" Janet asked. "Emily Jane Tate. The pediatrician says she doesn't appear to be premature at all."

"That's wonderful." His voice was hushed, and he felt a reverence he hadn't felt since the last time he had set foot in a church. He couldn't seem to take his eyes from the child but stood there staring at this remarkable new little being.

"I guess I got pregnant earlier than I realized." Janet sighed. "They want to keep her for a few days just to be sure, but...oh, Abel, I can't believe it! She's perfect, and she's healthy, and none of those bad things I was so afraid of came true."

He looked at Janet then and felt something deep inside him melt. "You're beautiful," he said huskily. She was tired and pale, there wasn't a smidgeon of makeup on her face, and her hair needed a good brushing, but she was, absolutely, the most beautiful woman in the world. "Your daughter is beautiful."

"You can touch her if you want," Janet said, her eyes brightening with the moisture of unshed tears. "It's okay. I keep needing to touch her myself. I can hardly believe she's real."

Gingerly he reached down with a single finger and touched one of Emily's tiny hands. He knew it had to be a reflex when her hand opened and then closed around his finger, barely spanning the distance between two of his knuckles, but it affected him to the very core of his being. Fighting back emotion, he gently stroked the backs of her fingers with his thumb. "She has one hell of a grip," he said, his voice thick.

And then, because it seemed like the most natural thing in the world, he leaned across the bassinet and kissed Janet. It was a sweet kiss, devoid of sensuality, but full of so many other things...things they were both afraid of.

He lifted his head a couple of inches and looked straight into her moss green eyes. "I have to leave for L.A. on Sunday. I should only be gone until Friday. Come with me, Janet. Bring Emily and come with me. You'll be safer there and I . . . Damn it, I don't know how I can leave you here with that monster on the loose. But I have to be in court. That's not something I can get out of."

"My dad will look after me, Abel," she said.

"I know he will! But I—" He broke off sharply and straightened. With a gentle tug he broke free of Emily's grip and strode to the window, staring out at the star-strewn night. These blinds shouldn't be open, he thought, and reached out to close them. Then he had no choice but to look at Janet again.

She had forgotten him, it seemed, for she was staring at her baby with the softest smile he had ever seen.

"Janet, I'll be scared to death the whole time I'm away. I can't leave you behind. I need to know you're safe. I . . . need you to be with me."

She looked at him, her expression still gentle. "I'm not sure it would be good for Emily to be exposed to so many people so soon. All that traveling by air . . . I'm not sure that's good for her at her age. And then there's this little problem of people wanting to kill you before you testify. Abel, what if Emily got in the way?"

He wanted to scream. For the first time since childhood— well, no, since Officer Burke had been killed—he wanted to throw back his head and scream with frustration and rage. He was between a rock and a hard place, and there was nowhere else to go. He needed her with him, but she might be at risk if she came, yet she was certainly at risk if she stayed behind. . . . God in heaven, there had to be some way to make her safe!

"Go with him, Janet." Nate stood in the doorway of the room. "If the doctor says Emily can fly, go with him. You're more at risk here than you will be there. Here, you're the target."

Janet looked stunned, as if this were the very last thing she had ever expected to hear from her father. "But . . . you'll take care of me here."

"I will," her father agreed, "but I don't seem to be real effective at it right now. I think you'd be safer away from here."

Something inside Abel felt wounded by Janet's reluctance to come with him. It was ridiculous to feel that way, but he felt hurt nonetheless. As if he were being abandoned yet again. And there was another hurt twisting inside him, too, one that forced him to say, "I'm not sure I can claim to be all that good at protecting anyone myself." He drew a deep breath, steeling himself for the admission he was about to make. "I just know I'm going to be worried sick if you stay here."

The sheriff approached his daughter's bed and looked straight across it at Abel. "She'll be safer there. Don't bring her back until I clean up this mess."

* * *

At first the pediatrician thought the trip would be possible, but then Emily developed jaundice—which, although it wasn't unexpected in a newborn, couldn't be overlooked. Abel had been in tight spots before in his life, but never before had he felt quite so much like a caged animal. He refused to look too closely at the reasons why he felt that way. There was nothing he could do but leave Janet and Emily behind and go to Los Angeles to testify.

Emily looked so small and alone in her tiny little diaper with cotton pads taped to her eyes so she wouldn't look into the treatment light that hung over her. He stood at the nursery window watching her as if he might find the answers to all the perplexing questions that troubled him.

"When are you leaving?"

He looked over his shoulder and saw Janet standing there, wearing a turquoise robe and slippers.

"In the morning."

She nodded and came to stand beside him at the nursery window. "Me too. But not Emily." She made a little sound that sounded like a teary laugh. "I hate the thought of leaving her here. That's ridiculous, isn't it? With all my fears that there would be something seriously wrong with her, I'm carping now because she has this minor little problem and can't come home for a few extra days."

"I don't think you're being ridiculous at all. Of course you don't want to leave your baby behind. You're not going back to the cabin, are you?"

She shook her head. "I'm going to move in with my folks again. Wendy suggested I come stay with her and Billy Joe, but so far she seems to have escaped all this stuff. I guess Doyle hasn't realized she's one of us. I'd hate to cause her trouble by staying with her."

"When I get back I'm going to find that son of a bitch if I have to track him from one end of the county to the other."

She looked at him, her eyes full of something he was afraid to identify. "You're coming back?"

"Count on it, Jan. I'll be back here just as soon as I'm through testifying."

"Maybe . . . maybe this whole mess will be cleared up before then."

"I'm coming back anyway." Doyle or no Doyle, there was something else here that needed clearing up. He could no more have stayed away than he could have quit breathing.

She was frightened. He saw it flicker in her eyes, and much as he didn't want to believe it was there, he saw it anyway. She was scared to death of him. She saw him as a threat.

Not knowing what to make of that, or how he could possibly deal with it, he returned his attention to Emily. In her sleep she wiggled her fingers. He was coming back. Beyond that he refused to consider.

Chapter 15

Abel took a roundabout route into Los Angeles, finally arriving on a flight out of Phoenix. He had told absolutely no one when he would be arriving. He caught a cab in front of the terminal and headed straight for Roger Vaillancourt's place.

Roger was the former Treasury agent, who these days worked for himself only as much or as often as he felt like. Being retired, he could take only cases that interested him. Roger could be trusted, and it was with him that Abel was going to spend the hours until he testified. The two men had planned it all out weeks ago.

The key on Abel's key ring let him into Roger's house in a sprawling suburban neighborhood. Trish Vaillancourt had left her husband nine years ago and taken the children with her. Roger didn't talk about it much or, apparently, see his children very often. Abel never pried.

There was a note on the kitchen counter, scrawled on a legal pad and addressed to no one, that said simply, "Back around seven. R." Abel glanced at his watch and decided he had plenty of time to shower. Traveling always left him feeling as if he'd accumulated a layer of grime.

He hadn't shaved since Janet had been taken to the hospital, and a stubbled face stared back at him from the mirror over the bathroom sink. Not quite a beard, it made him look dangerous and disreputable. He decided to leave it for now, because it would make him harder to recognize. In the morning, before he left for court, he would get rid of it.

He was just pulling on a fresh pair of jeans when Roger returned, noisily whistling a dirty ditty. The refrigerator door opened, a bottle clinked, and a satisfied "ah" wafted back to the bathroom. Grinning, Abel padded barefoot out to the kitchen.

"Lawdy-lawdy, it's the wild man of Borneo," Roger said by way of greeting. Leaning back against the counter, he raised his beer bottle in a toast and grinned. "When did you decide to go for the ape look?"

"I didn't. I figure it's a passable disguise until tomorrow morning. How's it going?"

"On what? On the stuff you asked me to do? Well, I managed to track down Warren Roth, formerly of the U.S. Army Green Berets. Got word just this morning. It seems the gentleman has taken up residence in Royal Palms Cemetery as of just six weeks ago."

Abel felt the skin on the back of his neck crawl. "What killed him?" Part of him hoped desperately he would hear it was a heart attack.

"Car accident. He evidently had a blowout and spun out right in front of a fully loaded semi."

A blowout. That might have been an accident. Then again... "Did he have any family?"

"Nope. Wife left him in the distant past, and I haven't come across any record of kids."

It fit the pattern, though, Abel thought unhappily. It fit too damn well. An event that might or might not kill. People survived blowouts all the time. Hell, it had probably just been intended as a scare, if Doyle had anything to do with it.

And Abel's gut said Doyle *was* behind it. That Roth had been his first target. And that time he had been successful. "What about Larry Doyle?"

"Now that was a little more interesting. This guy evidently doesn't like leaving tracks." Roger pulled a notebook out of his back pocket and flipped it open with one hand while taking a swig of beer. "Okay. Seems the guy never even came home after he was released from the POW camp. He turned up at the U.S. embassy just long enough to verify that his wife was dead and his kids had been adopted out. He demanded some inquiries, but my source says even the state department couldn't break the adoption seal." Roger looked up. "I don't believe that, frankly. For whatever reason, they didn't want this guy to find his kids. That smells to high heaven."

"Can you find out who adopted them?"

Roger grinned. "Try me. I figure I can have it in . . . oh, say a week?"

"That's good enough. Go for it."

"You got it. Okay, back to the guy. He wandered around Southeast Asia for a while, apparently mixing drugs and booze in epic proportions. And at some point he woke up and sobered up. Not sure why. Like I said, this guy doesn't like to leave tracks, and his past is real vague. All that's really clear is that he's been working as a mercenary for over twenty years now. He's turned up everywhere from Angola to Afghanistan, generally working as an adviser and training troops, although I gather he's been caught up in actual combat quite a few times. My sources say he's something of a mystery, a closemouthed hard-ass. He never, ever talks about his past."

"And where is he now?"

"Nobody seems to know. About two months ago he suddenly quit his advisory position in Central America and vanished like smoke. Claimed a family emergency and took off within forty-eight hours. Kind of abrupt. He hasn't turned up anywhere else yet."

"That's it?"

"That's it." Roger took another sip of his beer. "Does it help?"

"I think so. Mind if I make a long-distance call?"

"You know where the phone is. Say, I'm just going to order pizza for dinner. How's that sound?"

"Great. I haven't had one since I left."

Calling Nate Tate would also give him a chance to ask about Janet, maybe even talk to her. He'd seen her only this morning, just before he left Conard City, but for some stupid reason it had been the longest day of his life. Nor was he going to rest until he knew she was safe, at least for now.

It was Marge Tate who answered the phone, though, and told him that Janet and Nate had gone back to the hospital to visit Emily. She brought him up-to-date on the baby's health and the good news that the child ought to come home in just a couple more days. Everything else, she assured him, was quiet.

Perhaps too quiet? Abel wondered.

"I'll have Nate call you as soon as he and Janet get in," she promised him.

With that he had to be content.

But he didn't want to be content. He should have been mentally preparing for his day in court tomorrow, for his meeting with the prosecutors right beforehand and for his testimony on the stand. He should have been mentally reviewing everything he could remember about the people and events in question.

Instead, all he could think of was Janet.

Pretty damn pathetic, when all was said and done.

Nate called around ten-thirty. Janet, he said when Abel asked, had gone to bed. She was avoiding him, Abel realized. She didn't want to talk with him. Something inside him squeezed hard until it turned a piece of him into a lump of cold lead.

"Tell her . . . tell her I asked about her," he said to Nate.

"I will. Son . . . aw, hell, never mind. I've given up meddling. Marge said you had some news."

"Warren Roth is dead. It seems he had a blowout and collided with a semi about six weeks ago."

"It could have been an accident."

"Maybe."

"Then again, it fits with what you were saying about the way this guy doesn't seem really committed to what he's doing."

"I've been thinking more about that," Abel said. "It's as if . . . as if he's not comfortable with the idea of being an executioner. That doesn't really fit with the rest of what I have, though. It seems he's been working as a mercenary all over the world since he was released from the POW camp. Officially he's been advising and training, but Roger says he's also been in combat on occasion."

"Roger's the Treasury agent turned P.I. that you mentioned?"

"Yes."

"Well, there's a hell of a difference between killing in combat and setting out to stalk and kill in cold blood. And this *is* cold-blooded. I don't care how much of a grievance he thinks he has, stalking people who've never done a damn thing to him is sick."

"He may *be* ill. It seems he left his most recent post in Central America without warning. Something must have goaded him into action."

"Hmm." The wire hummed with silence as Nate thought about that. "I wish I knew if that was significant in relation to what's happening now. It may be he just got tired of whatever general or politico he was working for. Or it may be that something put a burr under his saddle about this other stuff. Wish I knew."

"Roger didn't get a clue as to why Doyle left, but if I know Roger, he's still trying to find out." From across the room Vaillancourt gave him a high sign. "Yeah, he's still checking it out. He's also going to see what he can do about locating Doyle's kids. He figures he can turn them up in about a week."

"A week?" Nate sounded bemused. "He wouldn't be looking for a job by any chance?"

"I doubt it. He likes the nightlife too much. What about the teddy bear and the note?"

"There were some latents on the note. I'm waiting to hear what they match."

"That seems funny. He doesn't seem like the type to leave fingerprints behind."

"That was what I thought," Nate agreed. "If they're his, they're there for a reason. He wants us to know who he is."

"Revenge is a lot sweeter if the victim knows it's revenge."

"I wouldn't know. I've never been interested in taking any."

Impossibly enough, Abel felt himself smiling into the receiver. Despite everything he had believed about the man when he had set out on his journey of discovery, he had come to like Nathan Tate one hell of a lot. "Neither have I, although if this guy hurts Janet..." He left the sentence incomplete. It felt awkward to say what he was thinking, as if he were exposing too much of himself.

"I could get interested in the possibility myself," Tate agreed. "So, you testify in the morning?"

"That's the plan. I was told before I left that I could expect to be on the stand for at least two or three days. Maybe longer."

"I don't envy you. Keep us posted."

"Yeah. I'll want to keep abreast of how Janet and Emily are doing, too."

"So far, so good."

When Abel hung up, Roger was watching him with apparent interest. "Who's this Janet?"

"Just a nice lady who's caught up in something that happened before she was even born."

"You never sounded that soft before, not even when you were talking about Louise before she cheated on you." Roger smiled faintly, even knowingly, then changed the subject. "I figure it wouldn't be real safe for you to stop by your place in the morning before court, so I had one of my suits and a couple of shirts cleaned and pressed for you."

"Thanks. I really appreciate that."

"Just don't get blood on 'em."

The attempt on Abel's life came just as Roger was dropping him off at the back entrance to the building that housed the prosecutor's offices. He arrived way too early for his appointment, figuring that if his enemies knew he was supposed to be there this morning, they wouldn't be looking for him more than an hour in advance of the time he was supposed to be there.

But they were. They also evidently hadn't expected someone to drop him off—certainly not someone with Roger's training—but had expected him to drive himself. The assailant had been lying down in the front seat of a gray sedan. When he heard Roger's car pull up, he peeked out the window, and immediately upon identifying Abel as he got out of Roger's car, he took a shot. It missed narrowly. Abel dived to the ground and rolled beneath a nearby pickup truck. Roger slammed his car into reverse and backed straight into the sedan, at once preventing the shooter from driving off and also stunning him enough that he and Abel were able to take him prisoner.

The assailant turned out to be the brother of one of the defendants and was himself a cop.

"Filthy," was Roger's sole comment.

By four that afternoon, the man who had tried to kill Abel had been persuaded, by means of a plea bargain, to roll over on the people who had put him up to the attempt. He named names, including his brother, and spilled the beans about the entire operation for which the six defendants were already standing trial. Abel still had to testify, but every word he said was now corroborated by a man who had been involved in the criminal activities. Thirty more people, suspects against whom the DA hadn't been able to develop a strong enough case to prosecute, were arrested thanks to the assailant's statement.

And Abel was safe. Now that he was no longer the sole witness, killing him would fail to accomplish anything.

It was as if a dark cloud had lifted from the back of his mind. Though he had accepted the risks and the threats as part of his job, he hadn't realized how much they had affected him. For months now, he had simply been unable to consider the possibility that he might actually have a future. Somewhere deep inside, he had believed he was going to die.

He returned to his apartment for the first time in months, dressed in some of his better clothes and went out to enjoy the night as a free man. The celebration wasn't quite what he had expected it to be, though. Instead of just enjoying himself, he kept wishing Janet was there. In the end, giving in to his melancholy mood, he wandered down the streets looking in shop windows at things he was sure would delight her.

She didn't want him, though. Of that much he was certain. Her having already gone to bed by the time her dad called him last night was a sure indicator of that. She must have known he had called, must have realized Nate would call back. All she had had to do was hang around until the call was placed.

But she hadn't. She simply hadn't wanted to talk to him. It didn't help to realize that she was wise to avoid him. After all, he didn't have a damn thing to offer her. Plus she had a child to claim her full attention right now. It wasn't as if he could even keep them safe from Doyle.

Hell, he was a failure. A complete and total failure. Nothing in his life could stack up to his inability to protect Janet. His inability to save Officer Burke. Getting a few corrupt cops convicted didn't even out the balance on this one. It couldn't come close.

That was when he saw the necklace. Knowing Janet's love of things Indian and Southwestern, he had paused to look into a store that carried items of Native American art and jewelry. All of a sudden he saw a necklace made of liquid silver and turquoise, tiny little beads of silver strung together in loop after loop. It looked like a shimmering river that led to a turquoise-and-silver pendant.

Without a moment's hesitation, he walked in, pulled out a credit card and bought it. The necklace was meant for Janet, and he could hardly wait to give it to her. He would tell her it was a congratulatory gift on the birth of Emily.

He also found himself buying some things for Emily in another store. Nothing much, just a receiving blanket and a soft nylon teddy bear to replace the one that Doyle had befouled.

Doyle. Abel paused midstride, then abruptly headed for a bus stop. Friday looked an awfully long way away. He needed to call the Tates to make sure Janet was still all right.

He needed to know. Now.

Janet sat in a rocker in the hospital nursery, holding Emily while she slept. The soothing back and forth motion of the rocker, the comfort of holding her sleeping daughter, made her feel serene as she had not felt in weeks. Not since Doyle had burst into their lives seeking retribution for events in the dead past.

Not since Abel Pierce had thrust himself into her awareness, a dark, mysterious man who seemed to have layers and layers of secrets that he exposed only when forced to by circumstance.

She was terrified of him. Something deep inside her seemed precariously balanced, ready to tip over the edge into involvement with him, and she couldn't allow that. She couldn't take that risk again. Right now she had to think of caring for her child in the most loving and responsible way possible. Falling in love with a man who would only hurt her would not be a responsible thing to do.

And he *would* hurt her. He might not mean to, but he wasn't going to stay; he was going to head back to L.A. Moreover, the primary reason for his interest in her had been Emily. She was sure of that. He'd needed to put some kind of closure on his last relationship, on his fatherhood that had never come to be, and he had naturally been drawn to a pregnant woman who could complete the last part of the cycle for him.

If he returned at all, it would be to finish out the drama by playing father to Emily for a while. But he wouldn't want to stay, because he wasn't really Emily's father. It was the same situation as with Louise, and he would back out of it for the same reason.

The only other reason he had hung around was a male need to protect a pregnant woman. She'd grown up with men to whom that kind of gallantry was as natural as breathing, and she had no trouble believing that Abel was the same kind of man. As long as he felt she was in danger, he would feel obligated to protect her.

Well, she didn't want that. She didn't want a man who wanted nothing from her except the opportunity to play benevolent protector. It would wind up exactly the way it had with Scott, with her feeling bruised and hurt because she had been used but never loved.

There was no way on earth she was going to allow that to happen again. No way she was going to fall in love with a man with so many private places. The private places might be nothing but bad memories, but they could just as easily contain secrets that could be harmful to her.

Somehow having Emily to think about had made her considerably more cautious. Any risk she took now might redound on her daughter. Nor could she allow Emily to become attached to someone who might drift away.

But as she sat there, rocking her sleeping daughter and telling herself she would be wise, all she wanted to do was weep. This was not how she had always imagined it would be when she bore her first child. She had always pictured a loving husband who would share the joy and responsibility with her. She had never dreamed that she would be sitting alone in the nursery, holding her baby and wishing for a man who was half a continent away, a man who probably hadn't spared a thought for her since he had left.

She hadn't imagined feeling so very, very lonely.

The woman and the baby were safe at the hospital. There were too many other people around that Doyle didn't want to risk hurting. It wasn't that he was afraid to kill—he'd certainly killed enough in his time—but he had scruples. Among them was not harming people who were no threat. None of the hospital staff threatened him in any way.

But he watched from a distance as Janet Tate came and went, saw the sadness on her face as she was escorted to and from her parents' home. She wanted her baby to be with her.

That touched him. He had disguised himself and gone to the nursery and looked at the newborn child himself, and had discovered that he didn't want to hurt that baby. So he would be sure not to. It was easy enough. As for the mother—well, watching the sorrow on her face, watching her hold her child with such longing, he finally decided that maybe he didn't want to hurt her, either. After all, the baby needed its mother.

And all of that troubled him. Instead of moving forward with his plans, he found himself halting. Waiting. Rethinking. He knew what he owed his wife and his lost children, but it had never before occurred to him that he might owe something to these people, as well.

Retreating to the woods, he thought it all over. Tested himself against the anguish that had been driving him steadily insane for nearly thirty years. The pain was as strong as ever, the betrayal just as bitter as ashes in his mouth.

Micah Parish, Ransom Laird and Nathan Tate had cost him everything that mattered and left him with nothing except an agony-filled, pointless existence.

Surely he deserved his revenge?

The only answer that came to him was a firm yes.

* * *

Janet watched her father talk to Micah Parish and Ransom Laird. The three men seemed to be able to communicate in single syllables rather than full sentences sometimes, often leaving her totally in the dark about what they meant. Seth was also there, as were Gideon and Sara Ironheart. Gideon was Micah's brother, and his wife, Sara, was a sheriff's deputy.

From what Janet understood, they had decided to remove all their families from the threat. They were to fly to Oklahoma with Gideon Ironheart, to stay with the brothers' relatives.

Sara was being fitted for a red wig and would shortly begin to impersonate Janet Tate. In a few days, when Emily got out of the hospital, Sara would don the wig and head out to the cabin with a lifelike baby doll. The idea was to draw Doyle into a trap. While Sara pretended to be alone, she would be heavily guarded, as well as ready herself to deal with just about anything.

The plan was not to remove the families all at once. It was agreed, finally, that the youngest children had to leave first, since they were most at risk from things like booby traps. Faith Parish and Mandy Laird would take their children as if on a shopping expedition and join up with Gideon, who would escort them to Oklahoma. A day later, Marge Tate would take her youngest daughters with her, and the older girls would leave separately later the same day. Janet was to follow as soon as Emily was out of the hospital.

It seemed like a sensible solution to her, to remove the families from danger and set up a trap. Lacking other targets, Doyle would undoubtedly go for the only one left—Sara Ironheart pretending to be Janet Tate.

But the thought made Janet uneasy in some indefinable way. Almost as if using her identity as a decoy was no better than using herself as one. It was not something she could have put into words. Understanding eluded her. The best explanation she could formulate was that even if it was Sara who was taking the risk, it would still be Janet who was being attacked. Whatever happened would be intended for her, and having someone standing in for her wouldn't change that fact.

Part of her wanted to snatch Emily out of the hospital and flee toward Oklahoma this instant. Another part of her grieved that she would probably never see Abel again. If he came back here at all when he was through testifying, he would find everyone gone except Nate, Micah and Ransom.

But he probably wouldn't come back, she told herself sternly, and battled back a wave of ridiculous tears. He wouldn't bother. All that stuff about coming back had just been talk. Men were full of talk. She ought to know that by now.

"All right," Ransom said, leaning back in his chair at the round oak table in the Tate kitchen. In the overhead lamplight, his hair and beard gleamed gold and silver. "Mandy and Faith pull out tomorrow morning, bright and early." The women and their children were at the church right now for a pancake supper, as were Marge Tate and her other daughters. They'd all felt that such a crowded, public place would probably be safe... which was not to say that it wasn't also crawling with deputies who were there to provide protection.

"Why not get them out now?" Gideon asked. "I can fit them all in my Suburban. Why don't I just pick them up from the supper and get them the hell out of this place tonight? We can catch an early morning flight."

Sara nodded agreement, as did Seth.

"Sounds good to me," Ransom said. "Anything they need, they can always buy after they get to Oklahoma. I'd rather do this than take them home for another night when anything could happen."

Micah agreed with a nod. "We need to get them out of the church hall and into the Suburban without Doyle seeing it, though."

"That's easy," Janet said, glad to be able to contribute something. "We've got all those old costumes from Halloween and school plays. We can probably find enough wigs and get enough other people to gather around to help that Doyle won't be able to figure out who got into Gideon's car."

"Good idea," Nate said. "I'll drive down there first and set it up. You follow fifteen minutes after me, Gideon."

"You got it."

"Meanwhile, Micah, Ransom, you bring your cars along with me. When we get the ladies and kids loaded into Gideon's truck, we'll all drive off as if we're taking our families home. That ought to cause some confusion. Gideon, you take Seth with you. He can watch out for a tail and bring your truck back from the airport.''

Everyone nodded.

''And, Sara, you take Janet to the hospital to see Emily. Stay there until I show up.''

Janet always went to the hospital directly after dinner to see Emily, so she and Sara followed the routine this evening, as well, leaving the house at around seven. Not until after dark would the others drive to the church.

Only when she was sitting in the nursery rocking a drowsy Emily back to sleep did Janet realize that they were all making a dangerous assumption—that Doyle wouldn't harm innocent bystanders.

A shiver trickled down her spine, and she wondered if they were being utter fools.

Late that night, when she was sleeping soundly in her old bed, the phone rang. She had an extension by the bed and reached for it groggily, forgetting that at night only her dad answered the phone.

''H'lo?''

There was a silence; then a gruff man's voice said, ''Janet? This is Abel Pierce.''

Abel. In an instant she was wider awake than she had been in her life, her heart hammering and her mouth dry. Not that he affected her... ''I'll...I'll get Dad for you,'' she stammered.

''No!'' The word escaped him explosively. Then, almost immediately, he apologized. ''I'm sorry. I didn't mean to yell at you. It's just that I want...to talk to you, too.''

Her heart hammered even faster, and she felt as if she were standing on a precipice with the wind tugging dangerously at her, threatening to pull her over at any instant. ''About—about what?''

Dumb question, Janet, she thought nervously as soon as the words were out of her mouth. About what? The one question that was incredibly awkward to ask of a man you weren't certain was even interested in you. The one question that might make him uncomfortable enough to say, "I forgot. Can I talk to your dad?"

But the question evidently didn't throw Abel off stride. Not much, anyway. After the briefest pause he replied, "I was thinking of you. Wondering how you and Emily were doing."

She and Emily. It *was* her baby he was interested in after all. Her heart sank. "We're doing just fine."

"I'll be back on Friday. I'm looking forward to seeing you."

Which "you"? she wondered. Just her, or just Emily? Oh, this was silly, she told herself irritably. The man wasn't interested in her at all, so she ought to quit analyzing his every word. Nor could she tell him that she was leaving on Friday and probably wouldn't see him at all. Her dad had been insistent that no one discuss the plan with anyone else, and certainly not with anyone on the phone. Awful to think that creep might actually be listening in. "That'll be nice," she said finally, not knowing what else she could possibly say.

"Yeah." Another silence. Finally he said, "Some guy tried to take me out on Monday morning."

Instantly Janet's heart climbed out of the pit of her stomach and into her throat. "Tried to kill you? Abel! Were you hurt? Did you catch him? What happened?"

"He took a shot at me as I was walking into the D.A.'s office. He missed and I'm fine, Jan. And yes, we caught the bastard. The nice part of it is, he agreed to testify against his buddies in exchange for a reduced charge. That means I can pretty much forget anyone else wanting to kill me, because I'm not the only witness anymore."

"That's wonderful!" Fear eased its stranglehold on her, and she drew a long, shaky breath. "Thank God. Thank God. I was so worried!"

She was revealing far too much, but she didn't care. All that mattered was that he was safe. A little warning bell sounded in the back of her mind as she realized how deeply she cared, but she ignored it. A certain sense of fatalism had gripped her. It was too late to prevent what had already happened. What she had to do was avoid getting in any deeper . . . and also prepare for the inevitable hurt.

"Then maybe you have some idea how worried I am about you," Abel said.

She hardly dared breathe. Not that it mattered. She couldn't think of any response that wouldn't sound like a plea for his love. She didn't want to do that. Never again was she going to allow herself to beg for anything.

The silence grew too long, and with it a feeling of awkwardness. Needing to end it somehow, Janet blurted without thinking, "Should I get Dad for you?"

"No. No, it's okay. Just tell him I don't have anything new to report yet. Other than that...I just wanted to be sure you and Emily were all right."

"We're fine." It almost hurt to say that. She wasn't fine. How could she be fine when he was so far away? How could she be fine when her heart ached this way and her mind wanted to run from the coming pain.

"Well, that's all I wanted to know. I'll see you Friday, then."

Eleven hundred miles away, Abel hung up the phone and stared into space. That had been the most painful conversation of his life, and never, ever, had he felt as alone as he did now.

Chapter 16

Friday morning Darlene Llewellyn and Sara Ironheart entered the professional building that was linked to Community Hospital by means of an enclosed bridge. Sara wore a blond wig and carried a doll, swaddled in a bright blue blanket, in a plastic infant seat.

Twenty minutes later Janet Tate, in the company of her brother, Seth, left the nursery with Emily, who wore a bonnet and was snugly wrapped in a pink receiving blanket. They crossed the bridge to the professional building and there entered the office of Emily's pediatrician. Almost immediately, Janet was ushered into an examination room. Seth waited just outside.

Darlene and Sara were waiting for her. The switch went easily, Emily exchanging her bonnet and blanket for the blue blanket and infant seat, and Janet exchanging her clothes for the blond wig and Sara's clothes. Sara was a little taller, but not so much that a few adjustments didn't correct the problem.

Minutes later, Darlene and Janet departed, carrying Emily in the infant seat. Together they went out to the parking lot, climbed into Darlene's car and headed out of town.

Fifteen minutes later, Sara emerged wearing a red wig and carrying the pink-swaddled doll. Seth walked beside her. Together they went out to the parking lot and climbed into Janet's Explorer.

No one was tailed.

"I wish you hadn't insisted on doing this, Dar," Janet told her best friend as Emily slept in the infant seat in back.

"So does Seth." Darlene flashed her a grin, then adjusted her grip on the steering wheel. "Aw, come on, Jan. This is probably the only exciting thing I'll ever get to do in my entire life...unless you want to count watching my brothers get braces."

"When are you going to start taking care of your own needs?"

"I just did." Darlene laughed quietly. "Seth thinks I'm crazy."

"You are. About him. Aren't you?"

Darlene didn't answer immediately, but she didn't have to. Her cheeks bloomed, pinker than Janet could remember having seen them since their early high school years. "We're just friends," Darlene said finally. "He's leaving in another week."

"So go with him."

"Janet!"

"Don't give me that, Darlene. You're crazy about him, and he's just crazy."

"What do you mean?"

"That his only objection to a relationship is that he's utterly convinced no woman can put up with his life-style. Convince him otherwise."

"As if it's that easy."

"Why not? If you want it, go for it. But he's more apt to believe you have what it takes if you do something really daring than if you simply say so. Anyone can *say* so."

"I don't believe you!"

It was Janet's turn to laugh. "Why not? If you have the guts to get involved in the middle of this mess to help me out, why don't you have the guts to go after my brother?"

"That's different!"

"Sure. Helping me, you only risk getting killed. Going for Seth, you risk getting hurt."

As soon as the words slipped past her lips, Janet felt as if someone had yanked her leash hard. Who was she to be advising Darlene to take big emotional risks? Hadn't she herself sworn never to do any such thing again? Hadn't she been virtually paralyzed on the phone with Abel because she had realized that she cared? How could she possibly be telling Darlene to take a risk she wouldn't take herself?

"I think he cares for me," Darlene said quietly. "Janet, I really think he does. But I'm not going to ram myself down his throat. If he wants me, he'll have to admit it himself."

Janet nodded, letting it go. Instead, she turned and looked into the back seat, where Emily was sleeping so contentedly. That little girl with her pink cheeks and thin red hair was worth every bit of the price Scott had exacted from her. Worth the pain and the humiliation. Worth every single tear Janet had shed. She would go through it all again, just to have Emily.

It was as if, right then, something heavy lifted from her shoulders. With surprising clarity she could hear her mother's voice in her mind, saying something Marge Tate had frequently told her daughters: "Even out of bad things, something good eventually comes. You just have to look for it."

Out of Scott had come Emily. And she wouldn't trade Emily for the world.

She was free of Scott at last. Free of the bitterness that had been plaguing her, free of the chains that had bound her to the hurt. Free to look forward.

If she survived.

Janet wouldn't let Darlene wait with her at the airport. The drive back to Conard City was a long one, and Dar would be making it alone. Janet was determined that her friend should get there before dark. "Besides," she argued, "nothing is going to happen to me here. All I have to do is squeal and a hundred people will run to my rescue."

Darlene finally agreed, persuaded that Janet would be safe in the busy departure lounge with a security guard within hailing distance. The only thing she insisted upon was telling the guard that Janet was being stalked and would he please be on the lookout for any man who seemed too interested in the mother and child. The guard, of course, was more than willing to be helpful.

Unfortunately, waiting alone for her flight gave Janet far too much time to think. She fed Emily and changed her, but the child went back to sleep almost immediately. Every so often a woman would stop to ooh over Emily, but mostly Janet found herself staring out the window and thinking.

She was the last of the family to leave. Even Wendy had been persuaded to take time off and go visit friends until things were cleared up, and Wendy had apparently never been targeted. If her dad was right, it wouldn't be long before Doyle discovered that everyone had left, and his attention would focus on the woman he believed to be Janet Tate. It was the hope of Nate and his comrades that they could limit trouble to the isolated cabin, away from innocent bystanders, and catch Doyle in the process.

Remembering how she had found Doyle in her bedroom with that knife, Janet wondered if it would be that easy. He seemed a very resourceful man, able to come and go at will despite their precautions. And still, some part of her couldn't quite accept the seriousness of the threat. Couldn't quite truthfully believe that this man wanted to kill her family. Kill her. Kill Emily. Not even after facing him in her bedroom as he held that ugly hunting knife could she fully believe that he intended to kill.

Denial, she found herself thinking, was an amazing thing. How much proof did she need that this man intended serious harm?

"Janet?"

Hardly able to believe her ears, Janet tipped her head slowly and looked up... into Abel's dark-as-midnight eyes. "Abel? What—"

"Miss?" The security guard was suddenly there, his hand pointedly resting on the gun that rode at his waist. "Is this man bothering you?"

Feeling almost dazed by Abel's unexpected appearance, Janet took several seconds to comprehend the question. "Uh, no. No! He's a friend of mine. Thank you, it's okay."

Abel took a seat on the other side of Emily and looked down at the baby with an expression so tender that Janet felt her throat tighten. "She's grown," he said quietly. "In just a week she's grown so much." With a smile he raised his head and looked at Janet. "What are you doing here? I didn't expect to see you until I got back to Conard City."

"There was another incident while you were gone. Somebody tampered with the steering system in Mandy Laird's car. She might have been killed, except that Ransom had decided to work on the engine and noticed that someone had taken a hacksaw to the steering linkage. It could have snapped at any time while she was driving."

Abel swore softly. "If I get my hands on that guy, he's going to be chopped liver."

"I think Ransom, Micah and Dad may beat you to the punch."

"So what are you and Emily doing here?"

"We're going to Oklahoma to stay with some relatives of Micah's. In fact, everyone's gone except the three men. We've all been thrown out." She tried to smile but couldn't quite manage it.

Abel frowned. "I can understand why they did it, but now Doyle will just sit back and wait. It'll make it harder to catch him."

"Except that Sara Ironheart is pretending to be me. They think they can draw Doyle out by getting him to take action against me. Or rather, her."

Abel nodded slowly. "That could work. God, I hope it does."

He looked so good, she found herself thinking. He'd been to a barber while he was away, and his dark, straight hair lay neatly. He wore black jeans and a black turtleneck, and right now he looked good enough to eat. She wished desperately that she could just crawl into his arms and feel his strength surround her.

Instead, he was looking at Emily, smiling in that soft way that made her wish he would once, just once, look at her with that kind of tenderness. If only he wouldn't continue to be so distant. If only he would reach out . . .

He bent suddenly, opening the leather carry-on bag at his feet. "I found something for you," he said. "It had your name written all over it, Jan. No way could I have walked on without getting this for you."

He took out a long, flat box and passed it to her. A name she didn't recognize was written in gold leaf across the black leather. "Abel?"

"Just open it, honey."

Honey. Knowing he really meant that would have been the only gift in the world she needed, but men often used that word indiscriminately. Gingerly she opened the box . . . and gasped when she saw the shimmering beauty within. "Oh, Abel! It's gorgeous!"

"It's perfect for you. Will you wear it for me?"

Carefully she lifted the strands of liquid silver and turquoise from the box and started to unfasten the clasp.

"Let me," Abel said. Rising, he stepped around behind her and took the necklace. She held her hair out of the way while he fastened the clasp. Silver glistened on her breast, shimmering with each breath she took.

Abel resumed his seat and smiled. "It's as perfect for you as I thought."

She looked up from the necklace and dared to meet his eyes. "Thank you. Thank you so much. Nobody's ever given me anything so beautiful."

"Maybe nobody ever appreciated you the way I do."

Her heart leapt, and feelings of joy she hardly dared acknowledge began to sparkle in her soul.

Her flight was announced then, and all she could think was that she didn't want to go. She wanted to stay here with Abel and explore these hardly-born, delicate feelings. She wanted to go somewhere with him away from the hurly-burly and get him to talk about what the necklace really meant. About why he had called her "honey." About what she really meant to him.

"Mrs. Condon?" A flight attendant bent toward Janet. "You can board first with your son. Let me help you."

There was just a brief moment left, and Abel seized it, taking her into a tight bear hug and pressing a kiss on her forehead. "Take care of yourself, Jan. Take care of Emily."

"What are you going to do?" she asked him, her voice breaking as her throat tightened.

"Go back to Conard County and find that son of a bitch."

"Mrs. Condon? Please, you have to board now. Everyone's waiting."

Blinking rapidly to hold back tears, Janet picked up Emily and walked toward the gate. The flight attendant followed with the diaper bag and Janet's carryon.

He was going to find the son of a bitch, he'd said. But he hadn't said he would be there when it was safe for her to return. She'd even had the half-formed hope that he would ask her to run away with him somewhere.

Instead he had said he was going to find the son of a bitch. He would have done that even if she and Emily hadn't been involved. It was a macho thing.

Her heart had been bruised once again. And perhaps it hadn't recovered from Scott as much as she had believed. Or maybe she'd been a hell of a lot more foolish than she had thought and had gotten far more involved with him than she ever had with Scott. Either way, it felt as if her heart had just crumbled to dust and were blowing away in the wind.

Abel's first stop upon returning to Conard City was the sheriff's office. Night had fallen, leaving the square almost deserted. The lights in the courthouse windows burned as the janitorial staff worked the evening away, but most of the businesses around had closed up and were dark. Hereabouts, most places didn't even bother with security lighting.

The thought struck Abel forcibly for some reason. The streetlights provided scant illumination, and the wind blew ceaselessly down abandoned streets. The only human sounds were those drifting faintly from Mahoney's Bar several blocks away, occasional snatches carried on the errant wind.

The sheriff's office was brightly lit, however, and cast golden illumination through the big front window onto the sidewalk. Inside, a deputy could be seen at a desk, reading a magazine. Only the top of the night dispatcher's head could be seen above the console.

The night wind must have been blowing right off the snow-fields that still powdered the top of the mountains, because it carried a sharply biting chill. Abel suppressed a shiver and entered the building.

The deputy looked up at once. His deeply tanned, weathered face betrayed nothing. "Something I can do for you, Mr. Pierce?"

Everyone knew him already; none of L.A.'s anonymity here. He scanned the other man's nameplate quickly. Deputy Beauregard. "I need to speak with Sheriff Tate."

"How important is it?"

"I've got some more information in the stalking case."

Beauregard sat up immediately and reached for the telephone. He punched in Tate's number but apparently got no answer. "Herb," he called to the dispatcher, "rustle up the sheriff for me."

"Sure thing, Beau." Herb, a young man who looked barely old enough to be working, leaned toward his microphone. Ten minutes later, he, too, gave up.

"Nate must be on the stakeout," Beau said. "Doesn't want to use his radio. Guess you'll just have to wait, Pierce."

Abel didn't like the idea; things could happen while he was waiting, and he wouldn't be able to do a thing to lessen the damage. Unfortunately, it was dark out there, and he couldn't act before dawn anyway, not to any useful purpose.

"Keep trying," Beau told Herb. "Every five minutes. As soon as it's safe, he'll be back in radio contact."

Herb nodded. "Consider it done, Beau."

Abel almost smiled at the youth's earnest eagerness.

"Help yourself to coffee, Pierce," Beau suggested. "There are some magazines on the table over there to pass the time with."

What Abel really wanted to do was get out to the cabin and get into the thick of it. Unfortunately, with no one knowing he was coming, that might be a foolhardy thing to do. He settled for a magazine and a lot of patience.

Nate resumed radio contact around midnight. When he heard that Abel was waiting for him at the office, he said he would be right in.

Thirty minutes later he arrived, wearing dark clothes and camouflage paint on his face.

"Come on back in my office," he told Abel. He snagged himself a cup of coffee on the way, then closed the door behind the two of them.

"I'm not trusting anybody right now," he said as he settled behind his desk and motioned Abel to take a chair. "The temptation to gossip might overwhelm somebody, and once word of what we're doing gets onto the grapevine, Doyle could hear about it."

"Janet told me at the airport."

"You saw her?"

"She was in the departure lounge with Emily when I arrived from L.A. today. I recognized her despite the wig." It kind of surprised him when he thought about it, because he hadn't been looking for her. But he had felt a kind of tugging beneath his breastbone, and his eyes had settled on the woman with the blond hair. His heart had apparently recognized her even before his brain.

The corner of Nate's mouth lifted. "I'm getting to like you, son, despite everything. She arrived safely in Oklahoma, by the way. I stopped and called on my way in."

Abel nodded, reluctant to admit the degree of relief he felt at knowing Janet and Emily were all right. "I hope it isn't common knowledge where they are."

Nate shook his head. "No one outside the three families knows, except you. So what's this news you have?"

"Roger found one of Doyle's children. The daughter. She's married, has a couple of kids of her own and is apparently curious enough about him to want to meet him."

"That could be useful. Only problem is, how do we get the word to Doyle? I could comb the mountains looking for him, but that's like looking for a needle in a haystack, even with a tracker like Micah. It wouldn't take a hell of a lot for him to stay one jump ahead."

"If he knows he's being tracked."

Nate cocked a brow. "What do you mean?"

"Well, he's primarily interested in what you, Laird and Parish are doing, plus whatever you have your deputies get up to. I'd probably have an edge with him, being Miles Bryant's son."

"You mean, set out to look for him yourself? But he's seen you with Janet."

"I'll pretend I'm on *his* side in this. It'd be easy enough to get that onto the local grapevine, wouldn't it? Or what about having your son-in-law carry the story up to the vets in the mountains that I'm after your hides because of what you did to my dad, and that I've been romancing Janet to get on your good side. Claim I'm writing a book that's going to ruin you."

"Hell, we could probably get that printed on the front page of the paper." Nate closed his eyes, tipping his head back a little, plainly pondering. "Next issue isn't until Monday, though."

The downside of a small community, Abel thought. No daily paper. "Any way we can. And with the women and children safely out of the way, there's not really any rush."

"Guess not." Nate sighed and opened his eyes. "Let me think about this. Come on home with me. I'll fix us some eggs and bacon, and we can talk it over."

The Tate house was still under surveillance, though not as tightly as when Marge and the girls had been there. Nate exercised a reasonable degree of caution when he entered the house, checking for signs of trespass and booby traps. "At some point or other," he said as they stepped inside, "he's going to figure out that we sent our wives and kids away. I'd be very surprised if he doesn't get angry and make a stupid move against Sara."

"He might. In the meantime, I still want to try to draw him out."

Nate set a skillet on the stove but didn't turn on the flame. Instead he reached for the phone and punched in a number. "Yuma, old son? Do you think you can come over to the house for a few minutes? I've got some ideas I want to bounce off you."

By the time the eggs, bacon and toast were ready, Billy Joe Yuma had arrived and joined them at the oak table.

"Yuma here," Nate told Abel, "was a medevac chopper pilot in Vietnam, and he spent nearly two years as a prisoner of war. He knows the vets on the mountains like his own brothers. You ask him what he thinks of your idea."

Abel met Billy Joe's gaze steadily. "There's been some evidence that Larry Doyle may have been hanging around with your friends."

Yuma nodded. "When he first arrived in the area. They see him from time to time, I found out this week, but he's not hanging out with them anymore."

"They'd probably get too suspicious. Anyway, what I'm thinking is, if we could get word to Doyle that I'm Miles Bryant's son—he was wounded and captured along with Doyle—and make him think that I'm after the same hides he is, he might try to get in touch with me."

"*Are* you Miles Bryant's son?"

Abel nodded. "To please my mother, I let my stepfather adopt me, which is why I have a different last name."

Yuma drained the last of his coffee, then mopped at some egg yolk with a piece of toast. "Okay," he said presently. "It's close enough to the truth that I won't feel like I'm out-and-out lying to them." His gray green eyes were hard as they met Abel's. "I won't betray their trust."

"I know. I'm not asking you to. My relationship with Bryant is real, and it ought to be enough to get Doyle's attention. He ought to at least want to find out what exactly I'm doing in these parts. I'd be real surprised if he didn't seek me out."

Nate popped a toothpick in the corner of his mouth. "Might work. Might work better than using Sara as a decoy... and I don't mind telling you, that doesn't sit at all well with me."

"Me, neither," agreed Yuma. "Okay. I was planning to go up in the hills tomorrow anyway, to take along some things I got for the guys. I'll just paint you with a tarry brush, Pierce. I can't guarantee that any of them will pass it on to Doyle, though."

"Sure you can. Just mention the names of the two guys who were wounded and captured. Somebody'll make the connection."

"Maybe."

"And I'll get it into the paper on Monday, either way," Nate said. "It'll get back to Doyle somehow. He's got to be keeping up with things around here in some fashion or another. He'd be a fool to trust only to his own eyes."

Abel nodded agreement. Reconnaissance required information, the more the better. If Doyle was half the soldier he seemed to be, he would be reading the paper and talking to anyone who might be able to give him useful information without betraying him or growing suspicious.

"Where's Seth?" Yuma asked Nate.

"Over at the Llewellyn place. Damned if he hasn't gone sweet on that Darlene."

Yuma cracked a grin, the first one Abel had ever seen him give. "Funny how women get under your skin no matter how hard you fight it."

Yeah, thought Abel. They sure had a way of doing that.

One in particular was downright infectious. His chest squeezed a little as he thought about Janet and wondered how she was doing. Wondered if she missed him half as much as he was missing her.

Wondered if he would ever find the gumption to open up the way a woman like her would need.

Wondered what the future held—or if he even had a future.

It was appalling for Abel to have to admit to himself that he was relieved not to have to protect Janet. The vision of red blood on oily gray pavement had never been as frequent as during the time when he had carried the responsibility for Janet's safety.

Intellectually he understood that no one could guarantee another person's safety one hundred percent. What had happened to Delia Burke might not have been preventable even if he had known she was going to be walking in on them. Given that her appearance had been an utter surprise...hell, he ought to be able to forgive himself. But he probably never would.

The sense of failure that lingered from that incident had carried over into his relationship with Janet. He had volunteered to protect her—no honorable man could have done otherwise—but he had felt inadequate to the task, especially after the teddy bear incident. And more so now, after Doyle had actually managed to get into the cabin with Janet.

Yes, it was a blessed relief to have Janet out of harm's way. God, he wanted her, though. Even though he wouldn't be able to make love to her again for weeks, he wanted her nearby. He wanted to see that soft smile of hers, wanted to hear her laugh, wanted to feel her silky skin next to his. There wasn't much he wouldn't have sacrificed just then to have her beside him.

But the wish was utter folly, and he was just going to have to get used to the aching emptiness her absence left behind, because she was not meant for him. He had nothing to offer her that she couldn't find in better shape somewhere else. What she needed and deserved was some young man whose life hadn't already been blighted by ancient bitterness and old scars. Some young fellow with a clean, shiny future ahead of him, not a cop who had come to resemble one of the street thugs he ought to be arresting.

She wanted to go back to school and finish her graduate program. No way would she want to come to L.A. with him, and he wasn't sure he could imagine being a cop anywhere else. Hell, he was an adrenaline addict, and he would probably go nuts if he didn't get his daily jolt. Somehow he didn't think he'd get it policing Conard County.

But part of him wanted a more peaceful life and kept toying with the notion that maybe he *could* give up undercover work so that he didn't have to live so much of his life on a knife edge. But until he was sure he could and would be willing to do that, he didn't feel he had anything to offer Janet and Emily.

It was different, this feeling he had for Janet, from what he had felt for Louise. Maybe because he hadn't really felt much for Louise at all. He'd been drawn to the home she provided more than he had been drawn to her. He couldn't once remember agonizing over what might happen to her if he continued to take risks. It had never occurred to him that he might owe her something more than a life spent waiting for his return.

But then, she'd never seemed overly concerned with whether he returned or not. They'd had a sort of distance in their affair, a careful separation that had protected them both from the worst emotional damage. When he came right down to it, Abel was a little surprised to discover that he had been more wounded by his best friend's betrayal than he had been by Louise's.

And by the loss of the child that he had believed to be his. But that, too, had been the loss of an idea, the loss of part of his notions of home and family. He had been crazy about the *idea* of being a father, which was a whole different ball of wax than being crazy about a particular kid. Emily was a different matter altogether. Emily had enormous dark eyes, smooth pink cheeks and a fuzzy thatch of reddish hair just like her mother's. Emily was somebody to love.

Hell. His thoughts were running around like a rat caught in a maze and getting absolutely nowhere. What he needed was for Billy Joe Yuma to come back down from the mountains with word that he'd spread the story to the vets. Then he would go back to set up camp in the old mining town on the side of Thunder Mountain. There he would wait for Larry Doyle to show himself.

He just hoped that Doyle came for him before he went for Sara Ironheart.

Chapter 17

Yuma returned just before nightfall on Saturday evening. Nate and Abel were getting ready to hit Mahoney's for a couple of beers and a sandwich when Yuma pulled into the driveway. Because Yuma was a recovering alcoholic, Nate immediately changed plans, instead choosing to invite his friend to stay for chili dinner.

"No thanks," Yuma replied. "I've got a ton of work I need to get done out at the hangar. The Huey's getting balky again, and I promised myself I was going to take care of it tonight."

He did come inside, though, to tell them what had happened. "I passed on the story about Pierce here being Miles Bryant's kid, and how I didn't like the way Pierce seemed to be out to get even with you, Parish and Laird. About how I figured you were using Janet to get close to Nate. I didn't want to lay it on too thick or make too much of a point of it, so I can't swear anybody was really listening, or that they'll think it's important enough to pass on. I kind of gathered that they had been wondering what Pierce was doing camping in that old ghost town, but I wouldn't say they had been significantly worried about it. As for Doyle...they run across him from time to time, more when he first turned up and not so much now."

"So we could wait indefinitely for the news to get around," Abel remarked. He wished there was some way to hurry things up, but knew from long experience on the streets that waiting was often the wisest course of action.

"Maybe not," said Nate. "The newspaper's going to publish the story on Monday. They're going to play it out like some investigative thing, saying they're on to you, Abel. I reckon your credit is going to be rock-bottom low around here by Monday afternoon."

Abel almost chuckled at that. It was the last thing on earth he was worried about.

"That's a beautiful necklace, Janet," Marge Tate told her daughter.

"Abel Pierce gave it to me." She looked down at the shimmering strands of silver and the turquoise-and-silver pendant that lay on her breast. Emily was sound asleep beside her in the little infant carrier as they sat on the porch and watched the Oklahoma sunset. The land here was hillier than Janet had expected, and far greener. Gideon and Micah's family was a huge one, encompassing second and third cousins as comfortably as brothers and sisters. Earlier tonight the youngsters had gathered around breathlessly to listen while Gideon told them of performing the Sun Dance the summer before last. He even showed them where his chest had been pierced.

Now the porch belonged to Marge, Janet and Emily, while the others crowded inside the big ranch house to watch a favorite TV program.

"It's nice here," Janet said. "Almost as nice as home."

Marge chuckled. "You're just prejudiced. Don't you think that necklace is a rather expensive gift?"

Janet didn't quite succeed in hiding a smile.

"Janet, you didn't!"

The younger woman didn't answer. Some things just couldn't be discussed with one's mother.

"Honey..." Marge's voice took on a note of concern. "Are you...involved with him?"

"I guess." Janet sighed and finally looked at her mother. "I think I care a whole lot more than I should. He's going to head back to L.A. as soon as this mess is straightened out, and I'll probably never see him again.''

Marge looked once more at the necklace. "I wouldn't be so sure about that, young lady. Men don't usually spend that kind of money on jewelry for a woman they don't intend to see again.''

"Except as a kiss-off?"

Marge drew a sharp breath. "Is that the kind of man you think he is?"

After a moment Janet shook her head. "No. Not in my heart. It's my brain that keeps telling me that's how I should look at this.''

Marge reached out and touched her daughter's arm comfortingly. "I hope your heart is right.''

"Me too. Oh, Mom, I just wish this mess would be over so we didn't have to be worrying all the time. I'm more worried now than I was there because I can't see with my own two eyes that Dad is safe. That Abel is safe. And do you have any idea how I'm going to feel if something happens to Sara Ironheart because she's taking my place?''

"That wasn't your decision, Jan."

"What difference does that make? None of this was my choice, but I could still wind up hurt. Damn it, I wish I could be there. I want to do something to help!''

"The whole reason we're here is so that your father and the others can address this issue without having to worry about us. This is the most useful thing we can do right now, and you know it, Janet. You don't have the training to be helpful, and right now you aren't in any physical condition to help, either. The most important thing you can do is stay out of the way and look after Emily.''

"I know. I know." Janet sighed glumly. "It's driving me crazy anyway.''

"It won't be much longer," Marge said. "I feel it in my bones. This is going to be settled very soon.''

It wasn't much longer. Monday evening, as Abel was sitting by his fire in a shack on the side of Thunder Mountain, Larry Doyle turned up.

With darkness had come a chill, so Abel had put on a heavy coat and thrown a few more logs on the fire. He was beginning to get the idea that even in the summer, nights could be cold hereabouts. The fire reminded him of Janet's hair, which led him down lonesome paths of thought that seemed perfect for the night and for the restless rumble of thunder from the mountain peak.

Doyle appeared between one breath and the next, arriving as soundlessly as a wraith. He stood on the other side of the fire, clad in woodland camouflage, looking like an apparition from a distant past. In the crook of his arm he cradled a shotgun. Abel didn't make the mistake of thinking the man wasn't ready to strike.

"Who the hell are you?" Abel demanded as if he didn't know. "What do you want?"

"To talk to you."

"About what?" He eyed the shotgun distrustfully. "Conversations at gunpoint aren't my style."

"Too bad," Doyle said. To reinforce his point, he leveled the muzzle directly at Abel. "You're Pierce, aren't you?"

"That's right."

"I hear your dad was Miles Bryant."

"What's it to you?"

The gun barrel moved menacingly. "Answer my question, Pierce. I haven't got a whole lot of patience."

He was tempted to try to take Doyle now, but it would have been pointless. They didn't have enough evidence to convict him of a single damn thing in a court of law. Not even the fingerprints found on the notes were his. So now that he had found the guy, he had to get the evidence they needed to put him out of commission for a long, long time. That meant biding his time and walking very carefully.

"Yes," Abel said. "Miles Bryant was my father. Why do you care?"

"Because I knew a Miles Bryant once. Tell me about him."

"What's to tell? He was career military, Special Forces. He was captured in Vietnam, spent time as a POW, and came home to die of complications of his wounds and the treatment he'd received."

"How'd he feel about that?"

"What is this? Twenty questions?" He didn't want to make this seem too easy to Doyle, who might become suspicious.

"Answer me, Pierce." He shifted the shotgun again.

Abel remained silent just long enough to make it clear that he didn't like this. Then he answered. "He hated the men he figured were responsible for leaving him to the enemy. He also always wondered who let word of the mission slip so that they were attacked when they arrived at their target. Somebody sold them out before they got there, and somebody sold him out after he was wounded. That's what he believed."

"And you? What do you believe?"

"That somebody is damn well going to pay for what happened to my father."

Doyle stood there staring at him, as if trying to decide what to make of him. "Was anybody with your dad when he was captured?"

"A guy by the name of Doyle."

"So that guy didn't sell him out?"

"Doyle? All I know is that this guy was wounded, just like my father. Maybe he was the one who talked about the operation and got them into all that trouble." That was a dangerous move, and Abel tensed in expectation of a blast from the gun.

But something about Doyle seemed to shrink a little. He didn't deny the accusation, and that seriously troubled Abel. All these years he had believed it must have been the young guy, Warren Roth, who had talked incautiously into the wrong ear before the mission. Could it have been Doyle? That would explain some of this madness, too. The man didn't want to leave anybody breathing who could accuse him of having breached security and jeopardized his comrades.

The hairs on the back of Abel's neck prickled as he realized that he might just have put himself on Doyle's list of enemies. Frantically he tried to think of a way to undo what he had just done.

But Doyle spoke then, as if he had discarded the accusation. "What are you up to?"

"Me? I don't see that it's any of your damn business, buster. Just who the hell are you?"

"The guy holding the gun. I wouldn't get difficult if I were you."

Abel was sitting on a log set on end, and he shifted his weight subtly until he was balanced to spring. Just in case. At the corner of his mind there flickered an image of blood on oily gray pavement. Not this time, he told himself. Nobody was going to die this time.

Doyle gestured with the gun barrel. "What are you up to around here?"

Abel figured he'd been as obstreperous as he dared for the moment. He needed to throw something out anyway, something that would draw this guy in a little further. "I'm researching a book."

"A book? About what?"

"About the guys who left my father to die in the jungle." Summoning all the anger he had felt as a child listening to his father talk of these events, he was able to snarl the words as angrily as Miles Bryant might have. "I'm going to ruin them!"

Doyle stared intently at him, then chuckled mirthlessly. "Ruin them? With a book? Get real, man. Nobody's even going to want to read it! Nobody cares about what happened then. Nobody."

"I do. So does Doyle's kid. The children of—"

Doyle interrupted him with a sharp exclamation. "What do you mean, 'Doyle's kid'? They're gone. Adopted out!"

"I found one of them. Hey, how do you know about that? Who the hell are you?" He took advantage of Doyle's astonishment to rise to his feet, but he was careful not to approach any closer, not with the shotgun pointed at him.

Doyle bared his teeth and pointed the gun right at Abel's stomach. "I'm Larry Doyle," he said. "What the hell do you know about my kids?"

Abel put up his hands in a placating gesture. "Don't get all bent, guy. I found one of your kids. Your daughter. She says she'd like to meet you."

Doyle shuddered as if a great wave of feeling ripped through him. "You're lying."

"I am not. Her name is Carlotta. Carlotta Nelms. She's married to a banker and has two small children, and she said she wishes they had a grandfather."

Doyle breathed a soft oath and closed his eyes for the merest instant. "You couldn't have found her. Even the State Department couldn't do that."

"I found her, all right. What I'd like to know is why the State Department said it couldn't. I have a sneaking suspicion that it had something to do with the fact that her adoptive father was a prominent diplomat."

Doyle swore savagely. "And my boy?"

"He was adopted by the same diplomat. His sister lost touch with him several years ago. I'm still trying to track him down."

"What was his name?"

"Andrew Eckhart."

"That was the diplomat's last name? Eckhart?"

Abel nodded, watching the man warily, trying to see any sign that this news would soften his resolve.

"Those men," Doyle said, "stole everything from me. My wife, my kids . . . my whole damn life! They're going to pay for it. They're going to pay the same price I did."

"What price is that?"

Doyle's eyes burned. "They're going to live with the loss of their families. They're going to have nothing at all left, just the way they left me!"

"You mean you're going to take them away from their families?" Abel shook his head. "There's no way on earth you can do that!"

"No, I'm going to kill them all. Wives, children . . . I'm going to take them away just the way mine got taken away!"

"That would be . . . foolish," Abel said bluntly. "In fact, it would be stupid."

Doyle glared. "Revenge isn't stupid."

"In this case it is. If you do what you're threatening, you won't ever get to be a grandfather to your daughter's children. Your family will disappear again, Doyle, but this time *you'll* be the cause of it!"

Doyle's face turned into a mask of fury, and before Abel could adequately dodge, he swung the shotgun around and pounded the younger man on the side of his head with the stock.

An explosion of pain filled Abel's head as he fell down a long, dark tunnel.

* * *

When he came to, he was bound hand and foot. At first he couldn't see anything at all and thought he must be blindfolded, but gradually he began to make out the ghostly shapes of shadows in the night and realized he was no longer in the shack.

His head throbbed violently, and his wrists and ankles were already sore from the ropes. How long had he been out?

The night was intense, suffocating in its darkness, and several minutes passed before he realized that the shadows he saw were the trunks of trees. Doyle must have dragged him out into the woods somewhere so that no one would find him.

The night was chilly. He shivered and wondered if hypothermia would kill him before morning. An ominous growl of thunder tumbled down the mountainside, reminding him that things could get worse. No lightning flickered, however, to illuminate his surroundings.

"Don't bother struggling." Doyle's voice came out of the night, a quiet threat. "The ropes will just get tighter if you do."

"Why are you doing this, Doyle? I didn't do a thing to you."

"Yeah, right." Doyle laughed quietly. "I saw you hanging out with Janet Tate."

"So?" Eyes closed, he battled a rising wave of nausea and silently begged Janet to forgive him. "She was just an easy way to get to her father."

"Come off it, Pierce! You were *living* with her. Tell me something I can believe."

"You can believe that. Her father didn't want to talk to me about what happened at the falls. I wasn't getting anywhere with the subject."

"Why would he talk about it? To let the world know what a despicable coward he is? Not Nathan Tate. Not Sheriff Almighty Tate who everyone thinks is so damn perfect. He knows he'd be ruined if word of what he really is got out in this county. That'd be the end of his long and illustrious career, I can tell you."

"Then let me go so I can write my book!"

Doyle laughed harshly. "Save your breath, Pierce. A ruined career doesn't come close to what they stole from me. Especially Tate. He was the senior man. He should have made sure they came back for me. We never left anybody behind. That was the tradition, man! Nobody gets left behind."

"Unless you can't find a piece of him to take back with you," Abel said quietly, abruptly changing tack. He was getting colder with each passing minute, and his shoulders ached miserably from having his arms bound so tightly behind him. With each movement he made, the rope bit more angrily into his wrists.

"Did they tell you that pile of horse manure?" Doyle asked. "Hell, we weren't even dead."

"But Warren Roth told them you'd been blown to bits."

"Yeah, right. Easy to blame someone who's dead."

"How'd you know he was dead?"

"I killed him."

That was almost enough to get the man convicted of murder, but considering that he wasn't going anywhere in the foreseeable future, Abel decided he had time to pursue further details. "He died in an accident."

"You have been busy, haven't you? Yeah, he died in an accident, all right. One I made happen. I shot out his tire. Got it on the first try. Not an easy thing to do."

For God's sake, Abel thought in disgust, the man was actually bragging about his prowess in killing another human being. He strained his icy fingers, trying to find a knot in the rope that he could begin to work with.

"Tell me about my daughter," Doyle said. "Why'd you hunt her up?"

"To round out the story," Abel lied. "So I could tell in her own words just what it cost because you were reported dead."

"She probably doesn't remember me at all."

"Actually, she does. Not real well, but she knows she had a father before Anton Eckhart. And she'd like him back in her life."

Doyle fell silent for a while, probably thinking about his daughter. Abel used the time to try to figure out what might be the key to ending this mess. He had been hoping that the mere discovery of Doyle's daughter would be enough to make the man change his mind, but it evidently wasn't making much difference at all. Too many years of bitterness and pain, perhaps, to be overcome so easily. But maybe there was another approach. He strained his brain cells trying to discover it.

Thunder rumbled again, a little closer now, it seemed. Abel didn't at all like the notion of lying on the ground helpless while a heavy storm pelted him. But then, he didn't at all like the notion of being helpless under any circumstances. He wiggled his fingers again, restoring circulation and seeking the elusive knot.

He wondered how Janet was doing in Oklahoma, wondered if she even thought of him. She had seemed pleased with the necklace, but what if she was only being polite? What if she really felt it was too extravagant? What if she had found the gesture tasteless?

But did any of that really matter? Whether she found him tasteless or anything else was insignificant beside the question of whether she wanted to see him again.

God, that frightened him even more than his current situation. Here he was, probably going to be dead before daylight, and the thing that scared him most was that he was scared to death that Janet Tate might never want to see him again.

Even stupider, he thought, was the way he was equally terrified that she *might* want to see him again. That she might feel even a little of what he was feeling. That he might have to take a chance.

Bullets were a hell of a lot less terrifying than the things that could happen to the human heart. Death was easy compared to losing someone you loved. Which was why he preferred not to love.

Lying there in the dark, half-expecting to have his throat slashed at any moment, he found his mind wandering over his past, testing all the hurts that had brought him to this point in his life, all the wounds that had made him into the man he had become. Perhaps if he had stayed in Okinawa he would have been a different person. He would have had his cousins nearby even when his father died. Even when his mother remarried. It wouldn't have felt as if his family had evaporated in the winds of time.

He would have had a stable place from which to weather all those changes. The way Janet Tate did. Even in the midst of what surely seemed like terrible upheavals in her life, she had the circle of her family's love to shelter her and provide a safety net. She was never *alone*. One way or another, Abel had felt alone all his life since the moment his dad had moved them from Okinawa to San Francisco.

But regardless of what had made him the way he was, the question became whether he was going to remain that way for the rest of his days. Or was he going to reach out past his protective walls and try to build the kind of life he truly wanted? Would he even live long enough to try?

Everything he had always believed without doubt had lately been called into question. It had started with his undercover work, which had obliged him to lie in order to achieve a good end. The ends justify the means? He had never believed so and was not sure even now that he would agree with that maxim, but that was how he had acted in his undercover work, and he had believed himself to be justified. So he had been forced to acknowledge that perhaps there were times when it was okay to lie. Times when it was okay to deliberately deceive.

That had troubled him and still did. As it troubled him that there were two sides to the story his father had told, that the men he had always believed to be without honor or scruple were men who were among the most honorable he had ever met. They could, perhaps, have acted better. But under the circumstances, they had done what they believed to be best. Could he continue to condemn them for that?

There was a rigid streak in his character that had made pondering these questions difficult. He didn't like that rigidity. It could be helpful at times, to be sure, but it could also blind him to things he needed to see. It could make him inflexible in his dealings with others. It could make it tough for him to reach out.

"Pierce?" Doyle's rough murmur reached through the night.

"Yeah?"

"You aren't lying about my daughter?"

"No."

"But you aren't really convinced that Parish, Laird and Tate are as bad as your dad said. You've bought their story about thinking we were dead."

Abel hesitated, wondering what the other man was getting at. It would be to everyone's advantage, he believed, if this man gave up his belief that there was no excuse for what had happened thirty years ago. "I'm . . . giving it some consideration, yes. It does make sense, Doyle. Tate says he had to get them out of there. They were under heavy attack, and when Roth reported that you and my father were dead, it would have been foolhardy to go back.''

''War is foolhardy.''

''It would have been different if you and my father had been alive.''

''You say that as if you believe it.''

''I'm beginning to.''

Doyle fell silent again. Thunder rumbled down the slope of the mountain, and Abel felt the fine mist of a rain on his cheeks.

''Tell you what, Pierce,'' Doyle said after a while. ''I'm going to test your idea.''

''Which idea? What do you mean?''

''You think they'd have come back if they'd known Bryant and I were alive.''

Abel hesitated, but only briefly. ''I'm beginning to, yes.''

''Well, I'm going to test that idea, Pierce. You damn well better hope you're right.''

Chapter 18

"I'm getting too damn old for this." Nathan Tate turned to look at his friends of more than thirty years. Micah Parish and Ransom Laird looked as tired as he felt after several days of keeping watch on the cabin where Deputy Sara Ironheart was impersonating Janet Tate. Crouching for hours in the woods while trying to remain silent and invisible was a task for younger men, or so Tate was thinking at this point.

And that damned Abel Pierce had disappeared, as well. He'd taken off for the mining camp on Saturday night, and no one had seen hide nor hair of him since. What the hell was he up to? Trying to track down Doyle on his own?

The three men were gathered around the desk in Tate's office, sipping coffee and eating eggs and bacon out of cardboard containers from Maude's Diner. Sara, as Janet, had come to town to run a few errands, leaving the cabin empty for several hours. It was an opportunity for Tate, Laird and Parish to take a breather, talk and eat a hot meal. Meanwhile, the house was being watched by other deputies and by Gage Dalton, the department's chief investigator. Gage was a man Nate would have trusted with his own life. If anyone approached that cabin, Gage would see it.

Micah spoke. "You're never too old to do what needs doing."

Nate tipped back his chair and scowled at him. "Maybe not you, you crusty old Injun. I've got a few years on you, though."

"And you've been out of shape longer."

Nate couldn't help it; he cracked a smile. "Too true."

Ransom smiled behind his golden beard. "I've got you both beat on that score. Steel legs. Indefatigable."

"Able to leap tall buildings," Micah agreed expressionlessly. "Faster than arrows."

"More powerful than a scooter," Nate added. All three chuckled and resumed eating. They were evading the issue, of course, which was that they still had no idea where Larry Doyle was or what he was up to, and that now Pierce had vanished, as well.

Ransom washed down some egg with a swig of coffee and looked at the other two. "What if Pierce has been working with Doyle all along?"

Nate had begun to wonder the same thing, and it didn't sit well with him. He'd been watching his daughter closely enough to know that she was getting involved with the man, and he himself was coming to like Pierce. Nothing about Pierce would have led Nate to believe the man was capable of this kind of duplicity. Stupid, when you thought about how Abel had been working undercover for years. Maybe this was just another undercover job to him.

The thought gave him heartburn.

"I wouldn't have marked him as that kind of man," Micah said. His dark eyes remained impassive.

"Neither would I," Nate agreed. "But let's face it—this guy makes his living as an undercover cop. If he sees the three of us as bad guys . . . well, you fill in the blanks."

Pierce had a strict code of conduct, a rigid moral backbone. Such a thing was good unless it got misdirected, then it could be hell to deal with.

"Sheriff?" Dave Winters knocked on the door and stuck his head in. "I found this under the wiper on your Blazer a minute ago. I thought you'd better see it."

Nate took the folded scrap of paper and opened it up.

I have Pierce. If you want to see him alive, you'll have to come get him. Alone.

Nate saw red. It was more than a man could bear to realize that Larry Doyle had been a few feet away sometime in the last hour. That the man had boldly come into town and slapped a piece of paper on the sheriff's windshield.

But that was what Doyle wanted, he reminded himself. To get them to act foolishly so he could get his revenge.

"What is it?" Ransom asked.

Nate tossed the paper to him. "It's begun. The only question now is just how Pierce is involved in this."

Abel figured he was probably going to die in a few hours, so he decided to use his time by thinking over past mistakes and figuring out how he could have done better. Wasn't that what you were supposed to do in the hours before your death? Besides, thinking about the past kept him calm, and his calm was driving Larry Doyle nuts. Other than a couple of hours early this morning when Doyle had completely disappeared, the man didn't dare wander too far away, for fear his victim was up to something.

Which was how Abel wanted it for the moment. He didn't want Doyle to wander off and leave him here to starve to death. When he figured out how to escape his bonds, it wouldn't matter anymore, but right now he wanted to be able to get a drink of water from time to time...and so far Doyle hadn't yet denied it to him.

What he didn't want to think about was whether Micah Parish, Ransom Laird and Nathan Tate would come to his rescue. He had begun to believe they were honorable men, to truly credit that they would have returned for his father had they known Miles Bryant was alive. But now that his own skin was on the line, a lifetime of doubts reared their very ugly heads. Why should any of those men put his neck in a noose to rescue someone he hardly knew?

Tough question. No answer.

So he figured he was going to die. He was rather surprised to discover how detached he felt from the idea. Had his life become so meaningless that he couldn't even work up a little concern that it might be over?

No. His problem was one of weariness. No matter how hard he tried, he couldn't remember a time in his life when he had felt he wasn't struggling against himself. Struggling to be honorable when he didn't feel like it, when no one else was being honorable and all that honor was getting him was a big black eye and a dump truck load of problems. Tired of fighting his desire for home and family, tired of fighting his need to be loved, because he knew damn well nobody could love him for long and he would just wind up hurt.

Hell, he sounded like a four-year-old.

But maybe his tiredness came from something else. Maybe he felt that he was at last about to get his due. Deep down inside him was the furtive feeling that *he* should have died in that shootout, not Delia Burke. Survivor guilt. It was a hell of a difficult thing to live with, and he was *very* tired of it. Guilt and common sense warred incessantly in him, and even when he managed to put the event out of his conscious mind, his brain would send up those sudden visual flashes of her blood on that oily gray pavement. Somehow that had fixed in his mind, the way that pavement had been oil-smeared. Dirty. It struck him as obscene, one of the most obscene things he had ever seen, as if life itself had somehow been defiled.

He chose now to remember that night and every detail of the events leading up to Delia Burke's death. It was an atonement of sorts, the only atonement he could offer.

There had been no warning that she was coming. That anyone was coming. Abel had been there pretending to be one of the street thugs with whom the cops were discussing an arrangement. His attention had been fully focused on trying to overhear every word that was said so that he could record it later and report it to his superiors. Maybe he hadn't been paying enough attention to other things.

No, he thought now, that wasn't true. He was blaming himself when there was no blame. Something had alerted Officer Burke to the presence of people in the warehouse. She had come quietly and stealthily, and it was only her misfortune that one of the cops had spotted her first. Even if he had heard her coming, Abel would have been unable to prevent what had happened then. Once the cops had seen another cop, one who could recognize them, they would have stopped at nothing less than killing her.

Before he had seen her himself, before he had been aware of anything except that something vital had gone wrong, before Burke herself had even made sense of the scene in front of her, one of the bad cops had leveled an automatic weapon at Burke and blown her away.

Red, red blood on oily gray pavement and blue eyes that would never see the sky again.

He was not to blame, and there hadn't been a thing he could do, and yet Abel still felt guilty. Guilty for being a survivor, guilty for not having done something anyway, guilty for having walked away from her body as if he had indeed been the thug he was pretending to be. It had been the only wise choice, but it still bothered him.

A death should be acknowledged. Someone's passing deserved more attention than a quick look over the shoulder.

And he wondered if his would get even that much.

Nearly a week after she had left Wyoming, Janet received a phone call from Darlene. Her dad had been calling her mom every day and passing along news, but she hadn't been able to escape the feeling that she wasn't hearing everything. Darlene confirmed her suspicions.

"I'm not supposed to be telling you any of this, Jan. I'm kind of surprised Seth told *me* and he'll probably never forgive me for telling you."

"Then don't tell me." Boy, wasn't that hard to say? Every inch of her was straining with impatient curiosity and not a little fear, but she didn't want to ruin Seth and Darlene's budding relationship.

"It doesn't matter," Darlene said. "He's leaving in a few days anyway, and I'll never see him again. Besides, there's no reason on earth why you shouldn't know about this, and if he thinks I'm a brainless twit who'll just follow orders, he's sadly mistaken!"

A Conard County Reckoning

Janet, with difficulty, refrained from begging her friend to just come to the point. "You're forgetting Seth is a SEAL. Following orders is second nature."

"Well, I'm not a SEAL. I've never even worn a uniform—"

"What about Scouts in third grade? Or being a candy-striper at the hospital in high school?"

"Janet, for heaven's sake!" But Darlene laughed in spite of herself. "It's awful having a friend who's known you your whole life!"

"It's awful having a friend who's bursting with news but not getting to the point."

"Oops." Darlene sobered immediately. "Okay, grab a chair. Here's the scoop. It seems Abel has been kidnapped by that Doyle guy everyone thinks is behind the things that have been happening to you."

"What?" The shock was so sudden, so unexpected that for a few seconds she felt faint. Her vision narrowed and there was a buzzing in her ears.

"He's been kidnapped. Actually, at this point there's some speculation that Abel may be in this mess with Doyle."

"But why? Abel would never—" She broke off, realizing that she was talking from her heart, not from her head. Her head realized she didn't truly know him well enough to say such things.

"I don't think Abel would, either, Jan. I really don't. I realize that none of us knows him well enough to be sure of that, but . . . I get the feeling he wouldn't participate in the kind of thing Doyle is attempting to do."

"I don't either, Dar. I just can't believe Abel would hurt innocent children!" And that was something she believed with all her heart. Nor, despite the cautious reminders of her brain, could she really believe that Abel would take revenge in this fashion. If he wanted to get even, he would do it face-to-face. Even his supposed book, according to him, was nothing but an excuse to meet the men involved. "But does anyone know why Doyle would have kidnapped him?"

"Yep. This is where it gets interesting. Doyle left your dad a note telling him that if he wanted to see Abel alive, he'd better come up to the old mining town—alone."

"Oh, my God." Fear gripped her so sharply that she could scarcely breathe. In the next room she heard her mother's voice and warned herself to keep her own voice down, keep it quiet. She didn't want her mother to find out about this. "Dad's going to do it." It wasn't a question. She knew her father.

"That's my impression. They're trying to work out a way that Seth and Micah can shadow him and protect him, but he'll probably go even if they can't."

"He will. He'll go." Abel kidnapped and her father walking into the maw of a deadly trap. Something inside her squeezed tight with dread, so tight she didn't know if she could bear it.

Abel. Abel might already be dead. There was really no reason for Doyle to keep him alive. Oh, God, she didn't think she could bear it.

Her hand tightened on the phone until it hurt. "I'm going to fly back up, Dar."

"Janet, no! Good heavens, Seth and your dad will have my skin for this! You stay there. With Emily. Janet, you can't be thinking of bringing Emily back up here?"

Never in her life had Janet felt so torn in two. Abel was in dire danger, her father soon would be, and she needed to be there. Needed to know that if there was something she could do, she would be there to do it. But Emily... She couldn't take her daughter with her, and leaving her behind seemed impossible. How could she bear to be parted from her? And what about what she owed her daughter? Was she being a good mother if she left and went to take chances with her own life? Who would care for Emily if she died?

Her mother. Her sisters. Emily would never want for a good home and plenty of love.

But Abel . . . Oh, God, it hurt so badly to think of never seeing him again! She didn't know if he cared two figs about her or ever would—even the weight of the beautiful necklace she wore every day didn't assure her that he saw her as someone special. She needed him to say it, needed it so desperately. What if he never did? What if he died and was lost to her forever? But was there anything at all she could do about it if she went up there? Probably not.

"No, Dar," she said finally, her voice thick with tears. "Don't worry about it."

"You're sure? I'd never forgive myself if you came back and got hurt."

"Don't worry about it. Just keep me posted, hmm?"

"Believe it. I know how angry I'd be if I were you and people were keeping me in the dark."

They talked for a little while about Darlene's brothers and her father, then said good-night. Turning, Janet found that her mother was standing there, watching her with love and sympathy. She must have heard most of the conversation.

"Mom—" Her voice broke, and she couldn't continue.

"It's okay, hon." Marge's arms closed snugly around her daughter, and Janet's face fell to her shoulder, soaking it with tears. "Sometimes a woman's lot is the hardest on earth. Men don't always understand that, but believe me, I spent years waiting for your father to come home, and I know. It's harder to wait and hope and pray while knowing nothing than it is to be in the thick of things facing all the danger."

"Then why don't we get into the thick of it?"

"Because we have babies who need us. Someone has to care for the children."

Another scalding tear ran down Janet's cheek as she silently acknowledged that her mother was right: someone had to care for the children.

Abel's throat was parched. Hours ago, Doyle had rebound him in chains and wrist shackles, saying he didn't want Abel to be able to work his way free. Then he had gone off somewhere and hadn't returned. He'd been gone too long. Something must be up. Overhead, the sky was a deep blue, and against it the tops of the trees looked dark and brooding. Chained and manacled as he was, he didn't have a whole lot of hope that he could get out of here on his own.

Since Doyle hadn't come back in a while, though, he had begun trying to slip the shackles off his wrists. Abel figured the man must have picked up these items in Central America or some other place on his travels, because he sure hadn't ever seen anything like this except in a Hollywood film.

As any cop knew, if the cuffs weren't adjusted just right, a determined person could slip them off, because a hand could be made almost as small as a wrist. But "almost" was the key word here, and he didn't seem to be succeeding. He took a break for a while, not wanting to try so hard that he caused his hands to swell, which would make it impossible to get off the manacles.

Abel was getting dehydrated; he couldn't even rustle up any saliva to swallow anymore. This mountain air was as dry as a bone, speeding up the process. There wasn't a whole lot of time left to dawdle.

Doyle's absence must mean he was expecting something to happen at last. Abel himself felt contradictorily convinced that Tate would show up in an attempt to free him and that the sheriff wouldn't bother. Why should he? Miles Bryant's complaints about Nathan Tate were as vivid in Abel's mind as they had been years ago, when his father had first engraved them there. Like mocking little demons, they kept resurfacing to remind him that there had been a time when Nathan Tate had not come to save a comrade.

And Abel wasn't even his comrade. Just an acquaintance who Tate probably didn't care much about one way or the other.

Then, of course, there was also the possibility that Tate would decide Abel was involved in this with Doyle. It was sure a possibility that would have occurred to *him* if he'd been in Tate's shoes.

So there were a number of reasons why Tate should refuse to come, and Abel found all of them perfectly reasonable. The only reason the man should stick his neck out was because of the kind of high-minded ideals folks didn't feel comfortable talking about anymore, things like honor and duty. They were the very things that propelled Abel Pierce through his days, but he had long ago learned that he was in rare company.

If the price wasn't potentially so high to both him and Tate, he would have been interested in seeing the outcome. As it stood, however, he wanted to get his wrists out of these manacles and get back down to his car at the mining camp so he could get to Tate before anything bad happened.

Finally, deciding that he was never going to get free this way, he grabbed the right manacle with his left hand and held it tightly. Then, gritting his teeth, determined to break loose even if it meant breaking his hand, he tucked his thumb into his palm and yanked.

He left a layer of skin behind on the edge of the cuff, but his hand was out. Not giving himself the chance to think about it, he grabbed the left cuff and yanked. Free. In agony from lost skin and what felt like a dislocation of one thumb, but free.

He gave himself a moment, practicing some of the meditation his uncle had taught him so long ago, clearing his head and preparing himself for action. Then he grabbed the dislocated thumb and yanked it back into place. Only sheer determination kept him from letting out a howl. The shrieking pain of displacement gave way to a throbbing pain at the base of his thumb. He didn't think it was going to be a whole lot of use to him for a while.

Then he rose to his feet, ignoring the numbness of long inactivity, and slipped away as quietly as he could into the forest depths toward the sound of running water.

He had a pretty good idea where he was. Through the treetops he could see a dike of volcanic rock that had weathered until the top of it looked like a mitten. That landmark had guided him on more than one hike through these woods.

At stream's edge, he knelt and drank the cold, clear water. Not only did it soothe his cracked mouth and throat, but in a relatively short time it energized him. Then, determined to prevent disaster, he began to trot downhill toward the mining camp.

Nathan Tate pulled his Blazer into the mining camp and parked it. He fully expected to have to wait, possibly for quite a while. It would have surprised him if Doyle hadn't chosen to exercise such a display of power, puny as it was.

The first note about Pierce had been followed by another, more specific one, setting the time and place. Doyle had allowed for the fact that Tate might not find the note right away, tucked as it was under the wiper of Marge's car. Nate didn't know if he'd found it right away, but he'd certainly found it soon enough to give him time to plan this escapade.

He found himself remembering what Pierce had said about Doyle having mixed feelings about what he was doing. That would certainly explain the lead time built into the note.

Uneasily aware that he was a clear target for a well-aimed bullet, Nate climbed out of the Blazer and began to stroll around the ghost town. Somewhere farther out from here, Micah, Ransom and Seth were all slowly converging on this location, sweeping the woods as they went for any sign of Abel Pierce. The theory was that they would arrive shortly and hold back until the situation had been assessed.

Hell, they might all be out there right now, keeping an eye on him from various vantages . . . which would explain the feeling he had that someone was watching him.

A crow's caw caught his attention. He wondered if that was Micah, letting him know he was there. No other sound, save the whisper of the wind in the treetops. Must have been the real thing and not Micah after all.

It was a risk to bring the three other men in this way. Doyle had been absolutely clear in his command that Nate come alone. On the other hand, he wouldn't expect Nate to obey and would be on the lookout for the others. That could lead to some messy problems if Doyle found any of the three men lurking out there.

But Nate knew Micah and Ransom and their skills, and he suspected that his son was every bit as good. Ransom was rusty, but not so rusty that he couldn't remember how to move silently and hide himself. Micah had kept his skills honed to a fine point. If anyone could secrete themselves out there and not be found by Doyle, it was these three. Even in Vietnam, when they'd all been at the top of their forms, Doyle hadn't been as good at this kind of thing as either Micah or Ransom.

And tucked in his pocket was a piece of information that had come from Roger Vaillancourt in Los Angeles just today. It solved the mystery of who had breached security and talked about the mission beforehand. Abel Pierce had a good friend in Vaillancourt. It made Nate feel a whole lot better about Pierce.

The ghost town remained silent. Wandering through its ruins, Nate found himself thinking about the people who had settled up here, hoping for wealth and the fulfillment of their every dream. It was mind-boggling, the amount of work that had gone into mining in days when the only help a man had was his own back and a mule.

The derricks, weathered dark gray, still loomed like strange skeletons. The pulleys that hung from them were rusted past use, and the ropes and chains that had hung there were long since gone. Beside each mine head were the piles of tailings, testament to man's fortitude and determination. All of that had been brought out of the ground by men.

The shacks themselves were generally just a single room with one or two windows and a fireplace. A couple of them boasted two rooms. Large families, perhaps, or businesses of some kind? It would be impossible to know now. This little town had lasted only a short time, and as far as he knew, no one had ever photographed it.

Until Janet, his sweet little girl, had become fascinated with the camp. She must have several thousand photos of this place, in black and white, in color, showing all the moods and seasons of the town. Through the eyes of her camera he had seen more life than he ever would have ascribed to a few tumble-down shacks on the side of a mountain. The collection of sagging buildings and collapsed chimneys had a personality of its own, changing moods and colors as vividly as any woman he had ever known. Without moving at all, without breathing or seeing, this place *lived*.

And he was damn well going to see that Janet got her photos published someday, even if he had to pay for it himself. She had captured something with her patience and fascination that most people never took the time to notice.

She also loved Abel Pierce. Nate had seen it in her eyes more than once. He didn't know how he felt about that, but he didn't suppose anyone was going to ask him.

"Tate!"

The shout brought Nate around, the back of his neck prickling uneasily. Doyle had found him.

Abel was out of breath from running in the high altitude. Even the weeks he had spent adjusting hadn't quite prepared him for the combination of thin oxygen, dry air and all-out exertion. He was parched again and finally had to pause to down more water from the stream.

As soon as he'd slaked his thirst, taking care not to drink so much of the frigid water that he would make his stomach hurt, he began running as fast as he could over the rugged ground toward the camp. He might already be too late to prevent trouble, but that wasn't something he was prepared to bet on. If he could get out of here and let Nate know he was free and alive, then Doyle would have lost his bargaining chip.

It struck him then, as he tore down the mountainside and tried not to sprain an ankle or break a leg, that he believed Tate would come for him. That Tate would do exactly what Miles Bryant had accused him of failing to do so many years ago.

And Abel Pierce, for the first time in his life, was actually trusting someone to put his neck in the wringer for him. It felt like shedding the layers of an iron coat. Like shedding some dark, scaly thing that had been clinging to him forever. He felt lighter and freer in some important internal way.

He also found himself wondering just exactly what was going to happen when Doyle found out that Tate *would* walk straight into a trap and put his life on the line for someone else. How would Doyle cope with the destruction of the anger and hatred that had driven him for so many years?

A familiar landmark warned him that he was getting very near to the mining town. He slowed down immediately, shifting to a quieter stride, in case this was where Doyle was waiting to trap Nate. It would sure be the likeliest rendezvous.

Just as he was getting close enough to make out the buildings through the trees, someone seized him from behind and clapped a hand over his mouth. Wild thoughts ran through his head, mostly about the most effective way to break the hold his assailant had on him. Then a familiar voice said, "Don't make a sound. It's me, Seth."

Abel gave a quick nod of his head, and Seth released him.

"You're getting rusty, Pierce," the younger man said sotto voce. "I could hear you coming for the last three minutes."

"Too much time pounding city streets. What's happening?"

"Not sure yet. Dad's talking to Doyle, and we're trying to close in on him without warning him we're nearby, so he can't slip away. Of course, a lot of that had to do with being worried about *you*. Now that you're here..."

"You don't want to startle him anyway. It might put your dad at risk."

"That too."

Since he evidently sounded like a herd of elephants crashing through the brush, Abel followed Seth's lead, moving very slowly and cautiously closer to the town. They split up by the outskirt. He could hear Tate's voice now, and when he peered around a tree, he could see the sheriff standing in the open, near the edge of town.

Tate called out to Doyle, "I'd've come for you if I'd had even the least inkling you and Bryant were still alive. I'd never have left without you."

"That's easy to say," Doyle responded. His voice sounded as if it were coming from everywhere, and Abel wondered if that was a trick of the woods, or if Doyle had somehow arranged to rig a sound system that would send his voice from several places at once. No, it couldn't be that. He wasn't hearing the echo effect that would occur when he wasn't equidistant from all the speakers. It must be a trick of the buildings and trees.

"Sure it's easy to say," Tate answered. "I'm standing here like the target on a firing range for no better reason than that you've got a hostage. Seems like I'd've been as willing to come for you as I am to come for Pierce."

"The danger was greater then."

"A man can only die once."

"No, Tate. He can die more than once. He can die every damn day of his life! You don't have any damn idea what it feels like to wake up every morning in a POW camp not knowing whether you'll be dead or maimed by nightfall. All I had to think about was my wife. My kids. They were the only thing that kept me going! I *lived* for them. Then I get out and discover they're gone. Gone! All because I was reported dead. I've been wishing I *was* dead ever since."

"I probably would, too."

"Not a day goes by that I don't think about them, Tate. Not a day. You might as well have put a bullet between my eyes that day at the falls. I wish somebody had."

"I wish I'd known that Roth wasn't telling the truth."

"You shouldn't have listened to him. He was just a scared kid."

"Maybe you're right."

Abel shifted closer, scanning the woods for any sign of Doyle. Just a flicker of movement was all it would take to betray his whereabouts.

"I *know* I'm right," Doyle argued. "Damn it, Tate, you should have questioned him more closely!"

"Now wait one hairy minute, Doyle! You weren't there. You don't know what kind of fire we were under. What was I supposed to do? Make him take an oath and cross-examine him at length? There wasn't *time.*"

Pierce brushed the raw back of one hand against something and sucked in a sharp breath as fire seemed to burn him. It was beginning to occur to him where Doyle might be. The only question was, what was the best way to handle it?

He listened intently, but Doyle had fallen silent, apparently troubled by what Tate had said. Until the man spoke again, there was little chance of locating him. Maybe Doyle was moving to a new position in order to confuse anyone who might have located him by his voice?

Finally Tate spoke again. "We found your daughter, Doyle. You could have a relationship with her, you know. She wants to see you."

"Too late for that," came the answer. "I'm in too deep now."

"Something could be worked out," Tate suggested. "Chances are, you could get a suspended sentence, since you don't have a record. I have some influence with the prosecutor."

There. Abel saw him, just a glimpse of movement at the window of a shack. He was in the town, hiding in a building, as Abel had suspected. The shack he was in acted as an amplifier and helped confuse everyone as to where his voice was coming from.

He had to slip around behind the building where Doyle was hiding, but he was no longer as worried about any noise he might make now that he didn't have to worry about Doyle hearing him and coming up on him from behind.

Moving to the left, he circled the town, keeping within the trees. Nate continued talking about how he was sure he could work out some kind of deal as long as Abel was okay. Hearing that, Abel felt another internal settling as he recovered more of the trust his father had deprived him of. Even now, Nate Tate was bargaining for his safe return. Risking angering or frightening Doyle into taking some rash action that might cost Nate his own life.

This man, Abel realized with absolute conviction, had not left Miles Bryant behind knowing he was still alive. This man would never do such a thing.

A few more feet and he would be at the door of the shack. He moved even more quietly now, wondering where the others were, whether they could see what he was doing and understand it. Or did they think he was going to the aid of Doyle?

His back prickled between his shoulder blades as he considered what an easy target he would make for Parish, Laird or Seth Hardin if one of them decided he was a threat. Damn, he was moving in plain sight in broad daylight.

But no bullet pierced his back, and he reached the door of the shack. Doyle was hollering something to Nate about how nobody could promise anything and his life was ruined anyway.

Abel felt a lot of sympathy for that last complaint. A whole lot. The man had lost everything, and it couldn't be patched up thirty years later, not even with a daughter and two grandchildren. But that was sure as hell no reason to get suicidal. Where there's life, there's hope, Roger always said. Roger had a boatload of maxims for every occasion....

Abel wheeled around the door, into the shack, and dived at Larry Doyle, catching him around the knees in a perfect football tackle before the man could do more than turn his head in astonishment.

Doyle was good, but he was almost fifty, and Abel had him under control in next to no time. He put Doyle facedown, his knee in the middle of the man's back, holding him where he was. Then he called out for Nate.

"I got him, Sheriff! We're two buildings behind you, slightly to your right."

Tate was there thirty seconds later, taking in the scene with a practiced eye. It took him only a moment to handcuff Doyle.

"I thought you were being held hostage," Nate said to the younger man.

"I was." Abel looked at his raw wrists and hands. "You know, this hurts like hell. Remind me never to get skinned alive."

It was as if a great bubble of tension burst, and Nate started to laugh.

Chapter 19

"**I**'m going to pick up Janet at the airport," Seth said to Abel as they came out of the sheriff's office two days later. Sam Haversham, the prosecutor, had agreed to a plea bargain in the Doyle case that would require Doyle to get psychiatric help in exchange for a suspended sentence. Everyone was pretty sure Judge Williams would agree. The murder of Warren Roth in Florida, though, was going to get him some hard time.

It was fair, Abel thought. He didn't approve of anything Doyle had done—and when he thought of the scare the man had given Janet, it made him mad enough to want to kill—but the truth was that Doyle was a tortured man, and he was no longer a threat.

"How come *you're* going to pick up Janet?" Abel asked. "I thought you had to head back to Virginia." The rest of the families had come back on an earlier flight, but little Emily had been acting colicky the past few days, and Janet had wanted to wait until she settled down. Abel figured those couple of days had lasted at least two eternities.

"Not for another week. I got my leave extended."

"Ah." Abel gave him a sidelong look. "Wouldn't it make more sense for me to pick up Janet and Emily so you can have more time with Darlene?"

"Darlene?" Seth pretended surprise but was betrayed by a faint flush of color. "What do you mean?"

"Well . . ." Abel hesitated, trying to determine the best tack to take. Fact was, he knew it would please Janet to no end if he could get Seth and Darlene together. He just didn't have any matchmaking experience. "I kind of thought she was sweet on you."

"Me? Nope." Seth dismissed the whole idea. "She's not crazy."

"What does that mean? Why should she be crazy?"

"I'm a SEAL. That's not very good husband material."

"Why the hell not?"

"Because I'm gone so much. Because I'm a cocky, arrogant son-of-a-gun who's used to having his own way and who gets wound up tighter than a spring if he's inactive for too long. I can get downright ornery."

"I never met anyone who couldn't. So, what you're saying is you're a man."

"I'm a trained killing machine!"

"I guess you could look at it that way. Do you kill women when you make love to them?"

Seth looked momentarily startled, then broke into a laugh. "That was underhanded, Abel!"

"Smarter than what you're saying, though. Why don't you ask Darlene what *she* thinks of life as a navy wife? She'd be the one who has to live it, so don't you think she should be the one to decide if she can or not?"

"I don't have the right to ask that of anyone. Do you realize how much hardship is involved? She'd be alone for months on end, having to deal with every single thing that comes along without any help whatever. And if there were children . . ."

"Women make it as navy wives all the time," Abel replied with a shrug. "I've known some. They're pretty special, to be sure, but they're out there. Darlene strikes me as the type who could probably do it. Just look at her, Seth. She gave up everything to come home and take care of her father and her younger brothers. If that doesn't require backbone, I don't know what does. So just ask her."

Seth stood at the curb, looking out over the courthouse square. Flowers blossomed in a riot of color in the carefully laid out flower beds, and the park benches were occupied by old men and young women with children, all of them enjoying the perfect day. "I'll think about it," he said finally. "While I go get Janet."

"I'll go get Janet," Abel insisted. "And tell your folks she may not be home tonight."

Seth shot him a sharp look, then grinned. "So you have an ulterior motive?"

"Damn straight. Now go find Darlene."

"I'll think about it."

A light, feminine voice intruded from behind them. "Why don't you just ask me right now, Seth?"

Both men turned to find Darlene on the sidewalk behind them. In her hand she held a bag from the dress shop up the street. Seth colored to the roots of his dark hair, and all of a sudden he didn't look at all like the killing machine he believed himself to be. In fact, he suddenly looked too young to be a SEAL. "You heard?"

"Enough of it," she said. There was a faint smile around her mouth and a wistful look in her brilliant blue eyes. "Is that your only reason for not asking me, Seth? That it might be too hard on me?"

He hesitated, as if he wanted to tell her there were a million reasons, but in the end he simply nodded. "That's it. It's not fair."

"What if I happen to think it is?"

Abel turned then, striding away to his truck. He knew exactly how this one was going to come out. Now all he wanted to know was how his own life was going to turn out.

The plane landed just as the sunset was painting the sky in brilliant streamers of red and orange. Abel waited, more impatient than he had ever been in his entire life. It seemed to take forever for the passengers to disembark, and he began to get edgy when Janet and Emily weren't among the first to appear.

But then she was there, a beautiful redhead in gray chinos and a turquoise blouse…and the necklace he had given her. His throat seemed to lock tight when he saw it, as if some part of him recognized that it was a symbol.

Her moss green eyes found him and lighted with surprised delight. Her soft lips formed his name, though he couldn't hear her over all the noise of other passengers greeting family and friends.

And then she was there, before him, Emily held snugly in her arm, a diaper bag over her shoulder, the baby seat in her hand.

He reached out, sure he must have the stupidest smile on his face, and took the diaper bag and the car seat from her. He wanted to take Emily. He wanted to take Janet. Things that had been locked up inside him for nearly his entire life were bursting to be free with a youthful eagerness that left him feeling utterly awkward.

"Hi," he said, feeling like a green fool.

"Hi," she replied, looking shy and happy. "Are you the reception committee?"

"The only one." At last, taking the biggest risk he'd ever taken in his entire life, he bent and kissed her gently on the mouth.

And suddenly it was all right. Everything was all right. Where before he had felt awkward and uncertain, he now felt confident and sure. Her lips were like a blessing to his troubled soul and a siren song to his heart.

When he lifted his head, she was smiling softly, and Emily was watching them both with her deep blue baby eyes.

Her luggage was a simple matter, just one bag to be claimed. The truck wasn't far from the terminal, and in a space of time that seemed endless and short all at once, they were finally there, locked inside, alone together.

Abel paused before starting the engine, then turned to her. "What would you say if I didn't take you back tonight?"

Her eyes widened, and she looked instinctively at Emily, buckled into her seat between them. "What do you mean?"

"What would you say if I kidnapped you and took you to the finest motel in this burg for the night?"

The corners of her mouth twitched and lifted. "What do you think I'd say?"

"I realize you can't...that we can't...that it's too soon, but I...I really need to be alone with you, Janet. To talk to you. I—I've missed you."

Her face softened into an expression of longing. "I've missed you, too."

"Then we can take this night for ourselves?"

She nodded.

He felt as if he'd just won the jackpot at Vegas.

"I need to go to the store and get some diapers, though," she told him as they pulled away from the airport. "I hadn't planned on being here overnight."

"I'll go out and get them while you and Emily are settling in at the motel."

When he braked in front of the motel office, he turned to Janet once again. She had agreed to give him the time, but it suddenly occurred to him that he might be forcing an intimacy on her that she didn't want. After all, they had only had one night together as lovers. "One room or two?" he asked.

"We hardly know each other." She smiled as she said it, and there seemed to be a joking note in her voice, but he decided it wouldn't be wise to make assumptions. Not now.

"Two rooms it is...." He started to climb out, feeling hurt because she felt they were still strangers, when her touch on his arm caused him to freeze.

"I was teasing," she said quietly. "Though Emily gets fussy during the night, and I don't want your sleep to be disturbed."

Slowly he turned his head and looked straight at her. "I don't mind."

The smile she gave him then could have lit up the night sky.

He had missed her. Janet hugged the knowledge to herself as she changed Emily and then settled down to nurse. Abel had gone out to get the diapers as promised, leaving her these quiet minutes to gather her scattered thoughts and emotions. She had half expected never to see him again; she had certainly never dreamed that he would come to meet her at the airport. The sight of him had blown everything else out of her mind, leaving her in a state not far from dithering.

He had wanted to spend tonight with her and had made it clear that it was not for sex. That made her feel good in ways she couldn't begin to put into words. For the first time in her life, a lover was telling her that *she* mattered to him, not her body. That it was her company he wanted, not her lovemaking.

That was the most special thing any man had ever told her. Looking down at her daughter's small face, she blinked back tears and tried to tell herself not to put too much importance on it. After all, he might just be getting ready to tell her that he wouldn't see her again and was gentleman enough to do it in person. It didn't necessarily *mean* anything.

Abel returned while she was still nursing. A receiving blanket preserved her modesty, but she was still a little unnerved when he sat on the edge of one of the two double beds and simply stared at her.

"Is something wrong?" she asked finally.

He shook his head. "I just suddenly realized that I don't think I've ever seen anything more beautiful."

Color stained her cheeks, and she had to look down.

"You know," he said presently, "we got together in kind of a funny way. Hell, we even made love before we had a date. We still haven't had one . . . although, if you'd like, after you finish feeding Emily, I want to take us out for a late dinner. Maybe we could call *that* a date."

She felt herself smiling but kept her gaze fixed on Emily. She didn't dare believe what she thought she might be hearing.

"If I'd met you in L.A.," he was saying, "I'd have asked you out at least six or seven times by now. I'd know if you like to play baseball, or if you watch football. We'd have talked about museums—I kinda like them myself—and what kind of books we read, and what our politics are . . . oh, hell. What I'm trying to get at is that we don't know each other in the usual ways."

And here it comes, Janet thought. The coup de grace. He was going to tell her that they had nothing at all in common. That what they had shared had been a simple human reaction to the danger they had faced, and that, nice as it had been, it was meaningless.

"There are a lot of reasons," Abel continued, "why wiser heads would probably tell me not to make too much out of this. But the truth is, Janet, I'm crazy about you. I'm head over heels for you. I don't think I want to face the rest of my life without you in it. You and Emily. I don't care that we're practically strangers. If it concerns you, I'll spend the next year rectifying that. What I feel—"

He broke off and shook his head. "It's all clichés. But what I feel isn't a cliché. It's as if—as if something inside me is connected to something inside you, and if the bond were to be broken..." He shook his head again, frustrated in his search for words. "It doesn't have to make sense to the head. It makes sense in here." He pointed to his chest.

She was looking at him now, and the tears were no longer prickling in her eyes, they were running down her cheeks. Emotion filled her, so intense that she could barely breathe, let alone speak. She drew a ragged breath.

"Oh, God, don't cry," Abel said. "I don't want to make you cry. I'll get lost if that's what you want. I can understand that you might feel I'm sort of crowding you. And you certainly wouldn't want to come back to L.A. with me. Why would you, when you live in this beautiful place—"

"Will you stop it?" she managed to interrupt him finally. "Abel, don't."

He looked wounded. His shoulders remained square, and nothing in his face changed, except that something about his eyes conveyed intolerable pain. Oh, heavens, he had misunderstood! She tried again, words tumbling from her throat. "It's crazy, but I love you, too. And of course I'll go to L.A. with you...." A sob choked her.

"You will?" His whole face began to lighten. "You really will?"

"I think so. It's just..." She hesitated, but she needed to express her one serious concern. "Are you sure...are you absolutely sure that it's not just Emily you want? I mean, you were so interested in my pregnancy, and after what happened with your girlfriend..."

"Good God, no!" he said with sudden vehemence. "I like Emily. I'm sure I'm going to love her to pieces, but I'm not fool enough to ask a woman to marry me because I like her *baby*. If

I need a kid that badly, I'm pretty sure I can make one of my own. Will you, Janet?''

"Will I what?''

"Marry me? Come to L.A. with me?''

Everything inside her hushed, as if the universe had stilled in recognition of the momentousness of what was happening. "My home is with you, Abel,'' she said quietly. It was the rightest and truest thing she had ever said in her life.

They never did get out to dinner. Abel ordered up pizza, and they ate on the bed while Emily slept nearby. When the baby fussed, it was already a toss-up which of them would be first to lift her and snuggle her close.

Janet found she liked that, that she didn't feel at all threatened by his interest in Emily. It was nice, in fact, to watch Abel grow steadily more besotted with the infant.

"I got Emily a new teddy bear,'' he said. "I think she'll like it.''

"I'm sure she will.''

"There's one thing…'' He hesitated and reached out to take Janet's hand. "What about Emily's father? Shouldn't he be part of her life?''

Janet thought of Scott and didn't feel even a single pang for that dead relationship. "I'm pretty sure he doesn't want anything to do with her. Some guys are like that.''

"Yeah. Fools. But…'' His dark eyes searched hers, as if he needed to find something there. "For Emily's sake, we need to be sure. If he doesn't…then I'd like to adopt her. Not the way I was adopted, to please my mother, but because I really want her. After all, she's part of you.''

The last niggling doubt seeped away, leaving Janet to face her future with nothing but joy. She couldn't help but throw her arms around his neck, and they came to rest entwined on the bed, the pizza box shoved ruthlessly out of the way. "I love you,'' she said. "And Emily's going to love you, too.''

He smiled, a smile that reached the depths of his black-as-night eyes and filled them with light. "Of course she will. We're going to have nothing but love in our home. You'll finish school in L.A., I'll quit working undercover so I don't have to disappear for days or weeks on end, and Emily will learn to sit, crawl, smile and laugh. Who could ask for anything more?''

A long time later, Janet said sleepily, "All we need to do now is get Seth and Darlene together. I just want them to be as happy as I am.''

"I think that's already been accomplished, sweetheart.''

"Yeah?''

He chuckled drowsily. "Yeah. The last I saw, she was asking him why he didn't ask *her* what she thought of being a navy wife.''

"Sounds like it's taken care of, then.'' A little bubble of laughter rose in her throat, but she was too sleepy to let it escape. She just wanted to lie there forever with her head on Abel's shoulder.

Who could ask for anything more?

*   *   *   *   *

WAYS TO *UNEXPECTEDLY* MEET MR. RIGHT:

♡ Go out with the sexy-sounding stranger
your daughter secretly set you up with
through a personal ad.

♡ RSVP yes to a wedding invitation—soon
it might be your turn to say "I do!"

♡ Receive a marriage proposal by mail—
from a man you've never met....

These are just a few of the unexpected
ways that written communication
leads to love in Silhouette Yours Truly.

Each month, look for two fast-paced, fun and
flirtatious Yours Truly novels
(with entertaining treats and sneak previews
in the back pages) by some of your favorite
authors—and some who are sure to
become favorites.

YOURS TRULY™:
Love—when you least expect it!

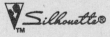

SPECIAL EDITION

Stories of love and life, these powerful
novels are tales that you can identify with—
romances with "something special" added in!

Fall in love with the stories of authors such
as **Nora Roberts, Diana Palmer, Ginna Gray**
and many more of your special favorites—as
well as wonderful new voices!

Special Edition brings you
entertainment for the heart!

SILHOUETTE® *Desire*®

Do you want...

Dangerously handsome heroes

Evocative, everlasting love stories

Sizzling and tantalizing sensuality

Incredibly sexy miniseries like **MAN OF THE MONTH**

Red-hot romance

Enticing entertainment that can't be beat!

You'll find all of this, and much *more* each and every month in **SILHOUETTE DESIRE**. Don't miss these unforgettable love stories by some of romance's hottest authors. Silhouette Desire—where your fantasies will always come true....

If you've got the time...
We've got the
INTIMATE MOMENTS

Passion. Suspense. Desire. Drama. Enter a world that's larger than life, where men and women overcome life's greatest odds for the ultimate prize: love. Nonstop excitement is closer than you think...in Silhouette Intimate Moments!

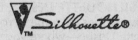

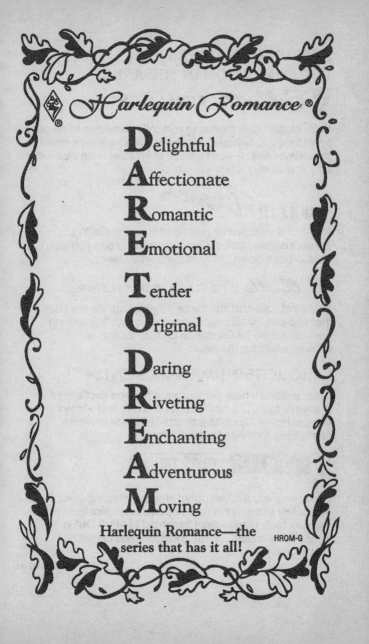

Harlequin Romance ®

Delightful

Affectionate

Romantic

Emotional

Tender

Original

Daring

Riveting

Enchanting

Adventurous

Moving

Harlequin Romance—the
series that has it all!

HROM-G

FIVE UNIQUE SERIES
FOR EVERY WOMAN YOU ARE...

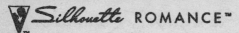

Silhouette ROMANCE™

From classic love stories to romantic comedies to emotional heart tuggers, Silhouette Romance is sometimes sweet, sometimes sassy—and always enjoyable! Romance—the way you always knew it could be.

SILHOUETTE® Desire®

Red-hot is what we've got! Sparkling, scintillating, *sensuous* love stories. Once you pick up one you won't be able to put it down...only in Silhouette Desire.

Silhouette SPECIAL EDITION®

Stories of love and life, these powerful novels are tales that you can identify with—romances with "something special" added in! Silhouette Special Edition is entertainment for the heart.

SILHOUETTE·INTIMATE·MOMENTS®

Enter a world where passions run hot and excitement is always high. Dramatic, larger than life and always compelling—Silhouette Intimate Moments provides captivating romance to cherish forever.

SILHOUETTE YOURS TRULY™

A personal ad, a "Dear John" letter, a wedding invitation... Just a few of the ways that written communication unexpectedly leads Miss Unmarried to Mr. "I Do" in Yours Truly novels...in the most fun, fast-paced and flirtatious style!